BOOKS BY TIM MCBAIN & L.T. VARGUS

*The Violet Darger series*

*The Victor Loshak series*

*The Charlotte Winters series*

*The Scattered and the Dead series*

*Casting Shadows Everywhere*

*The Clowns*

# COUNTDOWN TO MIDNIGHT

a Violet Darger novel

L.T. VARGUS & TIM MCBAIN

SMARMY PRESS

# COUNTDOWN TO MIDNIGHT

# PROLOGUE

Gavin Passmore waded through a cluster of decorative grass, a place where the foliage had overgrown the stone footpath in the yard. Blades of green brushed at the calves of his jeans. He'd have to get Daniel to give the landscaping a fresh manicure, get the shaggy stuff looking clean and prickly again.

Wait. Daniel? Or was the gardener's name David? Shit. He couldn't remember just now. Distracted.

He adjusted the phone against his ear and trudged up the hill toward the house. His eyes glided skyward from the ornamental grass to take in the mansion before him — his mansion — though he wasn't really seeing it fully, the details remaining distant. His throat was dry. Palms clammy. Heart thudding in his chest.

He reached the brick facade of the house and stopped in his tracks. Then he spoke into the phone, interrupting the drone of his agent trying to ditch the call.

"No, Jerry. I don't want you to call me back. I want an answer now, OK? Right now. I'll wait on the line. I want to know. This is… this is everything."

The producer would be calling any time now to let the agent know. The answer impending — his life, his career, hanging in the balance.

Gavin's agent clicked off the line to take the call.

He swallowed. Told himself he hadn't sounded desperate with the "this is everything" bit. That little waver in his voice at the end of his speech? Passion. That was all.

God. If he got this part… Cold bolts of adrenaline shot

down his arms and snaked through his hands at the thought. Made his chest suck in a big shaky breath and hold it.

If they could settle on the contract terms, this part would make his career. It'd be what *Fight Club* had been to Brad Pitt, what *Taxi Driver* and *Raging Bull* had been to De Niro, what Han Solo and Indiana Jones were to Harrison Ford. No more talk about a sitcom reunion, no more underwear modeling on the side, no more villain roles in bullshit Lifetime romcoms, no more fucking coffee commercials. He'd be the megastar he always thought he would be. Should be.

He'd earned some money in his career. Enough to support his lifestyle in any case. Now he had a chance to get what he really craved: Respect. Reverence. Oscar noms. Magazine covers. Fame of the highest order. Just like all the people at the agency had promised him over and over.

Mark. The gardener's name wasn't Daniel or David. It was Mark. Jesus. Who had he been thinking of? Maybe the car detail guy. He was here now. Gavin turned his head to see the small figure in the driveway in the distance, waxing the Mercedes.

He licked his lips. Blinked a few times. Listened to the screaming silence of the phone in his ear. Then he started walking again.

Gavin had paced up and down the length of the yard a few times as he waited for an answer. Milled around the gated section of the grounds. Now he changed his path. Walked toward the driveway to check on his wheels. He liked to look at his reflection in the silver surface of the hood whenever it was freshly waxed.

His face was beginning to show some signs of age at long last. It'd grown longer, or so it seemed to him. A slight droop creeping into that skin between his nose and cheekbones.

Nothing too bad yet.

In his profession, his face was his calling card. Headshots were sent around. The image of his visage piled up with the eight-by-tens of all the other wannabes at the various casting calls. Stacks of glossy photos for the casting director to sift through. An actor's voice was in many ways where their real talent either existed or didn't — but with the wrong face, it didn't matter. The director, the producers, they'd all look on that promotional shot when they decided who succeeded and who failed — stare at the eyes, the complexion, the smile, the bone structure. One face got plucked out of the pile, the rest got thrown away.

Fresh butterflies swirled in his gut as he stepped foot on the brick driveway. The sound of his footsteps grew grittier, bits of stray gravel crunching and scraping.

The smell of the car wax hit then. Acrid. Chemical in a medicinal way. The cleanest aroma in the world as far as Gavin was concerned. Beautiful.

But then the worker's technique caught his eye. He scrubbed a microfiber towel back and forth, smearing a film of wax around.

Gavin lifted the phone away from his mouth.

"Whoa… Hey, uh…"

Was this Daniel? David? Wait. Manuel? Something else? Fuck.

The worker turned and stared at Gavin, a deadpan look on his face. He had a bony brow, pitted cheeks over a big angular jaw. His head looked gigantic atop his scrawny cross country runner body, all sticklike. Couldn't be more than 25.

Gavin lifted his free hand and pantomimed a circular motion in the air.

"Circular motion. Um… Shit. Circular-o? What's the Spanish word for circular? Or, like, motion?"

He tried to think. Fucking language barrier.

"I speak English," the kid said with no trace of an accent.

Gavin gaped at him.

"Oh, right, of course. Sorry, I, uh…"

"We've met a bunch of times, Mr. Passmore, but… My name is Mark."

Wait. Shit. *This* was Mark. Who the hell was the gardener?

"Just, you know, use a circular motion. With the wax. That's the, uh, proper technique."

"You wax a lot of cars?" Mark said, his voice coming out as droll as the look on his face.

"Yeah." Gavin felt his head bobbing up and down. "Well, not personally. No."

"Got it. Consider it done. Circular motion."

Mark went back to waxing the car, and Gavin turned toward the house, his mind already replaying the awkward exchange. Was that racist? Assuming the car guy didn't speak English? Imagine if the tabloids got ahold of that. Should he try to say something else? Maybe suggest he was practicing for a role with a language barrier? That could bury it. Make Mark forget all about it.

Before he could go into damage control mode, he noticed a package on the stoop near the front door — a cardboard cube thrusting up from the marble slab. He must have been out back when the delivery was made.

Curious. He couldn't remember what he'd ordered, but that happened often enough. Late-night Amazon shopping got forgotten so completely that by the time the items arrived, it felt like he'd sent himself a present. Especially if he'd taken one of his sleeping pills. A little surprise, courtesy of Ambien. Still, this didn't look like an Amazon package. No smiley pointing arrow etching a black curve on the side or anything.

He scooped it up and tucked it under his free arm, grabbed the rest of the mail out of the box near the door, and took the pile inside. Flipping through the envelopes provided nothing of excitement — mostly junk mail to do with insurance and mortgage rates and the always thrilling electricity bill.

He passed through the foyer and living room, making his way into the kitchen as he picked out which mail to toss. Then he set the box down on the gleaming quartz of the island and looked it over again. The return address wasn't familiar and didn't feature a name. A P.O. Box in Dover, Delaware. Certainly not from Amazon then.

He realized, as he plucked a knife from the butcher block, that the phone call had mostly been forgotten now. The phone still smashed his ear flat to the side of his head, shifted over to the left side for the moment, but its silence seemed less important just now.

The tip of the knife probed the tape encasing the corners of the box. Then it slit down the seam at the top.

He held still and looked at the wounded package, at the freshly made slash that parted now like lips. He couldn't help but hold his breath as he went to peel the thing open.

His shoulder now pinned the phone to his ear to free both hands. His fingers approached the cardboard in what felt like slow motion, something delicate in the way they touched the thing at last.

The phone clicked back to life then, and Jerry's voice chirped in his ear. Something jubilant in his tone.

Gavin ignored him. Just for a second. His hands were

already moving now. Sliding to that part in the center.

He stripped away the top flaps. Then unfolded the second, smaller set of flaps to lay the chamber bare at last.

Or not.

A crinkled flap of packing paper still shrouded the contents of the box, the brown contours of wrapping material hinting at the knobby shape of what lay beneath.

He narrowed his eyes and leaned over the parcel now. Peered down into the compact cube. Rested his hands on the counter on each side of it. Moved his head closer as though zooming in on this open package until its open maw filled the frame of his vision.

He was breathless now. Rapt. Totally unsure of what this could be. Somehow drawn in by the mystery of this box.

He licked his lips. Pinched the papery sheath covering his boon, whatever it might be.

The voice in his ear sounded concerned now.

"You there, Gav?"

"Just a second."

He peeled the paper out of the way. Heard the faintest click as the detonation was triggered.

All that suppressed energy unleashed in a fraction of a second. Discharged. Set free.

The explosion thrust upward. Ripped outward. Impossible concussive force.

Shrapnel flung out of the box. Miniature nails leading the wave. Each one 10mm in length. A little more than a third of an inch. Tiny.

The flash came next. Impossible white fading to orange the color of flames. Flaring. Radiating in a halo from the focal point of the box.

Heat.

Violence.

Overwhelming.

It buckled the quartz countertop. Shot cracks up and down its length. Cratered the place beneath the package. Punched a blackened pit into the cabinets beneath. Smoke coiling up from the ruins.

The boom seemed to come just a beat later. A breathy whoosh trailed the force, almost a whistle.

A clicking bang interrupted it. Percussive. Sharp. Metallic.

And then that sigh of wind finally brought the full-throated rumble, drawing it out. It roared. Bellowed. The subharmonic thunder shook the house on its foundation, made the floorboards moan, made the windows rattle. Its vibration felt through the earth up to a mile away.

Gavin's face came apart even as the blast flung him back from the kitchen island. The bridge of the nose smashed flat to the skull. Cheekbones collapsing. Torn asunder. Hot nails ripping through teeth and eyes and flesh.

A human face going to splinters. A completed jigsaw puzzle fragmenting back into all those tiny pieces.

Shards of bone. Flaps of skin. Tattered meat.

Blown to bits.

*By the time you read this, I'll be dead, but what I've set into motion will only be beginning.*

*The first bomb has gone off by now. So it begins.*

*Starting at midnight tonight, a bomb will go off roughly every eight hours, and a target will be neutralized.*

*The targets are of no significance politically.*

*They are cultural icons. Celebrities. Actors. Reality TV figures and the like.*

*Be honest. Fiery death could make some of these folks more likable.*

*Doesn't that bland host of the karaoke show become more compelling after he's been blown to pieces?*

*How about the fashion model trying to break into the mainstream taking shrapnel to her jugular?*

*The juicy lead role of her dreams.*

*You piggies have a chance, however, to stop some of the carnage.*

*What better way to get attention to my message than to invite the police and public alike to play a little game?*

*Here's how it works:*

*Chunks of my journal are strewn about the city. Hidden. Each one contains clues to the next chunk, and likewise, each one divulges the details of one of the little toys I've prepared for one of America's sweethearts.*

*Clues for names. Clues for places.*

*Everything you'd need to locate and disarm one of the bombs is there.*

*All I ask in return is that you read the journal. Really read it. Consider what I am presenting.*

*Ironically, killing celebrities will make me a celebrity.*

*For the next 24 hours or so, as my bombs either go off or don't, I may well be the most famous person on the planet.*

*An unflattering photo of my face will be plastered in a box just over the news anchor's shoulder.*

*It will be worth it.*

*My ideas will be dissected and debated the whole world round, chunks of my journal translated into damn near every language on the globe.*

*The game begins.*

*Pour yourself a cup of coffee. And if you must sleep tonight, be sure to keep those DVRs rolling.*

*From Hell,*

*T. H.*

# CHAPTER 1

Violet Darger squirmed in her seat, walled in on all sides by auditorium seating filled to the brim. She swiveled her head to get a better view of the room full of cadets.

A little over 250 bright-eyed faces stared up at the stage, their bodies packed down in the theater-style seats. Smiling. Fidgeting. Coughing. Soft chatter filled the space with a whispery drone even as the ceremony continued on the platform at the front of the room.

After over twenty excruciating weeks of training, graduation had finally arrived for this class of FBI agent trainees. They'd earned it.

Each cadet had shot approximately 5,000 rounds of ammunition in the firearms course. They'd been punched in the face. Sprayed with mace. They'd spent hours being grilled by instructors on every possible procedure in class and also in practical settings. They'd run through the Capstone counter-terrorism exercise. They'd even investigated a kidnapping and a bank robbery in the mock town on campus known as Hogan's Alley.

Some hadn't made it. Two cadets had quit, and another pair had been dismissed.

Darger tried to imagine what that would feel like. Washing out of the program would be a brutal reality check. It was difficult to envision sacrificing so much, only to be found "not suitable" by the powers that be. And often, trainees were forced to quit their previous job before they began the grueling field training program. They'd have nothing to go back to.

Still, it might be worse to be one of those who had dropped out of training of their own volition. No one made it to this point without a tremendous effort. There was no waffling your way into the FBI. Being an FBI agent was a dream for every person in this room. Giving up on that dream would be heartbreaking.

Darger bounced her knee up and down. Let her eyes scan over the taut faces, the jittery smiles, the restless body language.

The tension in the room was beyond that of a normal graduation ceremony for good reason. The grads wouldn't just be receiving diplomas today. They'd each get an envelope containing their first assignment. Anything from Anchorage, Alaska, to Milwaukee to Honolulu to Jasper, Wyoming, was possible.

She watched the final trainee cross to the podium. Darger recognized the woman from the class she and Loshak had taught on crime scene profiling. Venus Jackson. She had the most upright posture Darger had ever seen. Spine straight, shoulders square. She already looked the part of an FBI agent. Subconsciously, Darger sat up taller in her seat.

On stage, Deputy Chief Wickett handed Jackson a binder filled with paperwork and forms and her shiny new credentials. A photo was taken. And then she received the envelope.

Darger held her breath. Watched Jackson stare down at the rectangle of white paper in her hands.

The agent peeled the top flap up and pulled out the sheet of paper inside.

Swallowed.

Darger remembered living through that moment. Standing in almost the exact place on stage. Clutching that piece of paper that held her first assignment. A single sheet of paper that seemed to weigh a thousand pounds. It felt so strange, to know that this wispy page held so much weight. It knew the next chapter of your life.

When she unfolded it, there would be Before and After.

Jackson licked her lips and opened the letter. Her eyes flicked back and forth across the page. Her eyelids fluttered. A subtle lift of the eyebrows. Surprise? Excitement? Alarm?

"Well, what is it, Jackson? Where ya headed?" one of the other newly minted agents called out.

Jackson blinked again, startled from her private moment. Her cheeks went pink when she realized she was still standing at the head of the auditorium, all eyes on her. But she recovered quickly, holding the letter high.

"New Orleans."

The room erupted in applause, as it had after every previous announcement.

The deputy chief stepped to the podium and spoke into the microphone.

"I just want to say again, how proud we are to have these fine ladies and gentlemen joining our ranks. I know that each and every one of you will make a valuable asset to the Bureau for years to come. Thank you."

There was more clapping as the formal portion of the graduation ceremony came to a close. The audience began to disperse. Family members of the new agents hurried over to congratulate their loved ones. The various instructors and supervisors headed for the refreshment area.

Loshak turned to Darger, eyes sparkling.

"Almost time for the best part of the ceremony."

"Are you talking about the badge-shaped sugar cookies?" she asked.

"You're god-damned right I am."

He rubbed his hands together, eliciting a snort from Darger.

"I still don't understand your obsession," she said. "They're good, but not *that* good."

"Hey, I'm not the only one." Loshak cocked his head toward the refreshment table. "Will you look at those vultures? They all know the cookies are coming out any second now, and they are ready to pounce."

Darger shook her head.

"See, I have a theory about the cookies — about why everyone talks about them. It's scarcity. They only get made for the graduation ceremony, right? For some reason, that captures all of your imaginations, turns you into raccoons clutching after something shiny. It's like Girl Scout cookies. You know that Keebler makes those cookies? You can literally buy most of them in the store under different names. Thin Mints are Grasshoppers. Samoas are Caramel Coconut Dreams or something like that. People act like the ones they buy from the Girl Scouts are somehow superior, because they've been made to believe they're scarce. Only available certain times of year. But it's not real. It's an illusion."

Loshak pursed his lips.

"Your analogy doesn't hold up. The badge cookies can't be bought at the store. They're made fresh, right here in the kitchens, and those ladies down there protect the recipe like a dragon guards its gold."

"You've actually tried to get the recipe?" Darger asked. She tried to imagine Loshak bribing a lady wearing a hairnet with a $50 bill or perhaps the promise of sexual favors.

"No, I just assume it's a secret recipe. It has to be." Before Darger could respond, Loshak elbowed her. "There they are.

Let's go."

Two women had appeared with trays of cookies and Darger could see the other FBI personnel holding back the urge to mob them before they could even set the trays down.

Loshak was already on his feet, making a beeline for the cookies.

"Who's the vulture now?" Darger muttered.

Loshak had already wolfed down half of his first cookie by the time Darger reached him. She poured herself a cup of punch.

"Don't forget to chew," she said.

"Keep cracking jokes," he said, shoving the second half of the cookie into his mouth. "All that yapping leaves no time for eating cookies, and that means more for me."

Darger chuckled and took a cookie.

Loshak scanned the room and gestured toward a slender dark-haired woman.

"Fabroa seemed to have a knack for the forensic psychology stuff," he said. "Where'd she end up, again?"

"Dallas, I think."

Loshak nodded and sipped his punch.

"I'll keep tabs on her. See how she matures these first few years. She could be BAU material."

"Looking to replace me?" Darger teased.

"Maybe," Loshak said. "I'm not sure I can stay partnered with someone who doesn't respect the cookies."

They stood near the door, and Darger became aware of one of the new graduates having a phone conversation just outside.

"Thanks. I kind of can't believe it's over," the man said and let out a strained laugh.

There was a pause.

"Uhhh... well. I got Cleveland." The man waited for the other person to respond. "I know, but it's not permanent, you know? They move people around all the time."

Darger cringed, wondering for the first time what this process must be like for someone with a family. It was one thing to sign yourself up for the FBI Academy roulette wheel. It was something else to expect your whole family to go along for the ride with you.

"No, that isn't how it works," he was saying now. "They don't take requests. And it's kind of a take it or leave it thing."

Loshak nudged her.

"So where'd you want to end up?"

Apparently she hadn't been the only one eavesdropping.

"I didn't care." She shrugged. "Not really."

"Come on. Everyone has a preference. They want exotic, like Hawaii. Or somewhere exciting, with a lot of action, like New York City."

"I wanted to be here. At Quantico, with the BAU," Darger said. "But no one gets that straight out of the academy, so I knew I'd have to work my way through those first few years. They could have sent me to Bumfuck, North Dakota, and I would have been happy."

"Ah! So North Dakota was at the bottom of your list."

"That's not what I said." Darger took a bite of her cookie before she went on. "Although it does seem very cold. And very rural."

"See, I knew you wouldn't want any of the quiet, out-of-the-way places. You wanted to be down there in the muck, getting your hands dirty."

"That's me. The Queen of Filth."

Loshak smirked, and then his eyes locked on someone

across the room.

"Is that Rodney Malenchuck? I haven't seen him in ages. I should go say hi."

Darger followed his gaze.

"I can't help but notice he's standing conveniently close to one of the cookie trays."

"A serendipitous coincidence," Loshak said, trying to sound innocent. "You coming?"

"I'll be over in a minute. I want to hit the ladies' room before everyone else has a bladder full of punch."

Darger went across the hall to the bathroom. As she was washing her hands, Venus Jackson came in, sniffling and holding back tears.

Jackson halted abruptly when she noticed she wasn't alone.

"Oh. Special Agent Darger." She wiped her sleeve across her cheek. "God, this is embarrassing. I swear I don't usually cry over this kind of thing."

Darger tugged a paper towel from the dispenser and passed it to Jackson.

"New Orleans isn't so bad, you know. Good food. Good music."

"It's not that." Jackson shook her head and looked down at her feet. "I'm just…"

"Overwhelmed?"

Jackson nodded.

"You're thinking: *I can't believe this is actually happening. I can't believe I'm an actual FBI agent.* And so there's excitement. And the relief of the grueling tests being over, finally. You made it through the pepper spray. You completed the mile-and-a-half run. You took the punches to the head and came out on the other side. But then there's doubt, too. A little voice that says,

*Wait. Me? I'm not an FBI agent. I don't actually know what I'm doing. They handed me an assignment and some credentials, but that doesn't magically transform me into a special agent. What if I'm not cut out for this? What if everyone figures out that I have no idea what I'm doing?'*

Jackson's eyes went wide.

"That's exactly it! How did you know?"

"It's called Impostor Syndrome. This irrational fear that you're less competent than everyone thinks, combined with a fear that you'll be found out. That everyone will learn you're a fraud."

"You had it, too?" Jackson asked.

"Oh yeah. I think everyone has it, on some level. I would bet that every cadet in that room has it, too. Well, maybe not the narcissists."

Jackson cocked her head to one side.

"Wouldn't a narcissist get weeded out during the Personality Assessment on the Phase 1 Exam?"

One side of Darger's mouth quirked upward.

"Not always. I actually think the Bureau lets some narcissistic personalities in. How else are they going to fill the upper management positions?"

Jackson let out a surprised laugh and hurried to put a hand over her mouth.

"Making jokes like that seems like the kind of thing that would get you into trouble around here."

"Oh sure," Darger said. "If an ASAC heard that remark, I'd probably get a formal reprimand. I think it's a requirement of any of the top brass jobs that you surrender your sense of humor."

Jackson stepped to one of the mirrors and checked her

makeup.

"OK, so if everyone feels this way — the impostor syndrome way — what do they do? Because I really don't know what I'm doing."

"Of course you don't. This is all new for you. But you'll figure it out as you go." Darger put a hand on her shoulder. "And if you want to know a little secret: the FBI is a bureaucracy like any other. Learn how to color in the lines the way your boss likes, and you'll be fine."

Darger heard Loshak's voice in her head: *How is it you can dish out this kind of advice but are incapable of following it yourself?*

Jackson dabbed at her eyes one last time and turned to face Darger. She put out a hand.

"Thank you, Special Agent—"

Darger took her hand, interrupting before she could finish.

"It's just Darger now. And it's no problem, Jackson," she said with a wink.

Jackson smiled as she wadded up the paper towel and tossed it in the trash bin.

Back in the auditorium, Darger paused inside the door, searching for her partner. She spotted Loshak hovering near the refreshments table and wondered if he'd been stuffing down cookies the entire time she'd been gone. But then he turned, and she saw the phone pressed to his ear and the grim set of his jaw.

Darger's spine straightened. A case?

He caught sight of her and started her way.

By the time he reached her, he was already ending the call.

"Uh-huh," he said. "We'll head out immediately."

He tucked the phone back into his pocket and met her eyes.

"We've got an assignment."

# CHAPTER 2

They'd lucked out and waited less than an hour for a flight to New York. Now Darger was slouched in the passenger seat of a rented Nissan, watching the heat distortion blur the concrete on the sides of the road.

The drive from LaGuardia airport to the crime scene in East Hampton would take over two hours. Darger got out her phone and scrolled through the briefing they'd been sent by the local field office.

Gavin Passmore. Blown to bits when he opened a package containing a bomb. And since the package had originated in New Jersey and thus crossed state lines, the case was instantly under federal jurisdiction.

"Says here this guy is an actor. Don't recognize the name," she said. "His picture looks familiar, but I can't place him."

Loshak nodded and merged onto Grand Central Parkway.

"Yeah, Agent Fredrick mentioned something about that on the phone. He been in anything I'd know?"

Darger found Passmore's profile on IMDB.com and ran down his list of credits.

"He was a regular on some sitcom for a while, but that was a few years ago, and I definitely never watched it."

"Well if you haven't seen it, I've definitely never seen it."

"He's also been a guest on a lot of stuff. All the shows that shoot in New York, looks like. *Law & Order. Blue Bloods. The Good Fight.*"

"Never seen any of those either," Loshak said.

"You've never seen an episode of *Law & Order*?"

"Maybe part of one here or there. But I can't watch shows about fictional murders when I deal with the real thing every day."

They passed a construction site where a large cube of steel and concrete was being erected. Probably another parking structure, Darger thought before returning to what Loshak had said.

"Now that you mention it, I haven't watched any of that kind of stuff since I became an agent. I thought it was the lack of free time, but I think you're onto something." Her eyes dropped to her phone. "Still, this guy looks too familiar. I must know him from something."

Darger left IMDB and simply typed the actor's name into Google. One of the results at the top of the page was a YouTube video of a coffee commercial. She played it and instantly recognized Gavin Passmore standing at a kitchen island. Steam coiled up from the mug in front of the actor, a smile that could only be described as cocky curling the corners of his lips. As he lifted the mug, Passmore's gaze locked onto the gleaming black surface of the coffee, and then as he blinked, his eyes pivoted to look straight into the camera — the brashness of the smile somehow intensifying. His voice came out deep and textured with fine grit sandpaper.

"He's the guy from those coffee commercials! The 'rich brew' guy."

At the next traffic light, she held out her phone for Loshak to see.

"Oh right… 'When I'm in the mood for a rich brew, I make a cup of Café Castro Midnight.'"

Darger chuckled at the impression, Loshak's voice having gone gravelly and low-pitched.

"Yep. That's him."

Even with the Nissan's air conditioner blasting, it felt like a city summer in the car — that August sunlight glinting off the concrete, angling through the windows, generally trying to scorch everything it touched.

They motored through the urban sprawl of the city. Apartment complexes and condos. Churches and liquor stores. And traffic. Unending traffic.

This was New York. Roughly seven million people crammed onto a 1400-square-mile spit of land. She averaged it out in her head. Five-thousand people per square mile. The residential buildings here were more like giant sardine cans.

Darger scanned the file again. It was short. So short she could read the entire thing in about five minutes. She wished she had more, but they were coming in on this one early. The team on the ground had only had time to send them the barest of details before she and Loshak hopped on the plane in Virginia. And now that same team probably had their hands full processing the gruesome scene.

She squirmed a little in her seat, antsy to get to the East Hampton home where the bomb had detonated. She tried to not look at the clock, knowing it would only annoy her to see how much further they still had to go. She made it a whole minute before caving. Eyes flicking. Numbers read. Sure enough, they still had almost two hours to go.

The further they drove, the less the buildings and houses crowded the sides of the highway. The trees filled in, and the neighborhoods she spotted through the greenery looked more and more suburban. Tightly packed houses instead of concrete behemoths. Here and there a brick wall divided the side of the highway with whatever lay on the other side. Probably apartment buildings. Or maybe a golf course or hotel. These people wanted to live near the big city, but they didn't want to see half a million cars zipping by on the expressway every time they looked out the window.

She checked her email, hoping for an unexpected update from the local field agents. Nothing. She tossed her phone into her bag and swiveled to face Loshak.

"So why does someone target a B-list actor with a mail bomb?"

Loshak shrugged.

"Could be anything. Professional jealousy. Angry ex-girlfriend. Or boyfriend. Maybe he had a stalker."

"Someone obsessed with the Café Castro guy, huh? I guess that sitcom had some big fans, even if it's been a few years. I saw some headlines suggesting there have been rumors of a reunion. But I wonder…"

Darger trailed off there. After a second, Loshak spurred her on.

"What?"

"I mean, it could turn into a serial thing. Lots of bombings do, you know?"

Loshak waited a second. Then let out a sigh and shrugged.

"There's always something so… ambitious about a bombing," Loshak said. "It takes research and effort and planning to make a bomb. So I can see where you're coming from. But we should probably let the evidence and background fill in before we start leaping to any grand conclusions."

"But if this was as simple as a personal vendetta, they could have taken him out with a gun. Or a knife. Hired goons with baseball bats." She gazed out the window and frowned. "A bomb is so over the top."

They were quiet for a few moments, and then Darger shook her head slowly.

"I have a feeling this is just the beginning."

# CHAPTER 3

On the far end of the island, they swapped the Long Island Expressway for a two-lane country road. They rolled through quaint little neighborhoods with yards bordered by picket fences and rose bushes. They passed vineyards and orchards and historic inns. The sprawling shingle style homes and Colonial Revivals with their expansive lawns were a far cry from the massive apartment buildings looming over the city just a couple of hours away.

When they reached East Hampton, the houses and yards grew bigger still. Set back from the road and landscaped to maximize privacy. Darger caught glimpses of some of the homes through the trees. Many were traditional, with cedar shake siding and shutters on the windows. Some were quite large, others were more modest. Darger figured they were all worth more than she could imagine. This was prime real estate.

Out of boredom, she pulled out her phone and glanced at the listings for houses for sale in the area. She let out a hissing breath.

"What?" Loshak asked.

"The prices on these houses. I knew it was an expensive place to live, but I don't think I realized how much. Here's a house that looks like the one I grew up in. 1.8 million dollars."

Loshak whistled.

Up ahead Darger spotted two New York State Police cruisers posted at the end of a driveway.

"This must be it," she said.

Loshak flashed his credentials, and the troopers waved them

through. The whole neighborhood was shaded by mature oak trees, houses tucked back into patches of wilderness. It was several moments before Darger caught a glimpse of the building as they wound their way up the long brick drive.

The house was a massive modern thing. All metal and wood and not a 90-degree angle to be found. Loshak brought them to a halt behind an Evidence Response Team truck parked among a dozen other vehicles along a circular turnabout.

Darger input the address into the real estate app.

"Holy hell."

"Now what?"

"The rent on this place is ten grand a month."

Loshak leaned forward and stared up at the behemoth of a house.

"Big place for a guy that lives alone."

"Good point," Darger said. "This listing says it has six bedrooms. Why does one dude need six bedrooms?"

They climbed out of the car and proceeded to the front of the house. The landscaping was as abstract and modern as the house. Boxwoods cut into perfect spheres. A water feature with a large glass pyramid that appeared to hover over a rectangular koi pond. The path leading to the front door was a manicured strip of green lawn inlaid with oblong marble pavers.

There were boxes of gloves, booties, and masks waiting outside the massive front door, and they paused to gear up.

"Ready?" Loshak asked, grasping the giant vertical steel bar that functioned as the door handle.

"Yeah. I feel like I'm entering a modern art museum instead of a house, though."

Loshak gave the behemoth of a door a shove. It was at least five feet wide, and instead of being hinged on one side, it pivoted open on an axis.

"No kidding."

The inside of the house was just as uber-modern as the outside. Everything white and angular. There was a carved statue in the living room that had to be at least twenty feet tall. Most of the height was dedicated to an intricately decorated post of wood, but at the very top, a female figure stood carrying a baby on her back. It looked like something that should be in the rotunda of the Smithsonian. In any other house, Darger was sure it would dominate the space, but here, with the vaulted ceilings soaring so high above, the wooden tower seemed almost delicate.

The place was swarming with people, which made sense considering the scene was only a few hours old. Darger spotted the insignias of at least four different law enforcement outfits: FBI, ATF, East Hampton PD, and State Police. The men and women bustled around with cameras and baggies and clipboards.

"Would you look at that?" Loshak said.

Darger turned to see him admiring the dining room table, which was another gargantuan creation of wood. One solid slab with uneven edges and actual tree trunks functioning as table legs.

"That's gotta be six or seven inches thick," he went on. "Probably weighs 800 pounds. Insane. Must be a redwood. I've seen live-edge tables before, but never on this scale."

"You have to appreciate how subtle they went with the decor," Darger said, eyeballing an abstract painting that took up most of the wall adjacent to the table. The canvas was an angry snarl of grungy black smears and splotches.

Loshak snorted.

"Right. Everything in here is cranked to eleven," he said.

Darger caught a glimpse of the pool out back. It fit in with the rest of the place in that it defied conventions. Instead of being round or even a rectangle, it had five sides, none of them equal. A reflection of the odd angles of the house. The pool was bordered by more of the spherical boxwoods, and another large statue stood watch over the northeast end. This one looked to be made of stone.

"It really does feel more like a museum than a place someone would actually live," she said, stepping over an orange ball laying in the middle of the floor. A few feet away, she spotted another. That was when she realized they weren't balls, but oranges. Then she spied the overturned bowl.

"I wonder why—"

The words died on her tongue. They turned the corner, the kitchen bomb site coming into view at last, and Darger's feet stopped beneath her involuntarily. A breath hiccuped into her lungs, and then her chest, too, held still.

She stood there, her eyes tracing over the wreckage over and over again.

Time seemed to stand still for a beat, everything going quiet.

The body was gone, of course. The autopsy was already underway according to the brief Darger had been given. But the remaining evidence still showed precisely where the blast had taken place.

The cratered kitchen island — a gaping wound in the quartz — exposed blackened cabinetry innards where the fireball had flared. The surrounding blood spatter and debris pattern displayed streak marks indicating where the victim had stood, the red and black marks on the tile floor interrupted by the place where the actor's bulk had taken the brunt of the blast.

The overall effect was beyond grisly. It looked impossible. More like a surreal art exhibition than a real live crime scene.

Soot marks stained the vaulted ceiling high above in a whirled pattern that resembled black clouds. Darger thought it looked like an impressionistic charcoal sketch — an abstract version of those ancient cave paintings, lines and shapes that seemed to signify something essential that was somehow just beyond her mind's reach.

A bitter smell still hung in the air. The tang of charred plastic that stung the inside of Darger's nostrils.

Finally, sound began to fade back into Darger's consciousness: little shards of quartz crunching everywhere under the bunny-suited feet tramping around the scene. Brittle sounds like broken glass, the pointed bits shrill where they scraped against the tile.

Darger took a breath. Glanced over at the large painting hung over the dining table, noting the similarity in color and form to the damage. Shades of gray to black on white. Anger and chaos and darkness.

She'd told Loshak she thought this would end up being a serial case. She hoped like hell she was wrong.

# CHAPTER 4

Darger squatted down, feeling overwhelmed.

She thought Loshak must be feeling the same, as he hadn't uttered a word either since they entered the kitchen area.

They'd seen hundreds of murder scenes between them. Stabbings. Shootings. Stranglings. Drownings. Bludgeonings. But this was something different. The damage left by the explosion was almost hard to fathom. Solid objects shredded into confetti in a single second. A quartz countertop rendered into pea gravel. What would the force of something like that do to a human body?

She knew the answer. She'd seen the photos. Passmore no longer had a face or much of a head at all, really. Skin, muscle, brain, and bone, all fragmented in a heartbeat.

Darger stared at a gummy puddle of viscera on the tiles near her feet. Blood had gathered in the grout lines, forming a strange series of nearly black canals that spread outward from the sludgy pool. What part of Gavin Passmore might that have been? It was impossible to tell. The blast had erased every recognizable detail.

She let out a long breath. It seemed loud, which made her realize how quiet the scene was. Aside from the periodic snap and click of a camera or the rustle of a plastic evidence baggie, there was a hush. Very little chitchat happening among those processing this area.

Darger's eyes were still locked on the splotch of human smoothie staining the tiles, half in a daze when Loshak broke the eerie silence by clearing his throat.

"I see Agent Fredrick out back." He gestured toward the wall of glass looking out on the pool. "Let's go see what she's got for us."

Darger nodded and rose to her full height.

She'd started to sweat as they'd stood there in the kitchen, observing the scene. Now the movement of the air on her skin sent goosebumps crawling over her arms. Her hands felt clammy inside the gloves. The mask over her face had gone especially hot.

They moved through the doorway leading out of the kitchen. Darger's legs felt slightly wobbly beneath her. Then the world seemed to pitch around her.

"Give me a second," she said, squatting down again.

Outside of the immediate crime scene, Darger ripped off her mask and basked in the sensation of the open air on her face. An air-conditioning vent blasted upward from the baseboard.

The cool air did not clear away her growing sense of unease, however. If anything, it had only strengthened.

That puzzled her.

Was it the scale of a bombing? The utter destruction possible with one small package?

She remembered what she'd told Agent Jackson about impostor syndrome. Could that be what was happening here? Was she feeling out of her depth?

"I hate bombings," Loshak said, swiping a gloved hand at his bunny suit.

Darger let her eyes slide over to him, wondering if he was saying this in earnest, or if he'd noticed she was rattled and was trying to get her to talk.

"Oh yeah?" she said.

"Most scenes end up looking kind of like the victim just

kinda keeled over. Even if there's blood everywhere. The body is more or less intact. And so is the rest of the place." He gestured back toward the kitchen. "But that? That reminds me of seeing the destruction after a tornado. Houses flattened. Trees blown into toothpicks. And you think, 'No one could survive this. They never even had a chance.'"

The thin sheen of sweat covering Darger's body was causing her collar to adhere to the back of her neck. She tugged at it, nodding along with Loshak's words.

"Thinking about Owen?" he asked.

That threw her. She whipped her head around to frown at him.

"What?"

"It's just that the last time we saw a bombing, we lost a lot of people, and Owen was almost one of them."

An image of Owen impaled on a piece of rebar flashed in her mind. She could still hear the sound of the explosion that had demolished the Atlanta motel room. See the smoke and dust and piles of debris.

"Right," Darger said. Maybe Loshak was onto something. Maybe the gnawing dread she was feeling was a lingering bit of PTSD. "I hadn't thought of that. Not consciously, anyway. But I do feel a little off-kilter, to be honest. Like this is all… too much."

It felt better to admit it. To have some sort of concrete explanation to cling to. Now she could move on. The tension she'd been feeling loosened ever so slightly.

"Anyway, whenever we're ready, we can get a more in-depth briefing from Agent Fredrick."

Darger inhaled, breathing easier.

"I'm ready."

# CHAPTER 5

Loshak led the way, and they passed through another doorway leaving the damage behind. Darger could still feel the blast zone behind her, her body somehow oriented to the wounded place in the countertop, the dark energy radiating outward from the detonation point. Even as they turned a corner and meandered toward the back of the house, a twitchy feeling deep in her ribcage stayed tuned to the direction of the wreckage like a compass needle.

They fell in with a group of bunny-suited techs, an exodus of traffic that filed outside through gaping French doors, venting into a side yard where law enforcement had set up a white polyethylene tent as a command center. The bright sunlight made Darger squint for a second, but then she moved into the shade beneath the canopy, the plastic-like tent material overhead crinkling and snapping in the breeze.

It smelled fresh out here. Clean. The green of the well-manicured plant life intertwined with a hint of a soil smell. No trace of the acrid burnt notes she'd smelled near the detonation point. Nothing blackened or scorched here.

Agent Beatrice Fredrick turned and greeted them from deeper inside the tent's chamber, her bunny suit wrinkling as she waved them over with both arms. She was probably around Loshak's age, with blonde hair cut short and a thick Maine accent. After making their introductions, she wasted no time filling them in.

"Do we have any more details on where the package came from?" Loshak asked.

"We're still working on it. We've traced it back to a drop box in New Jersey, as you know. And we know from the tracking information that USPS took possession of the package and scanned it at 7:48 P.M. on the 8th. We've already pulled surveillance from the area in the vicinity of the drop-off point to see if we can spot the person dropping the package. There's feed from multiple cameras, so we have high hopes that this will pay off." Agent Fredrick sighed and propped her fists on her hips. "The thing slowing us down right now is that the drop box is only emptied once a day, so there's a full 24 hours of footage to comb through."

Agent Fredrick walked to one side of the tent and plucked a tablet from the table there.

"We've got video of the explosion from the security cameras in the house, if you'd like to see it."

"Absolutely," Loshak said with a nod.

Swiping a thumb across the tablet screen, Fredrick located a folder of video files and selected one.

"This is 10:44 A.M., time of delivery."

The video was in color. Decent quality. A white USPS truck silently motored up the drive.

"No sound?" Darger asked.

Agent Fredrick shook her head.

"Only video."

The mail woman hopped down from the driver's seat, the box already in hand. She jogged up to the walk, pulled a device from her pocket, and scanned the label on the package. Then she rang the bell and set the package outside the front door before hustling back to her truck.

"You've interviewed the driver?"

Fredrick bobbed her head once.

"She was pretty shaken when she heard what happened. Spooked her to realize she'd been toting around a bomb in her truck half the morning. Our impression is that she's not a person of interest, but she's been told to stay in the area in case we need to question her further."

"Bombs aren't generally a woman's M.O. anyway," Loshak said. "But there are always outliers."

Agent Fredrick opened a second video, this one trained on the backyard and the pool.

"Passmore swam laps in the pool for a decent chunk of the morning. He was getting dressed in the pool house at the time of delivery, and then he paced around the grounds on his phone for a while after that. The box sat on the doorstep for more than an hour before he noticed it was there."

Darger squinted at the figure on the screen. Passmore was of average height with a lean build and wavy hair. He dressed casually, but in a way that still gave off a clear sense of wealth, even in this security video. What was it? The cut of the pants? The way every item of clothing was pressed to perfection? Something in his posture?

Fredrick returned to the feed showing the driveway and front door and skipped forward.

"Now we're at 11:37. This is when his car detail guy shows up to wax the Mercedes. Mark Trobiani. He was the one who called 9-1-1. Or I should say the *first* one to call 9-1-1. Six neighbors reported hearing a loud explosion in the minutes following the blast."

Now the actor stood at the edge of the driveway talking to the car detail guy for a few minutes. He circled one of his hands in the air, and then his brow crinkled, some embarrassed look flashing over his features.

Passmore still had the phone pressed to his ear as he pivoted away from the car and strode to the front door. He pinned it between his shoulder and chin and squatted down to pick up the package. The box slowly glided upward until the actor was practically touching his nose to its top, probably looking for a return label or some other clue as to what it was and finding nothing. Then he tucked the package under one arm, readjusted the phone to his ear, and went inside.

The nonchalant manner in which he carried the explosive unnerved Darger. It felt wrong the way he jostled it and held it so close to his body.

Agent Fredrick switched cameras again, this one showing an overhead view of the dining area and kitchen.

With the angle in reverse, they watched Passmore move toward them now, bringing the package into the kitchen. He cradled it to his chest, looking it over again. Then he set it on the counter while he searched for something to open it with in one of the drawers nearby. It was like watching a horror movie.

*Don't open it*, Darger thought, trying to will the man in the video to obey even though she knew it was impossible. *Don't open the box.*

Passmore finally retrieved a chef's knife from the butcher block. Moved to the package on the countertop.

Darger winced as he slid the tip of the blade between the flaps of the box and slit it down the middle.

The three of them waited for the lethal jack-in-the-box to spring to life. Their collective anticipation was palpable.

And then it happened. It was so fast. The blink of an eye. A single beat of the heart. Normal and then *BOOM.*

Except there was no boom because the video had no sound. And the silence seemed wrong. That much devastation didn't happen quietly.

The flash was so bright the entire camera flashed to white. And then a violent outward burst overtook the frame as the color seeped back in. Debris flung like dirt clods. Pulsating black smoke that dispersed almost as quickly as it appeared.

In the aftermath of the flash and the smoke, what was left was only the destruction. The crater and Passmore's figure sprawled on the floor amidst the chips and shards of gleaming quartz.

Agent Fredrick replayed the video, this time in slow motion. Worked through it frame by frame. Even then, it was impossible to see the moment of impact in the video. It was too fast. Too bright.

"Christ," Darger said. "We're lucky more people don't make bombs."

A few seconds after the detonation, someone else appeared in the frame. Creeping at first, the fear evident in the body language. Darger recognized the black t-shirt and cargo shorts.

"This is the car detail guy?" she asked. "Trobiani."

"That's right," Fredrick said.

When Trobiani saw the carnage in the kitchen, he froze. There was another beat before it dawned on him exactly what he was seeing. His hands flew to his head, and then he spun around and ran back the way he'd come. Agent Fredrick went back to the outside camera, where Trobiani could be seen making a phone call.

"He calls it in as soon as he's back outside."

"Any background on him?" Darger asked.

"He's been working for Passmore for six months. Lives in Hempstead but is originally from Staten Island. No criminal record. Seems well-balanced. But he's also been asked to stay in the vicinity, just in case."

"I'd like to talk to him," Loshak said. "Is he still here?"

Agent Fredrick gestured toward an ambulance parked off to one side in the driveway.

"He got a little woozy, probably mild shock, so we sent him over to the paramedics."

Loshak turned his head toward the vehicle. A pair of legs were visible where someone sat perched in the open rear door, feet dangling over the brick pavers.

Loshak turned back to Darger.

"Let's go see what he's got to say."

# CHAPTER 6

Mark Trobiani appeared to be typing something into his phone as they approached the rear door of the ambulance.

"Mr. Trobiani?" Loshak called out.

Trobiani hopped down from the back of the ambulance. A shammy cloth stuck out from one of his back pockets.

"I'm Agent Loshak. This is my partner, Agent Darger."

Trobiani nodded.

"Let me guess. More questions?"

"If you don't mind," Loshak said.

"I mean, I don't know what else I can tell you. I've told it about six times now." Trobiani sighed. "Don't really have anything new to add."

"Well, for starters, how are you feeling?" Darger asked.

"Oh, I'm good. It was just my blood sugar." He lifted one side of his shirt to show off an insulin pump. "Forgot to eat, what with all the excitement. Started getting kind of shaky. But the paramedics gave me some glucose gel, so I'm fine now."

"I'm glad to hear it," she said. "Instead of going over the incident again, why don't you tell us about Gavin Passmore. What was he like?"

"Ah. OK. Well… I guess I should preface this all by saying that I'm sorry that this happened to him. I mean, nobody deserves that. And I know he's got family. Friends. This is gonna be rough for them. But I'm not gonna lie. Mr. Passmore was kind of a jackass."

"In what way?"

"Like he could never remember my name, for one. And a

couple times he started talking to me in his half-assed Spanish. I'm Italian, man. I think he was getting me confused with the gardener. Daniel. He was born in El Salvador, but he's been in the US since he was like two and speaks perfect English, so I still don't know why Passmore would think he needed to talk to either one of us in Spanish. I kind of figure we were all just servants to him, so he didn't bother to remember our names or faces or whether we spoke English. Didn't need to, you know?"

"You'd think if you could live in a house like this, you could also afford some manners," Loshak said.

Trobiani shrugged.

"Maybe his problem was that he couldn't really afford it."

"What do you mean?"

Trobiani reached down and fiddled with one corner of the shammy cloth in his pocket.

"This is gonna make me sound like my nosy-ass Aunt Lynette, but I swear I wasn't eavesdropping on purpose. It's just that one time, I overheard him talking to his agent on the phone. He was kind of in a panic because he said he's got five different high-limit credit cards, and they're all maxed out. The agent must have said something about living more within his means or whatever, because then Passmore really lost it. Started screaming about how image is everything, and that he shouldn't have to downsize just because his agent was thinking too small."

He gestured at the house and at the freshly waxed Mercedes.

"That's when I started to realize that this — all of it — was just for show. All to appear successful… or more successful than he really was." Trobiani clicked his tongue. "Seems nuts to me. A single guy renting this six-bedroom house in one of the most expensive places in the country, just to give off some vibe that he's a big deal or whatever? And even worse, he's gotta drag me into it, too."

"How did he do that?"

"Well, I usually only work weekdays, right? But a couple of times, he paid me extra to come on a Saturday, in the middle of the afternoon, when he had guests over. Like, he easily could have had me do the car on Thursday or Friday. No difference. No extra. But I think he wanted me here working so he could show off. Like, *look at me, with my hired help*. He did the same with Daniel, the gardener I was talking about."

The phone in Trobiani's pocket chimed and buzzed. He pulled it out and glanced at the screen before tucking it away again, but the momentary interruption caused him to lose his train of thought.

"Shit. What was I talking about again?"

"You were saying that you thought Passmore hired you to come on weekends sometimes to show off."

"Right! Daniel told me that one time Passmore paid him to come pretend to be trimming the hedges around the pool, even though he'd just done it two days before. We were like props to him, man. Not that I minded so much. He did pay me extra and all. And the one time he had a check bounce, he made it right. So like I said… I can't really complain."

Darger considered whether being treated like a servant would be enough motive for murder. She thought in some cases it might, but here she doubted it. Trobiani didn't seem too bothered by it, all things considered. And if he did have an axe to grind with Passmore, he likely wouldn't have started out the interview describing the man as a jackass.

"Probably sounds like I'm judging the dude, but I figure it's his life. Just seemed kinda pointless to me. All that stressing out trying to convince people you're more famous than you really are? But I guess he was the 'fake it 'til you make it' type. And the way he'd been talking lately, he was convinced he was about to make it." Trobiani frowned. "Bad timing."

His phone buzzed again, and he blew out a breath.

"My girlfriend. She's kind of freaking out since she heard what happened. Texting me nonstop, even though I told her I'm fine." He started tapping out a reply. "Sorry, this'll just be a second."

When he finished and returned the phone to his pocket again, Darger tried to get him back on track.

"You seem to have a lot of insight into all of this. The idea that Gavin Passmore was desperately trying to keep up appearances."

"Most of my regulars are up this way. And believe me, Passmore wasn't the only one putting on a little show. But when you work around these types long enough, you start to notice the difference between the truly wealthy and the people who are just playing at it."

"Oh yeah?"

"Yeah, like Passmore was kinda cheap. A penny pincher, you know? Always demanding discounts or refunds. Like one time I vacced the car but didn't do the trunk, mostly because it didn't need it. Gavin demanded I deduct eight dollars from his next bill, since I hadn't done a full vacuuming. He *wanted his dime's worth.*" Trobiani chuckled. "That's what he said. And he'd go on and on about how that's how people attain wealth in the first place, by keeping an eye on every dime. But I've worked for some of the real old money families out here, and that just isn't true. These people, if you did their grocery shopping for the week and told them a gallon of milk cost ten bucks, they'd believe you. They ain't into the nickels and dimes, see? They probably haven't ever seen loose change. They'll tip you with a hundred because it's the smallest bill they got and think nothing of it. The truly rich people? Chumps like Gavin Passmore have no idea. No idea, man. They have so much money that any amount of cash on hand is like Monopoly dollars. It's a toy. Insignificant."

Darger glanced at Loshak. Wordlessly, they agreed that they'd gotten what they needed from the interview. Loshak put out a hand.

"Thank you for your time, sir. Sorry to put you through that yet again."

"Eh, it's no big deal," Trobiani said. "But does that mean I can go now? My girlfriend is hounding me about when I'm coming home."

"You should talk to Agent Fredrick about that," Loshak said, pointing her out near the command center.

Trobiani sauntered off, phone in hand.

"What do you think?" Loshak asked.

"I'd be surprised if he was our guy. He's too… relaxed. Too open."

"Agreed," Loshak said.

"I thought what he said about Passmore's agent was interesting. That they had an argument about finances and whatnot. We should make sure they're looking into him."

Loshak raised an eyebrow.

"Changing your mind on the serial angle?"

"I haven't decided either way. I'm 'letting the evidence tell the story,'" Darger said, quoting something Loshak always told the agent trainees in his classes.

He smirked.

"You want to head back inside and see if the techs have dug

up anything interesting?"

"Lead the way," Darger said.

# CHAPTER 7

Darger and Loshak went back inside through the large front door, but this time, they took a flight of stairs up to the second floor.

Their footsteps whispered over cream Berber carpet stretching the length of the hallway. Doorways on each side of the hall formed portals into fresh exhibits of the lifestyles of the rich and famous. Bedrooms with more expensive-looking furniture. Art and artifacts decorating the walls. A bathroom with marble covering every available surface aside from the toilet and glass shower walls. A bird of paradise plant in the window that stretched nearly to the ceiling.

In one room, they found an analyst with a laptop, scanners, and printer, surrounded by stacks of paper. He glanced up at them and sprang to his feet.

"Oh wow! Agent Loshak! I'd heard you were coming, but…" He stepped around the desk and put out his hand. "You probably don't remember me, but I was in your Advanced Crime Scene Analysis class when I went through the academy two years ago."

Loshak's eyes flicked to the lanyard with the man's credentials.

"Of course I remember you. Bill Crowley. One our best and brightest."

Crowley beamed.

"I just wanted you to know that your lecture series was my favorite part of training. I still think about it all the time. The way criminal behavior paints a picture of damaged psychology in action, consciously and subconsciously. Once you have a little insight into something like that, you start seeing it everywhere. In my other classes, I learned investigative techniques. In your class, I got a whole new perspective on the human condition."

"Well… that's wonderful to hear," Loshak said. "This is my partner, Agent Darger."

"Of course." The analyst's eyelids fluttered. "An honor to meet you."

"Likewise," she said, shaking his hand. She gestured at the stacks of paper littering the desk. "What is all this?"

"Various personal documents of the victim. Cell phone records, credit card statements, etc."

"Mind if I take a look?" Darger asked, jutting her chin at one of the piles.

"Be my guest."

Darger picked up the closest sheet. It was a statement for Passmore's American Express Gold card. Beside her, Loshak whistled at the balance amount. Trobiani had been right about the man's spending habits.

"That is some pretty massive debt," Loshak said.

Darger's eyes bugged out as she ran down the list of expenses. She paused on one.

"Three thousand dollars for wine?"

"That's a light month," Crowley said. "I guess he liked to throw big parties with an open bar. A few months ago he spent almost seven thousand on alcohol. And about the same on catering."

"Jesus."

"He also had a boat. Paid a few thousand a month to dock it up in Montauk. And then a few thousand whenever he hired a crew to take it out."

"Look at the minimum payment due on that card." Loshak jabbed his finger at a five-figure number in an outlined box at the top of the page. "What if Passmore was so over his head in debt that he started borrowing from someone unsavory?"

"Maybe," Darger said. "But they usually go for something a bit more low-key. A relatively subtle busting of the kneecaps so as to still give the person an opportunity to pay what they owe. Blowing the guy up doesn't leave a lot of wiggle room."

"Yeah, but maybe someone wanted to send a message. Use this public figure as an example. Pay us back on time, or we'll send you a present."

Crowley shook his head.

"The funny thing is, the victim was on the cusp of actually being able to afford all of this. Kind of ironic."

"What do you mean?" Darger asked, remembering that Trobiani had also said something about Passmore being on the verge of finally 'making it.'

"His agent says he was up for a role in a film by an A-list director." His voice lowered to something barely above a whisper. "He wouldn't name names, but he implied it was Tarantino. Would have been Passmore's big break. The agent kept repeating that it would have 'made his career.'"

Loshak's eyes glittered.

"The plot thickens. What if this is all motivated by professional jealousy?"

Darger was already shaking her head.

"Oh come on. You think someone offed this guy to keep him from getting the role? A rival actor?"

"Would someone really do that?" Crowley asked.

"Hey, look at the Nancy Kerrigan thing," Loshak said, shrugging.

The space between Crowley's eyebrows wrinkled.

"Who?"

"Oh, you sweet summer child." Loshak patted Crowley's shoulder. "OK. January 1994. The US Figure Skating Championships were being held in Detroit, Michigan. This would decide who made the Olympic team, right? The top two skaters for the ladies' singles were Nancy Kerrigan and Tonya Harding. A few days before the Championships were to begin, Nancy Kerrigan finished a practice session and was assaulted in a hallway of the arena. A guy named Shane Stant approached her from behind in a ski mask, took out an extendable police baton, and whacked her on the leg. He'd been hired by Harding's former bodyguard and ex-husband to carry out the assault."

Crowley's mouth hung slightly ajar.

"So what happened?"

"Oh they all got caught."

"No, I mean with the lady who was attacked?" Crowley clarified. "Could she not skate anymore?"

"Kerrigan didn't skate at the US Championships, and Harding got first place."

"Wait. They still let her skate after that?"

"At the time, they couldn't prove any involvement. Harding was later banned from the sport, and her Championship win was annulled."

"Jeez." Crowley blinked. "That's crazy."

"Even crazier, they both skated for the Olympic team later that year," Darger added. "It was a big thing in all the tabloids. Kerrigan took silver. Harding… well, there was this whole thing with her shoelace… she was a mess, really."

"Hard to imagine anyone being that committed to ice

skating," Crowley said, frowning.

Loshak held up a finger.

"Exactly. Now imagine you're a hungry young actor. Landing a role — a *juicy* role — in a Tarantino movie would very much be like skating in the Olympics. Maybe bigger."

Darger crossed her arms.

"Right, but they didn't send Nancy Kerrigan a bomb. There's a big difference between hiring a goon to bludgeon a knee with an extendable baton and building explosives."

"So maybe our guy doesn't want to leave anything to chance. Kerrigan got the goon treatment and still ended up skating. It's gotta be cut and dry."

"A bomb would be that," Darger had to admit. "Still… this is so big. So over the top. If you just need the guy dead, hire a hitman, for God's sake. Corner the guy in a dark alley. This is someone who wants attention. Someone with a cause, a set of beliefs they're trying to express with violence. The scale puts it beyond something personal, I think."

Loshak seemed won over by that, but his words remained guarded.

"Maybe. We'll have to wait and see what the evidence says. Speaking of which, let's go see if there have been any updates on tracking the origin of the package." He put his hand out again for Crowley to shake. "Bill, my man, it was a pleasure to see you. I hope we cross paths again soon."

"Thanks, Agent Loshak." Crowley's face turned pink, and Darger almost expected him to giggle like a schoolgirl. "And it was nice meeting you, Agent Darger."

"Likewise. Thanks for the help."

Back in the hallway with the giant bird of paradise, Darger elbowed her partner.

"You didn't actually remember him, did you?" Darger asked.

Loshak scoffed.

"Of course I did."

"I saw you read his name off his ID, you old fraud."

"I was just jogging my memory." Loshak's voice was pure innocence. "I knew the face but wanted to make sure I got the name right."

"You're so full of it," Darger said with a snort.

They reached the bottom of the stairs and nearly collided with several agents and techs jogging into the foyer. From the open door, Darger could hear a commotion outside: chattering voices, the slamming of vehicle doors, engines accelerating down the drive.

"Something's going down," Loshak said.

When they reached the door, they almost plowed into Agent Fredrick, who was trying her best to fight against the flow of people exiting the house.

"Oh good," Fredrick said, sounding out of breath. "You already heard? We're heading to his house in Jersey City now."

"Wait. Heard what?"

"We've identified our bomber."

She licked her lips.

"His name is Tyler Huxley."

# CHAPTER 8

Agent Fredrick filled them in as they wove around the agents, analysts, and techs scrambling about outside.

"The bureau has a helicopter waiting in Southampton that can take us to Jersey City in half the time it would take by car. I saved each of you a seat in the chopper."

"Sounds good," Loshak said, patting at his pants pocket and coming out with the keys to their rental car. "Can someone handle returning our car to the rental lot?"

"Absolutely." Fredrick gestured at a tall, thin man with glasses waiting near a black Ford Explorer. "Agent Jelani here is driving us to the heliport. He can take your keys and arrange a pickup on the car."

"Excellent."

They followed Fredrick over to the SUV, and Darger and Loshak slid into the backseat and buckled up.

"So how did they end up tracking him down?" Darger asked. "Was it the security video from the post office drop box?"

Fredrick twisted in her seat to face them as Agent Jelani put the vehicle in gear and started down the drive.

"It was. Because we had the footage from the house, we knew the size and shape of the package and could narrow it down from there. Anyone dropping a letter or a small envelope or one of those red, white, and blue Priority Mail boxes could be ruled out." She pulled the tablet out of a black carry case. "I have the video, if you'd like to see it."

"Sure."

This video was a step down in quality compared to what

they'd seen from the house security cameras. Grainy, black and white, with a low frame rate. The USPS drop box was on the right side of the screen. A man in a baseball hat approached from the left. The box in his hands indeed looked to be the same size and shape as the one left on Passmore's doorstep. The man in the baseball hat opened the pull-down door of the drop box, deposited the package, and then walked back the way he'd come.

Darger blinked.

"They were able to ID him just from that?"

"No. We have feed for the whole street." Fredrick opened another video. This one was full color and much higher quality. "This is someone's doorbell camera from maybe half a block down from the box."

The man in the baseball hat appeared. Darger could see now that he was wearing a camo t-shirt, black cargo shorts, yellow shoes. The hat was embroidered with the skull logo from the Punisher comic books.

"Look at his outfit," Darger said. "It's like he ordered the Domestic Terrorist Starter Package from Amazon."

Loshak smirked.

"Yeah. Except for the bright yellow clown shoes. Maybe combat boots irritate his bunions."

Passing by the stoop of the house with the camera mounted outside, the man turned a corner and disappeared from view.

"He's not moving very fast," Darger said. "Doesn't seem to be in a hurry at all. Ten seconds ago he dropped an IED in a mailbox, and he's as calm as can be."

Agent Fredrick selected a third video. This one picked up where the last one left off. Captain Clown Shoes entered the frame. Crossed in front of whatever building they'd pulled the video from. Disappeared.

Fredrick held up a finger.

"Wait for it."

About ten seconds later, a car rolled by. A silver sedan. Before it exited the frame, the license plate was clearly visible for several seconds.

"Nice," Darger said.

"Gotta love the availability of security footage these days," Loshak said. "A high-def camera in every pocket and one on every doorstep."

"We traced the plate, got his name and an address," Fredrick explained. "It appears to be current. Our colleagues in New Jersey are working on a warrant. We have SWAT and a Counter-IED team on standby. They'll be ready to go as soon as we get the green light."

They'd reached the heliport. Agent Jelani drove them onto the tarmac and right up to the edge of the hangar. Loshak handed Jelani the keys to their rental as they climbed out.

The helicopter sat on a small platform that was being dollied out onto the tarmac as they arrived. The metal platform shifted slowly over the threshold of the gaping hangar door. Moved out onto the concrete, following tracks embedded into the runway.

When it came to a stop, Agent Fredrick stepped up onto the metal surface and climbed in. Darger and Loshak followed.

Inside the chopper, they each donned a headset and took a seat. After flipping a couple of switches, the pilot cranked his head back to welcome them aboard and inform the group it'd be approximately forty minutes to their destination.

The door was sealed. The rotors started spinning, building speed, and within seconds they lurched off the landing pad and ascended into the air. The liftoff was a bit bumpy, the whole cabin vibrating like one of those Magic Fingers mattresses cranked all the way up. Rattling and rumbling.

Darger jostled from side to side in her seat. She dug her fingernails into the armrests. She'd never been a big fan of helicopters.

"Do we have any background on Huxley?" she asked, trying to distract herself by refocusing on the case instead of on the motion of the helicopter.

"He's got a lone prior, as far as we can tell — shoplifting from a hardware store about six months ago — so right now we only have the minimal details from that. Mugshot. A brief report by the arresting officer. It's not much," Fredrick said. "We're also looking at finding a connection between Huxley and Gavin Passmore that might speak to motive."

Once they'd reached cruising altitude, the ride smoothed out. Darger retracted her claws from the leather armrest covering and got out her phone.

"Let's see if our guy is on social media."

After a few false starts, she found him. He had a Twitter account that seemed to have been abandoned. His last update was a retweet of a Tom Brady meme from almost two years prior. His Facebook was more promising.

She found a few photos of Huxley — a fairly nondescript-looking Caucasian male in his late 20s. He had something of a hound dog look about his eyes, which were downturned and somewhat vacant, the flesh around them puffy and puckered. Other than that, he didn't stand out. Dark hair that he kept short. Clear skin. Not much of a smiler from what she was seeing. Clicking around his Facebook profile, she also found his employer and where he went to high school and college.

"According to Facebook, he went to high school in Queens.

A couple years of college at Nassau Community College. No degree. And it says he's a driver at QBF Shipping. One of those delivery start-ups trying to give UPS and the post office a run for their money."

"That's interesting," Loshak said. "I guess he'd have some insider insight into shipping — the logistics and how all of that works."

Darger scrolled through Huxley's most recent posts. Most were shared from elsewhere. Various memes. An article from *The Onion*. A 'Which *Reservoir Dog* Are You?' quiz. The most recent update Huxley had penned himself was innocuous and brief: "Drank two glasses of whiskey last night and got the spins. Shoooot. I'm getting old, lol."

Darger returned to the small collection of photos, studying the handful of selfies. In one of the photos, he was sitting next to an older woman on a sofa with an abstract printed textile that gave off a very 90s vibe. There was no caption on the photo, no one tagged but Huxley himself, but Darger thought she saw a family resemblance in the woman's eyes. Downturned and devoid of emotion.

She wondered if the woman was Huxley's mother. If so, she'd be a good person to talk to. Get some early life background on the bomber. His childhood. Whether he'd had friends or been a loner. Her gut said he'd be somewhere in between. The kind of guy who can blend with the crowd, socially. Is neither popular nor a pariah. It fit with the job, too.

Most delivery jobs were fairly stressful. A lot of accountability. The workers had to be motivated to run those routes day after day, keeping to a tight schedule. It wasn't a job for a slacker. And yet it would be quite solitary. There might be some time at the beginning or end of a shift where you saw the other drivers, the coworkers who did the sorting. But for the majority of his workday, Tyler Huxley would be alone. Plotting. Scheming. Is that where the fantasy started? Somewhere along one of his monotonous routes?

Fredrick leaned out of her seat to get a better look at the photos.

"He looks so… normal. One could even call him handsome, though he's not my type." She frowned. "But it's more than that. He looks… kind of gentle. Not the aggressive type, you know?"

"That kind of fits with the bomber profile, in a lot of ways," Loshak said. "Not that there's a type so much when it comes to physical features. But they lack some of the direct aggression that someone who uses a knife or even a gun might possess. A bomber's rage is almost… academic. A philosophy more than the visceral, immediate anger you get from a mass shooter. Look at the Unabomber. By all accounts, Ted Kaczynski was reserved and shy. Timothy McVeigh was the same."

Loshak sat back and stared up at the ceiling.

"Although, maybe it would be more accurate to say that they're better at keeping the fury under wraps. Better at hiding it. In any case, I can almost guarantee we'll find some kind of manifesto."

"I was hoping there'd be something on his Facebook," Darger said, shaking her head. "But this stuff is as normal as his photo. Some selfies. Some silly Buzzfeed quizzes. Some memes. I'm with Fredrick on this one. I was expecting to get at least a minor creepy vibe from Huxley, but his Facebook is so… sanitary. Sterile. I know you can't judge a book by its cover and how easily someone can manipulate or craft their image on social media, but so far this guy is just… boring."

Loshak shrugged.

"And maybe that's the scariest part of all. That they look like a hundred strangers you pass on the sidewalk and never give a second look. Indistinguishable from the rest of the crowd."

# CHAPTER 9

Darger spotted the Statue of Liberty and Ellis Island as they swooped over the city — choppy blue water surrounding the landmarks — before they finally landed at the heliport in Jersey City.

They hustled out of the chopper, everyone instinctively ducking under the still whooshing propellers, and Darger couldn't help but remember a news article she'd read. A man in a public park in Queens had lopped off the top of his skull with the props of his own RC helicopter in front of dozens of horrified bystanders. Just a relaxing afternoon of recreation.

Agent Fredrick moved out in front of the pack and pointed at a dark sedan parked at an angle beside the helipad. They ran for it. A metallic blue Chevy Impala waited for them, driven by a local Jersey field agent by the name of Laboda.

Through either a smile or gritted teeth, Laboda clucked out a greeting Darger couldn't understand, though the inflection somehow got across the gist. Then he wheeled them out of the heliport and into traffic, wasting no time.

"We've got a bit more background on Huxley," Laboda said, enunciating this time. "My partner emailed each of you the newest addition to the file we're assembling on him."

Darger opened her phone and found the updates on Tyler Huxley pretty light, considering she'd dug up some of it on her own. Like the fact that he worked at QBF Shipping and grew up in Queens. The only new information she saw was that he had a silver Ford Fiesta registered in his name.

"We put in a call to his supervisor at the QBF distribution

center. Huxley took the week off. Had a bunch of PTO saved up." Laboda took a hard right turn without using his blinker. "And get this. QBF serves the greater Long Island area."

Darger tensed.

"Was Passmore's house on his route?"

"Not his usual route, no. But sometimes the drivers end up covering part of another driver's route, like when they're on vacation. He would have delivered there a handful of times over the years."

"So that could be his connection to Passmore," Loshak said, his brow furrowing, eyes darting back and forth like that computer nestled inside his skull was already busy at work processing the new data. "That's huge."

Darger glanced back at the information on Huxley and noted that they'd tracked down his family — his mother and a brother — who still lived in Queens. Darger was anxious to talk to them. To dig into Huxley's history. But that would come after. First... they needed to catch their guy. Make sure he couldn't hurt anyone else.

Laboda drove them to a rundown neighborhood near a railyard. The house on the corner had a huge "Condemned" sign posted out front, a yellow plastic rectangle adhered to the front door printed with big black letters. The lower windows had been boarded up and all of the glass in the upper windows had been busted out. That set the tone for the rest of the street.

Broken-down cars in various states of rusty erosion occupied one vacant lot. Overgrown weeds sprouted up around the vehicles, their stalks swaying gently from the breeze of the traffic rushing past, leaves brushing at crushed fenders and shattered windshields.

Around the dumpy houses, the small yards were unkempt

and strewn with junk — random cinder blocks nestled in the grass and other shards of concrete poked up from the yards and gutters. Bits of broken glass glittered along the sidewalks. An old top-loading washing machine huddled in one yard with the lid hanging open to the heavens.

Here and there pedestrians wove through all of the decay. Hard faces. Narrowed eyes. So many people packed into this small area. The concrete teemed with them.

Laboda made another turn and then pointed out Huxley's house.

"Second from the last on this side. The little ramshackle one."

They parked along the curb, finding a spot a few houses down across the street. The steel slats of the roll-up garage doors alongside them were covered in layers of graffiti — a rainbow of jagged lettering scrawling countless obscenities on top of each other.

A few piles of tattered garbage bags were wedged into the corner of the lot, orange juice containers and piles of sodden cigarette butts leaking out of the torn places. The trash spilled down into watery potholes, cellophane bits floating around atop the mud puddles.

Law enforcement vehicles crowded the area, and Darger noticed the officers still occupied the vehicles, matching silhouettes visible behind the steering wheels and in all the passenger seats.

"Took us a little extra time to get the warrant given that it's a weekend." Laboda checked his watch. "Should be any minute now."

Agent Fredrick pulled a pair of binoculars from her bag to try to get a look in the windows. She stared toward the building for what felt like a long time, her mouth a grim line beneath the black bulk pressed to her eyes. Then she passed the binoculars around for the others.

When it was Darger's turn, she trained the lenses on the place and used the focus wheel to sharpen the view. It was one of the smaller homes on the street. A narrow shoebox of a house. She counted at least three different types and colors of siding. The windows were sparse and small. A blue tarp stretched over one of the upstairs windows on the side closest to them.

A tangle of vines crawled up the wrought iron posts on the porch. The shingles on the roof were crumbling and covered in patches of moss. The sidewalk out front was bordered by a chain-link fence with a gate that sat crooked on its hinges.

Darger counted four small satellite dishes jutting from the roof, the DirecTV logo visible on one.

"Why do you think he needs four dishes?"

"Too lazy to remove the old ones?" Loshak suggested.

"Probably."

Darger handed the binoculars to Loshak but kept her gaze on the house. She spotted the silver Ford Fiesta registered to Tyler Huxley parked in front of a pile of trash and old wooden pallets, which suggested he was home. But she detected no movement from inside.

Her anxiety built as they waited. She readjusted her position in her seat as if that might ease some of the tension.

"How is this going to work?" she asked. "I assume the SWAT team has been told our guy is into explosives?"

"They are under strict instructions not to touch anything. They'll do a rapid clear out and apprehend our suspect, if he's here. Then we'll take the bomb-sniffing dogs through. If we find any evidence of an IED on the premises, we'll send one of the bomb techs inside in the blast suit and bust out the MECV."

"That's the doohickey they use to safely detonate the bomb in?"

"Right. Stands for Mobile Explosive Containment Vessel."

Laboda's phone rang, and he answered.

"You got it? Beautiful. I'll let everyone know." Laboda hung up. "We just got our warrant, and we are officially sanctioned to rock."

He snatched a walkie-talkie from the dash.

"Agent Fitch, this is Laboda speaking. We've got the green light. I repeat, we are good to go."

From over the radio, they heard the SWAT team leader telling his guys to get ready.

Darger felt a fresh surge of adrenaline as she watched the SWAT van door slide open. Eight men in black gear hopped out. Two more men from the bomb squad waited nearby — one with a German Shepherd on a lead and another in a bulky green bomb disposal suit.

She tried to swallow the tension creeping up from her gut. She never got used to being at a live scene like this. Maybe no one did. The anticipation thrummed in the air. Jittery body language abounded — fidgeting limbs, shimmying shoulders, torsos squirming against the backs of their seats.

Darger slid her eyes over to Loshak and could see the artery in his neck throbbing. His eyes were on the house, unblinking. Well, at least it wasn't just her.

She knew the SWAT guys loved this. The buzz of energy in the air. The palpable sense of danger. That countdown to go time. Darger thought they were all a little nuts, frankly. She much preferred a quiet scene, after the fact. No wondering if someone was about to get hurt or killed. No pressure to make the correct decision in the span of a single heartbeat.

She blinked and saw that the SWAT team had reached the front gate. The man in front pushed it open and held it aside as the rest of the guys filed through. Half went to the front door. The other half slipped into the alley, heading for the back of the house. They disappeared around a corner, and then a raspy voice crackled over the radio.

"Team 2 in position. Ready when you are."

"Go, Johnny, go," the team leader said.

The team in front burst inside first, shattering the door with a battering ram and tossing a flash-bang grenade into the gaping hole.

The men rushed inside, and the radio buzzed with chatter as they searched and cleared the rooms.

"Living room clear."

"Kitchen is all clear."

The team leader's voice came over the radio again.

"Team 2, we've secured the ground floor, but I've got two sets of stairs here. I'll take the second floor with Latu. Jarvis and Mooney, you take the basement."

There was a long pause as the men traversed the stairways. Upstairs, two bedrooms and a bathroom were cleared. They waited to hear about the basement for several more seconds, and eventually Darger started to wonder if they'd lost the radio feed.

The silence was shattered by a voice.

"Furnace room is clear. We're moving onto the main—"

"Hands on your head! Hands on your head!"

Darger's entire body clenched. They'd found someone. Huxley?

She said a silent prayer: *Please let this go smoothly. Please let them get this guy without anyone getting hurt.*

"Hands on your—oh shit."

Darger held her breath, worried now that something had gone wrong. Each fraction of a second was measured out with the thud of her heartbeat in her ears. And then, finally…

"Jesus. Mooney, are you seeing this?"

"Yeah. Yeah I am."

Darger's chest hitched. Tried to breathe but she wouldn't let it.

"Goddamn it, Jarvis. Is it clear down there or what?" the team leader demanded.

"Well… I mean… there's someone down here, but… they're pretty dead."

# CHAPTER 10

Darger huddled with the others outside Huxley's house. Pacing along the sawhorse barriers planted in the front yard. Everyone fidgeting. Making idle conversation, their voices all sounding high strung with nerves, tight and a little clipped.

Inside, the bomb-sniffing dogs were making their rounds. A team of fierce-eyed German Shepherds doing multiple passes in each room for the sake of thoroughness. Thankfully the place was quite small at just over 900 square feet, including the partially finished basement. More of a shack than anything.

By the time the dog handlers were wrapping up, early word had come back on two fronts and circulated among the group outside. First, the dogs weren't finding anything — their work would be as comprehensive as possible, but with no signs of any explosive material so far, odds were now beyond 99% that there was nothing of danger here. Second, the tenant — the body in the basement — appeared to have died by a self-inflicted gunshot wound.

Darger tried to wrap her head around that. Tyler Huxley had shipped his bomb and gone home and killed himself? The notion intensified her queasiness, made fresh sweat seep from her palms and chest until most of her body felt clammy.

Finally, the dogs and handlers came out one by one and briefed Agent Laboda, confirming what everyone expected by now. No bombs or related materials were found, which was good… but to Darger it still felt wrong. Was a mid-list actor in Long Island really the only target here? The bomber already done in by his own hand?

With a hand signal from Laboda, the sawhorse barrier parted before them, and a flood of law enforcement advanced on the house. As she got in line to file through the front door with the others, Darger saw the guy in the bomb suit slowly shucking it off, piece by piece, just outside. He was covered in sweat but seemed in high spirits, a smile curling the place between his cheeks and chin. Probably any day you didn't have to get within arm's reach of something that might explode in your face was a good day in his line of work.

Inside, the light was dim. Peeling wallpaper drooped in the living room, and signs of water damage stained the ceiling brown above that in imperfect circles that looked cloudy. Pilled-up balls of lint coated the fraying carpet — the gray flecks looking like raisins dotting the pale brown shag. The furniture was sparse — it seemed Huxley sat on the floor with his laptop on a battered coffee table, a knee-high desk.

Looking ahead, she could see plates and bowls in the kitchen crusted with ketchup and the remnants of macaroni and cheese. Haphazard piles of dirty dishware and cutlery dominated the counter space, bulged out of the sink, some of the mess having taken up one corner of the cracked linoleum floor. Crumpled Burger King bags and cups intermingled with the platters. Red splotches seemed to adhere to all of the dinnerware — everything kissed with dried-out Heinz, the bright scarlet going dull and slightly brown as it dehydrated. It was a far cry from Gavin Passmore's gleaming quartz island.

An odor of dust and soup had persisted in the front room of the house, the smell shifting as Darger strode through the doorway into the kitchen. A weird food stench of some kind wafted around the piles of dirty dishes and fast food wrappers cluttering the space. It reeked like heavily processed meat seasoned with a pungent spice Darger couldn't place. Reminded her of uncooked hot dogs. The unidentified meat smell immediately made her think of the Jeffrey Dahmer case file — the neighbors had complained that his apartment smelled like chitlins, unaware that they were actually smelling the partially zombified bodies of his victims as they slowly decayed.

"Not to be morbid, but I gotta say, this whole deal is kind of an anticlimax," Laboda said. "And believe me, I'm not complaining. It's just I didn't expect the guy to have taken himself out already."

"It wasn't exactly what I was anticipating either," Loshak said. "The bomber types are usually pretty dedicated to their cause, whatever it may be."

The four agents made their way through the living room and kitchen and headed down into the basement where the body had been discovered. Cracks slowly opened seams between the cinder blocks along the stairwell. The other outer walls in the cellar were even older, or so it seemed, made of stone and mortar.

Three maps of New York lined one section of drywall that separated a cobweb-covered furnace room from the rest of the basement. Nonsensical graffiti covered another section of the stone in a bright red scrawl, though Darger couldn't make out much. She read what she thought said, *Dominion.*

"Just up here, we should find…" Laboda trailed off as they rounded the corner.

Darger saw the legs first. Sprawled. Feet clad in the yellow sneakers she'd seen earlier in the video of Tyler Huxley dropping the package in the mailbox.

The shotgun still lay on the corpse's chest. A Mossberg Persuader. Brand new judging from the still flawless matte finish of the pistol grip stock, the unblemished barrel protruding from it.

Her eyes moved on from the weapon. Saw the slack arms resting at his sides, elbows faintly bent. The relaxed pose of someone who fell asleep watching TV.

The stumped jaw was still intact. An angular bone with a plump bottom lip blooming out of it.

Everything from there up was gone.

He'd stuck the muzzle of the gun in his mouth. Blasted a pumpkin ball slug straight up through his palate.

Erased his face. Shattered the rounded dome of his skull.

Distributed his frontal lobe all over this section of the basement. A spray of skull fragments about the size of teeth.

This was more than a wound. It was obliteration.

Laboda sucked his teeth.

"Jesus H. Don't think we'll need the autopsy for cause of death."

They all fell quiet for the span of a few breaths. Stared down at the wreckage that had once been Tyler Huxley's face.

Blood gone tacky.

The smell of decay.

The medical examiner and an assistant descended on the corpse then. They fished a few items out of the pockets of his jeans — car keys and a balled-up Kleenex came out of the right front, his wallet came out of the back left. The assistant flipped open the wallet, pulled out the driver's license, and handed it over to Laboda.

"Huxley's license. No surprise there," Laboda said, before handing the ID card around. "But we've got his prints on record from that shoplifting deal a few months back, so we'll be able to use those to confirm the identity. Once word got around about the stiff in the basement, I called ahead, so the lab is waiting on the prints. Shouldn't take long at all to make the comparison."

While the M.E. continued her preliminary examination, her assistant squatted next to the body and began the fingerprinting process. Lifted the limp arm. Pressed the corpse's fingers to an ink pad and rolled them onto a white card one by one. The black smudges blossomed on the white paper, swirled with the identifying loops and whorls of his fingerprints.

"Can you tell how long it's been, doc?" Laboda asked the M.E.

She returned her thermometer to her kit and glanced up at them.

"Rigor mortis has dissipated, so I'd say it's been over 36 hours. How much over, we won't know for sure."

"Based on the timeline it seems like he dropped the package in the mailbox, came home, and within a few hours at most, killed himself," Darger said.

Everyone was quiet for a few seconds as they processed that.

"You think he started feeling guilty about what he'd done?" Fredrick asked.

Loshak frowned and scratched his chin.

"It's possible. I think it's more likely that he got scared. Knew we'd be coming for him." He shrugged. "It's not all that uncommon for domestic terrorist types to choose suicide over being caught."

Laboda blew out a breath.

"Well, I apologize in advance if we dragged you guys all the way out here for nothing. I mean, it's not exactly as if we need a profile now that the guy's dead."

Fredrick cleared her throat.

"I wouldn't be so sure of that," she said.

Darger's head snapped around to face the woman.

"What do you mean?"

Agent Fredrick aimed a penlight at a piece of lined notebook paper taped to the drywall off to one side of where the body lay.

"He left a note."

"A suicide note?" Darger moved closer.

Fredrick bit her bottom lip.

"Not exactly."

The side of the room where the note had been left was directly in the path of the exit wound. The gore slicked the concrete basement floor, and Darger had to step carefully to avoid slipping on the broken pieces of Tyler Huxley's head.

She found a clean area and leaned in to read the note without touching it.

The message was scrawled in spiky, aggressive lettering.

*By the time you read this, I'll be dead, but what I've set into motion will only be beginning.*

*The first bomb has gone off by now. So it begins.*

*Starting at midnight tonight, a bomb will go off roughly every eight hours, and a target will be neutralized.*

*The targets are of no significance politically.*

*They are cultural icons. Celebrities. Actors. Reality TV figures and the like.*

*Be honest. Fiery death could make some of these folks more likable.*

*Doesn't that bland host of the karaoke show become more compelling after he's been blown to pieces?*

*How about the fashion model trying to break into the mainstream taking shrapnel to her jugular?*

*The juicy lead role of her dreams.*

*You piggies have a chance, however, to stop some of the carnage.*

*What better way to get attention to my message than to invite the police and public alike to play a little game?*

*Here's how it works:*

*Chunks of my journal are strewn about the city. Hidden. Each one contains clues to the next chunk, and likewise, each one divulges the details of one of the little toys I've prepared for one of America's sweethearts.*

*Clues for names. Clues for places.*

*Everything you'd need to locate and disarm one of the bombs is there.*

*All I ask in return is that you read the journal. Really read it. Consider what I am presenting.*

*Ironically, killing celebrities will make me a celebrity.*

*For the next 24 hours or so, as my bombs either go off or don't, I may well be the most famous person on the planet.*

*An unflattering photo of my face will be plastered in a box just over the news anchor's shoulder.*

*It will be worth it.*

*My ideas will be dissected and debated the whole world round, chunks of my journal translated into damn near every language on the globe.*

*The game begins.*

*Pour yourself a cup of coffee. And if you must sleep tonight, be sure to keep those DVRs rolling.*

*From Hell,*

*T. H.*

Darger reached out, her gloved fingertips barely touching the edge of the paper. She turned the note over and found tiny lettering on the back.

*They say you're not just a pretty face. But I wonder what you'll do without it. Staring at yourself on screen, that looking glass mounted in every living room, like Narcissus staring into the pond. Rewind yourself. Replay yourself. An endless loop of you, you, you. Too stupid to look away long enough to eat or drink. Too stupid to live.*

From over her shoulder, Darger heard Laboda's voice.

"It's going to be a long night."

# CHAPTER 11

Goosebumps rippled over Darger's skin. Cold feelings crawling all over her, reaching inside of her.

*More bombs.*

*Christ.*

Her gaze stayed trained on that sheet of notebook paper. Blinking. Not really looking at it anymore. Some daze overtaking her body, her being, keeping her still. After a few seconds, a gloved hand plucked the note from the wall and the sheet of paper seemed to float away from her.

Laboda and Fredrick immediately pulled out their phones, putting in calls to their superiors to update them on this newest revelation.

Darger replayed the note in her head again, trying to parse it in any way she could. Read into it.

*Starting at midnight tonight, a bomb will go off roughly every eight hours...*

*For the next 24 hours or so, as my bombs either go off or don't...*

The simple math seemed to suggest three more bombs. One scheduled to go off at midnight, another at 8 A.M., and finally 4 P.M.

Around her, the scene grew frantic. Her colleagues scrambled to come up with a plan. She heard Laboda barking at another agent to tell the bomb squad not to leave. Fredrick was yelling something into her phone about contacting the Department of Homeland Security.

There'd been a brief calm once they found Huxley dead, a

moment where they'd thought the worst was over. But this note, with its promise of more bombs, more explosions, more death, had thrown everyone into a frenzy.

*More bombs. More victims. We have to find them before it's too late.*

A game Huxley had called it, and that sent a fresh chill through Darger's flesh. Icy tendrils roiled in her forearms, in her hands.

Her mind went to Leonard Stump. All his philosophical talk was a guise, a cover for the way he liked playing with people. Liked to capture them and hold them under a microscope like an insect while he pulled off one leg at a time. The place where he'd put a bullet in her prickled at the suggestion, but then she pictured him as she'd last seen him: in jail, looking frail and pathetic, an eye patch covering the place where his last victim had taken her revenge. The strange feeling in her scalp vanished as quickly as it had appeared.

*My wounds have healed, but Stump's eye is never coming back.* She took satisfaction in that. *Just like the broken bits of Tyler Huxley's skull will never piece themselves back together.*

Another wave of crime scene techs entered the basement then, and the frenzied energy in the tight space ratcheted up a notch. The air grew stuffy with all the people crowded down here — muggy — and it was beginning to feel cramped. The physical discomfort seemed only to feed the sense of dread Darger was sure they all felt.

The clock was ticking, and no one knew where to start. Had Passmore been a random target? Chosen simply because he was an actor on the rise? Or was he someone with whom Huxley had some personal connection? The latter seemed unlikely, she thought, but if the victims were being selected at random, it'd make their job even more difficult.

*He mentioned clues*, she reminded herself. It's a game.

Darger tumbled snippets of the note around in her head again. Tried to think, to get her brain to connect the dots somewhere.

There was something to the back side of the note. Something about the language. Vague and almost playful.

*Staring at yourself on screen, that looking glass mounted in every living room, like Narcissus staring into the pond.*

Darger figured that *had* to be a clue, but she had no idea what it meant. Perhaps one of the journals he'd mentioned was hidden near a pond? That hardly narrowed it down.

The atmosphere of the basement was becoming too much. The heat and stickiness and collective anxiety clouding her mind. Plus, the smell down here was making her stomach churn. The queasy feeling still lingering from the helicopter ride didn't help, either.

She backed up, retracing her steps up the basement stairs.

The techs and analysts were still swarming the ground floor, picking through the dirty dishes stacked on the countertops, opening cabinets and cupboards, sifting through papers and magazines and mail left on the coffee table in the living room. Combing the place for information. Anything that might tell them more about Tyler Huxley and who he may have wanted to target with one of his special deliveries.

Outside, the sun had partially hidden behind the skyscrapers along the horizon, casting a faint shade over the dumpy Jersey City street. The heat still radiated up from the asphalt the way it always did in the summer, though. No mercy.

A pair of techs and a photographer were across the street, processing Huxley's car. She watched the white-clad figures bagging fast food wrappers and what looked like hundreds of pages of articles printed off the internet. Another pair was tearing through the garbage cans, ripping apart the black plastic bags, and separating the trash from potential treasure.

Darger made a beeline for the abandoned garage across the street. She ducked around the corner and pulled off her mask and gloves. She closed her eyes and took a deep breath.

*Focus. Stop worrying about what everyone else is doing, and just focus.*

Darger brought up a photo she'd taken of the suicide note, swiping to the picture of the back.

*They say you're not just a pretty face.*

Well that seemed obvious enough. He was targeting celebrities after all. The pretty people.

The next line was, *But I wonder what you'll do without it.*

Images of the two faceless corpses she'd seen today flashed in her mind.

God, maybe this wasn't meant to be a clue at all. Maybe Huxley was just taunting them.

Her teeth ground together as she read the words a third and fourth time. If this was all they had to go on, they were screwed.

But then she remembered that they'd found one potential connection between Huxley and Gavin Passmore after all. Huxley would have subbed on the delivery route that served Passmore's mansion. If they could narrow down the potential victim pool to only locations where Huxley delivered, that would be huge. They needed to get more information about the routes he drove.

Darger inhaled, her ribcage quaking with adrenaline now that she had an idea on how to proceed.

A hand on her shoulder startled her from her thoughts. She

spun around and found Loshak standing behind her, one eyebrow raised.

"You OK?"

"Yeah. Just… I couldn't think clearly in all that. It was like being in the middle of a hurricane. Too much going on."

"Tensions are certainly running high."

He checked his watch. Probably calculating how long they had until midnight.

"Tension is exactly what he wanted."

Loshak ran a hand through his hair.

"Without a doubt."

Agent Fredrick joined them, her round face tense with concern.

"There's a task force meeting set for 2100 hours. In the meantime, we still have the chopper at our disposal. Any ideas on where we might start on all this?"

"I think we should talk to Huxley's employer and see if we can get his route information," Darger said. "So far that's the closest we've come to a connection between him and Gavin Passmore. And if he came across one target that way, it might be how he selected the others as well."

"I agree," Loshak said.

Fredrick nodded her head once.

"Let's go."

# CHAPTER 12

They soared over the Hudson River, and she saw the city from an angle she'd never seen before. A bird's-eye view of the towering skyscrapers. Instead of craning her neck to look up at the pointed spire atop the Empire State building, she was looking straight out the window at it. Down below, the streets were laid out in neat, square grids. The people reduced to dark specks on the sidewalks. Here and there a box of green that signified a park.

"Well?" Loshak said. "Aren't you gonna say it?"

Darger blinked.

"Say what?"

"That you knew along it was gonna be serial."

Darger leaned back in her seat, trying not to smirk.

"I'm too classy to say I told you so."

"Oh yeah?" Loshak scoffed. "Since when?"

Darger returned her attention to the scenery. There was something awe-inspiring about the city. The way it just went on and on and on, the buildings and the cars and the people. They'd poured all this concrete, little by little, let it flow over the soil and harden. Now it was a vast gray shell teeming with life.

"What do you think about this idea of him leaving us clues?" Agent Fredrick asked. "Seems kind of funny to go to all the trouble of building a bomb and picking out a target only to give us a chance to undo it all."

"I keep thinking about the Unabomber case," Darger said. "How Ted Kaczynski left what seemed like clues in many of his bombs, but it became clear that the point was to confuse investigators rather than represent anything meaningful."

Loshak nodded.

"Right. Several of the bombs included the initials 'F.C.' Kaczynski later claimed it stood for 'Freedom Club,' but I wouldn't be surprised if he put it there just to set the investigators on a wild goose chase. Truth is, I don't think he was ever going to do anything to increase his chances of being caught. He was happy as a clam, out there in that little shack, reaping destruction from a distance."

Darger adjusted her headset.

"So… what if that's Huxley's scheme? What if we try to follow these so-called clues, and it turns out it's all bullshit?"

"I don't know if we have much choice," Loshak said. "The only thing we can do now is figure out everything we can about the guy and hope he meant it when he said we could stop it."

The helicopter ride was smoother this time. And shorter, which Darger appreciated. Her stomach didn't quite have a chance to twist itself into a mess of flexing knots. Instead she experienced a slight wobbly feeling in the center of her abdomen that faded as they hopped out of the chopper and walked over to a dark-haired woman standing next to a sedan — this was their ride.

They pulled into traffic and almost immediately came to a standstill. Darger peered out the window. It felt almost claustrophobic to be down at street level again, surrounded by all the hulking towers reaching for the heavens. Glass and steel and concrete piled into great columns until they blocked out most of the sky.

"I always felt that one of the most frustrating things about Kaczynski was that his targets were, in many ways, random," Loshak said, continuing the conversation from the helicopter.

"When he was living in Chicago, he targeted people at Northwestern. He also sent bombs to Berkeley, where he'd taught. So maybe 'random' isn't quite the right word, but he'd never met any of the people he'd targeted. It would have been difficult to draw a line directly from Kaczynski to his victims, in most cases. They simply represented something he opposed: computer technology, genetics research, the airline industry, forestry. He'd read something they'd written or spot their name mentioned in an article, and then he'd literally look them up in the phone book."

Loshak paused and rubbed his eyes before continuing.

"So if you think about it, we're way ahead here by comparison. We already know who our bomber is. He told us when the next bomb would go off. He even kind of told us who he'd be targeting, at least in a general sense. Now it's just a matter of finding the *where*."

# CHAPTER 13

Twenty minutes later, they arrived at the massive warehouse, passing by rows of white trucks with the brown QBF fox logo. Floodlights lit up the corrugated steel building but left most of the parking lot in dusky shadow.

"The storefront is closed, so they said we should go around back to the loading area."

The driver followed these instructions, weaving through the murky lot and parking off to the side of two large semitrucks being unloaded.

Darger, Loshak, and Fredrick climbed out of the vehicle and approached one of the open rolling doors — a gaping place where light streamed out to compete with the twilight outside.

Darger peered into the slice of the building she could see, a glut of industrial features coming into focus. Fluorescent light glinted off smooth concrete floors. Trucks and boxes squared off in the center of the space. The steel rafters looked skeletal up above.

As soon as they passed the doorway and stepped into the light, a guy in a QBF polo shirt holding a clipboard spotted them and walked over. He was a middle-aged man with broad shoulders and a deep tan.

"You're the folks from the FBI?" he asked.

"That's us," Loshak said, flashing his badge.

"Jim Roth," the man said, shaking their hands. "Glad to have you. Wish like hell it were under different circumstances."

"You were Tyler Huxley's supervisor?"

"That's right. Goin' on five years now." He let his cheeks

puff up with air and blew out a breath. "Can't believe this… you know… stuff. Just… unimaginable. You hear people carryin' on about it on TV all the time, sayin' how they never would have expected it from someone they knew. Well hell, that's all I can think of. That I never would have put somethin' like this on Tyler, man. I mean, it's supposed to be the postal workers who get all disgruntled and open fire on a crowd of people at a mall or whatever, right? Us here, we're supposed to be laid back and shi—stuff."

Roth tried to smile, but it came across as more of a grimace. He scratched the back of his head.

"Sorry. That was supposed to be a joke, kinda, but I guess it isn't so funny."

"You knew Huxley well?" Darger asked.

"I don't know if I'd say that. The drivers spend so much time on the road, you know? This here is a real solitary job. Not a lot of interaction between coworkers. I'd see him every morning and evening like everyone else. But look, I got a few dozen other drivers under me, so it's not like we had a lot of heart-to-heart talks or nothin'. Besides, Tyler was a, uh — what do you call it? A wallflower, yeah? Real quiet guy. Always staying out on the periphery of things. Fading into the damn wallpaper."

He held up a finger.

"Listen, you all should really talk to Tina." He waved over a girl in one of the QBF polos. "Hey, Tina. C'mere for a sec."

The girl was in her late twenties, tall and thin. Darger tried to imagine her lugging around heavy packages all day.

"You started as a temp, right?" Roth asked. "Did the holiday run with Tyler?"

"Yeah." She blinked hard, had a shellshocked look about

her. The term *moon-eyed* sprang to Darger's mind. "I still can't believe this is happening. So weird."

"What'd you think of him?" Darger asked.

"I mean, I spent like two months riding his route with him. Never got any bad vibes or, like, an inkling that there was anything… *off* about him. Or whatever? I never felt unsafe, I guess you could say."

Darger nodded.

"It seems like you would have gotten to know him pretty well, spending all those hours together?"

"You'd think so, but he wasn't a big talker," Tina said. "At first I thought it was because he didn't like me or something, but then I realized that was just how he was. He lived up in his head. Kind of stayed separate from the rest of the world all the time, you know? Like he'd just be sittin' there all quiet, and he'd start laughing at something in his thoughts. Really laughing. Other times, he'd start doing these hand motions. Shrugging his shoulders and wagging his finger. Like he was debating something internally or something, going back and forth inside. He liked listening to podcasts, so that kind of filled the time more than conversation anyhow. And when we did talk, it was mostly about the stuff in the podcasts."

Darger raised her eyebrows.

"What kind of podcasts did he like?"

"Oh, all kinds, but I guess a lot of it was true crime stuff, now that I think about it. And he had, like, an almost encyclopedic knowledge of serial killers. One time he listed off the last meals of like a dozen different serial killers and mass murderers. I remember that because he said that John Wayne Gacy's last meal was like an entire bucket of fried chicken, and we kind of laughed about that."

"And how would you describe him, in general?" Darger asked. "Personality-wise."

"He was a little awkward for sure, but I think his quietness was more from not being interested in most conversations. If you got him talking about things he was passionate about, he'd talk your ear off." Tina cocked her head to one side. "And he had a real dry sense of humor. Witty, but... I don't know... strange."

Darger had hoped they'd find someone here who'd known Tyler Huxley well, but like many domestic terrorists, he was mostly a loner, and this particular job only exacerbated that.

"Did Tyler ever mention being a fan of any celebrities? Any actor or musician he talked about, maybe?" she asked.

"Uh... I remember him talking about one of the Marvel movies once," Tina said. "I don't remember which one, just that he'd asked if I'd seen it yet. I said I hadn't, and he told me I really had to see it in the theater to get the full experience. With any other guy, that would have been sort of a set-up to asking me out, right? But not Tyler. He just went on and on about how the effects sequences aren't the same if you watch it at home on DVD."

The supervisor's face lit up at that.

"I'm glad you brought up movies. It reminds me of something," Roth said. "I caught Tyler in a lie once."

"What kind of lie?" Loshak asked.

"He called in sick one time. Coughing. Hoarse voice. All that garbage, yeah? Anyway, that night, I took my wife out for dinner and a movie — no special occasion, it's just the kind of guy I am. Well, who the hell do we run into but Tyler Huxley. At the theater. Buying a box of peanut M&M's at the concession stand."

"Did you confront him?" Darger asked, curious as to what kind of excuse Tyler might have offered for his phony sick day.

But Roth shook his head.

"I figure about half the time people call in sick it's bull." His eyes slid over to Tina. "No offense. I mean, it's not like I never done it when I was young and dumb. Anyway, he almost never called in, so I guess I felt like maybe he'd earned a day here or there. This job ain't easy. We don't like to lose people."

"Did he ever mention anything about the people on his route?" Darger asked. "People he might have had issues with?"

"Not that I can remember. We get complaints from time to time. A driver dings a mailbox or something like that, but Tyler's record was spotless."

"Can we see a map of his route?" Loshak asked.

"Sure can. Tyler did most of the deliveries for Bridgehampton and Southampton."

He led them over to a computer where he pulled up the next day's delivery schedule.

Darger stared at the number of stops listed on the screen.

"One-hundred and eight stops. That's for one day?"

Roth nodded.

Darger's hopes deflated a little. One-hundred and eight stops and that was only the packages being delivered tomorrow. There had to be a thousand addresses making up the entire route, if not more. And there were a lot of the type of people Tyler Huxley seemed to hate living up there. If his next target was buried somewhere in the pages and pages of addresses, it would be like finding a needle in a haystack. And they only had until midnight to find it.

"Do you want to see his previous route, too?" Roth asked.

Loshak cleared his throat.

"His what?"

"Well, he switched routes about four months ago. Before he started doing Bridgehampton-Southampton, he was doing the Sag Harbor route."

"How many routes has he driven since he's been here?"

Roth tapped a few keys.

"This'll be his third route, matter of fact. He started out driving in Eastport."

Darger and Loshak looked at each other. They'd just tripled their search area.

And the clock kept ticking.

# CHAPTER 14

It was almost full dark out as they rode to the Jacob K. Javits building located at 26 Federal Plaza in Lower Manhattan. The task force would assemble on the 23rd floor, which served as the FBI field office in New York.

Lights glittered everywhere in this part of the city. The tiny squares of the windows glowing up and down the various towers, beating back the encroaching darkness one little slice at a time.

Darger stared down at her phone, at the map showing the three routes Huxley had run over his years as a delivery driver. Any of these might contain potential victims — but only if he stayed in his delivery area. The reality was, he could strike anywhere. He'd already used the mail once. He could target anyone that way. He could go global if he wanted to.

In hindsight, she felt stupid for pinning so much hope on the QBF angle. It was too easy. Too obvious. Huxley had called it a game, which implied they had a chance to win. But he'd stacked the odds in his favor.

Her nerves fizzled with frustration, anticipation. Heartbeat steadily increasing. Something horrible was going to happen, and for now they couldn't do anything about it. Nothing at all.

Darger's eyes went to the clock again. Measured out the countdown to midnight. Just over three hours left. How could they possibly find the next potential victim in that amount of time?

Loshak hadn't uttered a word since they'd returned to the car. She supposed he could be thinking ahead to the task force meeting, about the most pertinent details from the profile to get across to the group, but she thought he was probably thinking the same thing she was.

Three hours. Three measly hours to figure something out.

They had nothing.

And they were running out of time.

# CHAPTER 15

There was a Dunkin' Donuts around the corner from their destination, and Loshak loaded up with several boxes as was his ritual before almost every task meeting Darger had ever attended with him. When they reached the meeting room on the 23rd floor, there was a table already laden with an array of pastries and cookies.

"Looks like someone beat you to it," Darger said.

Loshak made room on the table for his boxes.

"Yeah, well. No one ever complained about too many donuts. Besides, it's a big group."

He wasn't wrong. Along with the primary group of FBI personnel, Darger saw a few guys from ATF and at least four different police jurisdictions.

A sheening oak table filled most of the conference room, its pale plank a little over twenty feet long. Agent Fredrick stepped up to the head of the table and raised her hand.

"If everyone could find a seat, we'll get started." She gave the room a stern look. "Now, before I hand things over to Agent Haslett from the forensics lab, I've only just been notified of a… development, I guess you could call it. And not a good one. The text of the suicide note we discovered in Huxley's apartment has been posted online."

A murmur spread through the room.

"I don't think I need to explain to anyone here how leaking this kind of information can jeopardize an investigation, and I'd like to believe that no one on this task force would do such a thing. But in the event that someone here has taken it upon themselves to interfere in this way, please be aware that you will be found, and you will be held accountable."

There was actually a smattering of applause from some members of the task force.

"Thank you," Fredrick said. "And now Agent Haslett will present his findings."

Haslett was a tall bald man with tortoiseshell glasses. He fiddled with the projector for a moment before beginning.

"This is a rendering of one the improvised explosive devices designed by Ted Kaczynski, the Unabomber." He gestured at the drawing of a bomb projected on the wall. "Based on the debris, we believe the device mailed to Gavin Passmore was quite similar to this one."

He pointed out various parts of the drawing.

"Here you have the pipe bomb portion. Three different sized steel pipes fitted inside one another concentrically and filled with ammonium nitrate and aluminum powder. The package is more or less booby-trapped, so that when it is opened, the tension applied to the switching mechanism here is released, which completes the electrical circuit provided by some lamp cord and two D-cell batteries."

The drawing became animated then, showing how a piece of cord attached to a flap at the top of the device triggered the detonation.

"When the electricity hits the hot wire initiator right here, it ignites the main pyrotechnic charge, which in turn ruptures the pipe, turning all that steel into shrapnel. We believe the package also contained additional projectile material, namely small nails and screws."

He displayed a series of photographs from Passmore's kitchen then. Holes in varying sizes that pocked the walls and cabinetry.

"The average speed of a fragment produced by a bomb like this is 2700 feet-per-second, which is equivalent to the muzzle velocity of a 30-06 hunting rifle. Each piece of shrapnel from a device like this is, in essence, a bullet."

The room was deathly quiet as that sunk in.

"What stands out to me here is that this was the design of the Unabomber's later bombs. His first seven IEDs relied on smokeless powder and match heads as the main charge. In other words, he started out with slightly less sophisticated, less powerful bombs. He moved onto the ammonium nitrite/aluminum mixture only after many years. Based on the level of sophistication, I believe our suspect would have made several practice bombs. Perhaps in the dozens. Usually we find that they start with more rudimentary IED designs, as was the case with Kaczynski. Once they get the hang of that, they become more daring. The chemicals being used are extremely volatile and there is a high risk of accidental detonation. In other words, this is not a sport for beginners."

An NYPD detective with a blond mustache raised his hand.

"Where would someone learn something like this?"

"We find that most bombers are self-taught. There's plenty of information out there for those who want it, unfortunately."

"What about the supplies for making the bombs?" another detective asked. "Would he need a special contact or source for that?"

"Most of the ingredients are harmless, individually. The pipe and lamp cord can be found at any hardware store or even scavenged if the bomber wants to avoid leaving any sort of trail. Ammonium nitrate is commonly found in certain fertilizers and cold packs. Aluminum powder is used in a variety of industries, including cosmetics. None of these things are illegal to buy or possess. It's only when combined that they become deadly."

Haslett took a drink of water before continuing.

"I understand the bomber has laid out a schedule of sorts for the forthcoming attacks. This leads me to believe that he will augment his prior method. First, I doubt he'll use the mail again, as it would be nearly impossible to orchestrate the opening of such a device at a specified time. The fact that he put forth a specific timetable suggests he'll be using timers." His eyebrows went up. "What I'd like to point out is that timed devices are almost always equipped with anti-tampering devices, so that should someone try to open or disarm the device, it will detonate regardless of whether the timer has initiated or not."

"Meaning we might have less time than he said? Like if he's left one of his packages sitting out in Central Park and someone comes along and monkeys with it… kaboom?"

Darger recognized the man speaking as the SWAT team leader that had stormed Huxley's house. Agent Fitch, she'd heard someone call him. Like many of the members of CIRG, he looked more like a guy that should be rappelling down the side of a building or maybe tracking the Predator through the jungle than your average FBI agent. His neck was a thick slab of muscle slightly wider than his skull, and his pale blue eyes gleamed with intensity.

"Precisely," Agent Haslett said.

"Well… shit."

Agent Haslett answered a few more questions before returning to his seat, and then Laboda stepped to the front, hitching up his pants as he went.

"First things first. I just got word from the latent print lab, confirming what we already suspected. Fingerprints from our stiff in the basement are a positive match for Tyler Huxley. The bomber is dead."

Laboda rifled through a manila folder for a few seconds before continuing.

"That's the good news. The bad news is that we were hoping to get a jump on identifying potential victims through Tyler Huxley's internet search history. Unfortunately, he did a top-shelf job of destroying his phone and laptop hard drive. That's thrown a wrench in things. To make matters worse, our attempt to narrow the scope by combing through Huxley's past delivery routes has yielded over five thousand individual addresses. Unless we can find a way to thin the herd in some way, it may not prove useful at all."

Smoothing his mustache, Laboda went on.

"We have managed to get his cell phone records, and we're working on getting his internet history stuff from his ISP, but it's going to take time, and it's going to be a lot to sift through. We also have a team going through his social media in the hopes that he sought out victims that way. Techs are still combing through the house in Jersey City as well."

The flaps of the manila folder parted again. Papers shuffled around.

"Dr. Farrow is finishing up the autopsy now. She has confirmed the cause of death was a gunshot wound to the head. Huxley's hands had gunshot residue and powder burns, all consistent with it being self-inflicted. So we're not expecting any bombshells from the postmortem… no pun intended."

"What about the gun?" someone asked. "Was he registered?"

Laboda shook his head.

"We have found no record of Huxley ever applying for a Firearms Purchaser Identification Card. We suspect it was purchased illegally or perhaps he bought it when he still lived in New York and brought it with him, which is legal."

Laboda glanced their way, an eyebrow raised as if to ask if they were ready. Darger nodded.

"Now I'll turn things over to Agent Loshak and Agent Darger, our profilers from Quantico. If you pay attention to anything said here tonight, this is where I'd focus. If we're going to thwart these imminent attacks, understanding Huxley's psychology is going to be the key."

This was one of the warmest introductions they'd ever received and not what Darger expected based on the region's reputation for blunt honesty peppered with a variety of four-letter words.

Darger went up first, giving a general background on Huxley and his psychology.

"Because we know who our subject is, we know the basics. Where he lived, where he grew up. He even left us a note, which gives some insight into his state of mind. After reading it, I think I can say with some degree of certainty that Tyler Huxley was likely a man filled with bitterness, resentment, and righteousness."

As she spoke, the subtle arrogance in Huxley's suicide note rang in her ears. *My ideas will be dissected and debated the whole world round, chunks of my journal translated into damn near every language on the globe.*

"Bombers often have this in common," Darger went on. "This belief that it's somehow their duty or responsibility to 'open the eyes' of the public at large. They are motivated by what they see as a mission, a cause bigger than themselves. They approach it pragmatically. Beneath the warped righteousness, these are men who feel overlooked. Sidelined. Held back by society in some way. Not allowed to reach the heights they feel they deserve. The bombings are acts of grandiosity, a sort of over-the-top compensation for their wounded egos."

Darger brought up a photo via the projector.

"Ted Kaczynski is a prime example. He showed a lot of academic promise as a kid. A mathematics prodigy, he graduated high school at fifteen and got into Harvard. His promise didn't pan out, though. A frustrated professor for a short time, he soon resigned and isolated himself in a Montana shack where he lived without electricity. He became increasingly convinced that technology was destroying the world." She shrugged. "OK. But how does murdering a secretary or a graduate assistant further that cause? How is killing anyone saving the forest? These acts did nothing to further his professed agenda. Because what really motivated him was fury and anger at his unfulfilled potential, great potential, in his estimation."

She swapped Kaczynski's for another.

"Timothy McVeigh. Very similar psychologically. On the surface, he claimed blowing up a federal building would spur a revolution, that was his motivation. But looking at the bigger picture of his life, the psychology underneath becomes clear."

Darger flipped to a new image, this one of McVeigh as a child, a vulnerable expression on his face.

"McVeigh was bullied as a kid. He tried to join Special Forces after his tour in Iraq and washed out on the second day. There we see the true motive, I think: he feels rejected and is lashing out. The bombing becomes a way of asserting his importance. The claimed cause is more or less an excuse to do what he's emotionally drawn to."

The next image showed handwritten text pulled from letters McVeigh had written.

"This is an excerpt of a letter McVeigh wrote to a childhood friend: 'I know in my heart that I am right in my struggle, Steve. I have come to peace with myself, my God and my cause. Blood will flow in the streets, Steve. Good vs. Evil. Free Men vs. Socialist Wannabe Slaves. Pray it is not your blood, my friend.' Here we see the violent fantasy, the grandiosity.

"In another letter to a friend, McVeigh wrote, 'I have certain other 'militant' talents that are in short supply and greatly demanded.'" Darger raised an eyebrow. "'Greatly demanded.' By whom? Again, we see the kind of grandiosity I'm talking about.

"So how does this relate to our case? In Huxley's mind, this is about advancing his cause, spreading his message. But psychologically, I think we can see that asserting his importance is a primary motivator. He feels ignored. Rejected. Well, bombs can't be ignored. And the grandiosity in the suicide note is consistent with the psychology common in this type of perpetrator."

She moved on to a list of social attributes common to the archetype.

"These men — and I say men because they are almost always male — tend to be loners. Like I said, McVeigh was bullied in school. Kaczynski has a similar childhood background. Shy, withdrawn, and all of that exacerbated by the fact that he skipped a grade and suddenly didn't fit in with his older classmates."

She used a laser pointer to highlight another item.

"Despite the fact that they struggle socially, romantically, and in their careers, these are men who have very high opinions of themselves. Their rage grows out of the perception that they cannot reach their supposed potential, something they blame the outside world and society for. They feel they've been done wrong. Treated unfairly. And they want revenge."

Darger gave a brief nod to Loshak, who took over from there.

"As Agent Darger has already touched on, these types of perpetrators like to claim all sorts of lofty ideals. They love to portray themselves as purists. As truth seekers. But to use Eric Rudolph, the Olympic Park bomber, as an example... He claimed to be carrying out his attacks to protest abortion, yet one of the places he admitted to bombing was a lesbian bar. How many lesbians do you think are getting abortions?"

There was a mute chuckle from the group.

"In all seriousness, if you really get down and parse their crimes, how they choose victims... they twist their rage into something resembling righteousness, but they are no different than a mass shooter who opens fire on a bunch of innocent people at a shopping mall. They get a thrill out of the chaos. A rush from feeling powerful. The violence allows them to finally feel... relevant."

Loshak cupped his chin in his hand.

"You may be surprised to learn that there are quite a few similarities between your more traditional serial killers and bombers. The anger. The inadequacy. They feel like victims, and they are compensating for that with these big displays of power and control. They want to prove to themselves and to everyone else that they *do* have power. They want to rub our noses in it. There's an irony to the fact that their violent acts stem from a feeling of powerlessness."

"Yeah, like, why not just get some therapy?" Agent Fitch joked. "Jeez."

Loshak smiled at the comment.

"Another thing — bombers tend to see their victims as symbols. Their anger is directed at society, but it's hard to lash out at society in a broad way. They end up choosing a figurehead or figureheads almost out of necessity. Some person or institution that acts as a lightning rod for their hatred. McVeigh focused his anger on the federal government, so he targeted a government building. Kaczynski's rage fixated on technology, on the destruction of the natural world, so he lashed out at scientists, a timber lobbyist, etc. Huxley's fury, I think, is being channeled toward fame. Celebrity. Success."

He gestured toward a photograph of Huxley's suicide note.

"Look at the language in the note, the sort of sweeping big picture talk, the grandiosity shining through from start to finish. The first attack had nothing to do with Passmore as an individual. This whole thing is epic in Huxley's mind, much bigger than one bomb, one victim. These crimes are a fantasy about power, about fame. These bombings let him tell the story — to the world if no longer himself — that he was important, that he was special. Like he said, he's a celebrity for today. A big one."

Agent Fredrick raised her hand.

"Speaking of the note… I had a question on that," she said.

"Go ahead."

"Well, I was curious if you think the promises he's laid out in the note — like the idea that we have a chance to disarm the bombs at all — are honest or not. I guess what I'm saying is, can we trust this scumbag?"

Stroking his chin, Loshak pondered this for a moment.

"*Trust* might be too strong a word. What I think we can put faith in is the fact that this is a game. He said so himself in the note. And a game doesn't work without rules. Of course, the fact that he is the designer of the game puts him at an advantage. There's no reason to cheat when you're the one creating the rules in the first place." Loshak ran a hand through his hair. "Something else I'd like to address is that I believe Agent Haslett is correct in assuming the rest of the attacks won't be through the mail. It leaves too much to chance, and Huxley wants his fifteen minutes of fame badly. Shock and awe arise from building tension, ever-increasing spectacle, like the structure of an opera."

Everyone was quiet for a second.

"I guess I'm saying that I think this is about to get a whole lot worse."

# CHAPTER 16

Amelia Driscoll felt the cool breeze of the air conditioner on her face. She basked a moment there, eyes closed, just inside the doorway of her house, enjoying the chilly touch.

The Florida humidity had been unbearable for seven days straight. Some vacation.

Somehow the flight home had been even hotter. And stuffy. All those sweaty people huddled together in a giant silver beer can with wings, the sun beating down on the metal, flaring its bright into the windows, the collective misery mounting with each ascending degree. Brutal. The sun's descent in the evening didn't seem to help things. No relief. Even asking the Uber driver to crank the air on the drive afterward couldn't sap the residual heat buildup from her being.

But this? This felt good. No more Florida. No more sweat plastering her back and hips into the coach seat. Just cold wind brushing at her cheeks and chin and forehead. Refreshing.

Finally, she opened her eyes and lurched to life again, placing the bundle of mail on the table — a stack of envelopes and one small box, none of which she would worry about for now. God, it felt good to be home.

A blur caught her eye — a smallish shape darting through the kitchen, a blond mop flopping around atop it. Her son, Lucas, had practically sprinted through the front door as soon as she'd unlocked it. Now he was careening around the apartment like a pinball. Why were eight-year-olds so hyper all the time?

She walked that way, getting her phone out as she did. Opening the fridge blasted her with a fresh wave of cool, and the

Fiji water she plucked from inside the door poured a little of the chill right down her throat.

After a few drinks, she thumbed through her contact list and tapped the name she sought. Her manager was probably annoyed that she hadn't responded to any of his messages, but she'd told him over and over that she refused to take business calls when she was on vacation. That was the whole point of going away, wasn't it? To get away from the real world for a while?

She glanced at the time while the line rang. It was late here in New York, but it was three hours earlier in L.A., and Tom usually worked into the night. Maybe that was his problem. For Tom, life was all work, work, work. She couldn't remember him ever mentioning taking time off.

Tom's assistant answered, as always.

"Hey Marcy. It's Amelia. We just got in from the airport, but I know Tom's been trying to get ahold of me."

"Of course. Great to hear from you. He's actually on a call with one of the execs from Universal. So it might be a bit of a wait."

"It's no problem."

The phone clicked and then went quiet. Amelia took another long drink of water.

"Mom, I'm going to open this."

She turned to see Lucas standing in the entryway near the pile of mail, one of the small boxes clutched in his hands.

"What is it?"

Lucas looked down at the cube in his hands. Squinted.

"Well… I *think* it's my new controller."

"What does the return address say?"

"There isn't one. But it was supposed to get here today, so

this has to be it."

"There's no label on the box?"

She took a step that way, but then she stopped herself. Thought she heard the click of someone coming on the line. Waited to hear Tom's voice spurt from the earpiece of her phone. But there was nothing.

Meanwhile, Lucas shrugged.

"Looks like part of the label got ripped off. I don't know. I'm going to open it."

"Fine. Go ahead."

Clutching the cardboard to his chest in a hug, the kid fingered the taped seam of the box with the opposite hand, tiny digits scrabbling there to find purchase. A fingernail caught and peeled the clear packing tape, curling it into a half-moon shape, but then his progress stopped abruptly. The tape wouldn't budge.

"Scissors are in the kitchen," she said, still half-listening to the silence in her ear even as she spoke.

Lucas nodded once and headed that way. He adjusted his hug on the box, bony arms hoisting it higher to keep it from sliding down toward his waist.

Amelia turned on her heel and paced through the living room. Flipped on a lamp there. The silence in her phone ear seemed to swell now — a vacancy, an abyss. The squish of her pulse became audible against the void.

She paced back and forth like that a few times, half watching the small figure in the kitchen out of the corner of her eye each time she passed the doorway. The boy had placed the box on the counter, rifled through a drawer, and now took the scissors to the tape.

She heard the snipping, only half paying attention as the

tape was sliced and parted. The cardboard edges scraped against each other, tape sort of swishing and lisping where it touched, crinkling as it bent.

Then the kitchen got quiet. Too quiet.

Amelia stopped pacing. Listened to the silence overwhelming both ears now.

"Everything alright in there?"

No answer.

"Lucas?"

She walked that way, and life seemed to flip into slow motion. Every breath stretching out. Every stride taking longer and longer.

That doorway into the kitchen framed her vision, the wooden casing partially blocking her outlook. It made her boy slide into view slowly, slowly, one piece at a time, a little more with each step. Just one shoulder, then the back of his head. Like the stylized cinematography in one of her movies — a slow zooming shot to build tension.

"Got the controller."

Lucas turned around and beamed at her, holding up the custom modded PS5 controller that had cost her over $100. He unsheathed it from a plastic cellophane bag, then turned it over in his hands a few times.

He looked up at her and crinkled his eyebrows, waiting for her to respond in some way.

"Oh. Oh, good." She stopped herself from saying more. Embarrassed now by that moment of fright, and somehow not wanting to admit to it out loud.

The kid darted away again, exploding through the doorway and building speed in the straightaway of the hall, that blond mop throbbing up and down again.

"No video games tonight, though," she called after him. "It's late, honey. You need to get ready for bed."

She pried the phone away from her ear. Thumbed the red icon to end the call. It somehow didn't matter anymore. Not tonight. Her career would still be there in the morning.

She took a deep breath, and delayed relief seemed to flood her being. God, that moment of tension had really gotten under her skin.

She walked into her bedroom and flipped on a lamp. Then she leaned into the en suite. Nudged the dimmer on the bathroom lighting all the way up and cranked the hot water handle on the shower. The water cascaded out of the showerhead and sizzled against the porcelain tile.

A shower would feel good. Wash away the grime of travel. She always felt a film of other-peopleness lacquering her body after huddling in airport terminals and packing in even tighter on the plane. Scrubbing it away would make her feel more alive again.

That was when she noticed the toilet seat. An open mouth gaping up at her. Water pooling down in its throat.

She turned to yell out the doorway.

"Lucas! For the thousandth time, if you're going to use my bathroom, at least put the seat down."

Before she could turn back to close the toilet, she saw something out of the corner of her eye. Her eyes had glided past it at first, but now they snapped straight back.

A box rested on the pillow of her bed. And not just *any* box. A Tiffany's box — she'd recognize the pale blue packaging with the white ribbon anywhere, even without the "Tiffany & Co." logo stamped on top in bold black letters.

A shaky breath rushed into her lungs. Right away her heart

beat faster.

She chuckled as she moved toward it. Nervous, breathy sounds whispering out of her, almost inaudible. And once again, her life seemed to switch into movie mode. The slow tracking shot as she zoomed in on something exciting.

Mike. It must be from him. They'd gotten into a fight before she left and hadn't talked since. That part wasn't unusual in and of itself. Mike wasn't big on the phone, either talk or text, so whenever one of them traveled, they were incommunicado for a few days. She'd gotten used to it over the eighteen months they'd been together.

But this? A gift waiting when she got home? This was above and beyond for Mike.

For just a second she felt guilty. She hadn't thought about him much while she and Lucas were on the beach or wading through the fanny-packed masses at Disney World. Too busy with vacation stuff to worry about the fight. Too busy living her own life to concern herself with a relationship that, to be blunt, seemed a bit half-assed and not long for this world.

She'd been waiting, she realized, for Mike to make a gesture like this. Something big and bold to renew her faith in the relationship.

And what if…? But no. It couldn't be a ring. The box was too big.

Still. Tiffany's? Maybe they should fight more often.

She lifted the box from the pillow. It felt heavy in her hands, a heft she hadn't expected that seemed to pull to one side in a swaying motion, almost like some liquid lurched against the walls of the container. Strange.

She caught a whiff of that subtle perfume scent that seemed to accompany all things Tiffany's related — warm amber and sweet vanilla wafting up to whet her appetite for fancy, sparkly things once more.

She pulled the lid off the box, and something clicked inside — a sharp metallic sound like cracking open a can of beer. Just as she got the lid out of the way, the blue cardboard jerked in her hands.

Fluid burst out of the box, jetting in all directions like a sprinkler. Lukewarm liquid doused her face. She dropped the box, and her upper body went rigid, neck and shoulders pulling upright in a flinch and freezing there.

The oncoming flood had made her eyelids snap shut before she could really see much. In her memory, the stuff had been pale yellow, almost the color of straw, but it'd been so fast that thinking about it now, she couldn't be sure.

She felt the juice collect and drain down her cheeks and forehead and went to work wiping it out of her eyes with her fingertips.

And for a second she thought she'd been pranked. Slimed or something like that. Maybe Mike had set up a hidden camera somewhere in the room.

But no. That didn't make sense.

*What the fuck?*

A pungent smell seemed to arrive then, finally breaking through her shock to make itself known. It reminded her of apple cider vinegar but stronger, danker, more chemical.

*Vinegar? Why?*

A faint motorized noise at her feet interrupted that thought. It sounded like a pulsing spray bottle, hissing and spitting out its rhythmic report. Even with her eyes still closed, she realized the box was still spritzing out its payload even now. Jetting more vinegar all over her rug and her shoes, the drizzling sound pattering her ankles and the bottom corner of her comforter.

She let out a squeal.

That was her brand new duvet cover from Neiman's.

She kicked at the parcel. Felt the box slide away, the sound muffled now underneath the bed.

She blinked a few times and tried to open her eyes. Heard spit sizzling between her teeth, frustrated sounds escaping her now like steam.

But then it started to sting.

And then it started to burn.

Real fucking bad, it burned.

The sting took hold in the flesh around her eyes first. Searing pain flaring up out of nowhere. Lighting her up.

It spread from there. Engulfed her lips and chin and cheeks and nostrils. Intensified into something white-hot. Blistering pain.

She gasped and gulped and backpedaled away from the bed, away from the box. Panic emptied her head of thoughts until only those bolts of pain and the dark were real.

She managed to peel her eyes open partially. Looked through slitted eyelids at a smeared world. Blurry shapes and contours huddled around her, the topography seeming to morph with every step she took.

Instinct moved her toward the bathroom. Used the colors as much as anything to guide her. The pale purple smudge was the bedspread. The brown splotch below showed her where the rug ended and the wood floor began. The glowing area signified the bathroom doorway, all distorted now so the hard lines of the edges had gone soft, almost making it more oval than rectangle. She could hear the crackle of the shower still pounding water onto tile, but she couldn't fully process it.

She hurtled herself through the bright threshold and groped at the vanity until her hands found the knobs. The faucet hissed as it jetted water into the sink.

Cupped handfuls of water flung themselves at her face. Slapped against her nose and cheeks and eyes before it fell away. The cold of the water brought no relief, though. Only seemed to make the hurt burn brighter.

She kept going. More water. Scrubbed her fingers at her eyes and nose. Trying to clear the fluid, flush the acid, whatever the hell it was.

The mucus membranes — the wet places — burned worse than the rest. Eyes. Lips. Nostrils. Fiery and gleaming. Some insane part of her half expected to see smoke rising from her face when her vision cleared.

Little by little, she was able to see some. The matte surface of the fogged-up mirror before her. Steam filled the room now. Tumbling out from behind the dark curtain where the shower's spray sizzled.

She could jump into the shower. Really wash this goo away. Clean.

She swiped her hand at her face, and her fingertips came away red.

Blood. It looked watered down. Other fluid diluting its opacity and thickness. Making it run down her fingers like cloudy pinkish water.

She swiped the wrist of her shirt at the mirror. Cleared the steam away with back-and-forth motions until her reflection became visible in the glass.

The bloody face there in the mirror did not look like her own. Not anymore.

The flesh seemed to bulge and sag. Pulling away from the

skull in baggy pouches.

Falling off.

Melting.

*Holy shit.*

Forget the shower. She needed to call 9-1-1.

She fumbled to get her phone out of her pocket. Eyelids blinking rapid-fire. Hands shaking.

The phone squirted out of her bloody fingers. Splashed as it belly-flopped into the toilet.

*Fuck!*

She scrambled back out into the bedroom. Tried to yell. Her voice came out raspy and whistling. Reduced to a quiet croak now.

Her vision started to blur again. Everything fading back to that smeared topography. Reality pulling away from her.

Amelia shambled down the hall into the living room, her arms held out in front of her, face drooping down her skull.

Lucas jumped back when he saw her. Mouth and eyes going wide. No sound coming out of his gibbering lips. Scared absolutely shitless.

And she stumbled near the landline there on the console table. Fell. Took out the lamp as she went crashing down. The bulb sizzling a split second. Guttering out like a snuffed torch.

The room plunged into darkness just as she hit down. The wood floor seemed to come up, thumping her good and hard. Cracking her on the chin. Making her teeth clack together. Spinning confusion into her head.

The dark reduced the blurs around her to shifting tendrils of gray and black like smoke. Shadows lurching for her. Cinching around her. Eager.

She tried to push herself up onto hands and knees, but the

strength had left her arms, left her legs. She squirmed there on her belly. Writhed like a worm drowning on the sidewalk in the rain.

And now she was hyperventilating. Passing out. In the dark. Face fucking melting. Falling off the bone.

The shadows opened wider then and swallowed her whole.

# CHAPTER 17

When they arrived at the building on East 14th Street, the entire block was lit up like a Christmas tree. The strobing lights of the first response vehicles flashed and flickered. Glowing red and blue streaks spiraling over brick and glass and concrete. Police. Fire. Ambulance.

Darger's heart thudded as they closed in on the scene of the latest crime. She could feel the misshapen muscle knocking in her chest, hear the blood beating in her ears. She looked up at the brownstone. Tried to steel herself for what they were walking into.

Something horrific had happened here tonight. Something almost unthinkable had taken place within the very walls she was staring at. Something Tyler Huxley had set into motion. She and the rest of the task force had been tasked with stopping it — stopping *him* — but so far they couldn't.

She swallowed hard at the thought. Heard a juicy sound in her throat. Tore her eyes off the building and turned her attention back to the street.

A uniformed NYPD officer was directing traffic away from the area but waved their car through when Laboda flashed his credentials out his open window.

"C-IED is in the house with their bomb-sniffing dogs now, double-checking there aren't any other surprises waiting inside."

Laboda parked on the sidewalk behind a fire engine. As they climbed out, Darger spotted the gurney being loaded into the back of an ambulance farther up the street. She couldn't really see any details through the dark and blinking lights, but Darger didn't imagine it was a pretty sight. From what they'd heard so far, this explosive device had been filled with some sort of corrosive acid that had left the victim covered with chemical burns.

She and Loshak formed a small huddle with Fredrick and Laboda several houses down from the victim's building.

Fredrick was giving the run-down on the victim. Amelia Driscoll. Thirty-four years old. An actress.

Darger searched the woman's name and found a Wikipedia bio which stated that she was discovered by a modeling agency at a Sbarro Pizza when she was nineteen. She'd parlayed that into acting.

"Was Driscoll conscious when the paramedics arrived?" Darger asked.

"It sounded like she was in and out," Fredrick said. "She'd wake up while they were working on her, scream for a bit, and then pass out again."

There was a whistle from the front door of the building. It was the SWAT team leader from earlier, waving them over. When they reached his position, he stuck his thumb in the air.

"It's all clear."

"Thanks, Fitch," Fredrick said. "I'm not sure you folks have been formally introduced. Agent Fitch here is overseeing all the CIRG activities on the task force. If you need anything from either C-IED or SWAT, he's your man."

The man's hand was so massive compared to Darger's, it felt like she was shaking hands with a baseball mitt.

"Shall we?" Fitch asked, gesturing inside.

Darger felt an eerie sense of déjà vu as they filed through the doors one by one. This home was nothing like the one belonging to Tyler Huxley, but the frantic, buzzing energy was the same. Techs and analysts flitting to and fro. Everyone on high alert, aware that the clock was ticking down even now.

They stopped first in a living room decorated with mid-century modern furniture. Under normal circumstances, the room was probably neat as a pin. Ready for a photo spread in *Better Homes and Gardens.* Just now, though, it was a mess. There was an overturned lamp on the floor and packaging from bandages, gauze, and syringes strewn about the room by hasty EMTs. Fitch pointed out a puddle of viscous fluid Darger couldn't identify.

"We've been warned to stay well away from any of the acid," he said. "Fucked up one of the paramedic's shoes, I'm told. And I don't know about you, but I'm not in a rush to find out firsthand what it does to human flesh."

"Where's the package?" Fredrick asked.

"She opened it in the bedroom. Ran into the bathroom, probably thinking she could wash it off. When that didn't take, she stumbled out here and collapsed at the feet of her son, who called 9-1-1. Paramedics found the victim here, semiconscious. Bedroom's back this way."

They followed Fitch further into the house, down a narrow hallway and into a bedroom. The group went silent as they passed through the final threshold. The area around the bed was cordoned off with police tape.

Darger's eyes went straight to what looked like smears of blood on the bedspread. One of the pillows was torn and sort of gloopy-looking where the acid had eaten away the pillowcase and lining. The stuffing inside looked gummy, the texture of gnocchi, Darger thought.

A large puddle of gray-black goo surrounded by shreds of

turquoise cardboard huddled half-concealed under one corner of the bed.

Fredrick's phone jangled, and she pulled it out.

"Mother of God," she said, clicking her tongue. "I asked Agent Warner to follow the ambulance to the hospital. Keep us updated on what's happening there. He just sent me a few photos of the victim taken in the ER."

The agents gathered around the phone. Darger's stomach turned at the horrific images on the screen. Raised patches and blisters marred the woman's face. Yellow and red and white. The flesh almost looked melted. Like when a piping hot pizza is tipped too far to one side and all the cheese and sauce slips out of place.

The phone jangled again as another text came through. Fredrick read it aloud.

"Warner says Driscoll is in surgery now. She's lost one eye for sure. They're trying to save the other. The major issue right now is that some of the acid got into her throat."

"Will she live?" Darger asked.

"The doctors are cautiously optimistic."

A photo of a healthy Amelia Driscoll hung on the wall, stylized to look like the Marilyn Monroe portrait by Andy Warhol. Darger didn't think she was going to look like that ever again.

And she wondered if that had been Huxley's intent. The bomb he'd sent to Gavin Passmore seemed designed to kill. But this one seemed designed to maim and disfigure. If Driscoll did survive, she'd carry the scars of this attack with her for the rest of her life.

Darger shook off the shock of seeing the photos and tried to remember what she'd been doing before that. She had the sense of a thought half-finished.

The bed, she thought. The shredded packaging.

"Did you guys see this?" she asked. "The light blue packaging the bomb came in?"

Fredrick squatted down, squinting.

"Looks like a Tiffany's box," Fredrick said.

Darger nodded.

"That's what I was thinking. The victim probably thought it was from someone she knew."

"Shit. If that box had been left at my house, my wife would tear into it without a second thought," Laboda said. "Huxley knew what he was doing."

"Where was the package left?" Darger asked.

"We think it was inside the house. According to Driscoll's son, they'd just arrived home from Florida. There was a pile of mail waiting, including one package, but it wasn't the Tiffany's box. The kid opened the other package himself. It was a video game controller he'd ordered." Fredrick glanced back toward the door of the bedroom. "He was out in the living room when he heard a commotion back here and then his mother stumbled out."

"If the Tiffany's box was left inside, that makes it even more likely that she thought it was from someone she knew," Loshak said.

"It also means Huxley probably brought it here himself," Darger added. "He must have known she'd be out of town. Maybe even knew when she was arriving back at home, which is how he knew approximately what time it would be opened and detonate."

"So he's stalking his victims beforehand."

"Seems likely."

"We should start canvassing the neighborhood. Maybe we'll find him on someone's camera again."

"Do we know if Huxley had GPS on his phone?" Loshak asked. "We could look at the history of his movements. Maybe figure out where he'd been the last few days. Narrow our search for the next targets."

"GPS was disabled, but we're working on getting cell tower data," Fredrick said, pulling out her phone. "It'll be slower than GPS, but it's something."

The conversation continued, but Darger was hardly listening. One of the frames hanging on the bedroom wall had snagged her attention — it was a Joli Minois cosmetics ad from a magazine with a shot of a much younger Amelia Driscoll.

"'Not just a pretty face,'" Darger said.

Loshak raised an eyebrow.

"What?"

"Huxley's note. He said, 'They say you're not just a pretty face.'" She pointed at the framed ad. "Look at the slogan on this makeup ad."

"'Joli Minois… Not just a pretty face.'" Loshak's eyes were glittering now. "OK. That's good. That means there really was a clue."

Darger's mind whirred at a million miles per hour now, replaying snippets from the suicide note. What else had he been trying to tell them?

*Staring at yourself on screen, that looking glass mounted in every living room, like Narcissus staring into the pond.*

Her eyes zeroed in on the TV mounted on the wall. She found the remote on a retro-looking sideboard below.

She turned it on, not sure what she was looking for. Only that the note had mentioned a screen. She flipped over to the

Blu-ray player. What if Huxley had left them a recorded message?

Darger pressed play. Driscoll's face appeared on the screen. A Joli Minois spot for some kind of waterproof mascara. The ad featured the victim splashing around in a fountain. After that was a clip of Driscoll in a few bit parts she'd done on TV.

"Did Huxley make this, you think?" Fredrick asked.

Darger pressed the eject button. There was a whirring sound from inside the sideboard. Darger opened one of the doors and squinted at the label on the disc, written in all caps.

AMELIA DRISCOLL REEL.

"No, I think this is hers."

*Rewind yourself. Replay yourself. An endless loop of you, you, you.*

It seemed Huxley had meant that literally. She tried to imagine the victim sitting in bed, watching this. Darger had a hard time imagining anyone doing that. She hated even looking at photographs of herself. Video was even worse.

Darger resumed her search, pressing herself against the wall and using the flashlight on her phone to illuminate the narrow gap between the TV and the wall. Nothing there.

She felt a surge of frustration and ground her molars together. There had to be something. She thought over the note again. She'd read it so many times, she pretty much had it memorized. It was the last line that struck her this time.

*And if you must sleep tonight, be sure to keep those DVRs rolling.*

She squatted down in front of the sideboard and studied the Blu-ray player.

Darger closed the tray and gave the device a tug. It moved a few inches, but the cords must have been tangled behind the sideboard, because it wouldn't budge further.

She flipped it upside-down, studying the back and underside.

Nothing.

What then? It had to be here.

Darger sensed the group bunched behind her now, but she didn't let it distract her.

She popped open the tray again, removing the disc and aiming her light inside. A sliver of white caught her eye.

A folded piece of paper had been wedged into the device. And a snippet of familiar black handwriting was just barely visible.

# CHAPTER 18

A breath rushed in through Darger's lips. Cool wind sucking back into her throat, into her chest. Scraping a little, a sound like leaves rasping over the sidewalk.

*This was it. This was the next clue. She'd found it.*

Her eyelids fluttered. Adrenaline sent a prickle of pins and needles down her arms.

She managed to refocus her vision on the folded sheet of paper. Forced words from her lips.

"I see something. A piece of paper lodged behind the tray, I think," she said. "I need a screwdriver."

"I've got one here," Fitch said, yanking a multitool from his belt.

He opened the screwdriver attachment and held it out to her. Darger tucked her phone away and took the tool in her hand.

A bedside lamp appeared to be the only source of light in the room though it didn't quite reach far enough, and without her trusty phone light, she might as well be working in the dark. Darger tried to use the faint glow coming from the TV, but it was too dim.

"Can I get some light over here?"

She heard several muted clicks and then three separate flashlight beams swept toward her and focused on the device in her hands. She worked the tray out slowly. As it popped free, she saw that she'd been right. There was indeed a small piece of paper tucked inside the player.

"Let's get a photograph of this before I take it out," she said.

Fredrick brought in a tech who took several pictures of the recorder and the sideboard they'd found it in. After the final flash, the tech handed Darger a pair of tweezers.

She gently slid the paper out, feeling like a kid again, playing the board game Operation. She knew the house had been thoroughly checked for more IEDs and had been cleared, but it was hard to let your guard down fully with someone like Huxley.

With gloved hands, she unfolded the note.

Black sharpie on white paper. The same jagged lettering as Huxley's suicide note.

*Hello from the gutters of N.Y.C. What a clever sheep you must be.*

*Clever enough to save her, I wonder? Or did she die screaming, with her face melting into a puddle? Haha. Oh I would have loved to see it.*

*But back to our game. Aren't we having fun?*

*I've left something for you in a secret place. Hidden from the prying eyes and greedy leers of the hungry crowd.*

*A hidey hole no one will find unless they are very smart. A slice of green cut out of the concrete. A place touched by family history of a very high caliber.*

*Before I go, let me leave you with these words:*

*And huge drops of acid*
*Poured down upon her head*
*Until her pretty face was gone without a trace*
*Yet the cats still come out at night to mate*
*And the sparrows still sing in the morning.*

*See you at the next job.*

# CHAPTER 19

Darger and Loshak stood just beyond the stoop of Amelia Driscoll's building, passing Darger's phone back and forth, studying the photo she'd snapped of the note before handing it off to the tech to be bagged and tagged. The apartment was crowded, and they needed space to think, but they wanted to stay close in case there were any developments.

Loshak used his thumb and forefinger to zoom in, as if making the text larger would suddenly reveal Huxley's intent.

"I'll tell you what, if the clue is as cryptic as the last one, we're fucked. I never would have tied that clue to the makeup slogan."

"And I only put it together after I saw the ad in her bedroom," Darger said.

Darger stared at the scrawled letters in black ink and sensed there was something here. Something she should see. A connection her mind wanted her to make, but she couldn't see it yet.

"Family history is the obvious lead," Darger said. "I mean, a lot of the wording is open to interpretation, but talking to his mom is at least a logical next step, right?"

"I was thinking the same," Loshak said. He looked at his watch. "Hate to go wake her up at this hour, but the clock is ticking."

Fredrick jogged over from across the street, looking like she had something.

"We found him on a neighbor's camera. Three nights ago." She whipped out the tablet again. "He shimmied up the fire escape on the back of the building. We lose him as he climbs out of frame, but he must have pried open a window and left the package."

Video of a man in black pants and a black hoodie played on the screen. He tucked the box under his arm, his body language looking fluid, almost serpentlike, as he hoisted himself up onto the wrought iron fire escape. Again Darger noted the yellow shoes as they lifted into view.

"Funny that he made the effort to wear dark clothes but then wore some day-glo, hi-vis shoes," she said. "Very smooth."

"Anyway, it confirms that he delivered the bomb himself," Fredrick said. "And suggests that he knew Driscoll's schedule intimately. Her son confirmed that she goes to bed at midnight every night. We already put a call into the phone company. They're going to send the cell tower records as soon as possible, but it'll still take a few hours."

"Did you send the newest clue to the forensic linguist?" Loshak asked.

Fredrick nodded.

"Dr. McAdams promised to call if she came up with anything."

An analyst appeared on the doorstep and waved a hand at Fredrick. The agent scuttled off.

Darger and Loshak looked at each other.

"What do you think?" she asked. "Should we go roust Huxley's mother from bed?"

"Let's ride."

# CHAPTER 20

Martha Huxley sat frowning at Darger from the sofa. Tyler Huxley's mother was a severe-looking woman in her late 50s. Her hair was dark and flecked with gray, and she wore a terry cloth robe.

Darger squirmed under the woman's gaze. There was a chill in the air that had nothing to do with the temperature. They were unwelcome guests here, and she didn't think it was solely about the late hour.

Darger swallowed.

"Again, we do apologize for waking you like this."

Mrs. Huxley's face was like stone.

"So you've said. And yet here you sit."

Darger shifted her focus to David, Tyler's older brother. There was a clear family resemblance between him and the late bomber, though David was a bit taller, his hair lighter, and he wore glasses. They'd lucked out to find him here. It would be good to get a history from Tyler's sibling as well as his mother.

"It's just that we don't have a lot of time," Darger continued. "There's a… schedule as it were. I wish it could wait until morning, but…"

"Let's get on with it then," Mrs. Huxley said, her voice sharp. "Or were you planning on just sitting there, gaping at us like a fish in a bowl?"

Darger wondered if Mrs. Huxley had cried when she'd heard about her son's death. Just now, she couldn't imagine it. Couldn't envision this woman shedding a tear for any reason, not even the loss of her youngest. She seemed too tough. Too hardened. Or maybe this was a grief reaction. Maybe she'd progressed past the denial and guilt and moved on to anger, and she and Loshak happened to arrive right in time to bear the brunt of it.

"Right. Well, Tyler left a note. A clue about another attack, I guess you could say. And he mentioned family. Family history." Darger splayed her hands. "So maybe you could start by telling us what Tyler's childhood was like."

Mrs. Huxley wagged a finger at her.

"Oh, no you don't. Don't you even go there."

"I'm not sure what you mean."

"You're going to try to paint it like I made him into some kind of monster. Well, I won't have it. My son had a wonderful childhood. We weren't exactly the Cleavers, but we did right by our own. Our boys wanted for nothing. Tell them, David."

"I would say we had a normal childhood." David nodded. "Yes."

"That's it?" Mrs. Huxley snapped. "That's all you have to say in your brother's defense? In *my* defense? You're just going to sit there while these two government thugs pass judgment on us? Call me a child abuser and your brother a monster?"

David closed his eyes.

"I'm a little overwhelmed right now, Ma. OK? I'm still processing all of this. And no one called you a child abuser."

Mrs. Huxley let out a dismissive puff of breath.

"Well I know that's what everyone's thinking! How am I going to show my face at St. Michael's after this? How do you think people are going to look at me?"

"I know this must be very difficult for you and your family, Mrs. Huxley," Darger said. "I can't imagine what you're going through."

When Mrs. Huxley turned her eyes on Darger, they were glittering with fury.

"No, you certainly cannot. And to have you coming in here trying to stir up more nastiness is really the last thing I need."

"Ma'am, if I may… I've lost a child myself, so I know a little of what you're feeling right now," Loshak said, coming to Darger's rescue. "And I hate to have to intrude like this in your time of grief. But the truth is, we're operating on very limited information right now. We have two people dead, another grievously injured, and a lot of unanswered questions. That's why it's imperative that we hear your side of it. Learn about who Tyler was."

Mrs. Huxley's expression softened a touch, and she nodded. She lifted a binder from beside her on the sofa, handing it to Loshak.

"I kept a scrapbook of everything he's ever done. Every drawing. Every report card."

Loshak opened it, revealing the standard preschooler's drawing of a house with a big yellow circular sun and lines radiating outward. Loshak flipped further in. As Tyler aged, he drew other things: cars, dogs, cartoon characters.

"He was interested in art, then?" Loshak asked.

"He was interested in many things." She gestured at a photo of Tyler dressed in an Air Force pilot costume for Halloween. "For a while it was airplanes. He wanted to be a pilot, but he's colorblind. So he gave up on that. And then he got into baseball for a while. Knew every fact and stat for all the players. And Tyler just loved movies and special effects. We took him to see one of the *Pirates of the Caribbean* movies when he was ten or eleven, and I think that's where that started. He asked for a camera for Christmas. We got him a little Flip camera that was popular at the time and not too expensive."

Her lips twitched, and Darger realized that this was Mrs. Huxley's rendition of a smile.

"He was so serious even then. So devoted to the things he was passionate about. He knew exactly what he wanted, and it always had to be the best. And he was very bright. Scored off the charts on the standardized test all the kids take in the third grade. I believe there was some suggestion that he should go to a special school for gifted and talented children, but it was all the way up in White Plains and Earl said it was too far, so nothing ever came of it."

"Earl was Tyler's father?"

Mrs. Huxley nodded.

"I should have insisted he go to that special school. It was where he belonged. Not in that toilet of a public school where nobody could see his potential."

"And what was his life like, socially?" Loshak asked.

"My Tyler was very popular in school. People were just naturally attracted to him. He had such a marvelous imagination. He always had girls fighting over him, wanting him to take them to the school dances, because he was also a great dancer. Of course that made some of the boys jealous. But people were always jealous of Tyler."

"Did he have many girlfriends?"

The woman waved her hand dismissively.

"He didn't really date much. The girls around here, they weren't up to snuff. And he was so much more mature than his classmates."

Mrs. Huxley glanced at Darger as she said this, as if judging her suitability for her beloved son and finding her lacking.

"I saw that movie about Richard Jewell, you know. The man

who discovered the bomb at the Atlanta Summer Olympics? He was a hero, but you people accused him of planting the bomb himself. Ruined the life of an innocent man."

Darger was confused at the sudden change of subject.

"I'm not sure I understand..."

"Well, of course you don't. It's obvious the FBI only hires imbeciles." The woman crossed her arms. "I'm saying Tyler could have been framed. Did you ever think of that?"

"Mrs. Huxley, he left a note admitting to—"

"Oh please. As if something like that couldn't be faked! People were always envious of my son. Of his talent. There are plenty of people who would love to take him down a peg, believe me."

"Ma'am—"

"You really have a lot of nerve to come into my home saying these outrageous things when you didn't even know him."

Mrs. Huxley seemed intent on talking over them now. Each time she interrupted, she got louder, more fervent.

Well, Darger could be loud, too.

"Be that as it may, Mrs. Huxley—"

The woman tried again to interject, but this time Darger ignored it, projecting her voice over the woman.

"—if you really want to help your son, then the best way to do that is by *answering our questions.*"

Mrs. Huxley's mouth popped open.

Darger sighed.

"I'm sorry for raising my voice, but we really just need to ask a few more questions."

"It's the day of my son's death, and here I am being shouted at in my own home," she said, her voice barely above a whisper.

Darger resisted the urge to roll her eyes.

"You're right. And I apologize." She swallowed her annoyance, deciding that Loshak might have better luck finishing the interview without her. "Does Tyler still have a room here?"

"Of course. I've always kept it just how he left it, in case he ever wanted to come back for a night or two. It gets awful lonely here when I'm here by myself, day in, day out." Her eyes went to a photo of Tyler hanging on the wall. "I always hoped he'd marry and have children. I so wanted grandchildren. But now…"

"Perhaps David could show me the room?"

Mrs. Huxley pressed her lips together.

"Tyler didn't like people going through his things."

Darger shot a look at Loshak.

"Ma'am, this will go much more smoothly if it's just us taking a look around. We can get a warrant if we have to, but they tend to make quite a mess when they tear through a place. I'd hate to have to put you through that."

"Fine." Mrs. Huxley frowned. "Take the lady to see Tyler's room, David. But you stay in the hallway and don't touch anything. Tyler would never forgive me if I let you in there to snoop, too."

# CHAPTER 21

David Huxley led Darger down a dim hallway lined with old family photos and a few small shelves filled with tchotchkes. He pushed a paneled door open, flipped on the light, and stepped aside.

"This is it here," he said.

Darger entered, letting her eyes wander the room, taking in the details. A blue plaid bedspread. An eclectic mix of movie and band posters coated much of the wall — Queens of the Stone Age, The Doors, the original 1974 version of *Death Wish*, John Carpenter's *The Thing* with the pale blue light exploding from MacReady's head. A small bookshelf filled with books, DVDs, and video games. The top was littered with a variety of collectible toys and figurines: Funko POP figures, WWE Superstars, *Muppet Star Wars*.

She sniffed, noting that the room smelled vaguely minty.

David hovered just beyond the threshold, having taken the instruction that he not enter the room literally.

The good thing about splitting up was that maybe now she could hear things from David's perspective. Mrs. Huxley had a way of co-opting the entire flow of the conversation and had barely let him get a word in.

"What's your take on all this?" she asked, still studying the room.

David rubbed the back of his neck.

"Honestly? I have no idea. It's… I feel like this has to be a dream, but I haven't woken up yet. I mean, I don't know."

Darger turned to face him.

"So you don't feel like Tyler was the type that would do something like this?"

"No. I mean, he had his quirks. But this?" He shook his head. "No."

"Is there anything in Tyler's history you would describe as traumatic?"

David shrugged and shook his head.

"No. I'd say his childhood was pretty uneventful. The worst thing that's ever happened to him would probably be our dad dying, but that was only a few years ago. He would have been 26 at the time, and I wouldn't say he seemed especially torn up about it."

"Can I have you look at something?" Darger asked, getting out her phone. "I'll warn you ahead of time, you might find it upsetting."

"It's not a picture of him dead, is it?"

"No. It's the clues he left. At the crime scenes."

She showed him the photographs of the two notes. His eyes crisscrossed back and forth over the screen, scrolling, reading the scrawled words. David's face blanched.

"Jesus. He really sounds insane."

"Does any of it mean anything to you? Give you any idea as to who he might target next?"

"No. I mean… it all seems pretty vague, I guess."

"Do you remember him ever talking about anyone? A particular actor or celebrity he might have been infatuated with or have some sort of grievance against… anything like that?"

The skin creased between his eyebrows.

"He was really into Charles Bronson when we were kids. But Bronson's been dead for years, so I don't suppose that helps." David winced. "We didn't really talk all that much these days.

I'm sure he mentioned movies and TV shows he was watching when we saw each other for holidays, but… I don't know. Nothing stands out."

"How did the two of you get along with each other?"

Again, David pondered this.

"We didn't really fight, if that's what you mean. But that was mostly because Tyler was always off in his own world. Doing his own thing. He wasn't really all that interested in other people, it seemed to me. In forming real relationships, I mean."

"Your mother made it sound like he had a lot of friends in high school. Was that an exaggeration?"

"There were people he'd hang out with, but I don't know if I'd call them friends, exactly. The thing you have to understand about Tyler is that he was sort of a schemer. A big talker. Good with words, you know? He always had a skill for talking people into stuff."

"Like Tom Sawyer getting people to whitewash a fence?"

"Sort of. I'm trying to think of an example…" He snapped his fingers. "When we were in middle school, there was this school contest. Whoever read the most books in each grade one semester would get a prize. A big jar of candy. Tyler got a bunch of kids in his homeroom to give him their book slips, figuring if they pooled their books, they'd win for sure. And by the end of the contest, he had twenty more books read than anyone else in his grade. So he got the candy. But then he refused to split it up with the kids who'd helped him."

"I don't imagine that went over well."

"Hell no. One of them ratted him out. They took away the candy and the win."

Darger raised her eyebrows. This wasn't exactly the image of the perfect son Mrs. Huxley had painted for them.

"What did your mother think of that?"

"She took his side, as usual. Praised him for being clever. Said that the rules for the contest as written didn't explicitly say you couldn't pool your resources. He had her snowed." David shoved his hands in his pockets. "He had this whole thing back then about making a movie, but it was just another scheme."

"How so?"

"Well, he got all these people all pumped up about it, other kids at school. He'd tell them he wanted to cast them in the movie or ask them to be part of the crew. Even had me signed on as his gaffer at one point. I didn't even know what a gaffer was, but it sounded important, so I liked it. Eventually I realized it was all talk. But it was an obsession for him… the script and shooting locations and how big the budget would be. Equipment he'd need. It's like he was dreaming out loud, and people were sort of taken with it, you know. It was infectious. They wanted to believe. So I don't think he was popular so much as he'd convinced people that he had something to offer. He manipulated everyone. I mean, even my ma fell for it. You heard her. Of course the movie never happened. None of it."

"Did he try?" Darger asked. "Apply to film school? Anything like that?"

"I don't think he ever even wrote a single page of script. It was just a fantasy, you know?" David blew out a breath. "He started telling himself this story, and then he started believing it, and pretty soon he's telling other people, too. Just a weird kid fantasizing out loud. But he could sound so passionate, so convincing, that he got a bunch of other people to join in. And that made it seem more real. Like it wasn't just a game of make-believe. He even got people to pitch in to buy some equipment. A camera and a tripod. Some lights. But he was just playing at it, all along. So to go back to your question about whether I thought he'd be capable of something like this… I mean, I never would have imagined him doing something violent. Blowing up the guy from that coffee commercial? Why? What's even the point? But then, in a weird way, maybe I'm not surprised. Because he always had something to prove, I think. Like he wanted the whole world to see that he was special. Does that make sense?"

"Yes," Darger said, thinking that it fit with the bomber profile exactly.

"One time I overheard him in the hallway at school, telling this story about how we went on vacation the summer before, and he started sleepwalking at the hotel and woke up in the middle of the night, pissing in one of the potted plants near the elevator. He had a whole little group around him, listening to him talk. The thing was, that story didn't happen to him. It happened to our cousin Christopher. He'd told us over Thanksgiving. And maybe that isn't such a big deal, stealing someone else's anecdote and making himself the main character, but I just always felt like Tyler wanted to give off the sense that his life was filled with fascinating things happening to him. Maybe he worried that if he didn't do that, people wouldn't be so interested in him." David paused and stared up at the ceiling. "Sometimes I felt like the only person who really saw that in him, saw him for who and what he really was."

"And what is that?"

"Manipulative? Insecure? A phony? Take your pick." He grimaced. "Shit. That probably sounds pretty harsh, considering… But I guess I'm just being honest."

"Oh, he's probably going to be called much worse. You might want to brace yourself for that."

"I'll be fine." He gestured back down the hallway. "Not sure about her, though."

Darger could feel for them. This family thrust into this tragedy against their will. Dragged into the mud simply because they shared DNA with a homicidal madman.

"You might get some media buzzing around, wanting a statement," Darger said. "My advice? Ignore them. Tell them 'no comment,' and keep moving. They'll lose interest eventually."

"That won't be a problem for me. Can't say the same about my mother. She's not the type to sit quietly until the storm passes. If they start asking pointed questions about Tyler… I mean, you heard her out there. She's got a hair-trigger as it is." David rubbed his eye sockets. "It's probably a petty thing to say, but I can't help but wonder if she'd be defending me with the same intensity."

"You think she favored your brother?" Darger asked.

"I have some vague memories, when I was very young, of her not having such a laser focus on him all the time. Seems like maybe it started once he took that test. The one in the third grade… that was it for her, I think. He sort of solidified his position as the golden child. The funny thing is, he never did that well on any of the tests ever again. He had a solid B average. Nothing special. Not that I did any better." He shrugged. "I think it was something she wanted to believe, though. Him being some kind of boy genius. Something that made her feel like she did right. And I guess it's always been important to Ma that we be… special somehow."

He stared at one of the posters on the wall and was quiet for a few seconds.

"She's always had this way of being either hot or cold to

people."

One side of Darger's mouth quirked upward.

"I guess I'd be cold then?"

David half-smiled.

"She's always been colder on women, for some reason. Guess it's a good thing she didn't have daughters." He glanced back in the direction of the living room. "Anyway, I should go check on her. For your partner's sake."

# CHAPTER 22

Alone in the bedroom, Darger took a closer look at Tyler Huxley's teenage possessions. It was like a time capsule from fifteen or so years earlier. She took photos of the rest of the posters on the wall: *The Matrix*, *The Black Keys*, *The Avengers*. Studied the books on the shelves: a set of the *Harry Potter* books, *Odd Thomas*, *One Flew Over the Cuckoo's Nest*, *Fight Club*, *The Giver*. A mix of reading he'd done for school and pleasure, she figured, snapping another photo.

The number of fiction books, however, was dwarfed by the true crime books that took up most of the shelf. Darger leaned in to look closer, finding books about a menagerie of famous killers: Bundy, Gacy, Dahmer, Manson, Zodiac, Son of Sam, Albert Fish. Lurid covers and titles. Lots of black and red.

So Huxley was a serial killer buff. Could that be significant? She didn't know.

She gazed around the room again. It was strange to think some of this useless junk might end up being important somehow. Then again, there might be nothing here. This could all be a waste of time.

But it wasn't good to think that way. They had to go through everything. Cover every base. There was too much riding on it.

She tried to find some pattern in the items. The DVDs and video games and books. Something that might apply to the clue he'd left in his suicide note. But his collection was so dated to his high school years and earlier, it was hard to see how it would apply now.

Darger shuffled through the video games. *Mass Effect*, *God of War, Red Dead Redemption.*

She photographed everything. At some point, she'd make a list and try to find if there were any connections. A particular actor or writer or someone else he might target.

Something flashed against the corner of the wall and ceiling, catching Darger's eye. Silvery light, almost rainbowed along the edges, streaming in through the window, twirling motes on the wall. She peered outside, spotting a row of planters on a neighboring balcony stuffed with metallic pinwheels that caught the headlights of the passing cars and reflected them all over the inner and outer walls of the apartment. She studied the dancing, spinning orbs of light for a moment before returning her attention to Tyler's room.

Her eyes moved to the dresser, strewn with random objects as if Huxley had only yesterday emptied his pockets here. Half-empty bottles of cologne and body spray. A pile of loose change. Several containers of mints and gum, which she realized now was where the minty smell was coming from. There was also a small spray canister of breath freshener. He seemed obsessed with bodily odors, specifically with covering them. So Tyler Huxley had been somewhat insecure. Though what teenager wasn't?

She tugged one of the drawers open and found polo shirts, jeans, khakis. Everything was organized and neatly folded. Darger couldn't help but think the clothes seemed bland.

As she went through his things, she flashed on that tattered corpse from the basement in New Jersey. She imagined the teenage version of Tyler. Wondered if he would have ever guessed this was how his story would end.

Then again, maybe he'd fantasized about doing something violent all the way back then. It wouldn't have been out of the ordinary — many serial killers detailed their recurring violent fantasies as having started as young as six or seven.

Darger felt around under the stacks of socks and boxers and undershirts in the various drawers, searching for anything that might have been hidden. There was nothing.

In the closet, she pushed aside sweaters and plaid button-ups and discovered a snowboard and boots tucked in the corner. Not helpful.

There was an old Adidas shoebox on the top shelf of the closet. Darger pulled it down and flipped open the top. Inside she found a Japanese manga book, a few spiral-bound notebooks, and at the bottom of the stack a DVD. Darger picked up the case and could tell from the lurid cover art and the giant "XXX" rating on the front that it was pornography. She glanced at the title — *Sluts and Butts and Butts and Butts! Vol. 5* — before tossing it aside.

"You know, I think the *Sluts and Butts and Butts and Butts* franchise really went off the rails after the third volume," Loshak said from the doorway.

Darger snorted, paging through one of the notebooks. Her heart started to pound when she saw the handwriting. She recognized that scrawl from the note they'd found taped to the basement wall. It was Tyler's journal.

It was a moment before she could get the words out. Could this be the crumb he'd left behind for them to find?

Finally, she turned to Loshak and held the book aloft.

"I think I found something," she said.

# CHAPTER 23

Back in the car they'd borrowed from Loboda, Loshak wove his way through Queens while Darger kept her nose in Huxley's childhood journal. It was sprinkling again, and the streets glistened under the streetlamps.

"Finding anything useful so far?"

"No. Lists of video games he wants. A list ranking of his favorite true crime books — he had a ton of serial killer books in his room, by the way. Another ranking list, this time of Martin Scorsese movies. It's not much of a baring of his teenage soul."

The entries spanned a period of time that would have represented Tyler's junior and senior years of high school, and Darger was struggling to find a link between the mundane descriptions of his daily life eleven years ago and his current crimes.

"I can't decide if we're on the right track at all," she said. "He did mention journals, but I was imagining something more... recent. I guess this could be what he meant by 'family history.' We did find it in his old room."

Loshak flicked on the blinker.

"I've been thinking about all the different things that could mean. *Family history*... maybe we're being too literal." He trailed off for a few seconds. "Speaking of, you get anything useful from the brother?"

They wheeled around a corner, and Darger felt the faint pull of centrifugal force before the car evened out again. The late-night traffic was sparse compared to what they'd seen earlier, but there were still cars in the lanes alongside them, still headlights gleaming from the opposite side.

"According to David, his brother was the favored son. Got a lot of extra attention. And their mom kind of built up this idea of him being special, but he never really lived up to it. Didn't really achieve anything or even try to, from the sound of it. He talked big. Had some scheme in high school about making a movie. David said it was a major obsession for Tyler, but in his estimation, his brother had never even written a single page of a script. It was all fantasy."

"That confirms what we said in our profile. How he's choosing his targets. Passmore probably seemed like a guy kind of living his dream. Getting to play the big celebrity."

They fell quiet after that, and Darger went back to skimming through the journal. More lists. A few nonsensical notes to himself about strategies to try in some video game. Finally she got to a string of entries that seemed to be more like traditional journal fare — recounting his day, talking about school. The details were sparse, though a girl's name, Emma, kept coming up.

"You got quiet over there," Loshak said when they came to a stop at another light. He gestured at the journal. "Find something?"

"Not really." Darger frowned. "There's a particular girl he seemed borderline obsessed with. Notes pretty much any time he sees her and whether or not they made eye contact or if she said anything to him. Keeps fantasizing about how once he gets his movie going, he thinks she'll take an interest."

"He really was pinning a lot on that, huh?"

"His brother said he kind of used the movie as bait for a lot of people. Acted like he had this big important thing he was going to do and would invite people along for the ride."

"Any chance the girl he was obsessed with is now an up-and-coming Broadway star?"

"I already looked her up online," Darger said. "She sells real estate in Columbus, Ohio."

"What else is in there?"

"Complaints about teachers. Complaints about the dumb, idiot jocks getting all the attention. Several pages of notes about what kind of equipment he'll need to make his movie with prices. Lights and microphones and special effects makeup. A list of action sequences he wants to shoot and what kind of CGI software that would require. Oh, and he has what looks like the start of a class report on GG Allin."

"The singer guy who used to roll around in glass and eat his own feces on stage?" Loshak asked.

"The one and only. It sounds like Huxley watched a documentary on him. He wrote about how the director of the documentary, Todd Phillips, is now this big Hollywood guy. And in the margin, he wrote, 'I need to find my GG. Someone so sensational they can't be ignored.'"

"Sounds like he decided to become that himself, instead."

"Yeah," Darger agreed.

She squinched her eyes shut, giving them a few seconds' rest from examining the journal.

"Did you get a sort of narcissistic vibe from mom?" she asked.

"Like the way she kept referring to him as 'my son,' as if he's an object that belonged to her?"

"That was part of it, for sure," Darger said. "It got me thinking… it's not uncommon for that type of parent to sort of split the family, especially their kids, into golden children and scapegoats."

Loshak licked his lips.

"She did seem to heap a lot of praise on Tyler. Less so with the son still there, living and breathing," he said. "In fact, she almost acted like he was a burden or something, despite the fact that he was there to try to comfort her."

Darger went on.

"Well, a lot of times, the golden child will respond to the parent in one of two ways: they either sort of achieve to please the parent, in which case they're accepting the parent's worldview and values, or they sabotage their own achievements to rebel against the parent."

"You think that's why he never tried to get his movie thing off the ground? He was sabotaging himself?"

"Maybe," Darger said. "It's all academic at this point, really. I certainly can't diagnose her with anything. And I doubt it'd do much for the case to fixate on it. There are plenty of awful parents in the world, yet most of their children don't send homemade bombs to people they saw on TV."

Loshak swerved to miss a pedestrian, though he didn't seem too perturbed by it. He kept the conversation going like nothing had happened.

"It gives us some insight on his psyche, though. Imagine a kid who's told all his life that he's a talented genius. Entitled to special treatment. Destined for greatness. And then he ends up having a fairly mundane, simple life. No fame. No fortune. No paparazzi waiting outside his door to catch a glimpse of him in his bathrobe. No awards lining his shelves. How do you think a person like that might react to realizing everything he's been told and dreamed of never came to fruition?"

There was a sticker on the cover of the notebook. The *Star Wars* Galactic Empire logo. Darger ran a finger around it.

"Well, a normal person would get over it, I'd think. Realize their dreams of great importance were a fantasy. But this guy? I guess we're seeing his response, aren't we?"

They were quiet for a few seconds, the squeak of the windshield wipers against the glass seeming to fill the car.

Darger looked down at the notebook in her lap and felt a fist clench in her gut. She found herself not wanting to go back to the high school journal. Something about it felt wrong, like they'd gone down the wrong track.

*Forget all the family stuff for a second. Forget the journal. Clear your head. Go back to the note.*

She pictured the black ink on the page. Spiky lettering. Aggressive.

*Hello from the gutters of N.Y.C. What a clever sheep you must be.*

The words repeated over and over in Darger's mind as she stared out the window. Fat flecks of rain struck the glass in a diagonal spatter. She watched the way the droplets reflected the lights of the glowing signs behind them. Glowing jewels in red and blue. Rubies and sapphires.

"Sheep and piggies," Darger said idly, a line from the first note coming into her head. *You piggies have a chance, however, to stop some of the carnage.* "He also mentions cats and sparrows. Could the repeated use of animal phrases be pointing to something?"

"Like a zoo?" Loshak suggested.

"Maybe."

Something struck Darger then.

"Didn't Manson use the term 'piggies' when referring to the police?"

"Yeah." Loshak scratched his chin. "And members of the

Manson Family finger-painted stuff about *pigs* on the walls, scrawling it in the victims' blood at two of the crime scenes."

On an August night in 1969, Charles Manson's followers broke into the Hollywood Hills mansion of actress Sharon Tate and butchered five people. The next night they killed two more in a house in Los Feliz.

Darger put a hand to her head, making another connection.

"So he makes what could be a Manson Family reference in his first note with *piggies*, after a crime involving an actor best known for a series of coffee commercials. The Manson Family famously killed coffee heiress Abigail Folger. The note is supposed to give us clues to Huxley's next victim, who happens to be a model-turned-actress," she said.

Loshak's head began bobbing up and down.

"Just like Sharon Tate."

"So maybe we were thinking of the wrong family all along. *Family history* could be an allusion to the Manson Family."

Goosebumps rippled over the backs of Darger's arms. Cold feelings shuddering through her.

"That makes sense," Loshak said. "His movie dreams couldn't come to fruition. But his true crime obsession showed him another way to get famous. A way he might actually be able to pull off."

The stacks of books in Tyler's room suddenly flashed in Darger's mind. Adrenaline sizzled in her veins now. This was starting to make sense.

"And maybe these references point to who he sees as his chosen family — the serial killers he worships."

Darger swiped through her photos to look at the newest note, reading it again. Her eyes went to the final line of the short poem he'd written. *And the sparrows still sing in the morning.*

There was something about it that seemed strangely familiar. She typed the eight words into her phone and hit the Search button.

"David Berkowitz," she said, the pieces finally sliding into place. "That was his poem. Huxley just changed a few of the words to make it fit an acid bomb instead of bullets. And look at this. One of his letters started with, 'Hello from the gutters of N.Y.C.' — another Berkowitz quote. Half of the second note is plagiarized from the Son of Sam letters."

From the summer of 1976 until August 1977, the self-proclaimed Son of Sam terrorized New York. He shot couples in cars, the eight attacks leaving six dead and seven wounded, and his letters to both the police and press taunted the public and whipped them deeper and deeper into a terrified frenzy.

"High caliber," Loshak said, quoting another part of the clue. "Before the Son of Sam nickname emerged, the papers had called Berkowitz the .44 Caliber Killer as it was such an uncommon — and large — caliber of bullet committing all the crimes. It's how they figured out the murders were linked."

Loshak's fingers drummed against his knee.

"OK… so where is he telling us to go?" he asked. "To the site of one of the shootings? And if so, which one?"

Darger searched for a map of the Son of Sam murders and found one. Jesus. The internet had everything these days. Studying the map, she inhaled.

"Look at this. Half of the attacks took place in Queens. Just blocks from here. Just blocks from…"

She and Loshak stared at each other.

"Huxley's old stomping grounds."

# CHAPTER 24

Flashlights sliced through the dark of night, lighting up sidewalks and benches, trees and bushes. Fredrick had called in reinforcements, and now they had five groups with K-9 units searching the various former Son of Sam crime scenes located on Huxley's home turf.

Loshak and Darger were with Group 3, assigned to comb the area around Bowne Park — a nearly 12-acre slab of green east of downtown Flushing, Queens. Gone dark for the day hours ago, the park consisted of a playground, basketball courts, a bocce court, and a kettle pond — an oval-shaped 2-acre aerated lagoon with two fountains, surrounded by a concrete retaining wall.

On the night of October 23, 1976, Carl Denaro and Rosemary Keenan were sitting in a car near the park when David Berkowitz opened fire into the vehicle. Keenan escaped with only superficial injuries from the broken glass of the car's shattered windows, but Denaro had taken a .44 caliber bullet to the head. He survived the attack, but part of his skull had to be replaced with a metal plate.

Darger felt a twinge of sympathy pain along the part of her scalp that covered her own metal plate.

"What did Fredrick say again?" Darger said. "That we're like ten blocks from Huxley's mother's house?"

Loshak nodded.

"This has to be it, then," she said, swinging the beam of her flashlight over the drooping branches of a willow tree. "This is the closest of the Son of Sam crime scenes to where he grew up.

Family history could have a double meaning."

"If there's something here, the dogs will find it," Loshak said, gesturing at a bloodhound sniffing around the edge of the nearby pond.

Each search party had been paired with two K-9 search teams, and then they'd parceled out dirty laundry from Huxley's house and given each of the dogs his scent in hopes of achieving faster results.

Darger checked her phone again, and her stomach clenched at how much time had passed since they'd solved the Son of Sam clue. It had taken a while to arrange the search parties, to call in the K-9 units, to collect the clothing from Huxley's home, and to issue instructions to each group. They had a little under five hours remaining to figure out where the next attack would take place.

She and Loshak spent several minutes carefully sweeping the area beneath a willow tree. Around the trunk. Up in the branches. Finding nothing of interest, they moved on.

"I wish we knew what exactly we were looking for," Darger grumbled. "I mean, this isn't a huge park, but the number of places you could hide something here… we don't even know how big it is."

"Or whether it's out in the open," Loshak added. "Or hidden in a bush or a trash can. Or shit… buried."

Darger checked the clock again. Seven minutes had passed since she'd last looked.

*Too much time. We're moving too slow.*

She felt her heart rate quicken at the thought that they might solve the clue and still run out of time. What a sick joke that would be.

From somewhere off to her left, someone's radio let out a

burst of static. She heard a rustle of leaves as an NYPD officer tromped through a nearby hedge in an awkward squat-walk, swinging his flashlight around like a cutlass. Another policeman flipped open the lid of a trashcan and peered inside before replacing the top and moving on.

Someone would find something. They had to.

She and Loshak reached the edge of a pond situated at one side of the park. There was a semicircular ring of benches and a concrete drinking fountain in the center.

Darger got down on her hands and knees and aimed the beam of her light under the first bench.

“This one’s clear,” she said, crawling forward to the next bench.

The rough surface of the concrete dug into her knees, and tiny pebbles stuck to the palms of her hand.

She focused the beam of her light on the underside of the next bench. The light glinted as it touched something there.

She froze. There was something metallic tucked behind the back left leg of the bench.

“You got something?”

“Maybe,” she said, scooting closer.

“Don’t touch it,” Loshak said.

Darger squinted, studying the object. Her shoulders slumped.

“False alarm,” she said. “It’s just one of those juice pouches with the silvery packaging. Capri-Sun, or whatever. When my light hit it, I thought it was something made of metal at first.”

She leaned back on her knees and dusted the dirt and bits of gravel from her hands.

“How come I’m always the one that ends up crawling around in the muck?” she asked.

Loshak smiled.

"Seniority."

"Yeah, well… Next time we—"

Darger was cut off by the distinct baying of a hound coming from across the pond. She and Loshak held still from the neck down, whipping their heads toward the place where the sound had come from. The barking cut off, and then they heard a human voice shout with excitement. It was too distant to make out the words, but they didn't need to. Loshak swung back to face her.

"Sounds like they found something."

# CHAPTER 25

She and Loshak jogged through the park, over to the far side of the pond. Darger saw other flashlights bobbing around them, everyone converging on the excited dog.

She wanted to run faster — to sprint ahead to see what the dogs had found — but the ground here was a bit uneven and slick with dew, and she didn't want to sprain an ankle or fall on her face.

They found a group clustered around a pair of park benches. Wooden slats and wrought iron arms and legs. A mess of flashlight beams swept around in the tight space under the horizontal seat support, stray light spilling up through the cracks and over the top, but there was nothing on or under the bench that Darger could see.

The dog lurched forward again. Pulled to the edge of the lead. The hound whined and scratched at the wood chips under the bench.

"I'm not taking any chances," Fredrick said and unclipped a radio from her belt. "I want the bomb techs to take point on this just in case whatever he buried down there is dangerous."

While she radioed for the bomb squad, Darger studied her surroundings.

This side of the pond was more secluded than the rest of the park, far from the streetlights that lined the edges of the grounds. Beyond that, the two benches were shaded by a maple tree, and Darger guessed the area would be entirely shrouded in shadow even in bright daylight. Right now, the area under the tree was nearly pitch black. She imagined Huxley here, on his knees, digging a hole beneath the bench. Hiding something there and carefully replacing the dirt and mulch.

*I've left something for you in a secret place.*

The minutes ticked by as they waited for C-IED to arrive. Finally, Darger spotted two vehicles roll up and park on the street. Agent Fitch and one of the bomb techs that had been at Huxley's house hopped out of a black SUV with a bomb-sniffing dog.

The rest of the group backed off from the area, giving the men space to work. The dog started near the bench, sniffing the ground, and then pulled away. The dog's handler redirected the dog back to the bench, but again the dog almost immediately trotted off in a different direction.

Agent Fitch gave his patented thumbs up signal.

"Dinah says there's nothing here," he said. "We're all clear."

"OK." Fredrick nodded at the crime scene tech standing next to her. "Let's start digging."

The tech got down on her knees and used a trowel to gently scrape away the top layer of wood chips. After that, she removed a thin layer of soil and placed it in a bucket, handing it off to another tech who sifted through the dirt looking for evidence. They repeated this process with each layer. Digging and sifting and digging and sifting.

It was a slow and careful process intended to minimize the chances of missing anything, but Darger couldn't help but feel a surge of impatience as she watched them work.

The tech with the trowel stopped.

"I've got something," she said. "It looks like a plastic baggie."

Fredrick put a hand up.

"Let us get a few photos before you dig it out," she said.

The two techs on excavation duty moved aside. The flash of

the camera lit up the gloom under the tree like flickers of lightning.

When the cameraman was finished, the original tech squatted down and used her trowel to loosen the area around the baggie. The plastic crinkled as she pulled it free. It was a gallon-sized bag, rolled into a tube for easier burying. Darger could see what looked like paper inside.

There was another moment of tension as they paused again to photograph the evidence. Finally it was handed off to Fredrick who squinted at the plastic-clad pages.

"You've got to be kidding me," she said.

"What is it?" Darger asked, the anticipation just about killing her.

Fredrick grasped the baggie by one corner and held it out for them to see.

"It's in code."

Loshak squinted at the symbols forming a rectangle in the center of the page. They were oddly familiar.

"I recognize that," Loshak said.

"Me too," Darger said. "It looks like the Zodiac letters."

Fredrick's head snapped up.

"You mean the Zodiac killer?"

Loshak nodded.

Details from the Zodiac case file flashed through Darger's head. She'd studied him closely in the academy.

Though he once claimed to have killed 37 victims, the self-named Zodiac Killer had five known murder victims in San Francisco between 1968 and 1969, killing couples parked at local makeout spots and eventually shooting a cab driver. He sent a series of menacing letters and ciphers to local newspapers and TV stations, demanding they be shared with the public and threatening bombings and killings if they weren't. He was never caught.

"He's doing it again," Darger said. "Mimicking another serial killer."

# CHAPTER 26

Once Agent Fredrick opened the bag and pulled out the sheaf of papers, they discovered that only the top page was in code. After that, there were around 25 pages of the journal Huxley had promised. The packet was hustled back to the task force HQ to be processed, copied, and distributed as quickly as possible. The more eyes they could get on these pages loaded with potential clues, the better.

The final sheet inside the plastic bag contained a schematic for what appeared to be a relatively simple explosive device, with the taunting phrase written in sharpie above it: *If you manage to crack the code, you'll be needing this.*

"The clue that tells us the next bombing location must be hidden in the coded text," Darger said. "Maybe there are hints in the journal as well, but I think the cipher is the key."

"I'm going to send it to Agent Remzi." Loshak tapped at the screen of his phone. "He's the best cryptanalyst in the Bureau as far as I'm concerned. If anyone can solve this thing, it'll be him."

While Loshak made the call, Darger turned back to her phone and studied the symbols again. She remembered reading that one of the Zodiac ciphers had only recently been decrypted. Fifty-one years the letter had sat shrouded in mystery before a team of amateur code crackers finally figured it out. Not a comforting thought, considering their deadline.

She gazed out across the pond and watched the bobbing flashlight beams of the C-IED guys leading the dog around the far end of the park. They were checking the rest of the park for signs of anything else Huxley might have left them.

Loshak walked back over to her, tucking his phone into his jacket.

"Remzi said he'd get to work on the code immediately."

She checked the time again, disturbed to see that it was almost 4 A.M. now.

Four hours left.

"Let's hope he can do it quickly."

# CHAPTER 27

It was just past 5 A.M. when they returned to the Javits building and rode the elevator up to the task force headquarters on the 23rd floor. Jittery feelings squiggled in Darger's middle despite the late hour, some unholy blend of overstimulation and exhaustion roiling deep inside as her eyes watched the floor numbers count upward.

As soon as she got into the conference room, she poured herself a cup of coffee. Sipped. Set the cup on the glossy surface of the conference table.

Then she moved to the whiteboard along the front wall. She grabbed a dry erase marker and used a section of the board to write out the encoded message. She stepped back and let her eyes trace over the symbols scrawled up there, blue ink smudged on the white. She tried her hand at decoding it herself, using the existing solved Zodiac ciphers as a guide, but none fit. After an hour, she had to admit that she was in over her head.

With one eye on the clock, she took another drink of coffee. She felt jittery as hell and more caffeine was the last thing she needed, but the long hours were beginning to weigh on her. She was at once completely drained and so filled with anxiety and anticipation that sleep was out of the question. Electricity burning bright behind her eyes, even if the flesh around them was growing sore with exhaustion.

Snippets of the Zodiac's threatening notes played in her head then, his repeated misspelling of *paradise* and all. They dredged up fragments of the fear she'd experienced back when she'd studied the case.

*This is the Zodiac Speaking.*

*I like killing people because it is so much fun.*

*When I die I will be reborn in paradice and all that I have killed will become my slaves.*

*I am not afraid of the gas chamber because it will send me to paradice all the sooner.*

Darger finally sat down with her copy of Huxley's journal pages and started reading.

*This is the Zodiac speaking. Ha-ha.*

Darger grunted. She continued reading.

*By now you're probably wondering why I did all this. Well, allow me to explain.*

*There is light and dark in every human heart, and we all choose our path. We all find our purpose. These pages will show you how I found mine.*

These few words formed a cover letter of sorts. Darger turned the page, and the journal began.

# CHAPTER 28

I witnessed a rape when I was about five years old. The memories are blurry. A little girl crying in a bedroom across the street. Whimpering. Moaning. Face all turning red. Fingers clutching at blue shag carpet. Bare mattress. Crawling under the bed to try to get away.

I witnessed a murder when I was 23 years old. Watched a masked person through the window next door. Drugged up and confused, he climbed the stairs, turned around on the landing, and lifted a revolver. Squeezed the trigger. Flames jetted out of the muzzle.

The pop was more metallic in person than it is on TV. Percussive and clipped-sounding. When I'd heard earlier shots that night, the ones that drew me to the window, I thought it sounded like a hammer smashed on the hood of a car.

The old man at the bottom of the steps bled out rapidly. Life seeping out between his fingers. Gone in 45 seconds.

This is what people are really like. This is what they really do to each other.

Cruel beings stomping around. Disturbed. Insane. Always hungry for more destruction. Always on the hunt.

Mindless violent raping world.

When bad things happen in real life, there's no cheesy music ending like a sitcom episode where we all say "sisters forever?" or some shit and everything is OK again.

No relief. No salvation.

The damage isn't undone. The conflict never ends.

The trauma persists. Festers. The dead don't come back.

You can feel the hatred, loathing, animal aggression surrounding us. See it like a red shimmer in the air. It's all around us.

This is the world we've made. We use each other. Break each other. Kill each other.

Mankind.

Restless creatures stalk the night. Every night. In every town.

Just turn on the TV. Watch a local news story about someone getting killed for $30, about some kid getting set on fire by his own parents. Fresh tragedy every fucking night.

We all just suffer, suffer, suffer. Ceaseless torment. Endless pain.

The great swells of humanity. A vast sea of misery. Real horror.

Someday maybe we'll all get wiped away. A black hole expanding to devour us. A big rain to wash it all away.

Maybe. If there is a God.

☾

The world is getting darker and darker. You can feel it in the air, in the wind. See it flicker against the night sky, trying to blot out the moon and stars.

Darker. Darker all the time.

You know it. You believe it. But what can you do?

When we look at the sky, we think we see the moon and stars, but most of what we see is nothing. Empty space. A vast, empty universe that stretches out into eternity.

So many people cower their whole lives long at what comes after death. They fear hellfire. They fear that deep down the universe wants to torture them eternally.

Like it fuckin' cares so much about them to bother.

The universe seems profoundly indifferent to me. Uncaring and cold. It's mostly nothing. Infinite emptiness. It doesn't give enough of a fuck about you to want to hurt you.

Can't you see that you're nobody? You're nothing. A grain of sand. A pebble on the beach.

And one day the darkness will win. The stars will expand and die. Burn out like light bulbs one by one. All life will wink out. Engulfed in black nothing. Endless cold.

Of course, mankind will probably have killed itself with global warming many thousands of years earlier, but still…

When I look at the sky, that's what I see: the darkness swallowing all.

☾

You fear Hell? Damnation? Guess what? We're already here. Already living it.

This is Hell.

We've made it. Built it here and now. We're just too dumb to see it.

Look around you. It's a mindless, violent, raping world. Cruelty. Brutality.

Walk down a city block and watch the crack fiends sleep on flaps of cardboard. Camped out on sidewalks and tucked back in alleys. All lean and hard. Angular. Sinewy. Crumbling teeth. Cheekbones protruding. Pointy hip bones jutting out.

Empty shells. Husks. Like the humanity got sucked out of them, left only the skin and bones.

Watch all the pedestrians stream past. Nobody helps. No one even looks at the bums. Nobody cares.

This is what we've made of this world. Skyscrapers that tower over the slums. Golden arches soaring over catastrophe. Human misery clustering on the concrete of every major city.

Go look up war videos on YouTube. Bombs raining down on exotic locations. Buildings and civilians blown to pieces. Hundreds of millions of military-related deaths in the 20th century alone.

In the United States, 136 people die per day from opioid overdoses. Too much pain to kill in this life. Too much suffering, misery, despair. The amount of medicine needed becomes fatal. The disease is too far gone.

Worldwide, a child dies from hunger every 10 seconds. They're born. They're hungry. They die. That's it.

This is what normal looks like. This is the pinnacle of humankind's progress. Every step of evolution working to lead us to this reality.

Mass death. Suffering. Cruelty. Brutality. Misery.

Hell is already here. We made it. We are living it.

# CHAPTER 29

We stumble through life, drunk on dreams. Filled to the brim with these fantasies of what we'll do and who we'll be. What we'll own. What we'll consume. If you really examine the human animal, really study people, you find that most of them — the rabble, the scum, the horde — don't even have their own dreams. They don't dare to. They copy someone else's dream. Wish they had someone else's life. Wish they were someone else. Motherfuckin' followers to the core. Bootlickers.

It starts young, too. Elementary school. The poor kids want what the rich kids have. The newest iPhone. The expensive name brand shoes. The designer shirts and jeans. They'd crawl over broken glass to have and hold these status symbols. They'd chug Drano.

Not to do anything interesting with, mind you. Just to mimic someone else. Ape their little ticks and behaviors. Reenact shit they've seen on TV. Just to feel better about themselves. *I want to be the guy with the iPhone Pro Max* is the height of what they can see for themselves, the absolute pinnacle of their ambition. Their deepest desire in life. Unreal.

Imagine having a life so dull that even your wildest fantasies would put everyone else to fuckin' sleep.

Ah, but sleepin' through life is what these people seem good at. The sleepwalkers. Easy to count sheep when you are one, I suppose.

☾

Behold the mission that opens in my head. More of a calling, I guess.

You want to change the fucking world? Kill the old dream. Kill the avatars of the old fantasy.

Celebrities. The gatekeepers who seem to keep us apart from their chosen ranks. Stars to be immortalized on film. Heroes to be worshiped.

Kill this dream and anything becomes possible. Real change.

Out with the old. In with the new.

The revolution will be sweet. Let the streets run red.

Fame is a religion.

Celebrity bodies turned divine by all the worship, all of the faith directed their way.

So I offer up a communion.

This is the celebrity body. Broken for you.

This is the precious blood. Spilled for you.

☾

Suffering is all around us, the primary product of our culture. And rather than doing anything to address it, we escape into fantasies about celebrities. We worship them. Wish we knew them. Wish we were them.

We picture ourselves lounging in mansions, cruising around in Lambos, engulfed in the tan flesh of harems.

Picture ourselves coked to the gills on the deck of a large boat, overseeing our fleet of minions zipping around on jet skis.

Picture ourselves rolling around in piles of money, our faces plastered on magazine covers, our faces broadcast on TV, our faces projected 30 feet tall on the theater screen.

In the face of all of that torment, all that suffering, we can only dream of fame and fortune. Hundreds of millions of people live in poverty, and we dream of excess.

So kill the dream.

That's why I'm here, why I was born. To kill the dream one celebrity at a time.

I can show you.

If we burn out the old way, we can build something new on the ashes. We can remake the world in a new image.

The old idols will topple. Die off like the dinosaurs. Reality will pierce the veil of tinsel at long last.

Kill the stars. Kill the dream.

The revolution will be etched into celebrity skin.

# CHAPTER 30

Cold feelings bloomed in Darger's hands and cheeks as she finished this chunk of Huxley's journal. She stared at the last page. Dazed. Blinked a few times.

Finally, she reread that final line.

*The revolution will be etched into celebrity skin.*

Visions of Passmore and Driscoll flashed through her head. Their famous faces broken beyond repair. Fragmented. Melted. Their beauty turned grotesque. Ghastly and shocking.

The journal's grim words seemed to match the damage done. Morbid. Callous. Traumatic and traumatized. Disturbing and disturbed.

And those icy tendrils snaked deeper into Darger's flesh. Reached down the lengths of her arms. The chill saturating her flesh until the conference room felt cavernous.

She placed the packet face down on the table, as though turning the text away from her might help her distance herself from the words. The back page gleamed accusatory white up at her, though, dared her to find the dark spots where the black lettering showed through the thin sheet of paper.

Tentatively, she reached out a hand. Fingertips reaching. Finding the sharp edges of the paper. Pressing ever so gingerly.

She scooted the packet over the glossy wood. Pushed it away. It hissed faintly against the surface of the table.

Darger's heartbeat thrummed. Pumped the cold all through her now. Like ice water threading her body.

The room seemed utterly quiet, utterly vacant. Motionless.

She got up and began to pace. Tried to clear her mind, to

think of anything but Huxley's dark words, but they seemed to echo in her mind.

*This is the world we've made. We use each other. Break each other. Kill each other.*

The thing was, he wasn't wrong. Not about that, at least. How many times had she cursed the evil acts people perpetrated on one another?

Huxley seemed at once to condemn the darkest aspects of humanity but also to embrace it.

Somewhere in her reading and musing, she'd lost her sense of how much time had passed. When Darger next looked at the clock, she was startled to find the hour hand approaching the seven.

She took a breath and felt a slight tremor in her chest.

Across the room, Loshak's phone jangled, and he nearly knocked it off the table in his haste to pick it up. He swiped at the screen and grinned.

"He's got it. Remzi decrypted the message."

Darger blew out a breath.

"We're cutting it close here."

"He says Huxley was using one of the pre-existing Zodiac codes, just slightly augmented. Still took a bit to figure, but it ultimately saved him some time."

Darger felt a slight surge of pride at that. She'd been on the right track in her amateur attempts to break the cipher after all.

Loshak waved Agent Fredrick and Agent Laboda over and opened the attachment Remzi had sent.

A photo loaded. Agent Remzi had printed out a copy of the Huxley clue and written in the corresponding letters above each symbol.

*Greetings from Hell.*

*If you're reading this, perhaps the game will proceed down the tracks.*

*Each explosion bigger than the last from here on out. Meant to kill, maim, destroy.*

*Some will live, and some will die screaming. Such is life in a universe that cares not.*

*To live is to suffer, to survive is to find some meaning in the suffering.*

*There are no facts, only interpretations.*

*Isn't it exciting to know that their lives are in your hands?*

*The stakes couldn't be higher. It's always dirkest before dawn.*

*Will you be brave? Will you race to the rescue? Or are you yellow?*

*Time to find out if you've got the goods.*

Darger read the note a few times. Realized that her lips were moving along with the words, little whispery sounds emitting from where her tongue touched the edges of her teeth.

She closed her mouth and read it again. Trying to pluck out a clue, a turn of phrase with a second meaning.

"Is that a typo on Huxley's part?" Fredrick asked. "*Dirkest* before dawn?"

"Could be," Loshak said. "Remzi said he double-checked that and the translation there is correct as an 'i', so it's not a mistake on his part, at least."

"Zodiac intentionally misspelled things in his letters," Darger said. "He always spelled 'paradise' with a 'c' instead of an 's'. Could be an homage."

Darger's eyes slid back up the disturbing stanza, finding the one line that stuck out to her as vaguely familiar. She read it out loud.

"'To live is to suffer, to survive is to find some meaning in the suffering.'"

"It's a Nietzsche quote," Loshak said. His voice seemed distant. Eyes glued to his phone. "So is the next line about *no facts, only interpretations.*"

"You think that's significant?" Fredrick cupped her chin. "Two quotes from the same guy?"

"Maybe he's pointing us to a book," Laboda said. "He had tons of books in his house."

"And at his mother's house," Darger said, thinking that maybe they were onto something now. Could Huxley have stashed something in one of the books lining his shelves?

"Hold up," Loshak said. He was still looking at his phone, but now his brow was furrowed. "That's not actually a Nietzsche quote — the line about suffering. It's a Gordon Allport quote commonly misattributed to Nietzsche."

Agent Fredrick clucked her tongue.

"Seems like every famous quote gets tied to Mark Twain, Abe Lincoln, or Friedrich frickin' Nietzsche."

Loshak ran his fingers through his hair.

"The main thing is, the line just doesn't have the same weight if it's attributed to Gordon Allport."

"Who the hell is Gordon Allport?" Laboda said.

"Exactly." Loshak took a big breath. "You want to know what I really think? I think Huxley got these quotes off Google. I think he probably thought it was a genuine Nietzsche quote, being that he probably put this together in five minutes."

They were quiet for a few seconds.

"So that's a no on the book idea?" Laboda said.

Loshak shrugged and then shook his head.

Agent Fitch came in from the hall, his biceps jumping as he cracked open a can of Mountain Dew from the vending machine. After studying the faces around him, he sensed the fresh tension in the room. The green can paused a few inches shy of his lips.

"Did I miss something?"

Darger ignored him.

"What about that last line? *Time to find out if you've got the goods.* Seems off to me."

Loshak nodded.

"Something almost hokey about it compared to the rest of the writing."

Fitch, now in the midst of a big slug of Mountain Dew, held up a finger, his eyes going wide.

"*Ultimate Food Fight,*" he said, wiping the back of his hand over his Dewed-up lips.

Everyone just stared at him.

"You guys have never watched *Ultimate Food Fight*? It's fucking great! It's a reality show. A competition, right? These families have to cook against each other, and then the losing team has to *get sloppy* in this, like, insane obstacle course made of food. Crawling on hands and knees through spaghetti and kiddie pools full of tapioca pudding and shit. It's incredible."

Still everyone stared at him.

"'You've got the goods' is the host's catchphrase. He says that to the winners."

Now everyone leaned forward.

"Dude hosts a few different shows, I think. Blond-haired guy. Kind of a smartass. Named Dirk something. Dirk Nielsen."

# CHAPTER 31

From the outside, the CIRG van appeared to be something like the standard UPS delivery truck. Oversized cargo bay. Low-key dark gray paint job with a single navy stripe. Otherwise unmarked.

The inside looked like something out of a spy movie.

Banks of monitors lined the wall, images from various satellite feeds flickering on some while streams of text fed endlessly on others. The console beneath the screens held enough colorful buttons, knobs, faders, and switches that it looked fit to record a Grammy-winning live album.

To Darger's disappointment, the agent manning the console — McAllister — looked like neither Will Smith nor Gene Hackman. He was a small, mousy guy. Bald and bony and slight. All his features were as petite as his frame save for the big buck teeth perpetually exposed by his curled top lip. He pecked at a keyboard there, muttered into his headset, eyes constantly flicking to a different monitor. Darger wondered how he could continue working as they flew down the road, juddering over potholes, racing around corners. She suspected trying to read and write during all of that would trigger her motion sickness.

She sat on a padded bench diagonal to the display of gadgetry. She pumped her leg — tension expressed in her pistoning calf. Across from her, Fitch held a hand to his ear, listening to some radio chatter, she assumed.

"Has anyone made contact with Nielsen yet?" Darger asked.

"Not yet. Bainbridge Tower is one of those cushy high-rise penthouses. Dude even has a private elevator, apparently.

Anyway, the front desk tried calling him. No answer. So then they sent someone up to knock at his door. Again, no answer. They're not sure if he's not home or just not answering."

She checked the time on her phone. If Huxley's suggested timeframe held remotely true, they had less than 30 minutes until this next bomb blew, a thought that made her stomach lurch. She wondered if they'd even get there in time, let alone defuse it.

She voiced none of these thoughts aloud, of course — not even to Loshak who sat next to her. It'd feel wrong to say it, to even indirectly suggest failure, with the bomb technicians prepping for the operation right next to her.

One of them was going to go in there, for Christ's sake.

That honor would go to Agent Michael Dobbins. He still had the short-cropped hair and chiseled features of a cadet fresh out of the Marines, but the faintest sag to the flesh beneath his cheekbones betrayed the illusion and hinted at his real age, probably somewhere in his mid-thirties.

He strapped himself into the EOD suit as they rode toward the scene, adjusting the black ballistic panels on the front which looked to be more rigid than the rest. The bulky green Kevlar blast suit instantly made Darger think of Jeremy Renner and Guy Pearce in *The Hurt Locker*, tottering around as if they were wearing fat suits.

If Dobbins felt any fear at the moment, his eyes didn't show it. He looked more determined than anything, Darger thought. A thoughtful kind of smile played at his lips now and again as he fussed with his gear. He toyed with the controls to the cooling unit attached to the suit. Fitch had explained how a system of capillaries pumped two liters of ice water through the Nomex body suit Dobbins wore under the armor. Dobbins tried maxing the settings, and when it got too cold he cranked the dial back and jogged in place for a second — Darger thought it looked like he had to go to the bathroom.

The agent next to him, Mike Alvarez, would be the voice in Dobbins' head, watching his every move through the camera in the EOD suit, talking him through the operation. After a round of mic checks, the dark-haired man typed furiously at the laptop sitting on his knees. The computer and the headset running over his ears and angling a microphone in front of his lips combined to make him look more like a telemarketer than a man about to head up a bomb disposal operation for the federal government.

Darger checked her phone again. They now had 24 minutes give or take. She swallowed. She hoped there was some amount of leeway to that detonation time, but nobody could know until it either happened or didn't. The whole thing knotted up her guts, made sweat bead along her brow. Her pulse thudded in her ears, quavered in her neck.

"We got an ETA?" Alvarez asked, looking up at the mousy guy behind the console.

"Current estimate is six minutes." He talked through those buck teeth, his voice strangely flat and emotionless, eyes swiveling just a little in a way that reminded Darger of one of those creepy antique dolls.

Alvarez nodded and swung his gaze over to Dobbins.

"You ready to rock, Dobber?"

Dobbins smirked before he responded.

"I was born ready, shitdick."

That got a big laugh out of Fitch, who stomped the floor in his excitement, his heavy boot a sledgehammer head thudding down next to Darger's foot.

"Fuck yeah," he said, shaking his head. "That's what I love about these bomb techs… you gotta have balls the size of goddamn grapefruits to do what they do. You probably gotta cart 'em around in a wheelbarrow, huh Dobbins?"

Dobbins opted to neither confirm nor deny the size of his testicles, instead rolling his neck back and forth and bouncing on his toes. His body language made him look like a fighter about to throw down in the octagon.

They sped through Manhattan, heading north. Darger wheeled around to look out the windshield and spotted the spire of the Chrysler building tinted gold by the rising sun. She went to check the time again, but it was a notification at the top of the screen that caught her eye this time.

"Shit."

Loshak leaned closer.

"What now?"

She showed him the screen of her phone.

"The stuff we found at the park got leaked online again. The code, the journal, even the schematics. It's all on there."

"When?" Loshak asked.

"Just a few minutes ago."

"Same account?"

"No. Another freshly created account." Darger considered this for a moment. "I think Huxley must have set it up to post automatically somehow. If someone was leaking it on our side, why wait until after we'd solved it?"

"Here's what I don't get," Fitch said, crossing his legs at the ankles. "Why go to all this trouble with the clues and whatnot and then leak them to the public? Doesn't that increase the odds of the clue getting solved and the next attack being thwarted?"

"Maybe. But it also creates quite a spectacle," Loshak said.

"Look at the views on that post."

It was already in the hundreds of thousands despite the post only being seven minutes old. Darger frowned at the screen.

"He's in the spotlight now for sure."

The procession continued past Central Park, which was already bustling with people jogging, biking, pushing strollers. Suddenly the van tilted underfoot and the engine whined as it lugged them uphill.

Everyone adjusted their position to compensate. Leaning in unison. The mousy guy splayed his hands on the console.

"I think that's it, right there," Fitch said, aiming a finger at one of the skyscrapers visible through the windshield. "Bainbridge Tower."

Darger shifted in her seat to get a better view of the fifty-story tower made of glass and steel. Luxury apartments with a priceless view of Central Park.

The grade leveled out beneath them. Their collective lean relented. Gravity once more pulling straight down.

The van zipped into a lane marked "Taxi and Limousine Parking Only."

Several police cruisers already hunkered in the narrow drive, lights spinning. Officers had blocked off the street and initiated an evacuation of the building, clearing the way for Dobbins to get up to the penthouse where the bomb would be.

The van turned parallel along the sidewalk leading up to the front doors. Parked between the cruisers.

That sickening feeling lurched in Darger's gut — the overwhelming inertia of stopping after all that forward momentum, the unbearable quiet surrounding them after the engine cut out. Every follicle of hair on her body tingled in that still moment, and her stomach fluttered rapid twitches like dragonfly wings.

Darger checked the time. Only 21 minutes now.

This was it.

# CHAPTER 32

The side door of the security van slid open, and bright morning sunlight glinted into the space. Dobbins stepped into the orangey glow, the lupine grin on his face conveying utter confidence.

"Welp. Going in," he said. "Just another day at the office, right?"

The others chattered platitudes around him like football players about to surge out of the tunnel. Messages that bordered on nonsensical, especially the stuff Fitch said.

"Go time, Dobber."

"Let's do this. Time to go get it."

"That's what I'm talking about, motherfucker. Now or never."

They circled him like vultures. Slapping him on the shoulders as they chanted.

He broke out of the circle after a few seconds. Moved into the open. Tottered up to the building in the blast suit. Legs kicking out choppy steps on the sidewalk, mobility limited by the bulky gear. Upper body swaying with each step. From the back, he looked a little like he was strapped into an inflatable sumo suit. Despite the clunky body language, he scooted right up the walk without delay.

He pushed through the front doors of the building. Disappeared behind the glare obscuring the pane of glass. Swallowed up by the shimmering brightness.

The others pulled back into the van. Closed the door. Cut off that orange sunlight all at once to plunge them back into the shade.

They huddled in the bluish glow of the monitors along the wall. Watched the feed from the camera in Dobbins' helmet.

He bobbed along, the image on the monitor rising and falling with his lumbering gait. Crossed the lobby. Entered the penthouse's private elevator with a special keycard. Then he stood motionless as the stainless steel box lurched upward, taking him toward the top floor in what felt like slow motion.

Dobbins narrated all of this, his voice sounding tinny through the speakers in the console.

"Elevator is on its way up now. It'll be a minute or so before we get to the top floor."

Darger couldn't help but picture Huxley's target as Dobbins rode up to his living space. Dirk Nielsen, reality show host extraordinaire. That smiling orange face perpetually telling audiences that one of his various shows would be back after these messages. Tan skin stretched over riveted musculature. Hollow cheeks. Blond hair that always looked freshly wet. Eyes just a bit too close together in a way that made him look like a bird.

"Has anyone been able to confirm whether Dirk Nielsen is in his apartment or not?" Darger asked.

Fitch shook his head.

"The first officers on the scene went up and hollered from the elevator. But since they had orders not to enter the apartment until the bomb squad arrived, they couldn't go in. For all we know the guy's blissed out on Ambien in there, completely unaware of what's happening." He nodded at the screen. "But I guess ol' Dobber is about to find out whether or not anyone is home right now."

The elevator reached the top floor, and the door drifted

open. The penthouse gleamed beyond the threshold, all glass and steel and sleek-looking. Modern. A little industrial.

"Exiting the elevator now. Entering the penthouse."

The cam once again bobbed with Dobbins' footsteps. Something of a foyer zoomed by — neon green running shoes pushed all the way to the side of a floormat — and then button-tufted leather furniture squared off the expansive living space, most of it pointed out at the seamless glazing facing the skyline, the window wall providing an uninterrupted view of the cityscape.

"Hello?" Dobbins called out. "Anyone home?"

His voice echoed off the polished floors and gleaming glass. There was no response.

Alvarez spoke up, the nearness of his voice startling Darger after so much silence in the van save for what came from the speakers.

"The front desk mentioned Mr. Nielsen receiving a flower delivery yesterday evening. We're thinking that's how Huxley got the bomb into the penthouse."

"Copy that. On the lookout for a bouquet of some sort. Here we go. Now entering the kitchen."

The camera wheeled hard to the left as Dobbins swiveled that way, the image blurring for a second and then sharpening into focus on the gleaming marble countertop of the kitchen island — bright white veined with smoky tendrils of dark gray.

His head rotated to the left and right, the cam sweeping past an oversized refrigerator that blended with the white shaker cabinetry around it. Dobbins did something of a double take, the feed on the monitor mimicking the motion, and then Darger saw what had caused the reaction.

A massive floral arrangement nestled in an antique metal

bucket sat at the end of the countertop to the right of the fridge. The thin stalks and velvety petals looked especially delicate surrounded by all the hard, glinting surfaces of the kitchen. An organic island in a sea of glossy cabinets and shining marble.

"The base on this thing is pretty hefty," Dobbins said. "I think this is it."

Dobbins trudged toward the flower arrangement. The camera seemed to zoom in on it.

He stopped just shy of touching the mass of flowers, though his thickly armored hands hovered on the sides of the screen now, drifting up and down with his respiration.

"I'm going to remove the flowers now," Dobbins said.

Pressure pounded in Darger's head, a squishing throb in her temples. It whoomped like a fan blade spinning inside her skull.

She tried to stop her eyes from flicking down to the phone in her lap. Failed.

They had six minutes. Give or take.

Dobbins lifted the large bouquet.

"Yep, there's definitely something here."

He set the flowers aside and leaned over the bucket that served as a vase for the flowers. There was a cardboard box inside the vessel.

Up close, thin beige lines became visible running around the package both longways and widthways, crossing in the middle. Darger realized it was bound in a length of twine.

"According to the schematic he gave us, we're supposed to be able to open the top of the box to disarm the anti-tampering trigger," Alvarez said. "Just be careful."

Darger chewed her bottom lip. What if they'd been wrong? What if Huxley wasn't playing fair? What if the merest disturbance set off the trigger and detonated the bomb?

Using a multi-tool, Dobbins snipped the twine. Brushed it out of the way. Then he slit the tape sealing the top of the box.

The tip of the blade punched through the clear layer. Disappeared into the cardboard crevice.

Dobbins hesitated with the knife like that. Took a couple of breaths. Cam rising and falling. Rising and falling.

Then he raked the tool toward himself. The metal sliced its way through the tape, lisping against the sticky plastic all the way from one end of the box to the other.

From there he quickly slashed the tape along the corners. Two clean swipes.

The cardboard flaps relaxed then. Pulled apart slightly. Like the thing had let out a breath.

Everyone in the van sat up straighter. Breath sucked in and held. Soundless.

Darger could somehow feel that they were all experiencing the same thing. A shared intensity prickling over their scalps, along their necks. Chest and palms vibrating with strange tension. Like the feeling had spread over the interior of the van, infected all of them.

Dobbins set the tool down on the countertop.

"OK," he said, voice going shaky for the first time. "OK. I'm going to open it now."

That was when the feed on the monitor cut to black.

# CHAPTER 33

Darger blinked hard and stared at the blank monitor. The van held tensely silent for that first jolt of shock, perhaps the span of a single heartbeat.

Then the panic hit.

A different kind of shockwave rolled through the enclosed space of the security van. Confusion rippling outward, throttling all of them.

Everyone in the vehicle flinched. Winced. Shoulders bucking backward.

Darger shot straight up. Her legs lifting her to her feet without her telling them to, some instinct standing her up for no good reason.

Fitch stood up a fraction of a second after her — the same inclination for action overtaking him. Their shoulders bumped, Darger getting knocked slightly off-balance, staggering on numb legs until she could right herself.

Gasps tore out of all the throats after that, as though on a timed delay, raspy sucking sounds full of surprise and fear.

The black screen just gaped at them. Empty. Nothing.

All the panicked voices rose then, finally able to find words and form them. The sounds tangled over each other. Cacophony.

"What the fuck happened? Did it blow?"

"I didn't hear anything. Shouldn't we have heard something? Is he OK?"

"Detonation or malfunction?"

Alvarez raised one hand like a kindergarten teacher. He

cupped the fingers of the opposite mitt over the microphone portion of the headset. The laptop perched on his knees wiggled slightly as he spoke.

"We've only lost the video feed," he said, his strident tone cutting through all the voices, drowning them out. "Let me see if the audio is still functional, see if he's OK."

Everyone took a breath, Alvarez included. His chest shuddered as the wind entered. Then he eased his fingers away from the microphone.

"Dobber. Are you there?"

Dobbins' voice crackled through the speakers of the console.

"Yep. I'm about to open this sucker up. Is there a problem?"

Another deep breath rolled in and out of Alvarez, hoisting his chest and then lowering it.

"We're flying blind now, brother. Video feed is down, but we can still hear you, so that's something. Anyhow, I think you should fall back. No need to risk your life for some rich asshole's property now."

Dobbins was quiet for a second. Breath huffing over the line.

"Is the building fully evacuated?"

Everyone in the van turned their attention to the crowd of residents across the street. People were still filing out of the front of the building sporadically.

"Looks like there are still some stragglers," Alvarez said.

"If there are still civilians inside, then we don't have a choice. With a big enough blast… well, I don't want to think about that. My point is, we're out of time, brother. I have to try to disarm it now."

Alvarez grimaced. Lips curling to reveal clenched teeth.

"Goddamn it, Dobbins. Always with the cowboy shit. Cocky son of a bitch."

"Hey, I'm here, and I'm all suited up. I can handle it."

"What'd I tell you?" Fitch muttered. "Huge fuckin' nuts, right? Wheelbarrow."

"OK, enough talk," the voice said through the speakers. "Opening the box now."

Everyone leaned closer to the empty video screen. Darger found herself squinting into the blackness as though the image might flicker to life there after all, as though she could will the feed to resume.

It stayed blank. A vacant rectangle.

Faint scuffing sounds emitted from the speakers now — the telltale noise of a cut cardboard edge scraping against something. Papery scratching.

"Tell me what you see, Dobber," Alvarez said.

"OK, after unfolding the four flaps from the top of the box, there's a rectangular plate beneath them."

Dobbins cleared his throat before he went on. Darger thought he sounded nervous for the first time, which she didn't like.

"Looks to be aluminum foil wrapped around flimsy card stock. I think I can see how it's attached to the bomb mechanism beneath. Looks like a very simple anti-tampering trigger."

Alvarez nodded.

"OK, based on the schematic, you'll need to clip the side wires to disable the trigger."

"Affirmative," Dobbins said. "Stand by for disarming."

Again, there was a beat of silence that seemed to stretch out. A hanging vacancy.

Darger could feel her pulse in her neck. She watched Alvarez who had his left palm cupped under his chin and pressed the tips of all four fingers into the cleft between his lips. He kept shifting the digits against his mouth, not quite able to keep them still.

Then the metallic snip of the wire cutters sounded over the speakers. Two sharp notes. Percussive.

Dobbins exhaled hard into the microphone. It sounded like a gust of wind blowing into a phone's mouthpiece, guttering and snapping, but Darger could hear some amount of relief in it.

"OK. Wires cut. Easy peasy. Removing the plate now."

Darger's eyes darted to her phone. Less than two minutes now.

She held her breath. Part of her waited for the blast, some thrust of deafening violence to break up all this tense quiet.

Something clicked. An odd sound. Almost musical.

"Plate removed. Eyes on the device now."

He swallowed. Spit sloshing in his throat. Then he fell quiet again. Quiet for too long.

"What are you seeing Dobber?" Alvarez said, his voice soft now. "Talk to me."

No reply.

The heads in the van began to swivel toward each other. Glances exchanged. Eyes narrowed. Concern mounting.

Fitch mopped the wrist of his sleeve over his sweaty lip and brow. Patting it there like a hand towel. He shook his head, and Darger watched fresh beads of perspiration weep down to replace the ones he'd wiped away.

"It's a thicc boi, alright. Several times more powerful than what we found in Passmore's kitchen."

He whistled before he went on.

"OK. Looks like we've got four… five wires," Dobbins said.

He seemed to be muttering to himself more than answering Alvarez's question. "And the timer trigger leading to a digital alarm clock."

He clucked his tongue against the roof of his mouth as though figuring something, tallying something up.

"Keep talking, Dobbins," Alvarez said, licking his lips like a nervous dog. "Tell me what you see."

Darger looked down then. The clock showed less than a minute. Her throat got tight. She shoved the phone down into her pocket, concealing it. She couldn't bear to look anymore.

She closed her eyes. Listened to her heart thunder out its terrified speed metal beat.

"Can you identify the power source?" Alvarez said. "Or the initiator?"

Another scraping clack echoed funny out of the speakers. A shrill sound that clipped off hard at the end.

Silence.

All the bodies before the console leaned forward. Listening. Anticipation mounting.

"OK," Dobbins said. "I just cut the power supply. Got it. The device is disabled."

# CHAPTER 34

Darger let out a breath. Chest heaving, huffing, expelling its contents until she was empty.

Her neck went slack then, tension draining away from her shoulders as well. Her head drifted down until her chin rested on her chest. She closed her eyes, and everything seemed to go quiet around her. All sound blocked out.

She stayed that way. Breathed. Weightless. Floating in the silence, in the stillness.

Relief washed over her in waves, the comfort somehow growing in intensity.

Then the sense of relaxation slowly shifted toward a kind of pleasure, something celebratory. A charge of jubilation welling up inside of her, spreading over her from the middle out.

Endorphins overtaking her head and body both.

She opened her eyes then, and the light was all around her, and the sound faded back.

Fitch arched his back until his head faced the van's ceiling, arms locked in some sort of Incredible Hulk pose. He crowed like a frat boy who'd just tapped a keg of Pabst Blue Ribbon.

"Woo! Boom, motherfucker! Bomber McFuckhead never stood a chance once we were on the case."

He straightened, revealing pale blue eyes glowing with some animal ecstasy, and pumped his fist in the air four times. Then his voice switched over to a sing-song delivery that weirdly reminded Darger of Oprah.

"We fuck-ing did it!"

The big guy started windmilling his arms, giving everyone

awkward high fives. The mousy guy behind the console made a face like Fitch had hurt his hand.

"Dobbins is the one who did it," Loshak said. Then he reached over and clapped Alvarez on the shoulder. "Dobbins and Alvarez did it."

Fitch's arms stopped cartwheeling, suspended in midair. He slowly lowered the limbs. Blinked a few times. His eyes went wide. Locked onto Loshak's.

"Oh, for… Don't get me wrong, now. Dobbins is the king. The king! We are merely his loyal subjects, you know, uh… doing the, uh, whatever subjects do. Serving the realm and whatnot."

He chuckled a little at his own lost train of thought. Then he arched his back again and howled like a wolf.

"Long live King Dobbins!"

# CHAPTER 35

As soon as the disabled bomb had been removed from the scene, the investigators swarmed in to have a look. Darger and Loshak were among the first wave, gearing up in booties, nitrile gloves, and PPE suits. They moved through the vast living space, footsteps echoing off all the gleaming surfaces. It felt eerie, Darger thought, to walk in the room she'd just watched on the security van monitor — bigger and brighter than she could have imagined with all the glass up here.

Streams of bunny-suited crime scene techs flowed through the lux space after that. The crowd seemed only to grow, as though a clown car had pulled up outside the building and techs just kept pouring out of it, eventually spilling into the mob upstairs. Bumping. Jostling. They looked like lemmings following each other around.

Camera flashes strobed over everything, the flickers of bright white coming in an unsteady rhythm.

Darger struggled to make her way through the kitchen, where the congregation seemed to be clustered tightest. She turned sideways. Tried to make herself as skinny as possible. Squeezed through the bodies clogging the doorway.

"Same building as Beyoncé," one of the bunny suits said to a small group. The ensuing *oohs* and *ahs* seemed to suggest that they were all deeply impressed by this fact.

Darger shook her head and kept moving. It was already the third time she'd heard the B-word.

The last of the euphoria still bubbled in her head like champagne, but the knowledge that Huxley's game wasn't yet finished was coming back stronger and stronger. Replacing the joy was the blend of gritty determination and anxiety she was more accustomed to.

The next clue was here somewhere, tucked within the walls of this unfortunately massive apartment. 5,500 square feet. Even with a crew this size, they could search all day and still come up empty, especially if Huxley was as sneaky about hiding this clue as he had been with the others.

But she would find it. She had to.

What they needed to do — what *she* needed to do — was figure out what hints he'd left them.

She thought back on the journal as she walked through the space. Studied Dirk Nielsen's possessions in hopes that some puzzle piece would fall into place the way it had when she'd been in Amelia Driscoll's bedroom and spotted the framed magazine ad.

Huxley's words echoed in her head.

*This is what people are really like. This is what they really do to each other.*

*Cruel beings stomping around. Disturbed. Insane. Always hungry for more destruction. Always on the hunt.*

*Mindless violent raping world.*

The ultra-modern dining space surrounded her now. She walked through it slowly. Scanned the details in the hope that it would trigger something.

A vaguely industrial-looking chandelier hung down from chains in the center of the space — all metal and sharp corners. The dining table and chairs looked like the expensive version of something from Ikea. Minimalist. Clean lines.

She brushed her fingers over the smooth surface of the tabletop. It felt cold. But it brought nothing to mind. Nothing here did.

Her eyes danced over another glass wall leading out to the lap pool running fifty feet along this side of the building. She moved through the doorway to walk along its edge. The water sloshed against the glass infinity wall, the wet noises seeming to dull the drone of the buzzing techs inside in a way that helped Darger focus.

*Fame is a religion.*

*Celebrity bodies turned divine by all the worship, all of the faith directed their way.*

*So I offer up a communion.*

*This is the celebrity body. Broken for you.*

*This is the precious blood. Spilled for you.*

When she reached the end of the pool, she paused to briefly admire the view of Central Park. A sprawling green rectangle dotted with trees and crisscrossed with bike paths. This was probably one of the best views in the whole city. She wondered how often Nielsen was even here to admire it with his multiple homes and "bi-coastal lifestyle," as one blog had called it.

They still hadn't even gotten in touch with Nielsen, though they'd at least confirmed that he wasn't in the apartment. At some point, he would find out about all of this, Darger supposed, though she didn't have time to worry about it now.

She headed back inside, passing a fitness room with a power rack and elliptical machine set at odd angles. Mirrors mounted on the opposite wall made doubles of the equipment and gave the illusion of stretching the room out. She caught a glimpse of herself there, hovering near the free weights. Her eyes looked tired. Red and hazy. Purpling bags puckered the flesh beneath them.

Yikes. She'd been up for over twenty-four hours now, and it

showed.

She ran into Loshak in the home theater. He was standing on one of the reclining seats, shining a flashlight into the projector mounted on the ceiling.

"Did you find something?" she asked.

"No. Just grasping at straws. Thought maybe since the clue at Driscoll's house was hidden in the Blu-ray player, maybe it was something similar here." He clambered down from the chair. "But I don't think he'll make it that easy on us."

"Me neither," Darger said and let out a sigh that turned into a yawn.

"Did you see the security footage of the floral delivery?" Loshak asked.

"No."

"Not much to see, really." Loshak shrugged. "Gal brings the arrangement in, leaves it at the front desk. She and the clerk who took the order are being interviewed now, but apparently this company specializes in doing more elaborate custom deliveries. One of their specialties is hiding an engagement ring in the arrangement. So it sounds like they wouldn't have found it all that extraordinary to allow a mystery package to be concealed inside a delivery."

Another dead end, Darger thought, though she didn't say it out loud. The fact that they were stuck playing out the world's worst scavenger hunt designed by a psychopath was starting to wear on her. But it didn't help anyone to voice her negativity out loud, so she kept quiet.

"Did you hear about the robo system?" Loshak asked.

She blinked. Stared into Loshak's face. It took a second for what he'd said to really register.

"Robo-what now? Robocop?"

Loshak snorted before he replied.

"The building has a robotic parking system for the residents' cars. Totally automated. It parks your car for you and can retrieve it in less than ninety seconds. Pretty slick."

"Huh. And here I am still parking my Prius with the cracked windshield manually. I could use a robot to clean it out, actually. Got like fourteen dirty coffee mugs in there right now, rolling around under the seat whenever I take a sharp turn." Darger rubbed her forehead. "Sounds like a slamming toilet seat when all that ceramic crap clangs together."

Loshak pursed his lips.

"Well… I wouldn't mention any of that on your application if you try to get a place here. Believe me, these people don't want their fancy robo system anywhere near your toilet car, Darger."

They went down the hall to a game room where a pair of pinball machines flickered orange light against one wall. A pool table and a row of arcade cabinets sat opposite them. The ping pong table seemed to take center stage — and a whiteboard nearby seemed to show a tournament bracket of some kind.

"You hear any of the talk about Beyoncé?" Loshak said, lowering his voice though no one was around.

Darger rolled her eyes.

"Oh, it's all I hear it seems. The bunny-suits are all atwitter to know that she might be somewhere nearby. She lives here, huh?"

Loshak's lips curved into a sly smile.

"Nope. Whole thing was a rumor started by a real estate agent trying to push some of the units. One of those enterprising types, you know? To stir up interest in the building, he started spreading the idea that Beyoncé was looking at the penthouse, about to snatch it up. The rumor sort of grew legs and took off from there. She never even had a viewing here. Probably never even driven past the place. Even so, there are people who swear up and down they've seen her in the lobby getting a complimentary latte from the machine down there."

Darger sniffed out a faint laugh.

"That's hilarious." Then she turned serious. "Do you think we could get a couple of those? Complimentary lattes, I mean. I could use the caffeine."

"Good idea," Loshak said. "I'll see what I can do."

# CHAPTER 36

Twenty minutes later they were still walking circles around Dirk Nielsen's penthouse, though now they were sipping their complimentary lobby lattes as they hunted for the next clue. The drink was too sweet, but Darger could feel the much-needed caffeine spread through her system — a strange jolt of electrical juice entering her bloodstream. Her eyes felt more alert. Back and neck just a little easier to keep upright. And that cloudiness that had begun to afflict her thoughts seemed to clear. The coffee didn't kill off the tiredness entirely, but it beat it back a good bit.

They walked past the exercise room again, glancing in at the mirrors and machines. She lifted one corner of a painting in the hallway next to the doorway and checked the back. Nothing.

Loshak sighed, frustration venting through his lips and nostrils.

"We can't keep searching randomly and hoping to come across it," he said. "This place is too big and crammed with too much crap. We're burning time."

"I know," Darger said. "I just can't figure anything from the last note that applies to Nielsen or this apartment."

"Let's have another look at everything he's left us. Maybe with a fresh jolt of caffeine running through our veins we can figure it out."

Darger followed Loshak to the living room where they plopped onto a white suede sofa.

There was a low rumbling sound, and Loshak put a hand to his belly.

"Wish I had a breakfast sammy to go with this," he said. "All this coffee is starting to piss my stomach off."

"Well, it's no breakfast sammy, but maybe this will help." Darger reached into her pocket and passed Loshak a small parcel wrapped in a paper napkin. "I saved it for you."

He unfolded the napkin and let out a tiny gasp.

"A badge cookie!"

His eyes glittered like a kid on Christmas morning spying all the presents under the tree. Darger started laughing.

"You've had this in your pocket this whole time?"

Darger shrugged.

"I figured there might come a moment when we needed a little morale boost."

Loshak looked at the cookie for a moment. Then he broke it in two and held out half toward her.

Darger slowly reached out and clutched the thin layer of baked good with the tips of her fingers.

"Fine. If you're going to twist my arm."

She took a bite of cookie. She hadn't thought much of them before, but after being awake for so long with so little food, it hit the spot.

"OK," Loshak said. "So the clue in Driscoll's house was found inside a Blu-ray player. And the hint that led you there was something about 'rewinding' and 'keeping those DVRs rolling.' So maybe we can cheat a little. Figure out if anything in the most recent note would apply to something in this apartment."

Darger nodded. Now that she had some sugar flowing through her veins, a fresh thought came to her.

"We know how he got the flowers delivered, but how did Huxley get up here to hide the next clue? The front door is guarded. Then there's the front desk to deal with. And that's just for the standard apartments. To get up here to the penthouse, you need a special keycard to access the private elevator. And while he might have bypassed any security measures by climbing Amelia Driscoll's fire escape, there's no way he climbed all the way up here."

She gestured to the view, which from this angle was a slice of pale blue sky and nothing else.

"Even the person delivering the floral arrangement with the bomb hidden inside only got as far as the front desk," Loshak said, nodding.

Then he stopped. He and Darger made eye contact.

"The floral arrangement."

They hurried into the kitchen. The space was still swarming with techs. Darger and Loshak went straight to the dismantled arrangement, which still lay on the counter where Agent Dobbins had put it. The bomb package itself had been removed from the premises and completely disassembled, so the clue had to be here, in the mass of flowers somewhere.

Loshak lifted the galvanized bucket, spinning it around to study it from every angle. Darger picked through the roses and ferns and clumps of moss scattered over the counter. She had been hoping to find one of those little cards stuck in the arrangement that said who the bouquet was from. The perfect place to tuck a clue. But it was just flowers.

She sighed, her mind buzzing with frustration. If she could just shut her brain off for an hour or two, maybe then she could figure it out. Her gaze wandered the stark kitchen, landing on the high-tech fridge with the giant LCD panel cycling through different screens: a list of fridge contents, a digital post-it note with a reminder to "refill Pepper's heartworm prevention pill," and then a series of photos. Nielsen at a red carpet event clutching an award. Nielsen posing with various actresses. Nielsen on a yacht, a glass of champagne in one hand. Nielsen standing beside a yellow Porsche.

Darger wondered what Tyler Huxley might say about a man who had photos of himself on the screen of his fridge. And then she slowly turned to Loshak as the realization hit her.

"What if the clue isn't up here at all?" she said. "What if it's hidden somewhere else?"

"Where?"

Darger walked over to the fridge and pressed the arrow to advance the screen to the photo of Nielsen and his Porsche. Snippets from the clue pounded in her head.

*Down the tracks.*

*Race to the rescue.*

*Are you yellow?*

"In Nielsen's car."

# CHAPTER 37

The private elevator made a swishing sound as it whisked them down to the first floor. Darger's fingers played with the bunched sleeve of her bunny suit, unable to keep still.

"We need access to Nielsen's car immediately," Fredrick was saying into her phone. "I don't need the owner's permission, I have a warrant!"

The building manager — a defensive-tackle-sized man with thinning salt-and-pepper hair and a suit that was somehow several sizes too big even for his oversized frame — met them in the lobby. He led them down a hallway and through a set of doors. They came out in the space age parking garage. A series of touch screens mounted on the wall allowed residents to tell the robo-parking system to deliver their car to one of the nearby bays.

"Under normal circumstances, only the vehicle owner has access to their vehicle, but we do have the power to override the system in the event of… well, when necessary," the manager explained.

Darger stared at the back of his head where a roll of fat seemed to occupy the place between his skull and baggy collar. Internally, she wished for less talking and more overriding, her teeth gritting a little to help her hold the feeling in.

Fingers as thick as cigars typed in an administrative password, found the entry for Nielsen's car, and told the system to retrieve it.

The screen showed the entire retrieval process on camera. A panel lit with blue LEDs under the car suddenly began to slide across the floor.

By now, Fitch, Alvarez, and their bomb-sniffing dog had joined the group.

"Oh, this is far out, man! I heard someone talking about this," Fitch said as they watched the car being lowered to the ground floor.

When the car was deposited in one of the marked bays before them a few moments later, Fitch balled his hands into fists that quivered with excitement.

"Far fucking out! Modern technology, man. Love it."

Fitch and Alvarez led the dog around the car, allowing it to thoroughly sniff and snuffle, checking for even a trace scent of explosives. The car had come delivered with the keys already inside. They opened the doors, and the dog continued its sniff search inside.

Finally Fitch stepped back.

"You're good to go," he told them.

The agents lurched for the car.

Under seats, tucked between cushions, nestled in the air-conditioning vents. Darger checked all of these places and more but found nothing.

While Loshak continued combing the interior of the vehicle, she and Fredrick checked the trunk, hood, and under the gas cap hatch.

More nothing.

"You know, even as crafty as he was, I don't think Huxley'd be able to get access to the interior. I doubt Nielsen is ever leaving this thing on the street unlocked," Darger said. "I think it has to be somewhere accessible from outside."

She and Fredrick shone their lights under the car, checking wheel wells and attempting to study the undercarriage, but it was difficult to see much without crawling underneath.

"Screw it," Darger said, flopping to the ground.

Loshak pursed his lips, looking amused.

"The techs have mats for that, you know. So you don't have to slide around in the dirt."

"I don't care if the bunny suit gets dirty," Darger said through clenched teeth. She wriggled deeper under the vehicle. "I'll have to find something else to wear to the prom, but…"

She angled her light into the various nooks and crannies. Around exhaust pipes and fuel lines and electrical wires. There were a hundred places the clue might be hidden, but she'd take this job over searching the entire penthouse any day.

"Hey, Fitch," she called. "Can I borrow one of those handy mirrors you guys carry around?"

"Sure thing." There was a scuffle of feet and then an arm appeared holding out a tactical mirror on a telescoping pole.

Darger scooted over to one of the rear wheel wells and used the mirror to study it from various angles. She caught a glimpse of something white and paused.

"I think I see something."

She reached for it but couldn't get her arm in far enough from this side, so she scrambled out from under the car. Squatting next to the wheel, she jammed her arm in up to the elbow, hand flopping around in the tight space, feeling around for it.

Her fingertips brushed against something flimsy. Another plastic baggie.

It seemed to be held in place with a strong magnet. A good yank pulled the baggie free and sent the magnet skittering over the ground.

"I've got it," she said.

Darger tried to push away from the vehicle but found her elbow was wedged against the inside of the wheel well.

"You need some help?" Loshak asked.

"Just a little stuck," she said, scrunching her shoulders until she gained enough room to maneuver her arm out from the inner workings of the car.

She held the small baggie with what she expected would be Huxley's next note aloft for everyone else to see.

"Righteous. Alright, Agent Darger!" Fitch said, clapping her on the back.

She wanted to let out a whoop of triumph but settled for a satisfied grin that made the exhausted muscles in her cheeks sting a little.

Still, they'd done it again. Huxley was going down.

# CHAPTER 38

A couple of deep breaths was all the time it took to wipe the smile off Darger's face. The jubilation of finding the clue tucked in the undercarriage of Dirk Nielsen's Porsche wore away quickly once she remembered that they still had to solve whatever riddle Huxley had constructed for them this time.

The note was scrawled in red ink. Spiky lettering on lined paper torn from a spiral notebook, all frayed on the left edge.

*Dear Boss,*

*How are you faring with my funny little games? Has anyone lost their head?*

*In a perfect world, this note would be written in the blood of my victims. Drain the phonies, yes. Use their strawberry red smears to rewrite the ways of this world.*

*Red ink is fit enough I hope. Ha-ha.*

*Imagine... these vapid TV personalities interrupt their self-worship long enough to see what further gifts the world must be trying to give them. They open a box and BOOM. Instant karma!*

*From Hell,*

*-Tyler Huxley*

Darger's eyes flitted down the page, still wrapped in the plastic baggie. The others huddled close to her, everyone reading. Her head bobbed as she started at the top again. As soon as she got through the letter a second time, she Googled the first line on her phone.

"'A letter beginning with "Dear Boss" was allegedly written

by the unidentified Victorian-era serial killer Jack the Ripper,'" she said, reading aloud. "Looks like that line about the red ink is a quote from one of The Ripper's other letters. And he began one of them 'From Hell' which Huxley has used to sign his notes numerous times now."

Jack the Ripper. The first truly famous serial killer, he terrorized London in 1888. Though some scholars believe he was more prolific, he killed at least five prostitutes, slashing their throats and then mutilating their torsos and genitals. He cut out one victim's vagina and took it with him. Like the Zodiac Killer, he was never caught.

"He was in London, right?" Fredrick asked.

"As far as I know," Darger said. "Hold on..."

Darger searched "Jack the Ripper NYC" and found a slew of articles on the subject.

"'Did Jack the Ripper move from London to New York City in search of fresh hunting grounds?'" Darger read. "'This is the question many were asking in 1891, after the gruesome murder of a Bowery prostitute named Carrie Brown. In a manner bearing a startling resemblance to the previous victims of The Ripper, Ms. Brown was found strangled and disemboweled in the East River Hotel.'"

"I don't imagine the East River Hotel still exists?" Loshak said.

"I doubt it," Fredrick said.

Darger's fingers were already tapping over the keyboard.

"But maybe we can find where it was," Darger said.

Her eyes zigged and zagged over the screen, searching for any mention of the building's former location.

"Found it. The corner of Catherine Street and Water Street in lower Manhattan."

"Let's fucking go," Fitch said.

# CHAPTER 39

While Fredrick stayed at the penthouse to oversee the scene there, Darger and Loshak were tasked with heading to the former site of the East River Hotel with Fitch and the rest of the CIRG team.

Darger ran inside to strip off her soiled bunny suit and wash the grease and grime from her hands. When she came back outside, Fitch and Loshak were waiting at the curb in the black CIRG SUV.

"Climb aboard," Fitch said, his eyes smiling. "NYPD is going to lead the way, motorcade style."

Darger opened the door and hoisted herself into the backseat. Before she could close the door behind her, Fitch was speeding away from the curb and down the street. Up ahead, their police escort swooped in front of them, sirens on, clearing the early morning traffic from their path.

With a sharp tug, Darger was able to close the door. She fastened her seatbelt. Sniffed the air. The interior of the SUV was filled with the distinct aroma of bacon and fried potatoes.

"What's that smell?"

Loshak tossed something to her from the passenger seat. She caught the strange package with both hands. It was oblong and wrapped in foil. And it was warm.

A breakfast burrito.

Darger peeled away the foil and took a bite. It was quite possibly the best thing she'd ever tasted, and she managed to scarf half of it before she had time to wonder where it had come from.

"Where the hell did you get burritos?"

Fitch held his half-eaten burrito aloft and waved it in the air.

"One of the residents of Bainbridge Tower ordered like 200 of them from the place down the street. Wanted to thank us for quote, *Putting our lives on the line to save theirs.*" He chuckled. "Rich people are hilarious. So dramatic."

He took another bite and kept talking.

"Anyway, the burritos are why I called dibs on driving the SUV versus riding in the van. McAllister won't let us have food around his precious equipment. He treats that console like he's married to it. Swear to God."

Even though the morning rush hour traffic had waned a bit, they still hit patches of road at a standstill. Darger's leg bounced up and down as she did the math. They had about six hours to find the next clue, figure out who the target was, and neutralize whatever device Huxley had left for them this time.

"You know, people think guys like Dobbins and Alvarez are crazy for volunteering to go in and disarm these things," Fitch said. "Even with the gear and the training, it's dangerous as hell. They all know that. But I think you gotta be a thousand times crazier to tinker with this stuff by choice the way a guy like Huxley does. I mean, you couldn't pay me to mess around with explosives for funsies. I won't even light off fireworks on the Fourth. Every year people blow their hands off or end up killing themselves by getting drunk and tipping the mortar over. All for a two-second boom and a little flickery light? Ain't worth the risk, homes. I guess what I'm saying is, I don't know where guys like Huxley get the 'nads. Like, at least the guys on the bomb squad can tell themselves they're doing it to save lives."

"Serving the greater good," Loshak said.

Fitch shoved the remainder of his burrito — a portion

roughly the size of Darger's fist — into his mouth.

"Exactly," he said, the food muffling the word. "That's the only thing that makes it worth it."

"Well, it's like we said during the meeting… most bombers have that same conviction. Albeit in a more twisted sense."

Fitch scoffed and several morsels of rice flew out of his mouth.

"Twisted is fuckin' right. I just don't get how this guy can blow up some random dude from a coffee commercial or douse some actress lady with acid and think that's somehow *good*."

Loshak crossed his arms.

"He's created a narrative that says fame and celebrity and all of these things we worship are ruining society. That's common among bombers, this notion that society is somehow on the wrong track, and they're here to more or less force us onto the right one."

"And they actually believe this?"

"I think a part of them does. But again, a large part of it is a story they're telling themselves to cover their true feelings of inferiority. Everyone does this, to some degree, but in less harmful ways. You might tell yourself that the reason Bob got the promotion and you didn't is because Bob's an ass kisser and your boss plays favorites. But underneath that, there's a part of you that wonders, 'Is Bob better than me, and that's why I didn't get the promotion?' We tell ourselves a little story to get past this small sense of rejection and failure. I think these guys have to create a really huge, over-the-top narrative to compensate for huge, over-the-top inadequacy."

Fitch chewed and nodded.

"K, but lemme ask you this… why go to all this trouble to create this big over-the-top scheme and then kill yourself?"

"There's a chance he was trying to martyr himself in some way," Darger said. "The bomber archetype loves to romanticize the great sacrifice they've made for their cause. Timothy McVeigh certainly had a bit of a martyrdom complex. He believed his execution would open people's eyes in a similar way the bombing had. That the public would be disgusted at the notion of his so-called 'government-sanctioned murder.'"

Fitch hissed dismissively.

"Please. That psycho can rot in hell for all I care."

Darger leaned back in her seat, trying to loosen a tight spot between her shoulder blades.

"The other explanation is that it was another power play. It's not uncommon for mass shooters to commit suicide to avoid being caught. It's yet another way to assert control. They choose who lives and dies. And they choose the moment and circumstances of their own death. I think in their minds, allowing themselves to be arrested would feel like losing or submitting. Giving up control. By killing themselves before they can be taken into custody, they control the outcome."

"Kinda like the ultimate 'fuck you,'" Fitch said.

"Pretty much."

They sped through Chinatown now, past the colorful awnings and banners written in English and Cantonese that offered jewelry, dim sum, souvenirs, Chinese herbs. Fitch had his window down, and Darger caught a whiff of fried food from one of the restaurants. She immediately imagined a piping hot bag of egg rolls straight out of the fryer, and even though she'd just eaten an entire burrito, her mouth watered.

When they reached the former site of the East River Hotel, everyone got out and took in their surroundings for a moment. Darger wadded the foil wrapper from her burrito and tossed it in a bin next to where they'd parked.

The area was now occupied by a small park with a jungle gym sandwiched between an apartment building and a storage facility. The water's edge was only a block away, the surface of the East River shimmering under the Brooklyn Bridge.

"What do you think?" Fitch asked. "Would he hide it in a park again?"

"That's where I'd start," Loshak said.

It took a few minutes for the NYPD to clear the area of civilians before they could begin their search. They spread out, using sticks to prod into the bushes and clumps of daylilies. Peering under benches and sifting through garbage bins. They spent nearly an hour picking through what felt like every blade of grass in the park, but the search was fruitless. Even the dogs came up empty.

Darger's frustration had her molars grinding again. She could picture the next chunk of the journal — another pack of pages stuffed into a freezer bag.

Was it here somewhere? Were they even close?

"Now what?" Darger said.

Loshak eyed the giant sign on the storage facility.

"What if he rented a unit in there?"

Darger turned to one of the dog handlers.

"Could the dogs detect a scent through a storage unit door?"

"It's possible," the K-9 officer said. "Depends on how strong the scent is. How thick and well-sealed the door is. There are other variables as well, but we can always try."

Loshak's gaze had shifted over Darger's shoulder. He frowned.

"Oh, this is cute," Loshak said. "We've got ourselves an audience."

Darger turned and noticed a small crowd forming near the police barricade. Several of the people had their phones out and appeared to be taking video of the park search. Apparently, the sensationalistic nature of Huxley's crimes was continuing to occupy the public's interest.

One of the people in the crowd noticed her studying them and waved a hand in the air.

"Hey, FBI lady!" A twenty-something kid with hair hanging in his eyes called out. "Are you looking for Jack the Ripper?"

Darger and Loshak glanced at one another.

"Now how the hell did he know that?" Loshak asked.

Darger had an inkling. She pulled out her phone.

"Son of a bitch." She held up her screen. "The newest clue got leaked again."

Loshak crossed his arms.

"Well, I think our theory about it being something Huxley set up is probably right. It's too consistent. Just a few minutes after we get the clue, it gets posted online. Like clockwork."

"But how?"

Loshak shook his head.

"Could just be on a timer. You know I'm useless at this computer stuff, but maybe there's a way he could have set it up to trigger like using a Google Alert. Anyway, leaking the clues and journals would ensure a certain level of public attention. That was clearly his goal with all of this."

Darger shook her head, a certain part of her almost impressed at the amount of detail Huxley had put into his plan.

"There are already hundreds of comments on the newest post." She scrolled through the comments, skimming mostly, then paused on one and chuckled.

"What?"

"Oh, people are posting their own theories about the clue. Some of them are just dumb. Listen to this one. 'Guys, what if Tyler Huxley is related to the Zodiac Killer? He used a Zodiac-inspired cipher in one of his letters. It's almost like he's trying to tell us something. Has anyone looked into his father's life? Could he have been in the Bay area from 1968-1969?'"

Loshak snorted.

"Here's someone pointing out the Jack the Ripper references. '*Dear Boss* and *funny little games* are references to the Jack the Ripper letters. I believe this clue is referring to the old East River Hotel, where a prostitute was murdered and many people now believe Jack the Ripper might have been the culprit.'" She thumbed further down the page. "And here's the resident nutjob saying that this whole thing is a false flag operation created by the FBI to improve their failing public image. Then someone else makes a joke about a poop knife."

"What the hell is a poop knife?" Loshak asked.

"Beats me," Darger said, eyes scanning the screen. She stopped and reread the last comment. "OK. Hold on. This one actually makes sense."

Loshak blinked.

"The poop knife?"

"No." She kept reading, realization dawning on her.

When she finished, she looked up at Loshak.

"We're in the wrong place."

# CHAPTER 40

Darger read the post out loud as they hurried back over to Agent Fitch's SUV.

"'Look at these references. The most obvious is *Instant Karma!* Then, *Imagine.* Both John Lennon song titles. Then we have a mention of "phonies," a term used repeatedly in *Catcher in the Rye.* All of these clues point somewhat indirectly to Mark David Chapman, who was carrying a copy of *Catcher in the Rye* when he shot John Lennon. Note, too, that he referred to his victim's blood as *strawberry* red. I think the clue is pointing to Strawberry Fields in Central Park.'"

Darger glanced up from the phone.

"The Jack the Ripper stuff was a decoy," Darger said. "And we fell for it."

"We don't know anything for sure yet. In fact, I think we should keep a group here to continue searching, just in case," Loshak suggested. "For all we know he might have split the next clue over more than one location. I'm going to call Agent Fredrick and have her send a K-9 unit and more backup to help us search Central Park."

"Good idea," Darger said.

They climbed into the SUV with Fitch at the wheel and took off. Blocks of concrete rushed past, but Darger couldn't bear to look out the window. Panicky feelings were roiling up inside her now. Peppering her with negative thoughts one after another: that they'd never be able to find the next bomb in time, that more would die by way of Huxley's contraptions, that this whole chase would never end. She leaned forward, tucked her head between her knees, and made herself take deep breaths.

A hand appeared in front of her face, momentarily distracting her from the borderline hysterical dread.

"You see a case of drinks back there, Agent Darger?" Fitch asked, his fingers patting around the floor near her feet.

Darger shifted her gaze to a box of Monster energy drinks nestled behind the passenger seat.

"Yeah." She snatched up one of the cans. "You want me to hand you one?"

"Please and thank you," Fitch said. "Help yourself to a can, if you'd like."

Darger waved her hand.

"I'm good, thanks."

"What about you, Agent Loshak? Care for a bit of liquid stamina?"

Loshak licked his lips.

"Don't mind if I do."

Darger handed them each a can. Loshak cracked his open and took a huge gulp. The scent hit her a few seconds later.

Her nose wrinkled.

"Smells like gummy worms mixed with cough medicine."

"I like it. It's crisp." Loshak shrugged. "Now I'll tell you what tastes like cough medicine. Red Bull."

Fitch chugged half his can in a single swallow, followed by an exaggerated *ahhh* sound.

"A sweet nectar," he said.

When they arrived at Central Park, the SUV slowed and parked. Darger took a few deep breaths. Nausea still lurched in her middle, but she forced the feelings of doubt from her mind.

Loshak leaned forward, staring out through the windshield. The John Lennon memorial was packed with people, some of whom were behaving oddly. Darger spotted two women on hands and knees, crawling underneath benches. She saw another man wielding a metal detector. A few yards away, a teenager got down on all fours so that his friend could stand on his back and climb a tree.

"What the hell is this?" Loshak asked as they regrouped on the sidewalk. "What are all of these people doing here?"

"I don't know," Fitch said. "I've never seen it this packed."

Darger's mouth dropped open when she realized what was going on.

"They must have seen the same post we did. They're looking for the next clue, same as us."

"Oh great," Loshak said. "That's just what we need. A bunch of dingbats from the internet getting in our way."

While they waited for the NYPD to clear the area, Loshak continued grumbling about the public meddling in their case.

"Can I just say how idiotic this is?" he said. "How do they know Huxley hasn't planted explosives here? We came armed with the CIRG team and bomb-sniffing dogs. These people are out here just asking to have a limb blown off."

"Anything to be part of the story, I guess," Darger said, getting out her phone to see what people were saying online.

The number of comments on the post had now tripled. There were links to YouTube videos. Someone was even livestreaming from the park. Darger clicked to open the livestream. The camera angle showed the exodus from the opposite side of the park. The camera wheeled around to show the man filming. He was in his mid-twenties and wore a baseball hat turned backward.

"As you can see, we are not the only people who came down here today, but now we are being forcibly removed by the fascist

NYPD, as if peaceable citizens don't have a right to convene in this public space," he said into the camera.

Darger glanced at the comments and immediately regretted it.

A user named Alt3r3dB3ast69 wrote: *Nice to see these rich liberal Hollywood cucks get taken down a peg, for once.*

"Yikes," Darger said out loud.

"What now?" Loshak asked.

"Oh, just that there are apparently some people among the public that are on Huxley's side."

Loshak let out a breath.

"Between that and people inserting themselves in the investigation like this, things could get nasty."

Darger stared at the people who had turned up in hopes of finding Huxley's next surprise. A babble of voices came from the crowd being ejected from the park, but one nearby rose above the rest.

"Why are you kicking us out, man?" a kid in a tie-dye shirt asked.

"This area is a potential crime scene," the officer explained.

"Because of the Huxley journal?" The kid scoffed. "Someone already found it, Chief. You're too late."

Darger took a step closer.

"Excuse me. What do you mean someone already found it?"

"The same guy that posted the solution. GinerSpaniel. He said he found the journal already. Came out here before he even posted the Strawberry Fields solution so no one could beat him to it. Everyone basically accused him of being full of shit, so then he posted a video of him with the clue. Scans of the pages and everything."

Darger went to her phone and searched for the original

thread. GinerSpaniel's post was now at the top of the page, with a long thread of comments. She got to the video he'd posted. A pile of pages in a plastic baggie, just like the others.

She pressed play.

"What's up, fucksticks? You wanted proof that I wasn't bluffing about finding the clue? Well here it is. Read 'em and weep, bitches."

He pulled the pages out of the bag and fanned them out on a desk.

"Shit," Darger said, squinting at the screen. "The handwriting looks right."

"You think there's any chance he's in on the whole thing? Like maybe he knew Huxley somehow?" Loshak asked.

"I don't know." Darger shook her head and scrolled through her contact list. "We need to call Fredrick. Figure out who this GinerSpaniel guy is and pay him a visit. At the very least, he's in possession of a piece of critical evidence in a major crime."

# CHAPTER 41

It was relatively easy to track down GinerSpaniel's information. One Patrick Dressel, aged 28, lived in a small brick house in Brooklyn owned and likewise occupied by his mother, Kathleen Manning. Or as Fitch had put it, "Dude lives in his mom's basement." He posted an average of 93.5 times per day on his social media site of choice, ClackSauce, regularly haunting various subforums on the site, their topics ranging from aggressive stock market investments to horror fiction to busty anime characters. Skimming some of the posts, Darger noted his recurring rants about being fired from his job at Arby's some nine months ago.

"Jesus. In a way *that's* his full-time job," Loshak said. "Posting, I mean. I wonder if I'll ever post 93 times on all social media platforms cumulatively. Like, in my entire life."

Barely forty minutes had passed since Dressel had shared the journal video online. Already his house was being surrounded by the SWAT team. Darger and Loshak sat in the high-tech van across the street with Agent Fredrick, watching the live feed from Agent Fitch's bodycam on one of the monitors.

The team huddled on the stoop before the front steps, their chests and shoulders heaving. After a countdown from 5 to 1, the battering ram swung into the door, knocking it aside with the crack of splintering lumber.

The squad of men in tactical gear stormed into the vacant doorway, their Kevlar vests and helmets making them look like a pack of bulky animals. They split into teams as soon as the threshold was breached.

The feed from Fitch's camera went choppy along with his gait. Chaos filled the screen. The moving limbs of the agents swallowed some by the shade inside the house.

Darger could make out what looked like a couch and loveseat. Plaid upholstery in beiges and browns. The one line of radio chatter she could pick up seemed to confirm what she was seeing.

"Living room is clear."

Action seemed to overload the audio and video feeds. Yelling. Waving hands. Assault rifles pointing everywhere.

Fitch thundered down a wooden staircase into the basement along with the others among his team. Feet thudding. Wood creaking. Camera jostling up and down.

The steps led them to an unfinished basement with a desk along one wall — a dim room lit by a single desk lamp and the dull glow of a computer screen. Concrete block walls. Exposed joists from the floor above. The sweaty can of Coke next to the laptop made it look like someone had just been there, but the chair behind the desk sat empty.

Fitch moved deeper into the concrete chamber. A pale slab of cement flooring filled the screen. Then the camera swept left and right. A furnace took shape ahead. Then the rounded white enamel body of the water heater.

Darger spotted movement at the bottom right-hand corner of the bodycam feed. Fitch must have seen it too, because he raised his rifle and shouted.

"FBI! Don't fucking move!"

The camera shook as he surged forward, causing the feed to blur for a moment.

Darger sat forward. Eyes squinted to slits. Trying to see what was happening in the dingy space.

Fitch stopped moving. The image on the screen came clear. Details filling in.

A man.

A man with his face pressed against the wall. He was attempting to jam himself in the small crevice behind the water heater in the back corner of the basement. He wore a pair of gray boxer briefs and a white t-shirt.

"Shit, man," he said, throwing his arms in the air. "Don't shoot me. Please!"

"Patrick Dressel?"

"Yeah, dude. Just please don't shoot me."

Fitch lifted one hand and waved his fingers.

"Alright. I want you to come out of there, nice and slow."

Dressel didn't move.

"I can't. Oh, God. Please don't shoot me!"

Fitch took a step forward.

"Move real slow, do what I say, and you'll be fine. Take one step to your right."

"I told you, I can't." Dressel squirmed. His body scraped audibly against the cinder blocks, torso slithering around, but his bulk didn't budge. "I'm stuck, OK? I'm wedged in here."

Fitch was silent for a second.

"Are you fucking kidding me?" the big CIRG agent said. "Believe me, kid. You're in deep enough shit as it is."

"I'm not. I'm not kidding you. I'm really stuck."

"OK. What *part* of you is stuck?" Fitch asked, and Darger thought she detected a note of amusement in his voice.

"My tummy… er, stomach area."

"Can you try to… you know, suck it in a little?"

"I'll try."

There was a faint grunting sound as Dressel tried to heave himself out of the space, but he didn't appear to make any progress.

"Hubler, cover me," Fitch said to the other agent in the basement.

He set his rifle down and approached Dressel. Fitch grabbed on to the crook of the kid's elbow.

"On the count of three, I want you to blow all the air out of your lungs, suck in that pot belly, and lean hard this way. OK?"

"OK."

Fitch counted to three. There was a faint rustle and then a scrape. With one final groan, Dressel popped free from behind the water heater. He stumbled out into the open, and the SWAT team cinched around him with their rifles, only easing back when his hands went up again.

"Holy shit, man. I thought I was trapped back there. Started to panic a little bit." Dressel brushed dust from the front of his t-shirt. "Fuck."

"Mr. Dressel, do you have any weapons in the house?"

"Yeah right. My mom won't let me have so much as a BB gun." Dressel scratched his head. "Is this about the stuff I found in the park? Because I swear I was gonna call the police about it as soon as I finished reading it. Jesus, if I'd known you guys was gonna bust in here like that, I wouldn't have touched the thing."

"What about explosives?" Fitch asked.

"Explosives?"

"Do you have any explosives in the house?"

Dressel looked bewildered.

"Hell no. What do you think I am? Some kind of psycho?"

"I'm going to need you to come answer a few questions," Fitch said. "Why don't you put on some pants."

"Look, I said I was sorry. Or maybe I didn't say it, but I am. Sorry, I mean."

"Pants," Fitch repeated. "Unless you want to chat with the FBI in your drawers."

A few minutes later, Dressel was led out of the house by Fitch and over to the SUV where Darger, Loshak, and Fredrick were now waiting.

Fitch opened the back door and ushered Dressel inside.

"Mr. Dressel," Loshak said. "We'd like to ask you some questions."

Dressel let out an audible gulp, his Adam's apple bobbing up and down.

"Um… OK."

"How old are you?"

Dressel fidgeted, flexing and unflexing his knuckles in a mincing way. His words came out slowly now.

"Twenty-eight."

"And what can you tell us about Tyler Huxley?"

He blinked. Eyes swiveling around, not looking at anything for long.

"Well, I can't really tell you anything other than that the guy seems like a real nutcase. I mean, you gotta be to go around blowing people up, right?"

Loshak leaned forward.

"And how is it that you know Tyler Huxley?"

"The same as everyone else. He's all over the news."

"You've never met him?"

"Met him?" Dressel's voice was shaking now. "No way."

"What about online?" Loshak asked. "Maybe you talked to him in one of your, uh, chatroom things?"

"No. I mean, not that I know of. What is this? I only found

the clue, like I said, and I was gonna call you, I swear." His eyes began to tear up. "Man, I didn't mean to cause any trouble. I just thought it would be baller as hell to find it, that's all."

"Baller?" Loshak repeated.

Dressel swallowed and wiped his eyes.

"Yeah, I mean… I figure I cracked the clue faster than like, the whole FBI and NSA and NYPD and whoever else is working on this thing, right? That's like… a totally baller move. There's gonna be clout involved in somethin' like that."

Darger crossed her arms, wanting to argue that most of the task force were running on little to no sleep and had been since yesterday morning. But it was pointless.

"It didn't occur to you that it might be dangerous to do what you did?" she asked.

"What do you mean?"

Something between a laugh and a scoff erupted from the back of Loshak's throat.

"Son, the man leaving these clues has blown up one person, grievously injured another, and attempted to kill a third. We have the bomb-sniffing dogs with us at every location, checking and double-checking to make sure there are no additional explosive devices."

Dressel chewed his lip.

"OK. That's fair. But it *wasn't* a trap or whatever, so… No harm, no foul, right?"

"And maybe you knew it wasn't a trap because Huxley told you so," Loshak said. "Maybe that's how you solved the clue so fast. You already knew exactly where it was."

Dressel's chin quivered.

"What? No way. I already told you, I didn't know that dude."

"Why don't you walk us through solving the clue," Darger said.

Dressel shrugged.

"It wasn't that hard. It was the thing about phonies that struck me first. I thought about how it was a funny thing to say. Like, I hadn't heard anyone use that word since I read *Catcher in the Rye* in tenth grade. And then I recognized the song titles, I guess, and the pieces all snapped into place." Beads of sweat had sprung up along Dressel's temples and upper lip. "So like… am I being detained or whatever? Because I was kinda planning on going back to bed. Been a long night."

"Back to bed?" Loshak raised an eyebrow. "You work the night shift or something?"

"Uh, well, I'm currently unemployed, actually."

Darger and Loshak exchanged a glance. As far as she was concerned, Dressel seemed to be exactly what he said he was. An unemployed man-child living in his mother's basement with a bit too much time on his hands. She could tell from Loshak's expression that he thought the same.

"You're free to go," Loshak said. "But a word of advice? Next time you have the urge to insert yourself into an active crime investigation: don't."

Dressel chuckled nervously.

"Right. Yeah. That's good advice. Uh. Thank you, officers. Err… agents? Whatever. Uh. Thanks."

Dressel hopped out of the SUV and scurried back into his house.

"Not the sharpest tool in the shed, is he?" Fredrick said.

"No. Which makes it all the more irritating that he solved the clue before we did," Loshak said. "That's just embarrassing."

"We're all exhausted," Darger said. "He had the advantage."

Fredrick's phone chimed.

"That's the handwriting analyst from the FBI lab. He says this sample is consistent with the others. It's legit."

Darger hadn't really had any doubts. Dressel might have had the pop culture chops to crack the clue and the balls to go dig it up, but the kid had been genuinely scared shitless in the interview. She thought he'd suddenly realized how far in over his head he'd gotten himself. There was no way he had the brass or the smarts to fake one of Huxley's journal entries.

Fredrick held the newly bagged evidence in the air.

"I say we head back to headquarters, dig into this latest packet he left us, and try to figure out the next target," Fredrick said. "Speculation is that this could be the last one, if Huxley meant what he said about it lasting for 24 hours. God, it'd feel good to have all this over with."

Darger nodded, trying to match Fredrick's optimism. But internally she was wondering how they would manage to do it again when they were all running on fumes.

# CHAPTER 42

I can't sleep at night lately. Too keyed up.

Electricity spins inside my skull. Like the filament of a light bulb burns in there. A white-hot wire that won't turn off. Won't burn out. Just sizzles away, slowly cooking the gray matter in my head like one of those hot dogs spinning on a gas station rotisserie — that collection of questionable sausages all plump and sweaty.

I toss and turn in bed. Twist the sheets around myself.

Doubts come and go. Negative thoughts come to me in the night like ghosts. Haunting. I try to shut them out, but they keep talking. Keep calling me.

Sometimes I think I should give all this up. These big plans. These explosive devices.

Just leave it. Move on. Live whatever passes for a normal life. But I know I can't.

The mission is too important.

Some of us have no choice. Something outside of us has chosen us, set us on our paths. So we endure the restless feelings, endure the crushing loneliness, the sleepless nights.

We sacrifice it all to make our mark. Spend ourselves in service of something bigger.

So here I am. Here I am. Open my veins. Pluck out my eyes and tongue and heart.

Take everything. I'm ready now.

Ready to go.

I get up sometimes in the middle of the night. Go up onto the roof of this ramshackle building. Look down on the city at night.

The wind is so cold once it hits about 3 A.M. Ghostly and dank. It goes right through your clothes. Goes right through you.

And all those lights in the city burn in the distance. They burn all night long. Just like the one in my head.

Glimmering spots dotting the purple. Flickering just a little, which you can see if you watch long enough. If you never blink.

The city makes more sense at night, I think. More than that. The city itself is *of* the night. Maybe I am, too.

We come alive in the dark. When no one's looking.

And it never really sleeps, the city. There are people milling about the streets and alleyways. Headlights swinging around corners, plunging into the dark. Even in the wee hours, the city throbs with life, teems with restlessness. Agitation. Disturbance.

All the freaks come out in the dark. The scum like me. The night sets us free, sets us loose.

We snuffle around. Watching the prey. Waiting for one of you to venture too far out into the shadows.

Waiting to pounce.

☾

There was a murder on the sidewalk outside my building. Dead guy just lying there. Face down on the concrete. Bulky torso pinning down both his arms to kind of arch his back funny. Made me think of a beached whale somehow.

The blood spread over the sidewalk. Ran down into the cracks like little troughs, almost like those tiny paper cups they used to put ketchup in at Wendy's. Except it slowly went darker as the sun got to it. Thicker and gummier. Almost black.

Someone put a jacket over the dead guy's face after a while. Some dated-looking windbreaker blocking out his features. Like that makes it not so bad.

They say it was a gang thing. The people out there talking, I mean. The lookie loos. I could hear their voices carrying on. Gossip peppering the wind like spores. Floating up to my window. Spreading like a fungus.

He was out there for a good five or six hours after dawn broke. Slowly cooking in the sunlight. I guess they were waiting on the medical examiner. Busy morning. Who knows how many bodies, you know?

There are some 20 or so murders per year here in Jersey City. Not bad for a town so small, desperate mobs of humanity all stacked on top of each other in shitty apartment complexes and disintegrating houses. Hell, I don't think all the residents could go out in the street at the same time if we wanted to. Too many people.

After the M.E. finally got to the scene, they bagged up the body and carted it away. The cops stood out there a long time. Talking. Milling around. Picking at their mustaches and whatever the fuck.

And then a couple of hours later they finally left, and the bloodstain was still there.

A dark puddle. Looked like someone spilled a whole bottle of cherry syrup and then the sun scorched it there. Blackened it. Adhered it to the concrete.

Anyway, I guess nobody comes and cleans that up. Like that's not someone's job, you know? I never thought about that before.

It's still there. The blood just crusts to the sidewalk. A man's life spilled onto concrete. And the world just carries on. Walks right over what's left of him.

You want to see peak humanity? Well, there it is. Just look at the bloodstains on the sidewalk.

☾

I sit at the diner down on the corner and listen to the idiots blather their heads off. It's one of those dumps with peeling paint and sun-bleached Formica everywhere. Holes worn in the upholstery seats of damn near every booth. Coffee strong enough to strip the varnish off furniture.

I hunker down in my booth. Scrawling in my notebook. Watching the people. Among the people, surrounded by them, but not really of them.

Separate.

So it's an older crowd, mostly. Retirees eating sunny-side-up eggs and toasted Wonder Bread slicked with pools of melted butter. Guzzling down gallons of sludgy coffee. They eat in slow motion. Too busy flapping their lips with a new list of complaints that sounds an awful lot like the old list of complaints.

It's uncanny how similar their observations are. Everything they say. Everything they think. It's like they are all the same shitty person. A many-headed hydra recounting the status of their 401k.

I find a recurring hilarity at the core of their shared philosophy. There are three tenets as far as I can tell:

1. I, the elder, should be able to do whatever I want. Anyone who obstructs my slightest whim is a morally abhorrent monster. Anything that prevents me from fulfilling my every minuscule desire "isn't fair."

2. Other people, on the other hand, can't just do whatever they want. Especially the younger generation. There are rules. Obligations. I would be remiss in my role as a boomer fucktard if I didn't try to guilt and shame anyone who doesn't conform absolutely, who dares to not serve me.

3. Other people, in fact, should generally be ashamed of themselves. Whatever they're doing, how dare they?

They are all convinced — utterly, wholly, absolutely — that the world, the universe, exists to serve them. It all belongs to them and only them. They cast themselves as the masters in their imaginations, see the rest of the earth's population as their unwitting slaves.

This is the idea that must be smashed, crushed, wiped off the face of the planet. And I will accomplish it by wiping away faces indeed, blowing them to little pieces.

Obliterated. Vaporized.

I stare down at the grimy tabletop in my booth as I listen to them prattle on. I don't dare make eye contact with the enemy, lest they try to engage me. You look at any of these windbags for even a fraction of a second, and you may as well be wearing a sign that invites them to launch into a humblebrag rant about their grandkid's academic achievements or some nonsense. Inane. Vacuous.

Not going to fucking happen to me. Believe me. I may be homicidal, but I'm not insane.

As it happens, I have a philosophy of my own. Just one tenet this time.

1. Don't talk to me.

But I bring all of that up to say this:

It's hilarious that grown adults act like life isn't fair. They even say it out loud for Christ's sake.

*It's not fair! It's not fair!*

All the old men growing red-faced and flustered at the Best Buy help desk, all the Karens filing their furious customer service complaints daily. Guess what? No one gives a fuck about you. You don't matter. There are a fucking million of you, or ten million of you, or billions of you.

The universe is indifferent. Cold and uncaring. Just empty fucking space stretching out forever. Black seas of infinity.

It. Does. Not. Care.

And you? You are nothing. No one. A bacterium.

Trust me. When you die, the world will go on, the universe will persist. It won't even blink.

# CHAPTER 43

Revenge becomes the only joy, the only hope.

When you really look at what we've made of this world, how can you not want to fuck it up? How can you not want to watch it crumble? How can you not gorge on violence, surrender to the appetite for destruction that must well in all of our guts?

Look beneath the surface. Underneath the glossy veneer of that celebrity dream that soothes you with false hopes.

They've got you convinced that if you follow orders, you can have a piece of that dream. Like if you work and slave and spend yourself, put something in, you'll get something in return. An implied transaction. Sleight of hand to make you docile, to keep you from seeing that your life is happening right here and now, ending one second at a time, and you're fucking wasting it in service of a diseased culture — a machine that mass produces suffering.

There is no peace here. There is no comfort in the crowd. There is no reward for obedience.

We're just restless animals. A hateful mob. Hungry. Disturbed.

Don't fight it. Embrace it.

☾

I spend my days hunched over shoeboxes. Tinkering with little mechanical contraptions inside them. Motion-activated triggers. Detonators.

No sleep now. Just stinging eyes poring over opened

textbooks, then back to the shoebox. Too excited to sleep ever again, I think.

Need to perfect my craft now. Develop my talent for improvised explosive devices.

Unleash the fury.

Big bang.

Peel faces off skulls. Cave in ribcages. Take heads clean off.

All by way of special delivery.

It will be perfect. Hideous. Profane.

And I will make it with my own hands. Will it into being. Set it loose upon the earth.

My spirit unleashed. Transmitted.

Detonated. Exploding.

I feel like a psychopathic MacGyver. It's such a blast.

☾

If there is a God, I must be God's lonely man. Some forgotten boy. I slipped down through the cracks in the sidewalk, the wounded places in the cityscape. Got washed down into the scum of the gutter. Sucked down some grate in the concrete with the piss and blood and rainwater.

Drain you.

In this life, I've witnessed rape and murder up close. Heard the whimpers. Watched tears leak down shiny cheeks, swollen and red.

Saw the forearm flex. The trigger squeezed. Watched the muzzle flash. Death dealt through the barrel of a gun.

I've been kicked in the ribs. Punched in the mouth. Beaten bloody. Spit on. Abandoned.

I'm nobody. Nothing. An ugly piece of trash.

But the scum always rises to the top, doesn't it? Eventually. Eventually. A film of bubbles emerges. A froth that drifts to the surface. It floats above all the rest.

☾

Waiting for a sign. Anything to tell me… to tell me… what? That I should do it now. Or that I shouldn't.

Sometimes I think I could forget all of this. Ditch the mission. Live a normal life somehow. Some way.

Find a place in the world. Find someone to kill the rest of my time with.

A simple life.

Maybe someone could find me. Pull me out of this mindset. Help me see a better way.

But I can't see it. When I try to picture it… I see the black of the sky again, the gaping dark between the stars.

Black nothing. Black dream.

Waiting for relief, maybe. A releasing of the tension. A ceasing of the restless pounding in my chest, in my skull — the thoughts that circle around and around in my mind like a hamster on a wheel. An end to that throb of energy that animates me, the electrical impulses traveling up and down my limbs.

Relief. Maybe that's all there is to wait for in a way.

# CHAPTER 44

A coldness had come over Darger again as she read. Icy prickles in her fingers and toes.

The previous entry was the first time she sensed true vulnerability in Tyler Huxley's words. Loneliness and desperation.

*Waiting for a sign. Anything to tell me… to tell me… what? That I should do it now. Or that I shouldn't.*

She sighed, wondering how different things might have turned out if he'd gotten that sign from the universe that told him to abandon his plan.

There was one page left. Darger turned to it.

*The circle closes. And so the story ends. We go through the motions now once more with feeling.*

*The human experiment is a failure. We tried and tried to etch order onto the chaos of the universe, but it cannot hold, it cannot win out.*

*Hitler. Stalin. Pol Pot.*

*Ted Bundy. John Wayne Gacy. Jeffrey Dahmer.*

*We keep pretending like this darkness isn't part of us, isn't etched into all of our DNA. But rape and murder have persisted throughout human history, and they always will. This is us.*

*The story is the same. Whether you wrote about it in a scroll sealed with wax 1,000 years ago, or etched the headline in inky newsprint 50 years ago, or post about it on your fuckin' blog today, the human story is the same.*

*Hollywood paints this picture of selfless heroes and harmony and the good guy winning, when our true nature is best represented by killers, thieves, liars, whores. The politicians who sell us out over and over for campaign contributions. The insurance company who decides they won't cover the surgery your grandma needs to survive. All those thousands of Nazis who followed their orders and shoved real live human beings into the ovens and showers. That's humanity. That's us. A brutal species. Look closer than what that silver screen shows you, and you can still see the bloodstains on the teeth, the chunks of torn skin trapped under the fingernails.*

*Me? I want something better. Am willing to sacrifice all for something better.*

*I'm just a hopeless romantic, I guess.*

*Look closer still. It's right in front of you. All around you. Hanging in the air. Written between the lines.*

*It's freeing, I think, if you can find it. You realize that nothing binds you. There are no rules. You are free, and you always were.*

Darger finished reading and squeezed her eyelids shut. All this reading on no sleep was taking a toll, and it felt like two handfuls of sand had been flung into her eyes.

Her brain tumbled Huxley's words around. Processing it all.

The last sheet had been different from the rest, both the framing of the message and the thickness of the paper itself. She thought that was significant. It seemed once more that the journal pages were handled separately from the clue, though that delineation was more implied than overt in this final case.

Did it mean anything? Maybe yes. Maybe no. They'd know for sure in about five and a half hours, she supposed.

*The circle closes. And so the story ends. We go through the motions now once more with feeling.*

Did that mean this was the end? One last clue to solve? One last attack to thwart? She almost didn't dare to get her hopes up. The constant running around from scene to scene was starting to get to her. She was pissed, tired, and she had a headache.

She'd downed two cups of coffee and three ibuprofen, but it hadn't dulled the throbbing in her temples.

And now the sun was shining directly into the conference room, reflecting off the polished tabletop, trying to stab through her pupils to get at her brain. Intolerable. She dug around in her purse. Found her sunglasses. Slid them over her eyes.

That was a little better. Solved the sun problem, at least. But it did nothing to solve the last clue.

Fucking Huxley and his games.

Beside her, Loshak slurped at another can of Monster. He'd apparently conned three more cans off Fitch. Darger pointed at one of the unopened cans.

"May I?"

He raised an eyebrow but slid it over to her.

The can cracked and hissed as Darger popped it open. She brought the aluminum cylinder to her lips and tilted her head back, letting the tangy concoction slide down her throat. It was sizzling and acidic and insanely sweet, and she did her best not to let any of it touch her tongue.

She chugged over half the can before setting it down. A syrupy tang lingered in her mouth. She grimaced at the aftertaste, but she thought maybe it had helped. A little. Or maybe it was just the adrenaline rush of choking down something so nasty.

Loshak nodded his approval.

"Crisp, right? Like I said."

# CHAPTER 45

After staring at the newest clue for some time, Loshak came up with the idea of looking over the originals, beginning with the note Huxley had left taped to the wall of his basement.

"So he starts right out with the Manson 'piggies' reference," he said. "And then, the note you found tucked inside the DVR at the Driscoll scene had the Son of Sam quotes."

Darger gestured at one of the evidence bags.

"That led us to the Zodiac cipher, which pointed to Nielsen's penthouse."

Loshak tapped a finger on the baggie Darger had fished out from the underside of Nielsen's car.

"And in the next one, he opens with the Jack the Ripper bit, which was probably just to throw us off." Loshak scratched his chin. "He got a little tricky with the Mark David Chapman thing since he isn't technically a serial killer. But he *is* a famous murderer. Close enough, right?"

"Sure," Darger said.

"So the key to solving nearly every previous clue was some kind of serial killer or famous crime reference." Loshak almost smiled. "I think it's fair to say that if anyone was equipped to solve such a clue, it'd be the two of us."

Darger picked up the most recent clue. The evidence bag crinkled in her hands.

"He mentioned three killers in the newest one. Six if we count the three genocidal dictators. Maybe there's some pattern to it."

Loshak stepped to the whiteboard and wrote down the name

of each killer mentioned in the newest clue. They tried a number cipher created by using the number of victims from each killer mentioned in the journal. When that failed, they tried finding a geographic area the killers might have had in common, specifically any connection to New York.

By the end, they were still right where they'd started. Darger stared up at the whiteboard, her eyes jumping from one set of scribbled ideas to the next. They'd made no progress whatsoever.

Still, her mood had improved. Talking it out at least felt like an attempt at moving forward.

Loshak read a passage aloud.

"'Hollywood paints this picture of selfless heroes and harmony and the good guy winning, when our true nature is best represented by killers, thieves, liars, whores.'"

The agent stopped there and shook his head.

"Hypocritical little pissant," he grumbled. "He's so damn offended by the way movies and society put forth these fantasies, like he's so above it all, and yet he's doing exactly the same thing. Except his fantasies involve actual violence."

Fredrick poked her head into the room.

"I just got a call from the documents experts. The forensic linguist and the cryptanalyst have gone over the newest clue a dozen times, but they haven't found anything of note. No hidden messages. Nothing that enlightens us at all."

Darger's shoulders slumped. She'd been hoping the documents lab would find something in the scans they'd forwarded over. Something the rest of them had overlooked.

"We're missing something," she said, rubbing her eyes.

Loshak slammed his fist onto the top of the table.

"Well I'll be damned if I'm going to let this little shit get the better of us. He's not as smart as he thinks he is, you know? He's got the mentality of a bitter fourteen-year-old who's mad because he doesn't get to sit at the cool kid's table in the cafeteria during lunchtime. It's pathetic."

"Whoa there," Darger said. "Is this because he called you a 'boomer fucktard'?"

Loshak squinted at her. He reached for his last can of Monster and cracked it open without breaking eye contact.

"I'll have you know that I've been told, on more than one occasion, that I have very Millennial energy."

Darger burst out laughing. Hard enough that tears sprang to her eyes.

"It's not *that* funny," Loshak said, still as grumpy as ever.

"Maybe the exhaustion is making me punchy." She wiped her eyes. "Sorry."

Darger sighed. Her eyes went from the manic scribbles on the whiteboard to the clock on the wall.

They still had time. They just had to keep working at it. It wasn't time to panic yet.

That would come later.

# CHAPTER 46

Darger bent over the sink in the ladies' room and splashed a handful of cool water over her face. She blinked at her reflection in the mirror, eyelashes all stuck together in clumps. She'd hoped the shock of cold water would be enough to squeeze a bit more brain juice from her mind, give her the tiniest edge to help solve the clue. But so far all she'd really gained was a wet splotch on the front of her blouse from where the runoff had dribbled off her chin.

When she returned to the conference room, all the chairs around the table were empty. She and Loshak had agreed to take a fifteen-minute break, and she was back a little early.

She stepped over to one of the windows and peered outside. The people below went about their day. Work. Meetings. School. Lunch dates. All the while, one of them had been marked for death, and they had no inkling. And up here, 23 floors off the ground, two FBI profilers were going crazy trying to figure out the who, the what, the where.

*Look closer still. It's right in front of you. All around you. Hanging in the air. Written between the lines.*

The fucker. Always speaking in riddles. Teasing them. Taunting them from beyond the grave.

*Written between the lines.*

She tried to force her mind to make some final intuitive leap. To see somehow *what* he meant for her to see between the lines.

Nothing.

She thought of another turn of phrase that struck her as out of place, a tactic that had helped on earlier clues.

*The story is the same. Whether you wrote about it in a scroll sealed with wax 1,000 years ago, or etched the headline in inky newsprint 50 years ago, or post about it on your fuckin' blog today, the human story is the same.*

Taken as a whole, the idea being expressed here made sense. Still, the bit about the scroll stuck out. She wasn't even sure why, but it did.

*Sealed with wax.*

She squeezed her eyes tightly shut. Let her mind go blank with just those ideas bobbing around in her head.

*Written between the lines.*

*Sealed with wax.*

Still nothing.

Grisly pictures opened in her head. She saw that melted pizza cheese flesh pulling away from Amelia Driscoll's cheekbone and jaw. Saw Gavin Passmore's face shattered and strewn about his kitchen — a bloody jelly flecked with cranial bits the size of teeth.

She swung her head back and forth like she might be able to shake the images off, get them away, get them out of her head.

And fresh doubt poured in. Doubt about all things in her life.

Doubt about Owen. Doubt about Luck.

Doubt about whether she'd ever have kids, have a family.

Doubt about the course of her life.

She knew it was the exhaustion. Lack of sleep did something to the mind. Made everything good in the world seem suddenly distant. Out of reach. But she just had to go a little longer.

Her eyes went to the clock. What horror would happen if they failed this time? What new grim image would haunt her nightmares?

Her hands balled into fists. Muscles flexing and shaking.

No. There was no room for *ifs*. They had to see it through and solve this thing. Had to.

It was like Loshak had said. They couldn't let Huxley win.

Darger crossed the room, past the line of evidence bags holding the originals. She connected her phone to the projector and brought up one of the photographs of the most recent clue. Maybe seeing it blown up twenty times its normal size would reveal something they'd missed before.

She rested her rump on top of one of the tables and just stared at it for several minutes. Scanning back and forth through the pages. Hoping something would jump out at her.

*I'm just a hopeless romantic, I guess.*

Darger smirked when she read that line. First, because only a psychopath would think terrorizing the public and blowing people to bits was somehow romantic. Second, because there was a bit of glare in the photograph that obscured the "p" in hopeless, so she always read it as "homeless romantic" before correcting herself.

When someone misheard the lyrics of a song, it was called a mondegreen. Darger wondered if there was a name for misreading a line of text in such a way that changed the meaning.

Loshak strode into the room with coffee and donuts from the place across the street.

"You want some fresh coffee?"

"God no," Darger said, shaking her head. "If I drink any more caffeine right now, I think my heart will explode. I doubt it's helping me much at this point, anyway."

Her eyes went back to the hopeless/homeless romantic line

projected onto the wall. She was about to tell Loshak about her text-based mondegreen when she froze.

She'd just noticed another subtle splotch of glare, similar to the one on the word "hopeless." It was further up the page. Not quite as noticeable. Her eyes scanned back and forth across the page. There was another one. And another.

Darger hopped down from the desk and snatched up the baggie containing the original. She opened the bag and flipped around to the page she'd been studying on the projector, angling the paper toward the sun slanting in through the window.

Yes. There was definitely something there.

"Hey, you really should be wearing gloves," Loshak said, his mouth half full of donut. "I mean, we already know who the perp is, and he's dead. But still. We're professionals here."

Darger ignored him.

"Did you hear me?" he asked. "Gloves, Darger."

She stuck out her hand.

"In a minute. Give me your coffee."

"What? You just said—"

Darger took a step toward him and snatched the cup from his fingers.

"Hey!" Loshak glared at her. "I can get you your own cup, you know."

Darger set down the sheaf of papers and dumped the contents of the cup over the page from Huxley's journal.

"Holy Christ, Darger!" Loshak's voice came out in a hiss, and he glanced over his shoulder toward the door as if he was afraid of making a scene and attracting the attention of anyone else. "Have you lost your mind?"

"No," she said and pointed at the page. "Look."

His eyes went wide and the expression of incredulity on his face vanished.

"What the fuck?" he whispered.

The brown liquid of the coffee had thoroughly saturated the page, tinting it a muddy tan color. But not all of it. In the center of the page was a clear outline of a large number "2" written in something that resisted the dark stain of the coffee. Wax, Darger thought. Huxley had left a hidden message in wax.

# CHAPTER 47

The full wax message read: *Mountain home of the 2 Gunslingers. Look in the latrine.* This time the clue required very little puzzling.

Everyone knew that the director of the epic western and best picture winner, *Two Gunslingers*, was Lucio Mancini. Everyone also knew about his mountain home in upstate New York where he edited all of his films himself. The cherry on top was that the house's street address was 2 Hideaway Lane, presumably the reason the number 2 was numerical in the clue unlike the movie's official title.

The Mancini mansion was one of many luxury homes nestled in the foothills near Lake Placid — a tranquil community in upstate New York which had once hosted the winter Olympics. The Adirondack Mountains formed a circular dome about 160 miles wide and a mile high, engulfing this region of the state with scenic forested peaks and lakes.

They'd hit the road in the CIRG van as soon as they knew the Mancini house was the target location, but the ride from the city out into the upstate mountains would take hours, even with the driver speeding the whole way.

The second wind of solving the clue had perked Darger up, and the nervous chatter as they embarked kept her up early on. Her molars once again gritted along with the jerky spasms in her jaw muscles, whole body gone strangely tense.

About twenty minutes into the ride, however, the conversation petered out. Everyone got quiet. A creeping sleepiness settled over all of them — they'd been up all night and then some by now. Outside, the sun ducked behind the clouds, rendering the sky dull and gray.

Something about the flitting green of the trees racing by on the sides of the road only served to enhance the tiredness, all that gibbering intensity of the urban sprawl falling away to nature, to acres and acres of untouched land.

The drone of the tires on the asphalt resolved into something steady as soon as they got out of the city. It seemed to lull Darger, pull her thoughts slowly down that drain at the back of her skull. The exhausted weight on her neck and shoulders grew and grew, made her feel like a marionette with the strings slowly going slack.

She gave in eventually. Slept in fits and starts as they chewed up ground. Her chin dipped, tucked against her chest, stayed there. The thinnest line of drool dripped down the crease at the corner of her mouth and pooled on her chin.

The security vehicle slowly and steadily mounted an incline. Climbed that tilting asphalt. Sleep pulled Darger deeper and deeper under.

And strange dreams opened in her head. Vivid. Nonsensical.

In one she was in the lobby at a McDonald's, waiting in line, gazing up at the menu now and again, though the words were all so blurry she couldn't read any of it. She realized that the back of the head in front of her in line was Tyler Huxley's.

He whirled on her just then, a pump-action shotgun in his hands. She recognized the weapon right away — the Mossberg Persuader they'd found in his basement.

The other customers screamed and dove out of the way, belly-smacking the gray tile floor and skidding over it on their torsos. The workers ducked behind the counter. Exaggerated facial expressions made all of them look surreal and cartoonish.

Disturbing.

Huxley lifted the gun as though to point it at Darger.

She pulled her own gun. Aimed. Fired. Fired again.

Again. Again. Again.

The gun bucked like some thrashing wild creature in her hands.

She had him dead in her sights, close enough range that she almost couldn't miss, but somehow all her shots went high and wide. Tore holes in that blurry menu.

Huxley backpedaled from her. Moved closer to the counter. Still bringing the shotgun up.

He swerved the barrel toward himself. Opened his mouth. Settled the metal under his palate.

His hand flexed. Squeezed the trigger.

The shotgun boomed. His head burst. Exploded. Red flung in all directions.

Skull vanished. Head reduced to a stump of chin.

And his headless body fell. Settled into that awkward final position, sprawled with the shotgun resting on his chest, just like they'd found his corpse.

Darger shook herself awake then. Heart pounding.

Her eyes swiveled everywhere. Took in sunlight, an orange glow replacing the gray beyond the windshield. She knew somehow that they were almost there.

She took a breath, ribcage shaking a little. Loshak watched her out of the corner of his eye, but he didn't say anything.

The sun glared overhead as the CIRG truck turned onto Hideaway Lane. Beams of that orange afternoon light filtered through the splayed limbs of the eastern white pines that dominated this section of the Adirondacks.

Chunks of gravel littered the dirt road, which had been

rutted into a washboard by rain and runoff. The truck juddered and crunched its way up the slope. Almost there now.

Darger rubbed a knuckle at her right eye. Felt the sandy sting there and made herself stop.

Loshak slipped on a pair of aviators next to her. The mirrored lens covered his red and puffy eyes. He took a slug of coffee, grimaced a little.

"Cold?" Darger asked.

"Worse. Gritty. How does that even happen? I've been making coffee for forty years. Never had it come out grainy like this."

Dobbins was all suited up again, his body swaddled in bulky Kevlar, though he kept his helmet off so he could guzzle down one of Fitch's energy drinks. The pungent bubble gum stench of Monster filled the cabin as soon as he cracked the top. Now he tipped the can back to shake out the last drizzle.

"I can't believe you guys can drink that shit," Alvarez said.

Dobbins shrugged and smiled.

"Keeps me frosty."

"I like that Ultra Purple flavor, man," Fitch said. "Tastes like purple Kool-Aid mixed with Fruit Stripe Gum. Fucking incredible."

"Hey, if it keeps you from zonkin' out on the job, you guys can drink zebra piss for all I care," Alvarez said. "Smells terrible, though."

Dobbins chuckled. Then he pulled on his helmet and started going through his warm-up routine — stretching, rolling his head from shoulder to shoulder to the extent the suit would allow, fiddling with the settings on the cooling system again.

Darger took a deep breath. Checked her phone.

Unlike the scenario heading into Dirk Nielsen's penthouse,

they would have a comfortable amount of time to disarm the bomb in the Mancini mansion. Over an hour. This building, too, had already been evacuated and secured by local law enforcement. On top of that, the New York State Police had sent their own bomb squad into the home already and located the explosive package — an Adidas shoebox nestled under a bathroom sink. *Look in the latrine.*

Somehow all of these positive developments didn't stop a plague of locusts from swirling around in Violet Darger's gut, stirring up a nervous froth. She wouldn't relax until it was over and done.

Even if there was some suggestion of this being the last bomb, they would need to search the place thoroughly once the device was disabled. This would be a much bigger building to sift through, of course. Googling the address had turned up an old Zillow listing for the property from years back. According to that, the square footage checked in at just over 11,000. Immense. Darger had flipped through some of the pictures, looking at, among other things, a spa room, a sauna, and a lot of taxidermied animal heads mounted on the walls throughout the house. It reminded her of an Aspen ski lodge decorated by someone who went on a lot of safaris.

She shook her leg again as she went over these thoughts, the cylinder of her calf flexing and throbbing, expending energy.

"Here we go," Alvarez said, looking out at the road ahead where the Mancini estate took shape.

The massive lodge-style house sat atop the hill ahead of them. Windows bracketed the stonework of the hearth and chimney, making about two-thirds of the front of the mansion glass panes veined with thin strips of wood, and the other third colorful rock and mortar clearly hand-built by a master stonemason. The glazing went right up to the roofline, too, revealing the vaulted ceiling beyond.

The CIRG truck climbed the last bit of road and then curled onto the driveway. The blacktop ramped upward at an even steeper grade, coiling around trees and shrubs. It took the house out of view for a few seconds, and then a final sharper curve spilled them directly in front of the detached garage with a steep staircase leading up a rock face to the main house.

The trees parted here for the house and yard, and that made the sun shine brighter. Darger squinted. Felt that sandy sting in her eyes.

Dobbins did that I've-gotta-pee jog in place again. Then he pogoed straight up and down a few times. Darger had to give it to him — he seemed more alert than any of them by a wide margin, and that was a good thing.

"OK. Go time," Dobbins said, adjusting his helmet one last time. "Let's do this."

# CHAPTER 48

The door of the truck glided open, and Dobbins stepped out onto the paved driveway. His exaggerated footsteps almost made him seem like an astronaut stepping down onto the surface of the moon.

He jogged in place again, the bulky suit bobbing along, and then he bounced on his feet and threw a flurry of punches into empty space. Shadowboxing seemed to be his go-to method of getting some adrenaline going.

Darger jumped out next, wanting to stretch her legs. She stopped just outside the van and noticed several New York State Police cruisers clustered on the other side of the sprawling driveway — they seemed to want to give the CIRG team their space. After a beat, she moved on.

The blacktop felt almost soft under her feet, as if the heat of the day had melted it a bit. Her ankles cracked and popped as she crossed the tilted ground, footsteps choppy, joints a little stiff from sitting for so long.

Then she moved off the driveway and into the grass, moving toward the tree line at the edge of the property. The fresh mountain air swirled around her, and the details of her footsteps faded into the background. She sucked in a big breath, held it for a beat, then let it out slowly. Even being a little warm the air felt somehow crisp after sitting in the stuffy confines of the CIRG truck for hours. Refreshing.

She closed her eyes and took a few more deep breaths. It smelled nothing like the city out here. Clean air in place of garbage and car exhaust. The vaguely sweet aroma of cut grass.

She turned then, let her gaze drift up the sloping land to the house.

The mammoth home seemed more imposing up close. A hulking structure at the top of the hill that seemed to lean over her. Threatening. Sunlight glared off all the windows, made the whole thing shimmer around the dull rocks of the chimney.

The others circled around Dobbins again, chanting positivity, doing that shoulder pat pump up again. From a distance, they looked like children, Darger thought, preparing for some game, some sporting event. These couldn't be the adults who kept citizens safe from the violent creeps of the world.

And yet… she had to admit that the CIRG guys seemed loose. Even now, Dobbins, Alvarez, and Fitch were laughing. That calmed her some.

They were pros. They seemed so goddamn competent. Had this streak of cockiness or pride without being obnoxious. Probably something they had to develop in order to do the job.

It reminded her of the innate confidence she'd observed in some medical doctors, particularly surgeons. A belief in themselves beyond what seemed reasonable, for people's literal lives were in their hands every day.

By the time she rejoined Loshak and the others, Dobbins was halfway up the staircase to the house. He turned back. Gave a thumbs up. Then he moved for the door.

Darger watched Dobbins head in. She yawned and stretched as he disappeared inside.

Then she reluctantly climbed back into the CIRG truck to watch on the cam feed. It seemed darker inside now, her eyes having quickly grown used to the sunlight.

By the time she sat down in front of the console, she realized that it smelled vaguely like a pet store inside the vehicle — the stench of exhausted human bodies secreting adrenaline in a confined space. Bodily and acrid. The stench was oddly familiar — like some kind of soft cheese, she thought. Baby Swiss.

Darger wrinkled her nose. Tried to focus on the screen.

The camera jounced along with the gait of Dobbins' footsteps. Glided through a rustic living room with exposed wood everywhere. Turned left into a back hallway.

The light grew dimmer and dimmer as the agent walked away from those windows on the front of the house. Shadows thickening. Bleeding the color palette to grayscale.

Dobbins moved toward the place where the bomb lay waiting.

# CHAPTER 49

The camera passed through a doorway — the pale wooden border of the jamb framing the screen for a moment. Dobbins knelt then. He'd reached the guest bathroom where the explosive device lay.

A brass faucet and sink slid past on the monitor in the back of the CIRG truck. Then the bomb swung into view.

The camera held there for a beat. Rose and fell in time with Dobbins' breath. Then the lens edged closer and closer to the device. For the moment Darger couldn't really tell what she was looking at.

It was housed in an Adidas shoebox. Tucked in the cabinet beneath the bathroom sink. The murky shadows there swathed the package, rendered the footage a little grainy.

"Shit," Dobbins said. "Looks like I'll be working in tight quarters here, so… uh… yay."

"We can't really see what you're looking at, Dobber," Alvarez said into the headset, his voice more subdued than before, just taking on that raspy edge of exhaustion. "Want to talk me through it or maybe get a little closer?"

Dobbins swallowed audibly, the sound strangely clicky through the tinny console speakers. He leaned forward, the camera pushing into the dark place underneath the sink.

"That close enough?" he said.

Darger couldn't tell if his tone of voice was expressing annoyance or just the discomfort of leaning into the cramped space.

The contents of the box grew blurry for a second as the

focus of the camera lens adjusted. The dark clouded everything. Then the picture sharpened into full detail.

A gray wad took up most of the box — an L-shaped sculpture or so it seemed. Dimples in the surface seemed to suggest marks where fingers had pressed it into this form. Darger thought that made it look like acne-scarred skin, except ashen and lifeless like a dead fish. A mess of wires poked into the gray substance like clay, crisscrossing as they ran to a few mechanical pieces along the perimeter of the box that Darger couldn't see as well.

"C4 charge this time," Dobbins said, breaking the silence. "Plastic. That seem weird to you?"

Though she wasn't any kind of explosives expert, Darger knew enough to know that plastic explosives were much less volatile than most types. So remarkably stable, in fact, that the Army issued it to the infantry. It was safe to transport. You could even set the stuff on fire without detonating it — something US soldiers did to warm their food in Vietnam. Anything short of a properly applied shock wave from a detonator, and it wouldn't blow.

"Harder to come by, maybe," Alvarez said. "Why, what are you thinking?"

Dobbins let out a breath. Seemed to think a few seconds before he answered.

"I don't know. This guy seems the impulsive, reckless, self-destructive type, right? Just seems… interesting, I guess, that he'd go with plastic here. Like he's being cautious for some reason?"

Everyone looked at each other inside the van.

"It could simply be that he's trying to impress us with his skill level," Loshak said. "He's varied the device at each scene so far, almost as if to say, 'Look at all the things I can do.'"

"Bottom line, Dobbins: if you're having second thoughts, we should call it off," Alvarez said into his mouthpiece. "I mean, everyone is safe. We could try to detonate it remotely."

Dobbins shook his head.

"No, I'm good. Just let me take a minute and get comfortable with it."

"Alright. But if you get cold feet, just say the word," Alvarez said.

The camera held there on the tangle of wires and parts. That hunk of mottled gray in the center of it all. The picture rose and fell with Dobbins' respiration. He breathed deeply, held the breaths for a moment at each apex.

Inside the CIRG truck, nobody moved. Nobody spoke. They only stared at that hypnotic image of the box on the screen, the edges of it pulsing faintly whenever Dobbins sucked in a breath.

Dobbins leaned forward again. The fat fingers of his gloved hands came into view, splayed on the wood on each side of the shoebox.

"OK," he mumbled to himself. "OK."

He held still like that for what felt like a long time, hovering directly over the bomb. His breathing seemed to grow heavier, perhaps due to the awkward position of sticking most of his upper body under a bathroom sink.

Darger felt something squirm through her middle — some muscle spasm reminding her of the tension to all of this. Dobbins was putting his head and chest directly over what looked like a couple of pounds of C4. Kevlar blast suit or not, it was insane.

"Ahh… I see what you did there," Dobbins said then, his voice all low and gravelly in a way that made him sound like

Alec Baldwin. He chuckled a little to himself.

His right hand rose from the wooden plank at the bottom of the vanity. Drifted within the borders of the shoebox.

His index and middle fingers extended. Stopped just shy of touching one of the loops of wire.

The two fingers traced along a red wire. Followed it from where it embedded in the mottled gray C4 to what looked like it could be a cellphone battery.

Then the fingers went back to the center of the box. This time they followed an orange wire.

"Tricky," Dobbins said. "He ran all of the wires through the C4 just to muddle up what we're seeing, but…"

Alvarez stared blankly at the screen, his mouth hanging open. After a second he responded, as though he'd forgotten for a moment that this was a dialogue.

"But what?"

"I've got it," Dobbins said. "I think I've got it."

Alvarez grimaced, but he didn't have time to say anything.

The beak-like nose of the wire cutters roved into the frame. Moved quickly. Confidently.

Dobbins snipped the orange wire. Hesitated for a moment, the tool floating in empty space above the tangle of wires.

Then he lowered his hand again and the bulky Kevlar of his glove got in the way. They couldn't see what he was doing anymore.

Darger hugged her arms to her chest. Squeezed herself into something smaller.

"Dobbins," Alvarez said, his voice going husky.

The wire cutters snicked again. Louder than before, as though they were cutting something thicker, something stronger.

That girthy Kevlar glove throbbed on the screen. Jerking and bobbing. Still working.

Dobbins gasped. Sucked in a big wet breath. The wind sounded hollow in the console speakers. Empty.

Everyone in the truck sat forward. Breath held. Eyes opened wide.

The wire cutters clicked like a dog's toenails on linoleum. It sounded huge in the quiet CIRG truck. Sharp.

Then everything went still.

Darger's arms quivered from hugging herself so tightly. Strange tremors jerking in her wrists and elbows. Pressing her flesh.

"OK," Dobbins said, his voice small and tight. "I got it."

# CHAPTER 50

Dobbins rocked up onto his knees, the camera wobbling and ascending along with him. He heaved in a big breath. Let it out. That wind rattling in the blast suit's microphone, sounding a little like dead leaves scraping over a sidewalk.

"Device deactivated," he said.

He started breathing heavy then. Panting in fast motion. After a second, Darger realized that he wasn't breathing funny, he was laughing. Wheezing out breathy chuckles.

"Dobbins does it again," Fitch said. "Unreal. Dude is just unreal."

The big guy clapped Darger and Loshak on the back, then rose from his seat. Gave Alvarez a high five. Then he drummed both of his hands on the edge of the console like he was doing a snare roll.

McAllister whirled around from his position manning the controls. His mouth curled downward so he looked like a hatchetfish.

"Um… the, uh, roughhousing… Not on the equipment. Please."

Fitch stopped his drumbeat, though he hardly seemed perturbed. He transitioned to air guitar, his mouth squealing out some high-pitched Randy Rhoads-esque solo.

Darger felt her chest hitch in a big involuntary breath. Throat opening so wide it tipped her head back like a Pez dispenser. Air surging to fill the void.

And then the endorphins hit. Bliss flooded her brain, coursed through her veins, made her follicles tingle. The feeling of champagne bubbles popping in her head came over her. The word *effervescence* sprang to mind.

Dizzy. She put a hand on the console to steady herself, eyelids blinking rapidly. It almost felt like a drug experience, some painkiller euphoria kicking in so hard it almost took her under.

"You alright?" Loshak said. He put a hand on the back of her arm as though he might need to leap in to stop her from keeling over.

Darger shook her head a little before she could get her mouth to form an answer.

"I'm fine. Just a little lightheaded. Can't believe he did it again, I guess."

"Yeah, this whole thing is…" Loshak trailed off there, seemingly at a loss for words.

Fitch had started to do his frat boy rooster crow again when Dobbins' voice cut through on the speakers. Sharp this time. Urgent.

"Wait. Wait. There's something here."

Everyone in the CIRG truck fell quiet, eyes once again fixed on that screen that fluttered slightly with the agent's breathing.

"Talk to me, Dobber," Alvarez said. "What are you seeing?"

"OK, you see this?"

Dobbins' chunky suit hand lifted onto the screen. His finger pointed at the back edge of the shoebox where the deactivated bomb still lay.

"When I changed positions just now, I noticed something. Here, I'll get closer."

The camera jostled back and forth a moment. Then it seemed to zoom forward into the shadows as Dobbins again stuck his head under the sink, this time angling himself off to the right of the box. He pointed the finger again, not quite touching the cardboard.

"Right here. Can you see that?"

The image clouded with shadows and then cleared, just like last time. Darger squinted to try to make out the details.

A tiny bit of white seemed to protrude at the back right corner of the shoebox. A triangular bit seemingly stuck to the side of the box. Maybe an eighth of inch showing — maybe less.

"Looks like a piece of paper?" Alvarez's voice went up as if it were a question.

Dobbins scuttled back from the sink. The camera pulled out and flashed to white, totally washed out for a second as the brighter light assailed the lens. Then the picture congealed again, contours returning as the contrast came back, returning to the normal bathroom view.

"OK. Here's what I think I see," Dobbins said. "It looks like the bottom of this vanity has a cut out beneath the device. A little compartment. Almost like a false bottom, you know. So this piece of paper is jutting out of there. I think it's another clue."

The silence inside the CIRG truck swelled again. Big and tense. Made Darger's skin crawl.

"He hid it right under the bomb?" Darger said, her voice soft. "Why would he do that?"

"Had the bomb gone off, the clue would be destroyed, right?" Fitch said. "So maybe it's like… a reward for figuring it all out."

Loshak raised an index finger as he chimed in.

"That could make sense. Huxley referred to this whole thing as a game. Perhaps this is our prize for completing the task he assigned."

Fitch nodded.

"And the dude seems eager as hell to spread his gospel through these journals. So this sort of ensures we find the next piece, right?"

Dobbins cleared his throat, apparently impatient with all the speculation going on in the truck.

"In any case, let's have a look, shall we?" he said.

The bloated-looking fingers of the glove moved to the paper. Gingerly poked until it peeled away from the side of the box. Pinched the flap between thumb and pointer. The bloated hand held there for a second as Dobbins took a few breaths.

He slid the paper out. Slowly. Carefully. It rasped against the wood and cardboard, sounded dry. Looked like someone tugging a sheet out from under a blanket.

Spiky letters revealed themselves on the page. Scrawled in thick black sharpie script.

Darger could just read the two words as they slid into view.

*Game over.*

# CHAPTER 51

The whoosh seemed to throw Dobbins. Lifting him. Flinging him.

Everything on the screen went blurry. Moving. Smearing past.

The camera lens shattered. All of it at once. Cracks stretching across it like broken ice atop a lake in winter.

Then the bright flash hit. Seared Darger's eyes. Flared through the fractured lens, through the monitor.

The explosion rattled in the speakers next. A boom and then an exhaled gust. Sounded like someone blowing on the mic again, crackling and growling.

Everything on the screen came apart.

Tiny motes burst everywhere. Traveling outward. Disintegrated bathroom bits and crumbled drywall flung like wads of dirt.

Then the sound and video cut off abruptly.

The screen went black. Vacant.

But the boom still roared around them. Thrummed its vibration through the ground. Through the building. Through the walls and floor of the CIRG truck. Rattled everything.

Fitch tried to leap into action. Lurched out of his chair only to be slammed to the quaking floor of the vehicle. Chest thudding the ground. Partially catching himself with outstretched arms.

He tried to push himself up and flopped down again.

The rumble seemed to build. Deep and booming. Growing louder, thicker, heavier.

And the shaking of the CIRG truck intensified. Turned violent.

The tremor knocked a mug full of pens and paper clips off the console. Bounced open the cooler door and tumbled cans of Monster out onto the floor, twirling them around on their sides.

Darger gripped the arms of her chair with both hands. Gritted her molars. Felt her bottom lip pull down into a grimace that exposed her lower teeth.

The shaking stopped all at once. A quick cut to stillness.

Silence.

Motionlessness.

Darger's skin contracted like a membrane. Pulled taut against the musculature of her body.

The quiet seemed wrong around them.

Empty.

Profane.

# CHAPTER 52

"Jesus Christ!" Alvarez said, his voice quavering. "That… that was a much bigger charge… it had to be…"

"Bigger than the plastic we saw?" Darger said, her voice coming out in a dry rasp.

Alvarez blinked and nodded.

"Had to be. It was… there had to be a second bomb."

"It was a trick," Darger said. "The whole thing. He played it off like a game with rules just for the chance to do this."

Fitch pushed himself up on wobbly arms as the others talked. Looked a little like a baby deer rising for the first time. He shook his head as though to clear the cobwebs.

"What's the protocol here?" Loshak said, eyes locked on Alvarez. "Do we wait for the NYSP Bomb Disposal Unit to clear the scene? Do we have time to do that?"

Alvarez's chin shook. It looked like he was having a hard time processing this. Probably going into shock. Mind retreating into itself.

"Dobbins," he whispered, teeth and lips oddly wet. "Oh fuck. Dobbins."

"I'll say this," McAllister said, glancing up from his control station. "Anyone even contemplating going in there now, whatever might be left of the building, should take a gas mask out of that locker over there. Explosions like this kick all kinds of nasty crap into the air, OK? Clouds of toxins, pollutants, carcinogens. It's no joke."

Fitch staggered to the locker. Ripped it open. Situated a gas mask on his face and adjusted the straps. He tossed one to

Darger, tossed one to Loshak. He looked at Alvarez's glassy eyes for a second and chose not to toss him one.

"You guys can wait for the State Police to clear the scene if you want," Fitch said, his voice muffled by the mask. "Me? I'm going in. Dobbins could still be…"

Fitch trailed off there. Jaw flexing a couple of times, making the sides of the gas mask bulge.

He strode across the truck. Ripped open the door. Bounded out into the wedge of daylight there.

And Violet Darger followed.

# CHAPTER 53

They rushed up the set of wooden stairs leading from the driveway to the house. Darger touched her palm down to the wooden rail every few steps, feeling the cool coarseness of the timber. She followed Fitch, his broad shoulders swaying as he climbed, heavy boots thudding down on the risers, legs thrusting.

She craned her neck to try to see the house, but the hill blocked most of the view from here. Hard to say how bad the damage was. Hard to know what she was heading into. She kept running.

She pulled the gas mask over her head. Secured it around her chin and forehead. Looked out at the world through the rounded edges of the visor, a black line cutting off the top of her field of vision.

She breathed. Heard that Darth Vader-like suction sound of the gas mask with every inhale. Felt her own breath billow inside the chamber around her face.

The staircase spilled out onto a landing and veered into a hairpin turn, zigzagging up the steep slope. They made that u-turn and zipped up the final set of stairs. The land leveled out at the top, and the immense house came fully into view at last.

Black smoke coiled from the top of the structure, a thick shaft twirling up from the roof. Ominous. Otherwise, Darger could detect no damage from here which surprised her some, given how violent the explosion had felt inside the truck.

The sun glared against all the big front windows. Painted the glass in blinding brightness. Made it impossible to see anything inside.

A stone footpath led to the front door. They hurtled toward that reddish rectangle that would lead them inside — the one pop of color on an otherwise solid facade of stone and glass.

Fitch hit the door first. Bulled into it with a dipped shoulder as he cranked the knob. The heavy steel thing flung out of his way like balsa wood.

He disappeared into the opening. A few paces later, Darger crossed the threshold as well.

A gray cloud filled the interior of the home. A roiling thing. Unsettled bits drifting, gliding, hovering. Dust and debris.

Darger gasped. Sucked in a big breath. The gas mask scraped and popped.

Fitch moved into the cloud. The gray swallowed him up.

Darger hesitated a second. Shaky breaths rasping through the gas mask. She took a couple of choppy steps forward. Then she too pushed into the murkiness.

The gray swirled around her like liquid. Obscured her vision. Disoriented her.

Still she advanced. Shuffling her feet. Her hands bobbed in front of her just in case, fingers going hazy as they dug into the smoke.

It felt like she was drifting through it. Gliding like the faux fog around her.

She pressed forward. Crossed a vast living space populated with suede furniture that she could only kind of make out. Moved toward where she knew the bathroom would be, where the blast would have taken place.

And pictures of Dobbins pulsed through her head. Memories of him gearing up in the back of the CIRG truck. Jogging in place to get himself pumped up. Always smiling, laughing. Always talking tough.

She swallowed. Felt a lump the size of a golf ball shift in her throat.

Something brushed against the small of her back. She turned. Expected to find Loshak.

Instead she saw Alvarez there. Just behind her. Eyes looking impossibly wide through the dull glazing of the visor.

The edge of the living room came into view in stages. First she saw the wood beam of the lintel hung over the doorway to the left, a dark line that seemed to float there, growing thicker and darker as the haze seemed to clear in the space around her. Then she saw the wall around it, the flat surface solidifying all at once.

Fitch's back took shape then. He was turning toward the doorway, legs wide, staying low. Darger sped up to close the gap between them.

Her heart thudded in her ears as they wheeled around the corner to the hallway, something distant in the sound of her pulse. A little hollow and uneven, like a partially flat tire wobbling along.

She knew that she must be going into shock, but what good did knowing that do her? She kept going.

The bathroom doorway should be just ahead. Should be. But a single step into the hallway was enough to see that it wasn't. Not anymore.

Sun shone down from the gaping wound in the roof above. A beam of light about six feet in diameter. It glinted on tendrils of swirling gray. Illuminated the damage in eerie light half-obscured by the smoke.

The walls where the doorway used to be were gone. Obliterated. Splintered lumber remained. Studs and plates. A sticklike frame Darger could see right through. A skeleton of what once was.

Some of the studs were gone entirely. Blown out or fragmented to bits. Others were fractured and blackened, large chunks missing.

She tilted her head upward to take in the damage above. More tattered lumber framed the hole torn in the roof, splintery bits forming a ragged edge where the explosion had sheared off the rafters above, damaged everything around the breach.

It was hard to envision the blast tearing upward and outward. Big enough to burst the high ceiling above.

Fitch kept moving forward, and she tried to keep up on numb legs. Blinking hard. Reminding herself to breathe, air hissing through the mask.

Fitch stopped short then. Head facing downward. Boots squeaking on the glossy wood floor.

Darger looked down to see what he was looking at.

The hole in the floor gaped back at her, a black hole leading down into the dark of the basement. This was an angry wound, bigger than the one in the roof. Charred wood formed the edge. Broken bits like toothpicks sticking out everywhere.

She stared into the void. Tried to make it make sense to her eyes, to her mind.

A bulk to her right caught her eye then. Made her turn her head that way in slow motion.

The dark shape sprawled. Draped over the remaining lumber where a wall used to be, the studs forming bars that probably helped hold him there, feet hanging over the edge of that hole into the basement.

She swallowed again. Felt that golf ball bobbing in the back of her throat.

Dobbins' helmeted head seemed to hang by a sinew. Laying all wrong on the blackened floor. Almost like it had been positioned next to the shoulders instead of on them, no longer truly part of the body.

Red misted the inside of the helmet's visor. The bright color stippling the safety glass. A vivid hue that stood out from all the drab shades of the smoke and debris around it. Angry red. Violent red. Almost glowing.

Blood had wept down the front of the blast suit. The wetness faintly visible through the chalky dust that had rained down on him, on everything. Chunks of tile and drywall littered the floor all around. Coated the dead body in white powder that looked like flour.

No one spoke. They just stood and stared.

And then Alvarez burst into tears. Nose wrinkling. Mouth curling. Cheeks contorting. Inconsolable.

He stumbled forward. Dropped to his knees next to the body. Buried his face in his hands.

The whimpers spilling out of him didn't sound like those of a hardened CIRG agent. They didn't sound like a grown man's sounds at all.

Alvarez wept like a child.

# CHAPTER 54

While a horde of crime scene techs flocked to the scene to process and search and catalog all that had happened, Darger and Loshak rode the fifteen miles to the nearest airport, ready to make the quick jump back to the city via helicopter. They sat in the back of a police cruiser. Quiet.

A numbness welled in Darger's being. That dead muscle feeling of physical exhaustion intertwining with the trauma of Dobbins' death. The sharpest edges of the tragedy somehow kept their distance for now. Like her fatigued mind couldn't process the reality, held the worst of the hurt at arm's length.

In its place she felt the dull ache of the loss in a more general sense — the distant kind of sadness that seeps the life out of the world. Saps the joy. Drains the color. It left her hollow and faithless and alone. Apart from everyone else. Empty.

Just her and the big nothing.

Darger didn't think. Didn't move. Just stared out the window through halfway-opened eyes.

Nothing in her head.

The thick green vegetation of upstate New York smeared past on the side of the road. A pastoral scene that rolled on and on for miles. The pluming foliage here reminded her more of where she grew up than what she thought of when she thought *New York.*

Her ears still rang. Piercing tones screaming from somewhere deep in the ear canals. Endless screeching. Pleading. Crying out for what?

She'd sat that way — vacant and motionless — for about an

hour when the thoughts finally came. Spiraling downward.

Memories.

Pain.

Pictures of Dobbins opening in her head. Vivid images. Violent.

His head mostly disconnected from the rest of him. Angled next to the shoulders. Dangling and strange. Helmeted. Crooked.

The thin lines of sinew still attaching the skull to the torso. Shiny strands of meat and yellowed connective tissue. Fibrous. Slicked with sticky red.

That red mist inside the visor. Blazing crimson contrasted with all the muted colors around them.

That white powder dusted over the suit, over the body. Some impromptu funeral rite performed by the explosion.

*Death.*

*Death.*

Her mind groped along the edges of Dobbins' absence. Tried to fathom how this funny, vibrant person could just be gone like that.

Here one second. Gone forever the next.

It made no sense. He had a wife and kids. He was good at his job. What did he do to deserve this ending to his story? How could he soldier on through all those years only to be snuffed out in a flash?

His whole life had led him to this. Only this. Each day another step toward the inevitable. The meaningless. The nothing.

Big nothing.

She pictured Alvarez again. Face cupped in his hands. Crying like a baby.

And no one could help him. No one.

Tears formed in Darger's eyes. Further blurred that smear of green rushing past outside.

But it wasn't her loss. It wasn't even Alvarez's loss. She knew that, felt its importance on some deep level that might only be open to her just now, in the midst of the trauma.

It was Dobbins' loss. His life snuffed out while theirs would carry on.

It didn't belong to them. *He* didn't belong to them. He never did.

The water edged over the rims of her eyelids and drained down her cheeks.

# CHAPTER 55

"It's strange," Loshak said, breaking the silence in the car. "The line between life and death is so hopelessly thin. Even in a job like ours, it stays impossible to fully grasp, impossible to wrap our heads around, impossible to accept. I can never… It's somehow shocking every single time someone takes that step to the other side permanently."

He blinked a few times before he went on. Eyeballs swiveling around in their sockets. Piercing empty space.

"We are incapable of imagining how it will feel when they're gone until it happens, you know?"

Darger nodded. Looked out the window again.

The air-conditioning suddenly made the car feel frigid. Cavernous. The chill seeped into Darger's flesh.

"In the weirdest way it gives me a kind of faith," Loshak said. "You feel it only in times like these, I think — almost something spiritual. When someone is gone, you feel that loss so deeply, so powerfully. It almost seems primordial.

"And it makes me think that we must all be connected somehow. This pain. This loss. It's not just intellectual. There has to be something more there, some energy connection. Like what they talk about in quantum physics, that all energy is connected, that it cannot be created or destroyed."

He scrubbed his hand at his hair. Fluffed it up on his head.

"I don't know. I guess I feel something like that sometimes. Mostly when I sit in the quiet alone and contemplate losing someone."

They fell quiet again after that. Listened to the tires hum on the asphalt, thumping every few seconds as they rode over a freshly patched seam, ribbons of black tar that still looked wet.

The rhythm of the white noise drew Darger out into a daze again. Eyes staring out at nothing. All thoughts fleeing her head once more. She drifted in the emptiness. Weightless. Untethered from this car, from this world.

Floating.

Her phone shrieked, startling her enough that she jumped a little. The ensuing jolt of adrenaline vanquished the daze she'd been in. The phone rang again, buzzed against her hip in her pocket.

She fished it out. Checked the display. It was Fitch. She swiped to answer it.

"Fitch. What's up?"

His voice sounded raspy in her ear. Cold and serious.

"He's still alive."

*What?* Darger squinted, her tired mind trying to process this sentence.

Still alive? He couldn't be. She'd seen him up close. Watched them zip the body bag closed.

The image of Dobbins flared in her head again. Posed among the skeletal lumber of the shattered walls. Head hanging by sinewy cords. Inside of his visor stained red.

Her lips fumbled for words. Tongue stuck against the roof of her mouth.

Finally she said, "Who?"

"The bomber. He just posted a video on the internet. Tyler Huxley is alive."

# CHAPTER 56

Darger's mind reeled. Thoughts flickering through her head like a slot machine whirring. Blinking. Spinning confusion.

She still held the phone in front of her face. Stared at the reflection of her open mouth there in the blank screen. Fitch had just hung up.

The mirror image of her teeth moved then. Mouth closing and opening. Lips popping. Throat clicking. But no words came out.

"What is it?" Loshak said.

His eyebrows scrunched down until they disappeared behind his sunglasses.

"Tyler Huxley is alive."

Darger replayed the conversation out loud. Voice soft. Everything distant. The world around her in a soft focus now. Strange and cold and quiet. The whole thing almost felt like an out-of-body experience.

And then before her conscious mind could catch up to what she was doing, she thumbed to the browser on her phone. Searched for the video. Opened it. Loshak leaned over to watch as well.

A masked face appeared on the screen. One of those creepy plague masks with the long black beak and beady eyes staring straight into the camera. He was still. Immobile to an eerie degree.

He sat before a wooden desktop. Hands moving now to lift something there, whatever it was crinkling off-screen.

He held a copy of today's New York Post up to the camera

— the utterly gigantic headline read in blood-red text, *Bomber Rips Through New York!*

Then he set the newspaper down. Held still for another few heartbeats. Chest just barely shifting along with his breaths. The frame utterly motionless save for a prism-like light glittering on the plain white wall in the background.

His hands rose finally. Gripped the sides of the false face.

He peeled the black latex away. That long beak buckling and rippling at his touch. Hair and skin spilling free.

And there he was. Tyler Huxley. His face on her screen. Coming out from behind the mask.

Smiling. Giddy. A twinkle in his eye.

Goose bumps rippled over her skin, a breath rasping into her.

*What the fuck?*

He spoke then, but she couldn't focus on the words. Her mind flashed to the corpse in the basement of the run-down apartment. That skinny body draped over the floor. That stump of jaw where the face had been.

She closed her eyes. Took a breath. Focused all of her willpower on listening now, paying attention. She opened her eyes.

She pushed the little arrow to restart the video, turning up the volume to hear his words.

This wasn't over yet.

# CHAPTER 57

Loshak hit the space bar on his laptop, and the video played again. They'd watched it at least two dozen times since they'd gotten back to their hotel, after watching it more than twice that many times in the helicopter that shuttled them back to the city.

Darger lay back on the bed, the comforter scratchy where it touched the skin on the back of her neck. Her hair was still wet from a quick shower, one that washed away that billowing dust from the Mancini mansion, brought a clean feeling to her skin, but somehow provided little relief given the circumstances. It was weird to see the beige spiral going down the drain, the physical remnants of the explosion washed away from her being, though the emotional effects never could be.

She closed her eyes and listened to the sounds of the video: that rustle of the moving newspaper again, the crinkling sounds having grown almost musical in their familiarity. Then came the scuffing sounds of the mask being pried free of his face. Finally came his voice.

"Look who's back from the dead. Truth is, I couldn't die. My mission is too important." He paused there for a big smile. "The bombings will slow — for now. But understand this… I'm just getting started."

The video ended, and Loshak clacked the space bar again.

Darger sat up. Forced herself to watch again. She scrutinized something different every time. Focused on his lips for this pass — wormy red lips, chapped skin marking out the segments strangely. Disgustingly to be honest. They looked like they might wriggle off his face and squirm around on the sidewalk in the rain.

The screen went black. Thumbs tapped the space bar.

She watched Huxley's eyes this time — dark pits for pupils, looked like he was in some state of arousal, possibly even on drugs. She heard snippets of the words as she watched, but these mostly stayed beneath her conscious mind now. His eyes flicked around in their sockets. Blinked twice. She looked for something in these details. Anything.

The video replayed like that five more times. Darger and Loshak huddled over the laptop. Neither of them said anything. They just watched. Observed. Over and over. Some strange trance overtaking them. They still had a little over an hour until the emergency task force meeting. What else were they going to do?

The details of the room behind Huxley started to intrigue Darger more and more. She took eight straight passes just looking at the top right quadrant of the screen, watching that little twinkle of silvery light dancing there as he put the newspaper down.

"Here's what I'm thinking," Loshak said. His thumbs still worked the space bar even as he talked, not breaking the rhythm. "The fingerprints. His shoplifting arrest was only six or seven months ago, right?"

Darger didn't reply. Just stared at the screen.

"He would have been well into the planning stage at that point. Well into setting all of this in motion. So the arrest was a setup. He found someone who looked enough like him. Probably paid the person to get caught shoplifting. Gave him his ID. Got those fingerprints — the wrong fingerprints — on the permanent record as Tyler Huxley."

Loshak stretched. Craned his neck up toward the ceiling.

"Death is the perfect alibi, right? The perfect way to make sure no one is looking for you. The fingerprints made it airtight. Reminds me of this case I read about. A woman in Brooklyn got caught trying to kill this other woman who looked remarkably like her. They both had dark hair and spoke Russian. They were able to figure out that she had befriended her doppelganger, brought her a cheesecake laced with poison, and planned to steal her life — not just her identity. She was going to take her name, her apartment, her job. Just kill her off and slide into her life. I guess they looked that much alike."

Darger's eyelids fluttered. She finally looked away from the screen.

"So why is Huxley revealing that he's still alive now?"

Loshak ran his fingers through his hair again as he answered.

"The same reason he announced his identity right out of the gate. He wants to take credit. That's as much a motivation as any other aspect of the crimes, I think — making sure the world knows *he* did this, knows who *he* is, that *his* face is plastered on the front page of every newspaper. He couldn't bear to do this anonymously. To hide in the shadows as an unknown Other like so many of the killers in the cases we work." He chuckled a little to himself, a bitter laugh. "The whole world knows his name now, and that's no accident. Despite all his talk, Tyler Huxley desperately wanted to be a celebrity all along."

They both fell quiet after that. Loshak offered to go get some coffees from the lobby.

"It'll be scorched by now," Loshak said, face puckering as if imagining the bitter taste. "But on a certain level caffeine is caffeine. I'd set up an IV drip if I could, but until then, the scorched stuff will have to do."

"Who knows?" Darger said. "Maybe we'll get lucky, and someone just made a fresh pot."

Darger's eyes drifted back to the screen as Loshak ventured out into the hall, the door clicking shut behind him. Now she manned the space bar. Tapped it with a choppy sound.

She watched the video loop over and over in the quiet room. For this run-through she found herself watching his hands. Long fingers. Glossy nails. Maintained and delicate. Maybe that made sense, she thought. Building bombs was a task that required finesse. This wasn't a crime fit for the sausage-fingered slobs of the world. Not at all.

But what did his hands really tell her? Or his lips? Or his eyes? How did any of the details in this video give her something actionable, help her forge a path forward?

Maybe they didn't. They probably didn't, in fact.

She hit the space bar again and again. It all felt singsong now. Every element of the video took on a rhythm through all the repetition, somehow made twee after so many loops.

Her eyes drifted over the details again. The rustling newspaper. The wormy lips. The black pits of his pupils. That little fluttery light in the corner. His graceful fingers.

Her eyes snapped back to that top right corner of the screen again — the place where the light fluttered just as he set the newspaper down. She watched for it. Waited for it.

Loshak came back in with two paper cups of coffee in his hands. He leaned a shoulder into the door and swiveled into the room.

"OK," he said. "So the coffee doesn't smell *great*, but—"

Darger yelped involuntarily. Interrupting him.

Loshak's eyes went wide. He lurched toward the laptop screen, sloshing coffee on the carpet.

"What is it?"

"There," Darger said. She tapped on the laptop screen. "I know what this is."

The light fluttered beneath her finger. Glinting through a window off-screen. Lighting up one little slice of the white wall. Sliding over the eggshell surface. Then disappearing.

Even after the light was gone, she just kept tapping. A million words raced through her head, but she struggled to get them to her tongue. Finally something came.

"Huxley went home."

# CHAPTER 58

Again the task force convened on the 23rd floor of the Javits Federal Building. The emergency meeting had been called late in the afternoon, interrupting a multitude of commutes, and stragglers were still filing in even as things got underway, a stream of them flowing off the elevator, speed walking down the hall, spilling into the room.

Detectives and special agents crowded around the glazed table in tall-backed office chairs. The room smelled vaguely of hand sanitizer intertwined with the burned stench of cheap coffee.

Darger tried to get comfortable in the bustling atmosphere. Eyes scanning everywhere. Watching all the keyed-up law enforcement officers twitch and play with their phones and likewise survey their surroundings.

She realized that most of them were functioning on as little sleep as she was, the bulk of them working all the angles of this case behind the scenes. Creases under their eyes spoke to that shared exhaustion.

The restlessness only grew as more people crowded into the space, a bodily stench adhering itself to that rubbing alcohol and burned coffee combo. Soon no one could keep still. Hands and forearms touched down on the tabletop before quickly fleeing. Fingers prodded at noses and brows. The leather chairs squeaked beneath fidgeting men and women in rumpled business suits.

Agent Fredrick had a sheaf of papers in front of her. She was highlighting something in neon pink, the lid clenched between her teeth. Her eyes darted to the clock, and then she cleared her throat and addressed the room.

"At this point, I don't need to belabor the ongoing shitshow this case has been from the get-go. Multiple deaths, both civilian and LEO. Internet shenanigans that have resulted in unwanted involvement from the public. And just to pop a green olive on top of the hot fudge sundae, our perpetrator is now officially at large. Thankfully, Agent Darger noticed a potentially identifying characteristic in the video Huxley released, and we're already planning our next move."

Lots of heads around the table turned Darger's way. Inquisitive expressions etched on all the faces. Then they snapped back to Agent Fredrick.

"The flashing light in the upper right-hand corner of the footage? We believe, strongly, that it comes from a pinwheel in a potted plant on a balcony near the apartment of Tyler Huxley's mother. The flashing was witnessed there by Agent Darger, and a few other officers who visited the mother's apartment verified seeing the same."

She flipped the pages in front of her. Finger tracing along text and finding something.

"So the news gets better. We've got multiple teams in place on rooftops nearby the apartment now. Recon Team 2 just got in touch minutes before this meeting officially began. They had eyes on a male inside the apartment, very briefly. They could not explicitly confirm the identity of the man, but he appeared about the right size, the right age for our suspect."

Everyone fell quiet for a second. Several officers leaned forward in their squeaky office chairs. Paranoid heads swiveling around.

"Are we sure the man they spotted isn't Huxley's brother?"

Loshak said. "He's been at the mother's apartment, and he could pass for Huxley from a distance."

Fredrick shook her head.

"The brother, David, should be off at school in Piscataway based on the class schedule he gave us." She paused to glance at her watch. "We're trying to track him down to get confirmation on that. So far he hasn't answered his phone."

"Have we thought about reaching out to his mother?" one of the detectives asked.

"Too risky," Darger said. "If he's there, she's likely been hiding him this whole time, right? She'd tip him off."

"That's our thinking as well," Fredrick agreed. "We're waiting on warrants at the moment, which we expect to have any minute. Confirmation that the brother isn't there would be extremely helpful, and I'm hopeful we'll get that from him directly. We want to move forward without letting the mom know — in case there's any chance of Huxley running."

They were quiet for a beat.

"Either way, we'll go forward with the raid. If he's in there, he's ours. If not..."

☾

From there, the meeting shifted into a tactical mode. Fredrick set up a map on an easel and drew red lines around multiple city blocks near the Huxley apartment. For the first time, it struck Darger how massive this operation would be.

"As you can see on the map, we're in the process of locking down three city blocks surrounding the building even now. Our hope is to take him by surprise to the degree that we can, but if he runs, he won't get far. We've got the FBI SWAT team and three local SWAT teams at the ready. It's going to be a massive operation, and we want to be good to go as soon as the warrant comes through."

She drew Xs at the front and rear of the apartment building where Huxley's mother lived.

"We'll have teams securing the exterior of the building — one on Barclay Avenue will cover the south-facing entrance, the other on 41st will lock down the north-facing entrance. That should do it. From there, the plan is to send a SWAT team in to lock down the hallways of the apartment building. FBI SWAT will serve as the strike team, breaching the actual apartment. Hopefully we take this shit heel by surprise.

"There's one more objective I want to be clear about. I've already talked to the teams on the ground about this, but it bears repeating. We want to do everything in our power to take Huxley alive. There could be additional explosive devices either at some point in the shipping process or rigged up somewhere, and we think if we can get him in an interrogation room, we can negotiate with him and potentially save lives. Ironically enough, a lot of these guys who taunt law enforcement end up singin' like Shania Twain as soon as we have them in custody, including our boy's hero, David Berkowitz."

She stopped then. Looked right at Darger and Loshak.

"I'd like to have the two of you on the rooftop across the street with the other half of the FBI SWAT team." She tapped the building on the map before she went on. "You'll be in good hands up there. I've got Fitch and a pair of snipers up there now, and they'll be expecting you. They were the team that spotted Huxley in the window."

Darger was surprised to hear that Fitch was still on the job. She expected him to go on leave after what happened with

Dobbins. But maybe what happened to Dobbins was precisely why he'd stayed. If Darger were in his shoes, she'd want to make damn sure they nailed the man who'd taken her friend's life.

The door burst open. All heads turned that way where Laboda stood in the doorway. His cheeks were flushed, and he was breathing hard, as if he'd just run a great distance.

"Just got word from the brother," he said. "He's at school, like we thought. Had his phone off until just now, being that he was in class."

Whispers hissed through the rest of the task force members huddled around the table.

"He also said we were right not to tell his mother," Laboda went on. "He thinks she'd cover for him, guilty or not."

"OK, people," Fredrick said. "You've got your assignments. Let's move out. We want everyone in position and ready to roll as soon as we get word on the warrant."

# CHAPTER 59

Darger's ballistic helmet sat on her lap as she rode across town in the back of the cruiser. She fidgeted in her seat, felt the awkward way the vest squeezed around her torso, squishing her abdomen like a corset.

She pulled at the armpits of the thing, fingers prying at one and then the other to no effect. Then she thought about asking Loshak to adjust the straps for her — an enthusiastic NYPD officer had pulled them too taut before they headed out — but looking over at her partner in the seat next to her, she thought better of it. An intense look occupied his features, eyes kind of zoned out, staring intently at nothing.

Instead she turned and stared out the window, watched the city blurring past — fifty shades of concrete. Glass and steel reaching up for the heavens, casting long shadows over everything below. Cars crowding every intersection. Pedestrians mobbing the sidewalk, all those people weaving around each other like ants swarming a dead bird.

Words from the journals echoed in her head as these images flickered by.

*You want to see peak humanity? Well, there it is. Just look at the bloodstains on the sidewalk.*

Pedestrians lurched along the sides of the car, pulsing with need. Hungry. Agitated. Darger tried to block out the words playing in her head.

*This is the idea that must be smashed, crushed, wiped off the face of the planet. And I will accomplish it by wiping away faces indeed, blowing them to little pieces.*

*Obliterated. Vaporized.*

She blinked a few times. Swallowed in a dry throat. But the words kept coming.

*The revolution will be etched into celebrity skin.*

Ahead, the rest of the law enforcement convoy stretched out as far as Darger could see. A snaking line of unmarked detective sedans and police cruisers pushing through the traffic, winding a tight path through the city. Almost like a funeral procession, she thought. In a way it was.

As they neared the building, a roadblock cut off the traffic around them. Wooden barriers stretched orange and white striped arms over the sidewalk, choking off the foot traffic as well, though some gawkers lined up along the perimeter to try to get a look.

They pulled up to the curb, brakes squealing faintly, car jerking to a stop, and the stillness of the ride ended abruptly.

Darger popped on her helmet and tightened the chin strap. Spilled out onto the sidewalk. Staggered a couple of steps.

Striding out of the car's air-conditioned comfort, she felt the humidity swell around her chest and legs all at once. Enveloping her. That city heat rising up from the concrete to grip her flesh.

The smell seemed to hit a second later — the clean scent inside the car replaced with a garbage stench out here on the street — the funk of juicy bags of trash cut with just a hint of a sharp sunblock odor.

The jarring change disoriented her for a few seconds, sucked her consciousness deeper inside of herself somehow, pulling her inward until it felt like she was looking out from a tunnel within her skull. Separate. Distant.

And then there were harsh voices and officers waving her on, funneling her toward the glass doors ahead. She fell in alongside Loshak and kept moving. Her mouth felt dry. Her pulse squished in her ears.

Though they were entering the building across the street from the soon-to-be-raided apartment high-rise, they did so through the rear of the structure, a block away from the raid target. The area in front of the mother's apartment would be kept clear until the SWAT teams were sent in to carry out the primary operation. Better to not tip him off.

If he was even still there.

Darger followed Loshak's lead through the glass doors. Potted plants reached leafy fronds over the furniture. Beat-up magazines crowded a coffee table. Everything swayed softly in the air conditioner's hissing wind. The chill clung to the backs of Darger's arms.

They got onto an elevator, and Loshak jabbed the button for the top floor. The doors closed, sealed them away from the world again, and the wind sound cut out to the faintest whoosh of the elevator car gliding upward.

Goose bumps rippled over Darger's skin as their car ascended. It was the quiet, she thought. The still moment growing unbearably tense. The tranquility somehow heightening the sense that all hell was about to break loose.

The elevator reached the top floor. Dinged. The doors slid open in slow motion.

From there, they pushed through a heavy steel door and climbed a set of concrete steps. Shade shrouded the dimly lit stairwell. Darger focused on the texture underfoot — cement painted glossy gray with black grip tape forming parallel lines on each tread.

Another big metal door squawked as Loshak elbowed the push bar and gave it a shove. It opened up to blinding sunlight, and they stepped out onto the roof.

Darger squinted. She could only see blurry contours at first, the dark of the bitumen roof shearing off against the impossible glow of the daylight. Various shapes huddled on the roof, jutting up from the black surface — air-conditioning units and the like, Darger assumed.

One of the shapes was moving funny, though. Looked like a tree branch wagging in the wind.

Then she blinked and everything sharpened into focus. It wasn't a tree branch. It was an arm.

Fitch was waving Darger and Loshak over to his position. He and two snipers were set up on the opposite side of the roof, kneeling to mostly conceal themselves behind the parapet. The CIRG agent had a laptop set up there, presumably to be able to watch the helmet cams as the strike team breached the apartment.

The blades of a helicopter whoomped overhead, a pounding sound that seemed to reverberate in Darger's head, out of time with her pulse. It must be part of the operation, she thought.

The agents made their way over to the others. Hot wind pushed on them with every step, an aggressive battering summer wind. Gusts that seemed angry. Wind this hot felt strange, Darger thought, like dragon's breath.

As they squatted into position near the others, the squad leader murmured something into a walkie-talkie, but Darger couldn't hear him over the sibilant blasts of wind. She realized after a second Fitch was talking about the helicopter.

"Someone tipped off the local news. Probably the mayor. He'd love to have footage of the SWAT boys kicking in the door plastered on every channel. Wants to look tough on crime with his reelection coming up. Law and order and all that."

He smiled at her, his sled dog eyes looking bright behind the clear visor of his helmet. He moved the walkie away from his mouth and spoke to her then, lifting his voice to be heard loud and clear.

"We got the warrant," he said. "They're about to go in."

# CHAPTER 60

Images twitched on the laptop screen. Darger watched over Fitch's shoulder as he clicked around to different body cams. Restlessly shifting from camera to camera even though the footage all looked roughly the same for now.

Black-clad men huddled in the back of an armored truck, something taut and nervous in their faces, in the way they carried themselves. Grim lines in their mouths, between their brows. Tension in the set of their shoulders.

Some flutter and jiggle to everything in the frame made it clear that the truck was in motion — rushing to the scene even now, rocketing over potholes and bumps in the road. That fluctuating quality in the video reminded Darger of ancient footage from the very first cameras — the black and white images all jerky and strange like a cartoon with frames missing.

Noise on the street below drew Darger's eyes away from the laptop screen. She peered over the parapet.

"Go time," Fitch muttered, half under his breath.

Three black trucks wheeled around the corner. Zipped over the asphalt. Skidded to a stop before the building.

Everything held still for a few heartbeats.

And then the cargo doors swung open on the back of each truck, and the men filed out. Anticipation seemed to waft off their upright backs and shoulders. Aggression, something like bloodlust entering the air, spreading, affecting Darger way up on the roof, a prickle over the back of her neck like rising hackles.

The chuff-chuff-chuff of the helicopter shifted overhead like a drum fill panned across stereo speakers. The percussive sound seemed to change pitch as it moved around, echoing funny in the hollow between the buildings, like the street was some steep valley made mostly of concrete and brick.

Darger glanced up. Squinted at the bright light above. Saw the news chopper banking overhead. Probably trying to get the money shot now, the trucks arriving, the best angle of the raid to come.

She turned her head back to the street in time to see the breach of the front door.

The first team had the Holmatro Door Blaster in place, waiting to fire. From this distance, it looked like a thick black bar extending across the door, simple, not unlike an anti-theft device stretching over a steering wheel. But Darger knew that just beyond that bar, the round pushing plate was flat against the door right beneath the deadbolt, even if she couldn't see it from here. The pneumatic pump would drive four tons of pushing force into the plate without a sound. It'd be like having a horse kick the deadbolt open, except with the power of an explosion.

The SWAT officers held quite still on the street. All the helmeted heads flicked back and forth between the officer next to the door and the commander kneeling next to the fender of the armored truck giving him hand signals.

Darger felt like she was floating above the scene. An observer. Weightless.

When the officer next to the door got the signal, he fired the Holmatro. The metal bar bucked once, and the door swung free. The only sound the device made was a faint thud when it clattered to the ground, its job complete.

The lead officer lurched for the building, the riot shield

strapped to his forearm forming a smooth wall that glided before him, his face pressed to the clear cutout in the matte black polyethylene armor. The shield was graded to withstand multiple shots from a .44 Magnum or .357 SIG, an impressive ballistic feat for something that weighed roughly ten pounds.

The rest of the officers filed behind him in something of a forced jog, bodies hunched, assault rifles cradled in their arms before them. They disappeared into the building's mouth one by one.

"First-floor hallway secure," a deep voice barked into the radio. The sound jarred Darger, making her realize how quiet the chatter had gotten for a bit there.

She turned to watch the monitor, where Fitch was still clicking around between cameras.

A narrow stairwell bobbed on the screen. Everything here rendered in shades of beige. Peeling wallpaper and floor alike.

Steps and risers scrolled endlessly upward like an ancient TV with the vertical hold broken. The frantic bouncing of the camera made Darger feel like she was watching some gritty police documentary, like COPS or something. After a second, she realized she basically was — live and in brilliant beige.

Yelling on the radio interrupted the thought. Multiple voices lifting, straining, tangling over each other.

"Down on the ground!"

"Get down! Now!"

"Hey! Hey! Face down! Face down!"

Fitch swore under his breath. Flicked to different cameras on the laptop until he found a piece of the excitement.

An older woman lay face down on the thin carpet of the hallway floor. Dyed black hair shorn close. Vivid blue shirt swaddling her torso, the sticklike arms coming out of her middle looking bony and out of proportion. Her pudgy middle trembled, lurching shaky breaths into her chest.

Two bags of garbage had plunked down on either side of her, and what looked like spaghetti sauce was trickling out of the mouth of one, red juice cascading over the yellow drawstrings and puddling on the floor. A miniature marinara waterfall.

Again the voices of the officers twisted over each other. Muddled and chaotic. Darger couldn't make out what was being said.

The SWAT officers helped the old woman up, her wild eyes flashing on the screen for just a second. Big and scared, pupils like sliced black olives. Then she disappeared into the door there, presumably shoved back into her apartment, out of the way.

The garbage remained face down on the carpet, the river of Newman's Own flowing freely.

"Second floor clear," a voice said finally.

The next few several floors went without a hitch. Within a few minutes, all six floors and the roof were secure. The streets outside were locked down as well, crawling with police, both SWAT and regular uniforms.

Now they'd send in the strike team.

Yet another group burst into the building, looking identical to the others. Riot shields out in front. Black tactical gear. Assault rifles. All swinging knees and elbows as they raced up the stairs, staying tighter in formation this time.

They clustered in front of the apartment door in question. Antsy. Shoulders swaying. Weight rocking from foot to foot. They looked like a high school football team about to rush out onto the field, crashing through some paper banner.

head. Do it. Now."

The prone figure put his hands on the back of his head.

The camera swung down. Finally gave a clear view of the perp — the back of his head, anyway.

Darger's eyes cataloged the features. Dark gray t-shirt. Navy sweatpants. Bare feet. Short brown hair. Average height. Slender build. It all fit.

It occurred to Darger that the hair was too dark and too short to be the brother's. Jesus. It was really him.

"It's him. We got him," the officer in the kitchen said. His voice had gone shaky with adrenaline, sounded tight coming out.

Heavy footsteps rushed into the room. Shuffled around in the small space between the fridge and the quartz overhang of the island.

More metallic sounds. More yelling.

"Rest of the place is clear," one voice said.

The camera angle made it hard to tell, but they must all be in the kitchen now. The entire strike team. Huddling. Crowding. A bulge of humanity jammed into the doorway. Boot treads making heavy sounds on the linoleum.

With an overkill of M4s pointed at the facedown figure, one of the officers stepped forward at last. Straddled the perp's back. He looked like an oversized toddler asking his dad for a pony ride. Instead, he wrenched the arms down one at a time and cuffed him. The click of the cuffs seemed to signal some release of tension in the room.

The agent administering the handcuffs stepped back. Big smile splitting his face. All teeth beneath the visor.

His grin spread to the others. Washed over the whole room. And they all leaned forward to look down at the man.

He looked smaller now. Squirming a little on the kitchen floor. Sweatpants fallen down enough to show just the top edge of butt crack.

"Fuck yeah!" the arresting agent said, high-fiving another. This too spread among the ranks.

After more excited chatter, they finally got the perp to his feet, a pair of officers looping a gloved hand into each of his armpits and lifting in unison.

As they swung him around, his face filled the laptop screen at last. Wide eyes blinking rapid-fire. His grim expression looked, Darger thought, quite a bit like the photograph on his driver's license. Feeble. Nauseous. Eyes all wet-looking. Like he had something hard wedged deep in his throat.

Except this wasn't Tyler Huxley.

# CHAPTER 61

A heavy feeling entered Darger's chest. Some leaden injection that sank down into her gut. Solidified there. Settled. Rooted her to the ground again.

No more soaring exhilaration. No more thrill of the hunt. No triumph of victory.

Huxley was one step ahead of them. Again.

She chewed her bottom lip. Tried to fight off the flashes of the explosion replaying in her head. That flickering death livestreamed on the laptop screen. Dobbins squatted down to get at the paper beneath the shoebox under the bathroom sink. Breathing one second. And then the flash and the bang, and he was gone. Gone. A curtain of black smoke spiraling over the frame.

Angry voices barked on the radio. Irritation plain in every syllable. The ends of the words bitten off. Chewed. Swallowed.

Word spread by way of profanity-laced radio chatter that the man they'd cuffed in the kitchen was Huxley's cousin from Ohio visiting his aunt in the big city. He'd come to town for what everyone had thought would be Tyler's funeral.

"Should we keep the building locked down for now?" one of the voices said on the radio.

Darger thought it was Laboda, but she wasn't sure.

"The fuck for?" Fredrick said. Her voice sounded gruffer than before. Tired.

"Well, uh… the light in the background of the video. Way I figure it, that'd shine in any of the windows around here, right? He could be holed up in one of the other apartments. Not hiding out at home, maybe, but somewhere nearby."

The radio chatter went quiet for a beat. Then a heavy breath rattled in the speaker.

"Maybe. That's smart. I mean, if the light in the video is even what we thought it was…"

Darger felt a twinge of blame. Was this her fuck up? Had she been wrong about the flickering light? She'd been so sure. Felt such satisfaction at figuring Huxley out.

Fredrick was still talking.

"The problem is we've only got a warrant for the mom's place, and we can't have a small army of SWAT officers locking down a couple city blocks indefinitely."

"Yeah. Shit."

To Darger's right, Loshak stood and stretched. His head looked small atop the elongated neck, like a featherless baby bird straining for its wad of regurgitated worm. She could hear creaking sounds coming from his back, a sequence of vertebrae cracking like knuckles. Normally, she might have made a joke. Something about how the old man's body sounded more and more like a rickety wooden ship every day. But nothing seemed funny at the moment.

She followed his lead. Straightened to her full height and tried to loosen her tense muscles. After huddling behind its concrete cover for so long, it seemed strange to rise up over the parapet. It made her feel exposed. Vulnerable.

Some of the strike team had spilled out onto the street now. Their formerly cocky body language sagged into slumped shoulders and hung heads as the confusion set in, the anticlimax of it all.

"Back to the drawing board, I guess," Loshak said, adjusting his helmet again. "Feels like he's close, though, doesn't it?"

Darger swiveled her head. Eyes scanning up and down all the buildings on the block. The bomber might be behind any one of the windows facing this little section of the cityscape.

Then again, maybe not. He could be miles from here. Could be anywhere.

The pinwheel turned over and over on the balcony across the way, jutting out of its potted plant. It was settled partially in the shade now, so the motes of light kicking off it weren't as intense as before. She stared at the neighboring apartments, squinting her eyes down as if it might give her the ability to see through the walls.

A flicker of movement caught her eye, but then she realized it was just a plastic bag tangled in the scaffolding that blocked off the row of apartments two down from Huxley's mother's place.

And then Darger was lurching forward. Grabbing the radio out of Fitch's hands. Speaking into it before she even knew what she'd say.

"Vacant apartments," Darger said. "Could we get a warrant to check the vacant apartments on this block? It's just these buildings right here that have a clear view of the light source. And how many vacant apartments would there be with windows on this side? A handful or less?"

Another prolonged silence. This time a deep chuckle rattled the speaker instead of a sigh.

"You think he's squatting, huh?" Fredrick said. "OK. That's smart. I'll get someone to contact the landlords for the buildings here. We might not even need a warrant if we can get permission from the building owners to search just the vacant apartments, but we'll run it up to the judge anyway. Cover all our bases."

Just then a loud bang drew Darger's eyes sharply to her left. Wrenched her out of the conversation.

A pale blue rectangle thudded against a concrete wall on the roof next door. The steel door shivered there like a tuning fork.

And then *he* emerged.

Tyler Huxley stepped into the doorway and looked both ways. His eyes seemed to snap to Darger's for a split second. Locking there. Fastening.

Then he turned and raced across the rooftop. Running away from her. Tennis shoes bounding up from the black rubber membrane coating the top of the building.

When he reached the end of the roof, he stepped up onto the stone ledge and leaped over the edge.

# CHAPTER 62

Fitch grabbed the radio from Darger. Growled into it. Explained what they'd seen.

But Darger couldn't hear him. Not really.

She blinked. Twice. Stared at the empty space where Huxley had been.

Nothing. Nothing. Just a stone edge cleaving off into the open, into the sky. A straight concrete line separating form from void.

*Did he... Could he just...*

Her chest shuddered. She sucked in a breath. Felt hot wind on her teeth, dry air roiling in the hollow of her throat. Realized that her mouth was open. Jaw unhinged.

And then she was moving. Rushing to the edge of the building. Stopping short at the thigh-high parapet wall there.

She still couldn't see him. Just that naked rock edge where he'd launched himself into the abyss from the rooftop next door.

Next her gaze drifted closer. She looked at the gap. It was about five feet to the next building, and the roof there was a few feet lower. Manageable.

Finally her eyes veered down all the way. Speared the emptiness between the buildings. Peered into the alley below.

A collection of shimmering mud puddles looked back at her like twenty eyes. The open dumpster next to them gaping like an open mouth. It all seemed tiny from up here. Ant farm features.

She backed up a few steps. Needed to get a running start.

Just as Loshak yelled, "Don't do it!" she moved. Lunged forward. Launched herself onto the parapet. Kicked off. Hurled herself into the breach.

A floating feeling came over her. Weightless. Adrift.

Wind blowing. Gravity sucking.

She kept her eyes up. Aimed up at the target, not at the ground.

The sky looked huge before her. A vast emptiness that stretched up, up, and away.

The wind a loud whisper in her ears, drowning out everything.

At last her vision wheeled downward. She saw the emptiness of the alley give way to the stone parapet, give way to the black sheen of the rooftop.

She soared over it. Easily cleared the gap.

And then the black terrain came rushing up at her.

She hit down. Hands first. Then feet. Rubbery roof hot against her skin.

Her ankles flexed from the impact. The momentum pushing her forward, off her feet.

She angled herself to the side. Rough landing on elbow and hip.

She rolled. Unblinking. The world tumbled around her — the view from inside a clothes dryer.

Light and dark. Roof and sky.

And then she stopped. Pushed herself up onto hands and knees. Took a few deep breaths. Eyes blinking down at the inky membrane.

Heat rose from the black surface. Coiled around her calves and wrists. Radiated to touch her chin and cheeks.

A couple of thuds landed on each side of her. Fitch and one

of the snipers. The second sniper clomped down a beat later.

Fitch lifted his head. His grin looked tilted. A crooked line beneath his visor. Ecstatic.

He chuckled then and clapped Darger on the shoulder.

"Goddamn, Agent Darger. I'd heard some of the stories, but…" he said. Then he turned to face the others and lifted his voice into a bellow. "Did you guys fucking see that? Let's go!"

They got to their feet. Dusted themselves off. Gray clouds wafted up from Darger's jacket like smoke.

Loshak spoke up from behind them.

"I'll just, you know, take the elevator down."

Darger turned. Saw him standing at the edge of the wall. One leg up on the parapet, though the knee was a little wobbly. He pulled his foot down from the ledge and stumbled backward, chuckling nervously to himself.

Then she swiveled back to where Huxley had leaped. Darted that way. Crossed the spongy rubber coating of this roof.

Felt it give under the balls of her feet. A little melted from the heat, she thought. Soft now like cream cheese spread over a rubbery bagel.

She reached the next ledge, the others alongside her. Together they peered over the edge.

Her eyes dipped low to check out the ground first this time. Another alley. Empty. What looked like steam rolled out of a vent down there, the streets themselves exhaling something toxic.

Then she scanned the next roof. Also empty. Shit.

She chewed her lip. Her right brain measuring, checking angles, doing rooftop geometry about another leap.

The next roof was lower still. Another ten feet down. It was a longer jump, though. Fifteen feet or so. Maybe twenty. But the height advantage made it doable, she thought.

"Son of a bitch," Fitch said.

Darger saw his arm flick up out of the corner of her eye. She looked where he was pointing.

Huxley was on the fire escape of the lower building, racing down the metal staircase. His neck snapped up as though he sensed them, his lizard brain craning his skull to point his eyes straight at them.

He stopped running. Froze there a second. Head looking up and then down. He was still a good fifty feet from the asphalt of the alley below. Maybe more.

Darger swallowed in a dry throat.

*Jesus, is he thinking about jumping from here? He'll shatter his legs like candy canes.*

Instead Huxley dove to his right. Hurled himself into an open apartment window there.

Fitch gasped. Spitty sounds whistling between his top and bottom teeth.

The bomber's torso disappeared into the opening. Swallowed up. But his waist caught on the windowsill.

His legs dangled there a second. Wriggling. Squirming.

And then the void sucked them inside like two spaghetti noodles.

# CHAPTER 63

Loshak stepped into the stainless steel chamber of the elevator. Jabbed the LOBBY button on the panel and watched the opaque plastic light up around the letters, glowing that pink-orange shade of salmon flesh.

Then he stepped back. Nestled his shoulders back against the wall.

The elevator door slowly shut, and a second later the box seemed to suck downward. Loshak tilted his head to watch the floor numbers count down in slow motion.

Part of him thought he should be embarrassed for not making the leap along with the others. Embarrassed that he'd even warned Darger not to do it. But deep down he knew he had nothing to be embarrassed about. He was an old man. Even in his prime, he'd been no elite athlete — always more brains than brawn. He knew that. He had no problem leaving all that rooftop chase stuff to the young hot shots. Anyway, the elevator was air-conditioned.

He tapped his fingernails against the steel handrail as gravity slowly slurped the elevator car downward. Sharp metallic clicks ringing out. The cold metal felt good against his skin after being exposed to the sun.

Then he thought about what he was doing. A handrail? In a public building? Probably covered with sneeze residue and traces of fecal matter.

He ripped his hands away from the metal and rubbed them on his Kevlar vest. Wished he had one of Spinks' moist towelettes handy.

When the elevator hit the ground floor, the doors opened and Loshak hustled through the lobby. He weaved around black leather furniture and moved for the brightness beyond the glass, eyes already locked on the SWAT trucks huddled outside.

He pushed through the front doors. Raced over the sidewalk. As he stepped down from the curb, his foot plunged ankle-deep into a pothole, soaking his sock and the cuff of his pant leg with muddy water.

"Shit," he muttered to himself, arms flailing in frustration.

OK. Maybe *now* he should be embarrassed.

He kept moving. Shoe making a sloshing noise with each step, leaving a trail of sodden footprints on the blacktop.

He zipped toward a cluster of black-clad SWAT officers who looked vaguely authoritative. One lifted a radio — Loshak realized it was Agent Fredrick — and then he heard Fitch's deep voice squawk from its speaker.

"Subject just entered a window in the apartment complex over here. Corner of Sanford and Bowne. We're in pursuit."

The SWAT officers all lurched to life then. Moving toward the building in question.

Agent Fredrick did a double take when she saw Loshak coming along.

"Agent Loshak. I assumed you went with the others." She studied him for a moment, frowning. "Why don't you take off your helmet and vest?"

Loshak only stared at her outstretched hand. Christ. Was he really just a useless old man now? Ready to be put out to pasture?

He imagined them snickering behind his back as he'd strapped into his gear earlier. *Look at old man Loshak. Still going through the motions.*

Then Fredrick held out a headset.

"We're setting up a temporary command center at the 109th precinct, a few blocks from here. Our raid is turning into a chase, and I could use a contact there helping to keep things coordinated. Someone with easy access to maps, satellite feeds from the news chopper. That kind of thing. Hopefully we won't need it, but now that this thing has gone mobile, we've got to be ready to change gears on the fly."

OK. That made sense. Loshak nodded along with the words, trading his tactical helmet for the proffered headset.

"I'm on my way."

# CHAPTER 64

The old lady ripped wads of wet laundry out of the washer and shoved them into the dryer. Socks. Underwear. A couple of ratty towels.

The TV blared in the living room, getting louder as Burt cranked the volume. Some newscaster babble practically screaming. Distorting as it pushed the speakers to their limits. She huffed and then yelled to be heard above it.

"Burt! Instead of turning the volume on the TV all the way up, why don't you adjust your damn hearing aid for once?"

After a beat the old man's usual refrain sounded out through the apartment.

"WHAT?"

She closed her eyes. Squeezed a clump of dewy socks tighter, hands balling into fists, a little moisture dribbling down onto the open dryer lid. Wet socks. A makeshift stress ball, she thought.

The volume on the TV lowered slightly.

"Suz?" he called. "You say something?"

Damn him. It was one thing if he wanted to go through life deaf, but the grandkids were coming today. He should be present for that.

Suzy was about to repeat her hearing aid request when the man crawled through the window.

He sort of fell into the room as much as anything. Slithering over the sill on his belly. Balling up on the linoleum floor like some animal that walked on all fours. Untangling his limbs and picking himself up.

He looked right into her face. Eyes wide. Almost innocent-looking.

Suzy shuffled back from the gaping maw of the dryer. Sank back toward the doorway. Dropped a few of the socks as she did.

He stepped forward. Just one step.

Instinctively she threw a wet sock at him. Flung it forward like a chest pass in basketball. Pushing with both hands.

It flopped against his chest. Fell to the floor with a limp splat. Left a moist mark on his t-shirt.

They both stopped. Dipped their heads to stare at the soggy sock imprint on his shirt. Then stared at each other.

Suzy's jowls quivered. The soft skin along her chin and neck shaking like a Jell-O mold.

Her voice seemed to grow inside of her. Building up like steam in her chest. Rising. Taking a surprisingly long time to actually reach the surface and spill free.

"Blast him, Burt! It's a prowler!"

She could just see her husband out of the corner of her eye. Still perched in front of the blaring TV.

He didn't exactly spring to her rescue.

The old man shifted in his La-Z-Boy. Cocked his head to one side and then the other. He lifted his voice in that way only someone hard of hearing does.

"WHAT?"

The old lady backpedaled through the kitchen. Hands clutching her chest. Wads of loose skin dangled from her upper arms like a pair of turkey waddles.

Huxley stalked forward. Slow and steady. Hands up. Every movement delicate. Almost like he was afraid to spook her. Afraid she might lurch for some shotgun just out of sight.

"Burt! It's a creeper! Cold cock him!"

The old man tilted his head again. Brought his middle finger to his ear. Twiddled with the hearing aid lodged there.

"You say something, Suz?"

"My God, Burt. Do something! He means to ravage me."

"No," Huxley said, a hint of disgust in his voice.

The prowler picked up speed then. Turned sideways to sidle past the old woman. Slipping through the doorway.

He reached the open beyond her. Darted across the living room. Hurdled the coffee table. Let himself out the front door and into the hallway.

Burt looked from the open doorway to his wife and back.

He fingered the remote control on his arm rest. Muted the TV.

"Who da hell was that?" he said, his voice finally approaching a normal volume.

Suzy picked up the newspaper from the coffee table. Rolled it up. Swatted Burt on the head a few times like he was a misbehaving dog.

"You idiot!"

Burt held his hands out, trying to fend her off, but she kept on the attack.

Cords stood out on the old woman's neck. Lower teeth exposed.

"Wait," Burt said, no longer dodging the rolled-up newspaper she wielded.

He sat forward in his chair. Pointed at the TV screen. "It's him."

The photo from Huxley's driver's license hovered over the left shoulder of the news anchor. A shadowy border ran around the perimeter of the picture. Made him look all the more sinister. Jagged red letters declared him the "Celebrity Bomber" under the photo.

The old couple read the closed captioning, a stream of text crawling beneath the newscaster's chin. It described the attempted SWAT raid underway. Announced that they'd now go to live footage of the scene in progress.

They watched in eerie silence as the screen cut away to the hovering helicopter cam. It soared over their block. Drifted in slow motion. Angled its lens down at the rows of asphalt and concrete.

The bright and hollow sky formed a glowing border against the concrete edge, the line where the towers gave way to the heavens. The wind whipped all the flags around. Everything on the ground shimmied a little from the moving air, but the helicopter's shot stayed smooth like a Steadicam.

The SWAT trucks still huddled in their positions in front of the apartment building. But the officers themselves were racing down the street on foot, black-clad and helmeted so they looked like ants with assault rifles swinging before them.

Burt stood. Pointed.

"Suz. That's… that's our street. That's our building. Right there. They're… they're running this way."

Suzy clucked. She whapped Burt on the back of the head with the newspaper again.

"The goddamn bomber was in our apartment, you dumb son of a bitch. I told you to cold cock him, didn't I? You could have been a hero! But noooo—"

A series of thuds behind them interrupted her rant. Stopped her rolled copy of the Times in midair.

Their heads swiveled back toward the kitchen doorway. Watching. Listening.

It sounded like more thudding in the laundry room. Hands and feet clattering on the linoleum.

"Another bomber?" Burt whispered.

Suzy whapped him again.

A man and a woman appeared in the doorway of the laundry room. The man was huge and dressed like the SWAT officers on the TV. The woman wore dress clothes and a bulletproof vest that said 'FBI' across the chest. More thumps sounded behind them.

"Where'd he go?" the FBI agent said, her voice flat.

Both old people pointed at the open door.

# CHAPTER 65

Darger didn't wait for further explanation. She bolted for the door. Tore it open. Led the small brigade of SWAT officers out of the apartment.

They piled out there into the hall and stopped. Held still.

In unison all their heads swung to the right and then the left. Scanning. Listening.

No signs of Huxley either way.

The rows of apartment doors stretched out before her. Seemed endless in this moment.

Darger swallowed. Felt some uneven lump bob in her throat. Fresh tension settled over her neck and shoulders.

The speed and noise and relentless drive of the chase had given way to this — a quiet moment of uneasiness, of confusion. Her skin crawled in the eerie quiet of this vacant hallway.

Huxley could have ducked into any one of these apartment doors. Or he could have hit the stairs and made his way two flights down by now.

Fitch muttered something into the radio. Talking low and fast, like maybe he didn't want Huxley listening in if he were near.

Hopefully the cavalry was in the process of surrounding the building already. Blocking the exits. Perhaps securing the ground floor. Of course, Darger knew it was optimistic to think that. They'd probably just now gotten confirmation of the address. But maybe they'd make it in time.

Without speaking, the crew fanned out to search both ends of the hall. Darger and Fitch moving left. The others heading right.

Cautious steps jabbed forward. Made soft scuffing sounds on the thin layer of carpet out here.

Heads swiveled. Eyes scanned everywhere.

A quiet intensity seemed to occupy this time and space like a trembling wave in the air. Darger could feel its prickle on her skin like static electricity lifting the hair on her arms.

She listened for any kind of footfalls in the distance but heard nothing. The carpet would deaden the sound some, but if Huxley were running, she would hear it. If he were even on this floor anymore.

"Stairs are this way," Fitch said. "Let's roll."

As she turned, Darger's mind whirred. The idea that Huxley might barricade himself in an apartment flashed there once more. She could picture it. Him holed up in a random unit, huddling behind some futon, his hand cupped around some old lady's mouth even now.

But no. It wouldn't make sense. Once the SWAT officers surrounded the building, he'd be trapped like a rat in a cage. No way out. No hope for escape.

Huxley was too smart to let that happen. Too crafty. His only hope was to get to the ground — to get out — before the backup could arrive and secure the exits. And he would know that better than anyone.

Fitch used one massive forearm to bash the heavy door of the stairwell open. Funneled them into an off-white stairwell that smelled like sawdust. Stale. Shaded and dingy.

And then they were on the steps. Feet pounding down the declining slope. Racing, racing.

Their footsteps clattered louder as they picked up speed. Echoed in the narrow stairwell. Heavy boots clomping against the laminate stair treads. All those clapping sounds tumbling over each other like swelling applause.

They wrapped around a landing onto another staircase. The battering rhythm of their footsteps changed with the turn, slowed, then settled back into a galloping groove.

Hot breath plumed against Darger's teeth. Heart hammering in her chest.

The careening chase had flushed her face with heat. Plumped beads of sweat along her hairline, sent them streaming into her brow, down over her cheekbones.

She curled around the protruding handrail at the next landing. Another floor down. Closer now. Closer and closer.

Two more staircases put them on the ground floor. The door to the lobby jolted out of the way at Darger's touch.

And then they ran toward daylight. The sun gleamed into the glass doors at the front of the place, lighting up the fronds of potted plants and stretching glowing patches over the cement tile floor.

The light was blinding after being closed off in the murky stairwell.

Darger could see movement outside the building, but she couldn't make out the details. Just a shapeless writhing in the glare.

She didn't slow. Didn't think. She ran for the door, raced for the brightness. Pushed two sets of glass doors open. Found herself vented out onto three concrete steps.

And then she saw what was writhing.

A crowded city sidewalk lurched and throbbed with pedestrians. Bustling people packed shoulder to shoulder, the tightly jammed bodies snaking past each other in all directions. Everyone in a hurry. Everyone preoccupied.

Cars whooshed past. Horns blared. All the voices on the street collected into a many-throated drone. Reminded Darger of standing near a cornfield, hearing all the bugs trill and warble together, a perpetual call, endless and meaningless.

None of the heads turned to face the small mob of law enforcement gathered on the concrete steps. Even with the rifles in their hands, no one noticed them.

This was New York after all. No one cared.

Darger scanned the crowd. Watched the bodies cluster at the corner, waiting for traffic to stop. Watched the torsos twist and tilt and jockey for position in the throng. Sharks swimming in their constant swells.

She looked for his face, for his tightly cropped dark hair, for his red t-shirt. Eyes darting, flitting, fluttering over the roving horde. Waiting for something to pop out. Anything.

Too many faces. Too many people.

Huxley wasn't there.

# CHAPTER 66

Darger pushed into the teeming mass of humanity. Felt like she was wading into an angry sea, fighting her way through the current.

Waves of human bodies flung at her. A surging flood of knees and elbows that kept crashing, thrashing, swerving, crushing. Limbs flailing every which way.

The sounds of the mob grew louder as she moved. Car engines growling. Brakes squeaking. Rubber soles pattering at the pavement, scuffing here and there.

Voices chattered everywhere. Cacophony. Something aggressive in it all. Hard voices. Strident tones. Like you had to project an edge at all times to make it out here, to even stand a chance.

Darger waded deeper into the crush. Slipped through the mosh pit. She thought if she could get to the curb, she might be able to stand on a bench or newspaper box and get a better view, but progress was slow.

The collective body odor seemed leathery to Darger up close. Animal skin. The stench rising from all those bodies to cook in direct sunlight. A little smoky. A little tarry. Mingling with the funk of that faint garbage smell this neighborhood always had.

Fitch screamed into his radio to get backup here pronto. The crowd noise kept swallowing him up, so Darger could only make out about half his words. Something about getting eyes on Huxley with the news chopper before they lost him for good.

That was smart, Darger thought. Turning the nuisance news

helicopter into another set of eyes? Maybe the media could do them some good for once.

Her own eyes drifted up to the little slice of blue between the towering buildings, scanned the hollow sky, just for a second. Nothing there yet.

The crew of law enforcement split up again. Half the party veering left and half veering right. All of them weaving through the foot traffic, the various pedestrians forming wedges that splintered the group further and further.

But that was OK, Darger thought. They could cover more ground that way. Get different vantage points from within the mob.

Fitch started yelling at the crowd. Waving his assault rifle in front of himself, though he kept the barrel angled up. That seemed to part small sections of the mob, but not enough to matter. They'd need more than the handful of them to manage this many pedestrians. Hell, they'd need a dozen or two just to get everyone's attention.

When she finally parted the last line of the throng, Darger clambered up onto a blue USPS collection box, holding onto a lamppost next to it to balance on the rounded top. She turned back toward the crowd.

Her eyes flitted over faces and torsos. She sought red above all else now. The bright red of his t-shirt would be the easiest way to spot him, she thought. Somewhere in this mess of people, it waved even now like a bull fighter's cape.

She saw scarlet hats, brick red shirts and shorts. But she didn't see Huxley.

She hopped down from the mailbox and kept going. Squeezing through gaps in the mob. Pressing her body against sweaty strangers when she had to. Using her arm to pry openings between torsos where none existed. Levering idiots apart. Creating space.

Her heart punched in her chest. Beat so hard she could feel the vibration of it thrumming in her neck, in her jaw.

But she willed herself to stay calm, to not let the frantic gnawing in her gut overtake her emotions and make her overlook something. Vigilance. Attention to detail. Focus. She needed these things now more than ever.

Soon Darger heard the chuff-chuff-chuff again. That weird accelerated backbeat of the helicopter's rotor pounding up above. She glanced skyward. Saw the drifting black thing, its blades slicing at the air over and over.

Something metallic clanged behind her. She turned in time to see Fitch jump up on the mailbox as if it were a hickory stump. He cupped a hand next to his mouth and yelled.

"News chopper has a possible sighting. He's heading northwest from our position."

Fitch took a second to orient himself, glancing at the sky, pivoting his arm like the hand of a clock until it was pointed in the correct direction. He jumped down, and they all headed that way.

They knifed through an increasingly tight cluster of pedestrians. The throng seemed to thicken as they drew up on the intersection, all those people waiting to cross the street. Darger felt like she was a salmon swimming upstream.

In the distance she saw a big group of additional SWAT officers crossing one of the barriers, moving in from where the raid had taken place. Guns raised. Aggressive moves. The black clothing made them look like swarming wasps. They seemed to be having more luck getting some control of the crowd. The rabble backing up, dispersing, retracting into itself like reversed footage of a spreading puddle.

She realized then that her hands were shaking. Fingers trembling. Palms clammy and tingling. The adrenaline spike of the chase had somehow intensified with all the people around. All those faces in the crowd. All the bumping and jostling for position.

Fitch and the others tried to yell for the people to clear out of the way again, but it was no use. Too much noise. Too much confusion.

And then she saw him. Just a flash of red at first, and then a glimpse of his face.

She got lower, using her legs to push through another clump of torsos. Weaved around a baby stroller. Stepped around a black fire hydrant with a silver top.

He seemed to sense that she was closing on him. Picking up speed himself.

She watched him get hung up. Some hard-hatted construction worker with shoulders about a man and a half wide blocked his way. They did the awkward back and forth dance before Huxley finally got around him. That got her to within a few paces.

And then the bomber spilled out into the street. Running. Not waiting for the light like everyone else.

Tires screeched. A cab jerked to a stop just shy of the collision. Its nose brushed at Huxley's legs, and the bomber's palms slapped flat against the hood for a second before he ran onward.

The cabbie shook his fist out the window. Yelled "Fuck-ah-you!" in a thick accent Darger couldn't identify.

Darger, too, broke out into the open of the crosswalk. Gaining on him. She could feel Fitch pull up alongside her.

Huxley entered another mess of people on the other side of the street, but her eyes were locked onto that red shirt now. They had him. She could feel it, little motes of excitement bubbling in her head like a gin fizz.

Her confidence shook when she saw the tunnel mouth taking shape ahead.

The entrance to the subway was like a gaping mouth in the sidewalk. Human bodies seemed to froth at the delta of the thing, some bubbling out onto the street, some being sucked underground.

Huxley hit the stairs at a dead sprint and dipped out of view.

# CHAPTER 67

Darger clenched her teeth. Felt her molars gritting. Jaw flexing in staccato bursts.

She drew up on the stairs without slowing. Hoping to catch a glimpse of him as she peered down the staircase. No luck.

She flew down the stairs. Fitch and the rest picking out paths on either side of her. All of them bumping into angry New Yorkers as they descended. Feet clapping against the cement.

"Watch it, moron!" a middle-aged office worker yelled after getting shouldered out of the way, shaking his briefcase around for dramatic effect. Then he turned. Eyes going wide when he saw that it was a SWAT officer rushing past. Going wider still as they drifted lower and locked onto the rifle in the officer's hands. Instinctively he covered his crotch with the briefcase, no longer using it as a prop to express rage. His voice got tight and quiet, and he muttered, "Oh, shit. Uh… sorry."

"FBI," Fitch yelled periodically. "Get out the fuckin' way!"

The light changed as they got down to the concrete floor underground. Yellow. Artificial. Darger realized that it was somehow always night down here. Always.

They jumped the turnstile. Elbowed through more weirdos.

The ground opened up before them at last. Not so packed in the space beyond the gate. Crisp clicks and slaps sounded from their footfalls, echoing about the larger concrete chamber like bats.

They kept moving. Swiveling their heads for any sign of Huxley.

He couldn't slip away now, after they'd been so close. Could he?

A spindly homeless man leaped up from a slab of cardboard he'd been sitting on. A knit cap shrugged down low on his brow. Fingerless gloves jutted out of a long plaid coat that looked not of this century. Something black and cloudy like soot rimmed his wild eyes. Gibberish spewed at top volume from his lips.

"Hurry, hurry about. Coppers gonna cop, way I figure it. Strike like copperheads, you know? Snake in the grass. Gas, Grass, or Ass. Nobody rides free. Not in this life, bub."

He chuckled as he lurched into their path. Bumping Darger. Sending her ricocheting into one of the SWAT officers. All of them banging into each other like bowling pins.

The bum's voice went louder still. More shrill. He threw his hands up over his head.

"I am not resisting arrest! I am not resisting arrest!"

Still he jumped into them, thrashing and bouncing like he was trying to start a circle pit at a rock concert.

Fitch gave him a shove, and the guy flew back like he was on roller skates, barely managing to keep his feet. Darger and all the SWAT people rushed past, and Fitch dusted his hands off theatrically as he rejoined them.

"Little crowd control trick I learned at the academy."

"Huh. They didn't teach that one when I was there," Darger said.

With the homeless guardian dispatched, Darger's focus returned to the growing crowd near the tracks. Eyes once again scanning bodies. Seeking out shades of red among the shirts.

And then she saw it — a glimmer of crimson visible through a gap in the crowd.

Her steps grew choppy as she thrust herself that way. Bulldozed through a family of tourists in matching I HEART

Instead it was this rectangle of wood that stood in their way. The thinnest barrier between them and the objective, between them and the end of all of this.

Another Door Blaster was fastened between the lock and the doorknob. The circular plate bucked the door with its silent explosion. This time kicking up splinters where it snapped the wood around the deadbolt and tore the door out of the jamb. Made the heavy oak thing look like some plastic toy.

The SWAT team rushed into the opening. Single file. Face first into the breach, into the danger. Angry. Zealous. Exuberant.

The edge of the splintered door got clipped by the edge of the riot shield. Bounced off the wall once and then stayed the hell back, out of the way.

The last of the men charged through, his camera showing the backs of the others as they parted. Darting all directions. Left. Right. Straight ahead.

Fitch switched cameras in time to see the perp belly-flopping onto the linoleum in the kitchen. The body cam bobbed then as the SWAT officer ducked back.

A bowl plunged out of the perp's hands as he went down. Dive-bombing alongside him. Broth and noodles flung everywhere. A strange ramen wave arcing in the air. Slapping down on the floor.

Bowl and spoon shrieking as they hit down. Clattering. Crashing.

All seemed quiet for a beat after that. Darger could hear the breath of the officer wearing the body cam. Could hear the tiny metallic sounds of his hands adjusting their grip on the M4. And then the yelling started.

"Freeze! Hands on your head. Hands on the back of your

NY t-shirts. Slithered her hands past the last few bodies standing in her way to grab the blood-red garment.

Fingers scrabbling over soft knit fabric. Grasping. Balling into fists as she gripped as hard as she could.

He jerked. Tried to pull free. But she had him now. She had him.

She spun him around. Pulled him close. The red shade of the shirt was just right.

But it wasn't him.

The scowling face of a teenage girl glared at her instead. Mouth puckered. Eyebrows knitted together in anger.

"Sorry," Darger said, letting go and turning back the way she'd come. Breathing heavy now. Eyes swiveling everywhere. Taking in the panorama as she whirled all the way around.

People in all directions. Big and small. Young and old. Everyone moving and talking and jostling.

Too many people.

She backtracked a few paces. Found Fitch and some of the others.

"Got anything?" Fitch said.

Darger just shook her head.

The big man heaved out a sigh.

"Goddamn it. We know he's here somewhere."

They stood and watched the rabble for a second. Powerless. Hopeless.

A train pulled up. Another complication.

All those milling people clustered tighter near the tracks as the subway cars slowly eased to a halt before them.

Darger started in among them, not wanting to get blocked out. Her arms wrenching forward, reaching out before her almost like they were swimming through the humanity.

The doors popped open, and waves of people vented from the train, runnels of them flowing through the mob. Some members of the SWAT team bulled their way into the crowd. Tried to shout at people to make room, let them through.

The people in front of Darger started filing on board. The crowd pouring into the metal tube. Disappearing.

Darger felt her pulse banging in her neck again. Unsure of what to do next.

"Do we think he's getting on the train?" Fitch said.

Shallow breaths rushed in and out of her. Chest shuddering. That heat still flushing her face, even in the cool of this underground chamber.

"I don't know," Darger said. "Maybe."

"Damn it," Fitch hissed. "I don't want to split up, but we might have to."

The last of the commuters had gotten on board, though plenty of people still lingered around the tracks. Darger's eyes looked everywhere, looked everywhere.

Nothing.

"We've got to get some of our people on the train," Fitch said.

The two sides of the subway door in front of them started sliding closed. Fitch shoved his arm in the gap before it could fasten shut. He gripped the black rubber on each side and pried it open. Waved two of his men through even as the car jolted into motion.

"You two search the train, yeah?" he called after them. "We'll keep an eye on things here at the station."

Darger nodded. Watched the pair of SWAT officers jump on the train just as it slid away. It rattled down the tracks, building speed, and then it was gone. Sucked into the tunnel.

As soon as the sound of the train had faded away to nothing, Darger saw him.

The red shirt came clear as he detached himself from the crowd and walked toward the front of the platform. Something determined in his stride.

Darger lunged that way, Fitch and a handful of the others right with her. All those feet pattering at the cement, skittering to get around commuters.

Huxley moved right up to the ledge, the place where the gray cement gave way to bright yellow warning paint, everything pocked with those bumpy treads to avoid anyone slipping this close to the rails.

Darger bumped into an old man. The collision turned her some, but she didn't break her line of sight. She steadied the man, putting both hands on his shoulders until he was rooted to the ground again, and kept going.

She broke into the open. Closing on him.

Huxley jumped off the platform. Disappeared behind the concrete edge as he landed on the tracks. Plunged out of view.

# CHAPTER 68

Darger froze there, fifteen feet shy of the edge. Some strange pulse fluttering in her head like a strobe light.

Everything felt slowed down. The fluorescent bulbs buzzed overhead, their insectile hum seeming to grow louder in this prolonged hush. It echoed funny in this concrete box. Rebounding off the walls. Shuddering in the hollow. Made the chamber feel empty. Tomb-like.

She blinked. Thoughts finally awakening in her head.

*I can't let him get away. Can't.*

She charged up to the edge of the platform. Gazed down into the shaded spot below. It took a second for the contours there to sharpen into focus.

And there he was.

Huxley bolted down the center of the track. Stepping from plank to plank, the wooden railroad ties thudding out hollow sounds. There was a hitch in his step — maybe he'd busted his ankle when he jumped down — but he was moving pretty good. Advancing toward the deeper shadows where the tunnel swallowed all of the light.

Darger leaped down. Falling. Plummeting. Arms drifting up on each side of her like she meant to spread her wings. Swoop out of trouble.

She stared down between her feet. Locked her eyes on the crisscrossed lines of the tracks and ties. Made damn sure she gave the third rail a wide berth.

Her feet stabbed at the gravel, and she folded up on impact. Hips and knees bending her into a squat. Hands touching down to steady her. The rocks were cold against her palms. Jagged like teeth.

The others came down around her. Multiple SWAT officers hurling themselves off the edge. All those boots punching the rocks, grinding out gritty sounds.

Darger rocked forward and launched herself into a sprint. Found her steps choppy. Lurching until she, too, fell into a stride that placed her feet only on the wooden ties. Smoother that way.

She kept her eyes on Huxley as she found her footing, though she wasn't really seeing him for now. Just following that flitting shape ahead — the solid thing churning toward the darkness.

She grew more confident in the mechanics of her running with each step. Feet finding the wooden beams like step stones on a footpath. Accelerating. Feeling her way toward a sprint. Faster, faster.

It felt good to be in motion again, to be proactive again. Coursed a prickle of energy through her limbs. An airiness shooting through her, bubbling upward like carbonation.

A couple of the SWAT officers whooped beside her, sounded like frat boys howling at a kegger, apparently sharing that jubilation Darger felt. This wasn't over, but they were all getting some kind of second wind. Hungry again. Riding a wave of mounting determination.

They ran. Rocketed forward. Elbows pumping. Legs pistoning.

The tunnel mouth was a black hole before them. A vacancy. A circular cutout in the tile and concrete with a gaping nothingness at its center. They ran into that yawning maw, left the station behind.

Almost instantly the tunnel felt too small, too tight. A cinching sphincter around them. The tight quarters triggered Darger's claustrophobia, made her think about a train ramming its way down this chute like a cleaning rod shoved down the barrel of a gun.

Squeezing. Crushing.

But she pushed the fear down. Took a deep breath in. Let it out slowly. Her chest quivered on the exhale, but she felt better.

She'd been in tighter spots than this.

Her eyes danced over the tiled ceiling and then shifted lower. Sharpened on the bomber at last.

Huxley looked ghostly up ahead. Translucent like he was made out of darkling gauze. The black hole where the light from the station ended was encroaching, spreading. Engulfing more and more of the bomber's details in charcoal tones. Shrouding him in phases.

Better to get him before the tunnel went fully dark, she thought. She bit her lip. Pushed herself harder.

The sound of crunching gravel poured out in a strange beat beneath all of them. Throaty and percussive. And the noises cast strange echoes down here. The tighter quarters intensifying the reverb. Made everything sound wet, like they moved in some damp cave.

The dark thickened further as they pulled away from the platform of the station. Leaving all the light behind. The rounded ceiling above grew indistinct. Murky and featureless.

The shadows grew above and below. Opened. Deepened.

Darger could see the line where the light ended, that stark divide where the dark took over entirely. It made her chest tight, made her stomach clamp shut. She hurled herself toward it even if it terrified her.

She breathed. Pushed herself. She was mindful of the third rail and the 600 volts of direct current running through it even now. A line of death waiting about eighteen inches to her right. Oblivion just one touch away.

Huxley crossed that borderline at the light's edge first. Absorbed by the gloom.

She could just barely see him. A blackness running. A silhouette with arms and legs moving like liquid in the dark. Made her think of a spider skittering over the wall at night.

And then she crossed the line as well, and the dark became total. Complete. It devoured her.

One of the SWAT officers beside her whipped out a flashlight. The beam pierced the murk. Shined off the subway tile lining the arch overhead. Swung down onto Huxley's back.

He seemed smaller when the light glared on him. The glowing circle exposed him. Split the shadow to show who he really was, what he really was.

*Just a man.*

They were gaining on him. That little hitch in his step seemed more pronounced now. And that might be the difference here, Darger knew. That small weakness giving them the opening they needed.

The wounded prey gets taken down.

She ran up on him quickly. Closing the gap faster and faster. Almost within arm's reach.

He veered left hard without warning. Ducked into the wall.

Gone.

Just gone.

All of the SWAT officers started yelling at once. Panicked. Agitated. Shocked.

"Lost eyes on the target!"

"What the *fuck*?"

Stutter-steps chopped at the gravel. The jumbled rhythms matched the chaos in their cries.

The flashlight swung wildly as soon as Huxley escaped its circle. Flashed its gleam over the concrete tunnel wall. Brushed back to the spot where he'd disappeared. Holding steady on a black rectangle there. A cleft in the concrete.

A side tunnel.

# CHAPTER 69

*Not again.*

Darger took a few steps closer. Stopped and stared.

A small doorway gaped in the smooth concrete wall. A rectangular hole. Roughly cut around the edges as though it'd been chiseled there, chipped into existence one hammer stroke at a time. It formed the mouth of the utility tunnel.

The flashlight speared a little way into the shaft beyond the opening. Swung up and down slick-looking cement walls. Revealed a much smaller tunnel than the one housing the subway tracks, wide enough for perhaps two men to walk side by side, but only just.

The tunnel floor sloped downward about ten degrees. Appeared to grow smaller as it descended. Tighter.

Darger swallowed in a dry throat. Hoped her mind was playing tricks on her with that last detail — some neurosis-based optical illusion making the shaft appear to shrink as it advanced. She didn't think it would make much sense.

"Son of a bitch," Fitch said. "There's a maze of utility tunnels and drain-off mains down here. A mess of interconnected shit that runs under half the city. How much you want to bet our boy has maps of all this shit? Knows exactly where he's going. Maybe even has multiple exit routes ready to go."

"Maybe," Darger said.

Being prepared for this would fit the profile — the meticulousness with which he'd seemed to organize and execute his plan. But she hoped they had him on the run now finally. Improvising. At a disadvantage.

"Either way, he's on the run, and we've got to press it," Darger said.

She led the way through that chipped-out place in the cement. Shot forward into the dark tunnel.

The flashlight's beam shined past her to light the way in a swinging flicker. It couldn't quite reach far enough to vanquish the dark. Illuminating one little chunk of the way at a time, the rest cleaving off into shadow.

They ran for a while. Darger tried to force herself to focus solely on the path ahead, to not think about those concrete walls all around her, encasing her, entombing her. She tried.

The subtle downward slope felt wrong. Made every step she took feel like it went on just a little too long, the ground perpetually lower than her sense of balance expected. It strengthened that roiling panic in her gut. Made her feel like one of these times, she'd go to step down and the ground wouldn't be there at all.

The swamp smell came first. Filled Darger's nostrils with the reek of bog. Algae. Mud. Funk.

Wet patches of concrete appeared on the floor next. Puddling in some spots. Gleaming wherever the flashlight's beam touched it. Little flecks of black interrupting the sheen. Matte pebbles of some kind, duller than the rest. Oblong.

"Rat shit," Fitch said, explaining the pebbles. "Look out for 'em. Fuckers are supposed to be as big as terriers down here. Bigger. I heard they swarm anything that moves in the lower tunnels. Emboldened by the dark or something. Meaner, you know. Don't know if it's true."

"Lovely," Darger said through gritted teeth.

She scanned for large rodents as she ran, be they sewer rats or Huxley. No sign of anything four-legged, and still no sign of him. He'd gotten a pretty good jump when he darted into the tunnel, but with his gimpy ankle she figured they had to be gaining on him.

That was all well and good if the chase kept to a single path like it had so far, but how long would that last? So far the tunnel hadn't branched or connected to anything else, but it would inevitably. She guessed they'd worry about that when they got there.

The floor leveled out after that. The wetness and rat feces receding. The dry clap of concrete replacing the wet slaps their footfalls had become.

A deep rumble built up somewhere behind them. Growling and throbbing. Mounting in tension, in volume. It made the hair prick up on the back of Darger's neck.

She turned back. Realized a train was bearing down in the big tunnel. The rumble built to a roar. A tremor vibrated through the cement. Strengthening until it felt like the floor shuddered underfoot.

The clank of metal pounding against metal pulsed at the center of it all. Train wheels banging the tracks like hammers. All of it getting bigger. Louder. Deafening.

It whooshed past the small utility tunnel. A rectangle of lights flickering at the end of the tunnel, glowing dots flitting past like the checked yellow lines in the middle of the highway. The pull of the train sucking audibly at the doorway like a snuffling hound.

And then with a final whoomp it was past. Trailing away. Gone.

Darger refocused on the tunnel ahead. Running into the open space where the flashlight sliced a wedge out of the darkness.

Utility pipes hung along the ceiling now. Dark snakes running up above them. Dead-looking metal. Rusty and dripping.

Hissing steam leaked somewhere ahead. Its sibilance piercing, somehow instantly identifiable. Darger realized it was growing warmer and warmer as they moved forward — that cave-like coolness of the underground passage giving way to the steam heat running through here.

The tunnel curved to the right at a subtle angle. Widened into something of a long chamber before them.

The room housed a series of machines of some kind. Huddling things. Girthy. In the half-light Darger thought they looked like bulky generators of some type, though they made no noise. She didn't pay attention to them for long.

Her eyes drifted lower almost at once. To the oblong slabs laid out alongside the machines, darker than the rest.

Sleeping bags.

Little orange embers glowed above some of the bags. The cherries of cigarettes hovering in the dark.

The flashlight swept that way just in time to see a man sit up in one of the bags. Scraggly beard. Haggard bony face. Squinting eyes shielded by his outstretched hand.

A quick look around showed there were around twenty people nestled in this little chamber.

"People actually sleep down here?" Darger asked.

"Not a big surprise, I guess," Fitch said. "Steam keeps it warm, a steady temp year-round, you know? A bunch of 'em got run off after Hurricane Sandy. Tunnels all got flooded and shit."

The homeless scuttled back like beetles. Crab walking on palms and feet. Trying to slide away into the shadows. Sleeping bags still cocooning their lower halves.

Darger winced inside. They probably thought some kind of raid was happening. Police batons. Handcuffs. More abuse headed their way after a lifetime of it, an existence that had led them here, living in this dank rat hole beneath the city.

Down in the dark where no light shines.

"Did someone just run through here?" Darger said, her voice coming out harder than she meant. Accusatory.

The haggard man in the spotlight blinked hard. Eyebrows crunching down.

"What?"

Darger took a breath before she tried again. Smoothed out the tone of her voice.

"Did you hear someone run through the tunnel before us?"

"Uh… yeah. Yeah, a fella just flew through. Kicked over Kevin's lantern and busted it, the son a bitch. Hell, with the lamp burning it ain't so bad down here. We can play cards. Read a newspaper or something. But in the dark? There ain't nothing to do but drink and smoke, you know? Drink and smoke and sleep."

He pulled out a half-pint bottle of Jim Beam. Settled it between his teeth. Tipped his back and took a slug.

"This guy — the lantern kicker — he went this way?" Darger pointed down to the far end of the chamber.

"Oh yeah. He went that way. Kept on truckin'. Real wiry guy, it looked like to me. Limping like a pony with a broken leg. Wearing a, uh, red t-shirt."

# CHAPTER 70

Darger lurched forward once more. Fitch and the others followed. They zipped across the chamber. The vagrants thinning out as they advanced until only barren spaces lay between the hulking machines here.

That hissing steam sound grew louder now. The sticky warmth wrapped itself around them like a wet blanket. Breathing on them. A soggy heat like Miami in the summer.

Darger ran. A sheening surface filled the tunnel before her. Wet concrete again. Looking slick and shining back a green hue where the flashlight touched it as though the surface were being overtaken by some layer of algae or mildew. Glistening. Organic.

At first, Darger thought the tunnel dead-ended before them. She saw only the smooth cement surface of the wall. No way forward.

Then rusty rungs took shape in the center of the barrier. Ruddy stripes accenting the green. A ladder made of rebar looping out of the concrete. Ascending into a cement tube about the width of a manhole.

Darger reached the wall. Stopped herself with her hands out in front of her, touching the slimy wet for a second. She looked up into the shaft where the ladder led.

A circle of light shone at the top. Yellow light. Unnatural. Some kind of soft utility light, she knew. Some safety code thing, she figured. The kind of meager bulb that didn't really light up an area so much as shift it the few degrees from pitch black to shadowy.

They climbed. Hands looping around the rusted metal rungs. Feet pinging when they landed and pushed off.

Darger felt the grit of corroded metal coat her fingers like powder. Pictured the dried blood shade adhered there now. Couldn't wait to wipe her fingers off on her vest.

She pulled herself up onto the floor above this one. Crawling into the tightest section of tunnel yet. Fingers finding not cement but angular metal beneath her.

Amber light angled from a single bulb on the ceiling. Revealed a shrouded version of what she was feeling with her hands.

A steel grate filled the area underfoot. It formed the floor for this next section of the utility tunnel.

Darger got to her feet. Smeared her hands against her vest a few times. Waited a second for the others to pull themselves up onto the floor here.

She leaned forward. Cupped her hands around her knees. Heart pounding. Mouth open. She focused on her breathing.

So far she'd managed her wind pretty well, the adrenaline helping her avoid fatigue. But the chase was finally catching up with her. Pressing the first twinges of weakness into her limbs.

She closed her eyes. Sucked in great lungfuls of breath. Held them at the apex for a beat. Deep in and slow out.

The humidity didn't help her respiration any. The air felt thick and hot in her throat. A soup that smelled like swamp.

The last of the men made it up, and they took off again. Moving into that yellow light. Single file now.

The grate clanged along with their heavy footsteps. Loud and distinctly metallic. The noise reminded Darger of a cowbell keeping time with a drumbeat.

The tunnel grew hard angles now. A sharp turn to the right

was followed by an equally sharp turn to the left. After that, three fat sections of pipe made bottlenecks. Clogged most of the tunnel. Everyone had to turn sideways and sidle past, Fitch and a few of the big guys sucking in their guts to avoid contact with the hot metal.

The collective obstacles made this section of tunnel feel slower than what they'd experienced so far. Darger could feel the frustration amplifying in the crook of her jaw, the muscles there flexing in angry spasms.

And all the while, the shaft grew warmer and wetter. Muggy. Miserable.

Darger kept running. Kept pushing. The more weariness bloomed in her legs and in her lungs, the harder she pressed herself.

She was setting the pace, setting the tone. She had to want it more than anyone else. Work harder than anyone else. Let that passion spread to the others.

Here and now, for this one little slice of time, the officers in this tunnel shared a mission. A righteous cause. A calling.

With Agent Darger leading the way, they would not be denied.

# CHAPTER 71

Sergeant Burke of the 109th precinct led Agent Loshak down an empty hallway. The precinct's basement seemed dated — sported yellowing drop-ceiling tiles and cheap flooring that reminded him of a high school hallway. It also seemed utterly vacant. Dusty in a way that suggested no one came down here much.

Their footsteps clattered and echoed around the empty space. Clapping sounds that shuddered as they rang down the hall. Something about the quiet made Loshak uncomfortable.

"So you're the, uh, map guy, huh Burke?" he said, sounding a little dumb to himself but happy to break up the silence.

Laughter hissed out of the short man, though Loshak couldn't tell if it was coming from his mouth or nose. His bushy salt-and-pepper mustache twitched.

"Map guy. I guess you could say that," Burke said. "I've always been fascinated with the tunnels. Probably been down in the lower tunnels three, four dozen times over the years on various assignments, so I've gotten familiar with where the old maps are, how to read them. Not to mention navigating the mess down here in the basement. That kind of thing."

Loshak nodded, and the quiet blossomed around them again until the agent could hear his pulse pattering in his ears. He felt sweat slick his palms.

"Got the lay of the land and whatnot," he said, trying to keep the conversation going.

Sergeant Burke chuckled again.

"Well, so few people come down here these days aside from

me, what with everything being digitized, that I suppose it's become an assumption that this basement and these maps are my domain." He opened a door that led into a dim room. "Here we are."

A second later the fluorescent bulbs winked on overhead.

Evidence boxes cluttered the small space. Haphazard stacks of cardboard set in uneven rows.

Burke wove his way through the maze of containers, turning sideways to squeeze between a couple of crooked towers of them. He disappeared into the gap and came back a few seconds later with a long metal tube in his hands.

"Yes. Here we go," the little man said, a smile curling the ends of the bushy mustache. "Help me hang this, would you?"

Loshak took one end of the metal tube and together they hung it on hooks along the wall at the front of the room. Burke pulled the handle in the center of the tube, and the map unrolled to cover much of the wall. Reminded Loshak of his school days.

Clear overlays showed various tunnel systems in different colors — a series of weaving lines like a diagram of the circulatory system. The subway system was rendered in black lines. Utility pipes appeared in a dull red. Water was blue. A few other layers veined the map in orange, purple, and green.

"Okie dokey," Burke said. "Where are we…"

He ran his finger over the map in ever-narrowing spirals until he found what he was looking for. The tip of his index finger did a rat-tat-tat on a location on the map.

"Main Street-Flushing station. That's where he jumped onto tracks, yes?"

"That's right, heading west," Loshak said, remembering what Fitch had relayed over the radio before they'd lost contact.

"Right. Right. And then you said he took off down a side tunnel heading south?"

Loshak nodded.

The sergeant's finger traced down the line. Found the intersection.

"OK. Looks like he ducked into a little utility line here. Some of those are awfully narrow. Crawling room only in a few spots."

"Yikes," Loshak said.

*That ought to do wonders for Darger's claustrophobia.*

Burke's finger followed the red line a ways, twisting and turning along with the meandering path of the tunnel.

"This tunnel houses some generators it looks like. Backup emergency-type stuff. Nothing active. Also has pipe access. Could be a warm one. Steam, you know?"

Loshak nodded. Watched the finger as it progressed over the glossy map.

"Looks like it comes out… here." He clucked his tongue against the roof of his mouth. Did another rat-tat-tat on the map. "Ah. One of the abandoned subway stations."

"Abandoned?" Loshak said.

"Yep. 91st Street Station. They stopped using 'er back in 1959. Riding the 1 train, you can still see it for a few seconds. Guess it's full of trash. Mole people."

Loshak didn't say anything for a second.

"Mole people?"

"Oh yeah. Big time."

Loshak licked his lips.

"Let's leave that aside for now. Do you think we could get to the station before him? Cut him off?"

Burke got quiet. He now worked two fingers at the map, one on each hand. Tracing various lines. Breath whistling through his nostrils.

He clucked his tongue against the roof of his mouth again, and his fingers stopped abruptly on the map.

"Yes," he said it almost under his breath the first time. "Yes. I know a shortcut."

# CHAPTER 72

Movement caught Darger's eye. Silvery fluttering filling the tunnel before her. It looked like heat distortion somehow made opaque.

She squinted. Scanned the throbbing shapes ahead, the hazy dance of light and dark, still not quite able to discern what she was seeing.

She blinked hard as though to clear her eyes of some obstruction. Squinted harder. And then it made sense.

Steam billowed out of one of the pipes that ran vertical along the wall. A roiling cloud spewing out at about shoulder level. The leak angled up toward the ceiling, moistened the pipes and cement up above so it all looked like a sweaty beer can.

They slowed again. Ducking low. Pressing their backs against the opposite wall. Sidling past.

Darger glanced up at the steam as she moved under it. Liquid smoke, more or less. Spitting and sniffing endlessly. Rolling ever upward.

The heat was impossible now. It saturated her clothes. Felt like it was beading on her skin. The droplets congealing out of the air, plumping into jewels on her arms and along the rim of her top lip. Disgustingly warm.

"Didn't have 'takin' a schvitz' on my to-do list when we were planning the raid this morning, but..." Fitch said. "A little sauna sesh. This whole operation went in a classier direction than any of us could have anticipated. Feels like I'm at the spa."

"Yeah, especially with all the rat turds sprinkled everywhere," Darger said. "That's like the New York Transit

Authority's version of caviar, right?"

That got a chuckle out of a few of them.

They got going again once everyone had made it past the broken pipe. Feet jangling against that steel grate again. Pounding on that steel drum that only played one note over and over.

Condensation dripped down like rain now. Murky droplets the shade of merlot gathering on the pipes overhead. Drizzling in a steady downfall.

Some of the thick drops splatted down on the back of Darger's neck. Lukewarm and nasty. Probably streaking rust smears down into her shirt, like daubs of red-brown fingerpaint running the length of her spine. Other droplets pelted the rounded top of her helmet, made little flicking sounds when they hit the Kevlar shell and burst, hanging a mist in the air all around them.

The swamp smell intensified again. Pungent and earthy. A pond scum stench with a hint of urine tang sprinkled on top for good measure.

Scratching sounds scrabbled around them now. Rats, Darger thought, though she still couldn't see any. Fleeing rats, not used to all of the commotion down here. Huxley running through had probably stirred them up, and now the additional foot traffic was flushing them more thoroughly. Some mass exodus. Little pink feet clambering over the steel grate, toenails rasping at the cement walls.

She clenched her teeth and kept going. Tried not to think about the rodents. Tried not to think about the overwhelming humidity. Tried not to think about the concrete walls closing in, cinching tighter and tighter until she couldn't breathe, until they crushed her limbs snugly to her torso, squeezed her ribcage until it quivered and splintered, compacted her into a tiny cube and spat her out in some landfill somewhere.

She blinked hard. Bit the inside of her lip until the hurt exploded. Let the pain pull her back into the moment, out of the negative thought loop and into the here and now.

She tasted blood. Just a little.

But it worked. Sharpened her mind. Refocused her eyes on the concrete and steel edges of the narrow passageway in front of her.

Breathe. Just breathe and run.

She strained harder whenever she focused. Twitched the muscles in her legs a little bit faster. Feet bounding up from the steel grate with a renewed bounce.

And she felt the surge of desire spread through her to the others. Heard it in the increased tempo of all the pounding footsteps. Like a song speeding up, hitting harder at the chorus.

Passion was infectious. Fury. Intensity. Sometimes Darger thought it was all she had to give.

It felt good to have the cavalry with her, though. Fitch and the others had her back. Nothing like last time — when she was on her own.

All these officers, and all their guns against a single unarmed man. They had the upper hand. No question.

Another sharp right took them to a straightaway. The steel grate floor ended underfoot. Transitioned to a concrete ramp that sloped downward at a sharper angle than before.

They descended once more. A dank cement rectangle easing them deeper into the earth, into the strange world of tubes snaking around beneath the city.

More of that green fungus textured the wall in patches here. Slimy and glossy. The emerald shapes sported rough edges where the green slime gave way to the black of the wet concrete, uneven borderlines, little isthmuses connecting larger blobs here and there. They looked like continents, she realized, the wall a sprawling atlas.

She tongued the wound in her lip as she ran. Those faint flashes of pain kept her focused somehow, even if they were muted compared to the initial bite. The sting more annoying than anything.

She kept her eyes wide open. Refusing to blink as she stared at the next section of tunnel, the cement surfaces where the flashlight swept around.

Breath spilled through her lips. Sucking in and heaving out. Muggy air scraping over her teeth. Its heat cloying in her throat.

They rounded a wide corner. Came out on another straightaway.

Darger's gaze pierced the empty space before her. Angled deeper and deeper down the concrete shaft.

Shadows writhed in the distance. Looked like black smoke roiling and bucking. Elongating to touch both sides of the tunnel at once. Dancing everywhere.

Darger lifted her arm. Pointed.

Her footsteps grew choppy underneath her. All of her consciousness zooming in on that inky movement ahead.

The flashlight lurched and reached further down the tunnel. The beam growing as it crawled over the slimy floor. Drifting upward from there. Spearing the empty space.

The beam stretched after the shadow. Grasping for it. Finally reaching it.

The shadows shrank back finally. The image coalesced there. Becoming solid when the light laid it bare.

It was Huxley.

# CHAPTER 73

Something flexed in Darger's chest. Muscles squeezing like a fist. Cinching tight around her ribcage. Constricting her breath.

Her heart hammered away inside that rigid torso. A frenzied muscle. Felt like a wild thing in a cage, trying to beat its way free.

She kept her stride. Didn't slow.

Kept her eyes locked on the dark figure ahead. Unblinking.

The flashlight bounced up and down on Huxley's back. A jostling strobe effect. Made it look like the bomber was shaking around somehow, like a purposely frantic shot in an action movie. The kind that sometimes gave Darger motion sickness in the theater.

She forced herself to breathe. Fought her rigid muscles for control. Sucked in air. Humid, swampy air. Better than nothing.

Huxley loped ahead of them like an injured gazelle. Favoring that left leg. He was still moving pretty good, though, considering. His arms pumped at his sides, two hands slicing the air around him like blades.

He rounded a corner. Drifted to the right. Disappeared.

Darger set her jaw. Molars quivering against each other.

She listened. Like she might be able to hear the bomber's footsteps over her own, over the heavy boot treads slamming down right behind her.

Her chest started to compress again. She could only take shallow breaths as she approached the corner where Huxley had moved out of view. Shaking with the effort.

She hit the corner and watched the next stretch of tunnel

slide into view in slow motion as she made the turn. Unveiled left to right as though a curtain were pulling out of the way, as though the concrete shaft were opening before her.

She saw the light first.

A glowing square lay at the end of the tunnel, a little higher than the floor they ran on now. Maybe a hundred yards down the tube. Probably less.

And then she saw the staircase congeal in front of it. Details filling in as she drew closer.

Galvanized steel stairs with mesh inlays. The stairs led up about eight steps to the glowing opening. Harsh fluorescent light gleaming in from the next section of tunnel, whatever it might hold.

It was a doorway. The way out of this tunnel and back into the main subway system probably. If there were people out there, Huxley might be able to get lost in the crowd again.

Her eyes drifted lower. Found the bomber's jerking figure. A dark shape moving toward the light.

He was closer now. They'd gained on him. Narrowed the gap.

Some ferocious feeling pushed Darger harder still. Maybe some killer instinct kicking in. Knowing how close they were now. Ready to finish this.

Something like bloodlust.

She bolted after the scrawny man. Felt the officers just behind her, keeping up. Maybe they felt it, too. Contagious like so many things were in battle.

She bounded. Muscle fibers twitching out long strides. Chewing up the ground between her and the target.

Huxley's back got bigger as though she were zooming in on it. She drew to within twenty feet. And then ten.

Huxley glanced back. Wide eyes. Gaping mouth. Tongue lolling like a slice of ham.

Darger felt her own mouth moving. A grin forming there that felt wolfish. She licked her lips.

They had him. He wouldn't make it to that glowing light in time. They'd finish it here. In the dinge of the tunnel.

By now they'd probably gotten the task force reorganized in any case, hopefully swarming into every subway station around for miles. Pouring in like flood water.

Wherever this tunnel came out, they'd be there. They had to be.

The bomber's hands moved then. Broke out of the pumping motion. The right paw reaching in front of him. Clawing at the waistband of his pants.

Darger zipped up on him. Just about getting to within arm's reach.

Huxley looked back again. Eyes still as big as moons. Mouth still yawning.

Darger's eyes moved to the right hand as it came into view again. Saw the dark object clutched in his fingers about the size of a big pack of gum.

Huxley lifted the item. Slowly raised it over his head.

His face showed no expression. Dead eyes. Drooping jaw.

Darger got closer still. Finally she could see what he held.

It was a standard garage door opener. Charcoal gray body. Steel gray buttons. Little chrome clip on the back.

Now Darger's eyes expanded.

A detonator.

She needed to tell the others. Needed to—

Huxley fingered the button.

# CHAPTER 74

It happened in the space of three heartbeats.

The air shuddered first. Overpressurized. The shock wave unleashed. All that energy released in a microsecond. Forcing outward in a sphere of destruction.

The concrete cracked somewhere behind Darger. Even in that fraction of a second before the sound wave of the explosion could catch up, she could hear the walls bursting. Shattering. Thick crunching and rumbling like thunder.

Then came the flash. A fiery light flared over the dark of the tunnel. Pushed outward from the detonation point. Lit the space in blinding orange for a single second. Less. Reflected strangely off the wet concrete of the floor, of the walls, of the ceiling.

Darger turned back. Felt like she was moving in slow motion.

The walls of the tunnel crumbled some seventy feet back. Falling. Piling.

Giant concrete shards toppled over each other. Looked like chunks of jagged ice shifting in an arctic sea.

Powdery bits of pulverized cement flung everywhere. Puffing and roiling in cloudy spirals. Hanging over everything. Growing thicker and darker.

All of them had turned to look now. Black-clad bodies twisting that way. Helmeted heads pivoting. Everyone staring back as the tunnel closed behind them. Darkened. Choked with debris.

The second blast hit four heartbeats later. Twenty feet closer.

This time the concussive wave rolled off the detonation point and knocked Darger back a step. The wall fractured with a sound like a giant spine being snapped.

She faced the flash fully. Saw it light up those cement shards as they ground against each other like shifting continents. Tectonic plates.

The tunnel was collapsing in on itself.

On Darger and the rest.

Slabs of concrete rained down from both sides. Huge chunks falling on the men in the rear of the group. Closing them off in rubble, in that ever-undulating cloud of debris.

The men tried to scramble. Too late.

Darger gasped. Watched a concrete chunk the size of a coffin come down at an angle. Take out a black clad agent at the shoulder.

Gone.

They both seemed to vanish into the pile. Buried. Swallowed up in heaving dust clouds.

The blast wind blew a hot gust into Darger's face. The exhale seeming to come just after the first thrust of the explosion, tailing after that orange blaze of the flash.

Fitch lifted a gloved hand as though to shield his face from the heat. Darger squinted. Squinched her lips tight. To her, it felt like sticking her face into a wood-fired pizza oven. It was mercifully brief, at least.

And then all was dark the way they'd come. The cement shaft caved in to the point of being sealed off from the yellow light. It plunged that way into darkness.

One of Fitch's men lay face down in front of the pile of jagged rubble. A vaguely visible dark bulk. But the dust cloud roiled there like smoke. Drifting downward. Quickly settling lower until it cloaked the fallen figure. It shrouded him and everything else that way. Left only vague contours of cement visible through the billowing gloom.

Closer, the light from the doorway glittered on some of the dust motes fluttering around, giving a sense of the particles still drizzling down.

Darger kept backpedaling away as she took in all of this. Fitch and a couple of the others did the same just a few paces beyond her. Only four of them left.

She wheeled her head to look for Huxley. Found him halfway up the steel staircase.

And then the third blast flung her like a rag doll.

# CHAPTER 75

Footsteps echoed everywhere in the parking structure. Loshak and Burke ran down the shiny concrete slope toward the cruiser, their shadows looking long and jerky under the yellow lights.

Burke yelled into a walkie talkie the whole time, the chatter streaming out too fast for Loshak to make out most of the words, especially with the little man zipping away from him. Burke's legs jittered beneath him. He had incredible speed for his stature, Loshak thought, and the agent couldn't help but feel old again as he lagged behind.

When he got to the car, Loshak had to put out his hands to stop himself. Palms pressed flat against the glass of the passenger side window. A bolt of pain shot through his bad wrist, but it faded quickly.

He pried open the door. Plopped down in the seat. The pint-sized officer was already snugged in place behind the wheel.

"Got two more officers headed our way," Burke said. "Figure we might need the backup."

"That's smart," Loshak said.

"Hopefully they'll be quick about it. They're upstairs, but I told 'em it was urgent. As urgent as it gets."

The small mustached man checked his watch. Then he pumped his knee and sort of chewed on his mustache, his bottom lip coming up over the bottom tip of the prickly hair and shifting about in fast motion. Something about the convulsive mannerism reminded Loshak of a ferret.

The agent wheeled his head around to stare out the back

windshield. Eyes dancing over the steel door where the officers would soon emerge.

He blinked. Swallowed. Heard his pulse as a hollow thrum inside his head.

Nothing in the scene behind them moved.

"Two minutes tops," Burke said, eyeballing his watch again.

They waited.

# CHAPTER 76

Time slowed down.

The blast struck Darger most solidly between the shoulder blades. A stiff punch that knocked her off her feet. Tipped her top half forward. Laid her out flat in the air.

She flew like that. Horizontal to the ground. Like a baserunner diving to slide into home, except her arms were swimming a little, clawing at the air like she might be able to regain her balance by way of a doggy paddle.

Weightless. Floating.

She looked down. Watched the wet cement floor zooming past underneath her. Blurry gray. Shiny with moisture.

The emotions hit then. Defeat ripped and scratched inside her gut as she soared in empty space.

Pain. Loss.

She'd failed.

He'd been a step ahead of her the whole time. Ahead of all of them. Maybe several steps.

Tyler Huxley always had a plan. Always.

And then the orange flash gleamed everywhere. Impossibly bright light shooting down the length of the tunnel, touching every surface. It made scads of the wet concrete twinkle and glisten, patches glowing and then relenting to darkness in weird flickering patterns.

The light speared Darger's pupils. Searing pain blazing into her skull. It blinded her for a split second.

She blinked away the afterimage. Drifting blotches and whorls slowly clearing.

And then she was coming back to the earth. Slamming down onto her belly with a jolt. Ribcage smacking flat and taking the brunt of it.

Something cracked there on the right side. Shot bolts of pain all through her torso. Electric tendrils of misery surging through meat and bone.

She bounced once. Touched down again.

The pain in her chest flared harder on the second impact. Froze her breath in her lungs. Teeth biting down so hard it made her eyes water.

Reality blinked to black and came back a few times in rapid succession. All the sound guttering out to silence and returning as well. Rolling blackouts of unconsciousness.

Light and dark. Anesthesia and agony. Her reality winked on and off like a strand of Christmas bulbs until the lights inside her skull came back on and stayed that way.

And still momentum shoved her forward. Skidded her over the wet concrete like a slip 'n slide. Belly down. Arms splayed out in front of her like useless sticks.

The blast roared behind her now. The low-pitched boom made the floor shudder beneath her. Cement rippling and buckling like flimsy plastic. Vibrating in convulsions.

The sound was more ferocious up close. An angry bellow. Violent and meaningless. Impossibly loud.

The walls cracked and perforated around her then. Crevices opening and snaking everywhere. Splitting like torn seams. The tunnel's structure fragmenting into jagged chunks of concrete with pointy bits of rebar jutting out.

Collapsing in on her. Caving in.

Everything went to pieces. Splintered. Disintegrated. The world itself no longer solid, no longer whole.

Dust plumed everywhere. Thick clouds of gray going black. A growing murk enveloping all, lurching and swooshing.

She spun onto her back to be able to see the approaching destruction. Crab walked backward as she watched the debris twist around itself.

The tunnel cinched shut behind her. The circle tightening and closing. Rubble spilling down to close the gap where the opening had been.

An avalanche of industrial material advancing. Encroaching. Racing her way to fill the tunnel.

She watched it devour the other SWAT agents one by one. Covering them over in concrete shards and inky dust clouds roiling like smoke.

Trampling. Engulfing. Pummeling down.

And then the crushing blackness swallowed her.

# CHAPTER 77

The police cruiser boomed down the ramp of the parking lot, tires squealing as it wheeled out onto the street. With the flip of a switch, the siren screamed to life, sending out its warbled, twirling song. Another thrown switch brought glowing movement to the lightbar on top of the car, flashes of red and blue.

Loshak gripped the ceiling handle in the passenger seat. He double-checked his seatbelt with the opposite hand. Watched the driver out of the corner of his eye.

Sergeant Burke jammed his foot down on the accelerator. Hunched over the wheel. Chittering his teeth like some kind of overgrown chipmunk in a bad mood.

The man drove like Evel Knievel.

They weaved through traffic at top speed. Jerking to the left and right. Flying through red lights. Braving a trip across the yellow line into the opposite lane. Narrowly missing cars from every angle.

Loshak managed to peel his eyes away from the treachery playing out on the road. He cranked his head back toward the backseat. Locked eyes with the two uniformed officers back there, one and then the other.

"Does he always drive like this?" he said.

They both nodded emphatically. Then they hunkered down in unison as the car tore around another tight turn and fishtailed coming out of it. The back end skidded around underneath them for a while before it smoothed out.

Loshak was glad to have the others riding along with him

and Burke — four extra hands, a couple of extra guns. They'd reported the information about the abandoned subway station to Agent Fredrick, and the SWAT team was en route to the location even now. But Loshak had a feeling that the map nerd Burke would somehow get them there first, especially with the way he drove. Better to have some backup.

The cruiser gunned it through another intersection. Tires bouncing over rutted spots in the asphalt. Horns blaring around them.

Burke hissed laughter — that sibilant wheezing that either came from his mouth or nose or both at once. Just as quickly the laugh cut out. The man's face went rigid, eyes swiveling everywhere.

"Almost there," he said. "Our tunnel access will be on the next block."

At least it was almost over, Loshak thought. The agent watched the pedestrians blur past on the side of the road, all the faces seeming to smear together as the car bobbed and weaved and zipped and darted.

And then the blasts shook the earth — three total, hitting one after the other. Deep resonant booms bubbled up from below. The concrete shivered. Rocked the car so hard it bounced and bottomed out once.

All the traffic around them did a strange stutter in reaction to the explosions beneath them. Cars jerking. Heads turning. A collective sort of double take rippling through this section of the public, like their hearts had all skipped the same beat.

All four law enforcement officers in the car looked at each other. Foreheads creased. Mouths reduced to grave lines. A wordless exchange of concern.

Burke's mustache twitched atop those chittering teeth. He

still hunched over the wheel, eyes wide now with morbid wonder. When the small cop spoke this time, his voice came out as a gravelly whisper.

"Mercy. I hope we're not too late."

# CHAPTER 78

Darger coughed out a cloud of dust. Blinked a few times. Stared into the smoky wall hung up around her like fog.

The world looked sideways. Tilted and broken. Sheared-off concrete edges set at odd angles along the floor. Clumps of broken wall lying all around.

She lifted her head. Propped herself up on her elbows. Watched the listing ship of the world right itself some.

She took a few breaths. Let her inner ear settle.

Then she brushed at her chest and belly. Swept wads of pulverized concrete off herself. Chalky powder peppered with chunks had settled over all of her. Like someone had dumped multiple bags of flour on her, except gray and lumpy. Some of the pieces bigger, almost baseball-sized.

She stopped and breathed again. Needed to take it slow. Let herself come back little by little.

She could only vaguely feel the bruises covering her body for now. She knew from experience the real pain would come later. Settling over her in intensifying waves as the hours progressed.

Her ribs were another matter. Probing fingers elicited sharp torment and a spasm there. She'd cracked one. Maybe two.

Breathing deeply made it feel like someone was jabbing a pitchfork into her side and twisting. So she sucked in shallow breaths. Kept it to a dull ache.

Her pulse pounded in her ears. But that was OK. It meant she was still here. Still alive. That was something.

Finally, she craned her neck. Braved a look beyond her immediate area.

The rectangle of light still streamed in through the open doorway at the top of the steps. Murky and partially obscured by the smoky dust. The glowing beam lit up the swirling dirt, showed how tendrils of it twirled and braided about in the air.

She turned around. Saw the heaping rubble where the tunnel had been. Chunks of shattered concrete. Twisted steel rebar. It choked off the opening with wreckage. Clogged it completely.

Darkness cloaked the area. None of the others were there that she could see. Maybe they were still there in the pile, still alive.

Someone.

Anyone.

She sat up and everything got woozy again. Her vision turned runny along the edges like raw egg white.

Her chin dipped. Sank down toward her chest all at once. Everything tilted and darkened.

She caught her head just shy of her sternum. Took a few deep breaths to steady herself.

Something moved in the corner of her eye.

It was him.

Huxley stirred where he lay at the bottom of the steps. Dust motes shifted in the light around him.

He got to his hands and knees and then pulled himself to his feet. Climbed the stairs on wobbly legs. Slow steps. Both hands gripping the rail.

A dark shape moving into the light. Flowing. Looking like black smoke now. Like even the light could no longer remove the shadow from him. Not anymore.

He stumbled on the third step from the top. Dropped to one knee.

His right hand scraped off the rail and clutched his ribcage. He stayed there. Kneeling. Breathing. Chest heaving.

Darger forced herself up. More bits of concrete tumbling away from her, handfuls of dust spilling like she'd just been buried at the beach.

She staggered for the staircase. Feet gritting over the bits of wreckage. The remaining tunnel seeming to sway back and forth around her with each lumbering step.

Her numb fingers fumbled at the holster at her side. The cool of the gun pressing into the heel of her hand.

They wanted him alive, yes. She would try that.

If not…

A moan behind her stopped her in her tracks.

She turned. Scanned the choked tunnel mouth again.

Now that she was standing, she could see Fitch lying near the edge of the rubble. He looked small now. Swathed in shadow.

His body seemed crooked. Sprawled at some strange angle.

But his chest rose and fell. He was alive. Breathing.

Her eyes drifted lower.

His left leg was gone from about mid-thigh down. The femur jutted from the tattered edge of meat — the bone itself protruding about eight inches and splintering into a pointy edge like a harpoon.

Blood pulsed out of what was left of the thigh. Sheets of watery red throbbing out. Sliding over the bone. Puddling outward in the gravelly debris.

She looked back just as Huxley wobbled through the doorway and moved out of sight, still tottering and slow. Then her head snapped back to the fallen figure.

Fitch moaned again, hand feebly patting curled fingers at

the wounded thigh. Like he might be able to stanch the blood flow that way, might be able to hold his life in somehow.

The red jetted over the back of his hand. Sticky stuff clinging there. Viscous. The shade made it look like dirty motor oil.

An involuntary breath snuffled into Darger's mouth and nose. Sent a fresh twinge of pain through her cracked ribs. A grimace curling her lips, wrinkling her nose.

Her heart beat faster. Pulse pounding in her temples, in her ears.

Her head swiveled to the open doorway and then back to the sprawling wounded man. Little wet sounds lisped with every throb of blood venting itself from Fitch's wound.

She could chase Huxley or help Fitch. Not both.

She took another breath and chose her path.

# CHAPTER 79

The cruiser wrenched to a stop in the middle of the street. Sergeant Burke jammed it into park and bolted out of the car in one motion. He streaked across the asphalt, oblivious to the traffic flowing past.

Loshak shook his head. The small cop was already standing over the manhole, waving them over, before the agent had even undone his seatbelt.

The others bustled out of the car. Hustling out into the wind of the passing vehicles.

One of the uniformed officers from the backseat set traffic cones around the car. Loshak and the other uniform jogged over to where Burke stood.

Between the four-way flashers, the cones, and the light bar glowing, Loshak thought there'd be plenty of notice that official police business was going to be occupying this section of road for a stretch. Nevertheless, the New York traffic honked off and on, the drivers apparently pissed they had to swerve into another lane to get around.

*Oh, sorry about that, dickface. We're only trying to stop a guy from blowing your goddamn face off.*

Now all four of them stood near the manhole. Burke spoke — looking for all the world like he was yelling, mustache shaking furiously — but Loshak couldn't hear him over the roar of the traffic. Maybe it didn't matter. The next step was simple enough, right?

A pry bar tilted one edge of the manhole cover upward. Two of the officers got their fingers into the opening and together they rolled the metal disk out of the way. Looked heavy enough. It was hard for Loshak to believe that manhole covers were stolen on a regular basis — sold for scrap.

The dark hole now gaped between their feet. A perfect circle of nothing — or so it appeared.

Burke shined a flashlight down into the opening. First the beam revealed the steel rungs of the ladder leading down. Then it swung into the hollow and Loshak could see the concrete floor some fifteen or so feet below.

"This tube will get us right into the station. Not a problem."

Burke waggled his eyebrows as he said it. Then he gestured for the others to start down with a firm dip of the flashlight.

Loshak lowered himself into the opening. Fingers gripping the gritty rim of the hole. He let his feet kick down into nothing before his toes caught the metal rung.

Then he descended into the dark place, whispering little half-formed prayers that they weren't too late.

# CHAPTER 80

Darger's knees touched down in wet gravel. Lukewarm blood soaking through her pant legs right away. Adhering itself to fabric and skin.

It felt syrupy. Half-congealed already.

Fresh blood kept flowing into the puddle. Gushing from that wide-open wound. Gliding over the exposed bone. Hissing a little with each pulse. A slushy sound.

Up close the femur looked even more wrong. Broken down the vertical length of the bone. Whittled into a jagged, spiky thing. Yellow marrow exposed through the cracked side.

Her hands moved to her middle, fishing under the seam of the Kevlar vest. Fingers scrabbling at her belt. Finding the buckle. Unclasping it.

Fitch coughed and then scowled. Head turning to one side and then the other.

Darger half expected to see red appear on his teeth — signs of internal hemorrhaging — but the incisors stayed white and clean even if the face around them looked pained.

She pulled at the leather belt. Felt it slither free of all the belt loops one after the other. An odd release of pressure there.

"You should have left me, Darger," Fitch said. He didn't make eye contact. "Should have… gone after him. What good am I going to be to anyone now?"

But Darger knew he was wrong. She didn't know what to say, so she didn't say anything.

Her hands worked quickly now. Moved lower.

She looped the belt around his upper leg — careful not to

touch the jutting bone. Cinched it tight. A makeshift tourniquet.

One more surge of blood drizzled free. Surged into the red puddle with that babbling sound. And then the bleeding stopped.

They both held quiet then. Fitch's chest heaved. Darger's shallow breaths sounded like a panting dog's.

Fitch looked down at his missing leg. At the belt binding the wound there.

He blinked a few times, lips opening and closing, but Darger couldn't read his expression.

"I'll probably never dance again," Fitch said finally. He coughed again before he went on. "I mean, I never danced before, but still…"

# CHAPTER 81

Footsteps sounded beyond the doorway. The clatter of shoes on cement, gritty thwacks echoing around, somehow growing louder without really sounding like they were getting closer.

Darger turned away from Fitch and lifted her gaze to the top of the steps. Stared at the light streaming in the doorway. For a split second she expected to find Huxley's blood-red shirt there, the bomber coming back to try to finish them off.

Instead Loshak appeared in the rectangle of light. He stood up straighter when he saw her, then jogged down the steps, shoes clanging on the metal.

A few other officers filed in behind him. Their flashlight beams sliced into the gloom like glowing blades, swinging around with jerky flourishes.

As he drew up on them, Loshak's eyes snapped to the place where Fitch's leg used to be, rested for a beat on that jagged length of exposed femur, and then slid up to find Darger's gaze.

"Just… just you two, then?" he said. He kept his voice low as though he didn't want the others to hear just yet.

Darger nodded once.

Loshak stepped away. Said something into a radio, again keeping his voice low. Then he came back.

"Rest of the cavalry will be here any minute," he said. "I've got an EMT unit on the way to help Fitch."

The others came closer now. All eyes locked onto Fitch's wound. Nobody said anything for a beat.

"Don't worry. We're gonna get you help, buddy," Burke said, swallowing hard.

Fitch smiled up from his place on the floor. Something angelic in his face now.

"It's OK. I don't feel it anymore," he said. "The pain, I mean. Some endorphin rush kicked in or something. Made it so I don't really feel nothin' at all. Crazy how the human body works, you know? Such an intricate machine."

The men gaped at the tattered meat around the protruding bone. Glassy looks in all their eyes.

"It'll be alright. I'll be alright," Fitch said, his voice going softer. "Hell, I'm one of the lucky ones when you think about it."

He gestured at the clogged tunnel, and they all looked that way. The gravity of what had happened here settled over all of them.

When Burke swallowed again, it was audible against the stark silence.

The EMTs arrived shortly after that. They loaded Fitch onto a stretcher, hauled him up the steps and away.

The rest of the task force arrived and began searching the abandoned station and the various tunnels snaking off of it. Burke and the others drifted that way, eager to aid in the search. Soon it was just Darger and Loshak left in the mostly crushed tunnel.

"They'll search the tunnels," Loshak said. "Maybe they'll get lucky, but..."

"But you have your doubts."

"I think he lost us. Gone in the tunnels, in the dark. I thought we were getting here in time." Loshak rubbed his fingers at his brow as he went on. "When I first climbed down into the empty subway station, I heard scuffling, you know? Thought maybe it was him, that I'd gotten here in the nick of time. I drew my gun. Stalked toward the sound. But then I saw a rat tail slithering through a cluster of crumpled chip bags. It was nothing. He was already gone."

"The rat got away this time," Darger said, her voice tight and small.

The two of them stood and looked at the passageway choked with debris.

# EPILOGUE

The second the plane touched down in Virginia, Darger checked her phone for any updates on the case. The news about the investigation had been sparse.

First, they'd tracked down an ID on the poor bastard who'd wound up a corpse in Huxley's dingy basement. Ricky Fuller was the unlucky man's name — a 26-year-old from Trenton who'd worked on and off in construction since graduating high school. He'd been reported missing by his mother in the hours after the first Huxley bombing. An officer in Trenton noticed the resemblance and got word to the task force.

Next, after an exhaustive three-day search, law enforcement had officially cleared the tunnels. There was no sign of Huxley. Their bomber was officially considered at large, and the manhunt would shift gears now.

Huxley had been moved to the top of the Most Wanted list, his face plastered on post office bulletin boards and the front pages of newspapers. Posted and reposted across the internet. Splashed on the TV screen of anyone watching the nightly news.

With all that publicity, Darger prayed they'd get a lead sooner rather than later. She tried not to think about how the Olympic Park Bomber had managed to remain at large for five years, hiding out in the mountains of North Carolina, only venturing among mankind to pick his meals out of dumpsters.

A little chill rippled over her skin as she thought about it now, looking out the window.

Tyler Huxley was out there somewhere. Hiding. Plotting his next move. Watching from somewhere no one could see.

"We'll find him," Loshak had assured her. "It's only a matter of time. He can't hide forever."

*But what if they didn't find him*? The question seemed to echo in her skull.

So did a tiny voice in the back of her mind that kept trying to say it was her fault. That she'd made a mistake, not going after Huxley when she had the chance. But no. She'd saved Fitch's life. The doctor in the emergency room had told her so.

"He was likely minutes from death when you stopped the bleeding. Maybe less." He had glanced back at the curtain cordoning off Fitch's bed. "I couldn't believe he was even awake then they wheeled him in here."

If she had to do it all over again, she'd make the same choice. Because Fitch being alive was one of the few pieces of good news they had, at this point. That and the fact that Amelia Driscoll was going to survive her attack.

Still, they'd lost four of Fitch's men, which brought Huxley's victim count to six, counting Gavin Passmore and Agent Dobbins.

The sun was dipping below the tree line when Darger finally parked her car on the street in front of her house. She couldn't wait to get inside. To shuck off her grimy travel clothes. To take a long hot bath and sleep in her own bed.

Sleep. She almost wept at the idea of getting a full night's sleep, uninterrupted.

She'd managed a few hours of off and on slumber on the lumpy hotel mattress, a restless kind of sleep which had done nothing for her sore and aching body. Her cracked ribs had throbbed in time with her pulse all night long.

Darger climbed the front steps, pausing before the door to pull out her keys. She slid the key into the lock, but before she could turn it, the door kind of just swung open on its own.

She stopped. Listened.

This wasn't right. Couldn't be right. There was no way she'd left the door unlocked.

Her hair pricked up little by little. Insects crawled over her skin.

This was wrong. Something was wrong.

Her hand drifted toward the partially open door. Hesitated just shy of the wood.

An image of the bomber flashed through her mind. Tyler Huxley. Bony shoulders twitching inside that red shirt as he ran.

Was it possible?

*Be rational*, she thought to herself.

How would Huxley know who she was or where she lived?

Her landlord, maybe… except he hadn't called or texted. Unless there was some kind of emergency, he wouldn't just let himself in like that.

Besides, where was his car? Her eyes strayed to the curb. Scanned for the big obnoxious Hummer the landlord drove, a hulking forest green box with wheels. Her vehicle was the only one parked outside.

OK. Well… someone had obviously broken in. She doubted that person was still here, but…

Darger's fingers found the butt of her gun. Slipped it from her holster.

She took one step inside. Pushed the door. Watched it glide out of the way.

Her eyes scanned the interior of her apartment, searching for anything out of place. Anything that might have been taken or rifled through. Her gaze landed on a package just inside the door. A plain box with no address or postage marks on it. The heavy feeling of dread in her gut intensified.

Jesus, Huxley really had been here.

And he'd left her a present.

She stutter-stepped backward through the doorway. Wheeled around to face the street.

She should call Loshak. No, 9-1-1 first. Then Loshak.

But first she had to get away from the house. Away from whatever was in that box.

And then she heard something. A clatter coming from the kitchen. She turned back.

*He's still here.*

Darger's palms went cold. The Glock suddenly heavy and awkward at the end of her arm.

Huxley was in her apartment.

She swallowed.

Took a shaky breath.

Then she tiptoed forward. Crossed the threshold again. Feet light and soundless.

She had to take him by surprise. Couldn't give him a chance to make any kind of move. Not this time.

She picked her way toward the kitchen. Choosing her steps. Trying to remember which floorboards squeaked and which didn't.

When she reached the kitchen doorway, she flattened herself against the wall. Closed her eyes and took a deep breath.

She could still hear him in there. Running water. Opening cabinet doors. The fucking creep.

Darger counted to three. Exhaled. Whirled into the kitchen, gun raised.

"Freeze!"

The man there spun around, eyes going wide when he saw

the gun aimed at his chest.

"Oh shit."

"Owen?" Darger hissed. "What the hell are you doing here?"

He held a wooden spoon aloft.

"I was going to surprise you." He gestured at a pot on the stove filled with what looked like marinara. "I made dinner."

Darger didn't realize she still had her gun pointed at him until he cleared his throat.

"Could you uh… point that thing somewhere else? Hell, I knew sneaking in here would get a big reaction, but… I was *trying* to be romantic."

Darger's shoulders slumped. She set the gun on the counter.

"Jesus. I'm sorry. I'm just a little… tightly wound."

"Things went bad, huh?"

"Really bad."

"I caught some of it on the news. They have any idea where he might go?"

She shook her head.

"Well, his face is plastered on every news outlet from here to Alaska. They'll find him sooner or later."

"That box by the door?" she asked, still feeling aftershocks of paranoia. "That's yours?"

"Sure is." He stirred the sauce on the stove and then turned to raise an eyebrow at her. "Oh… you didn't think it was… did you?"

Darger shrugged.

"Christ, you really are tightly wound." He moved over and pulled out one of the stools. "Here. Sit. You want some wine?"

"God, yes."

Owen poured her a glass and set it in front of her. She took a sip. Waited for the alcohol to start untying the knots in her nerves. She watched him putter around the kitchen for a few minutes. Running water into a pot for the pasta. Rinsing fresh basil leaves. Slicing a loaf of Italian bread.

"What did you do with your boat. And your cat?"

"Clancy's at my mom's. As for the boat…" Owen sighed. "Well, remember the engine troubles I was having when you all were down there?"

"Yeah."

"I got the part I'd been waiting on. Did the repair. Got her running again. Did a leisurely cruise up to the Florida Keys. And then she died on me again." Owen tore open the end of a box of pasta. "Mechanic said, in his opinion, that I'm at the point where I either need to rebuild or replace the entire engine."

"Ouch."

He nodded.

"So I decided to take a little break from the sailing life." He swung around to face her, leaning his back against the refrigerator. "To be honest, I think I might be through with it."

"Really?" Darger was genuinely surprised to hear this.

"Really. At least as a full-time thing. Think I'll sell the boat, and if I ever get the urge again, I'll rent instead of buying." He scratched his chin stubble. "Honestly, I was getting kind of restless. Turns out a life of luxury is fuckin' boring."

"It's OK," Darger said, trying not to smirk. "You can admit that what you really couldn't stand was being away from me."

Owen laughed.

"Hold on, now. I thought I was the cocky one in this relationship."

Darger thought about how spooked she'd been when she discovered her door open with the mysterious box inside and was suddenly relieved to have Owen here. The notion that Huxley was out there somewhere was too unsettling to face alone.

She pushed herself up from the table and went over to him. He was dumping dry spaghetti into the boiling water, and his back was to her. She wrapped her arms around him and buried her face in the space between his shoulder blades.

"I'm glad you're here."

"I know."

Now it was her turn to laugh, and it came out muffled because of the way her face was pressed against him. He swiveled around, snaking his arms around her waist and giving her a squeeze.

"Careful. I've got two cracked ribs."

"Sorry." He loosened his grip. "So it's cool that I just showed up like this, unannounced? You're not going to kick me to the curb?"

"No, but I'm going to make you earn your keep."

A sly smile spread over Owen's face.

"I assume you mean sexually," he said, waggling his eyebrows.

Darger choked out a laugh.

"Don't flatter yourself. I'm talking about manual labor. My washing machine has been making a weird noise, and the toilet flapper leaks."

Owen's smile faded, which only made Darger laugh harder. Too hard. There was a twinge of pain in her ribs, and she groaned.

"You shouldn't have made that comment about a life of luxury being boring," she said, clutching the sore place.

"Well, I suppose there are worse fates than being Violet

Darger's manservant."

For some reason, that brought to mind an image of Fitch writhing on the ground, the lower half of his leg gone. She winced. Worse fates indeed.

"You alright?" Owen asked. "Did they give you any pain meds?"

"It's not that. It's just…" She swallowed. "What if we don't find him? Huxley, I mean."

"You will."

"How can you be so sure?"

Owen tucked a lock of hair behind her ear.

"Because once you get your teeth in something, you're like a Doberman. Ain't nothing in the world gonna make you let go."

The center of Darger's forehead creased.

"Um… thanks?"

"You're welcome." Owen kissed the top of her head. "Now who's hungry?"

# COME PARTY WITH US

We're loners. Rebels. But much to our surprise, the most kickass part of writing has been connecting with our readers. From time to time, we send out newsletters with giveaways, special offers, and juicy details on new releases.

Sign up for our mailing list at:
http://ltvargus.com/mailing-list

# SPREAD THE WORD

Thank you for reading! We'd be very grateful if you could take a few minutes to review it on Amazon.com.

How grateful? Eternally. Even when we are old and dead and have turned into ghosts, we will be thinking fondly of you and your kind words. The most powerful way to bring our books to the attention of other people is through the honest reviews from readers like you.

# ABOUT THE AUTHORS

**Tim McBain** writes because life is short, and he wants to make something awesome before he dies. Additionally, he likes to move it, move it.

You can connect with Tim via email at tim@timmcbain.com.

**L.T. Vargus** grew up in Hell, Michigan, which is a lot smaller, quieter, and less fiery than one might imagine. When not click-clacking away at the keyboard, she can be found sewing, fantasizing about food, and rotting her brain in front of the TV.

If you want to wax poetic about pizza or cats, you can contact L.T. (the L is for Lex) at ltvargus9@gmail.com or on Twitter @ltvargus.

LTVargus.com